LAURA BEATTY

Laura Beatty's debut novel *Pollard* won the
Authors' Club First Novel Award in 2009 and
was shortlisted for the Royal Society of Literature
Ondaatje Prize. She lives in Wiltshire.

ALSO BY LAURA BEATTY

Pollard

LAURA BEATTY

Darkling

VINTAGE BOOKS
London

1 3 5 7 9 10 8 6 4 2

Vintage,
20 Vauxhall Bridge Road,
London SW1V 2SA

Vintage is part of the Penguin Random House group of companies
whose addresses can be found at global.penguinrandomhouse.com.

Penguin
Random House
UK

First published by Vintage in 2015

(First published in Great Britain by Chatto & Windus in 2014)

www.vintage-books.co.uk

A CIP catalogue record for this book is available from the British
Library

ISBN 9780099584148

Typeset by Palimpsest Book Production Ltd, Falkirk, Stirlingshire

Printed and bound by Clays Ltd, St Ives Plc

Penguin Random House is committed to a sustainable future for our
business, our readers and our planet. This book is made from Forest
Stewardship Council® certified paper.

A double dedication for a double book:
To Ivo and to my Brilliana

'. . . as the wakeful bird
Sings darkling, and in shadiest covert hid
Tunes her nocturnal note.'

Paradise Lost, Book II: 38–40

'A note in my edition says that 'darkling' is 'not yet poetic'. In fact it is the reverse of poetic in the context from which Milton took it:

The hedge-sparrow fed the cuckoo so long
That it had it head bit off by it young
So out went the candle and we were left darkling.

The word 'darkling' is instinct with tragedy, though it also suggests 'darling' – 'little dear'. Its darkness is also the darkness of belonging to a powerless opposition.'

Tom Paulin, *The Secret Life of Poems*

CONTENTS

LIST OF ILLUSTRATIONS

All images used by kind permission of Edward Harley. All photographs, except of Brilliana and Brampton Bryan Castle, taken by Ivo Beatty.

Map by Laura Beatty.

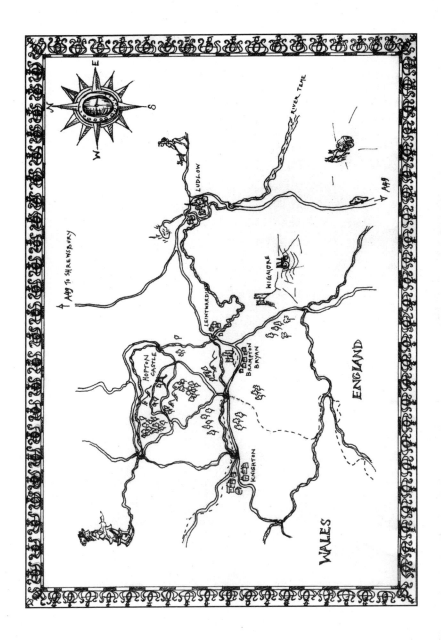

PART I

THE WELSH MARCHES

THE SOUTH EAST VIEW OF BROMPTON BRIAN CASTLE, IN THE COUNTY OF HEREFORD.

To the R.t Hon.ble EDWARD Earl of Oxford and
Mortimer, and Baron Harley of Wigmore, Owner of
these Remains, This Prospect is humbly Inscrib'd, by
My Lord Y.r Lordsp. most Obed.t & Oblig.d Serv.ts
Sam.l & Nath.l Buck.

THIS CASTLE belonged for some Ages to a Family
of Distinction call'd Brian de Brompton. In the days of
K. Edw.III. Robert de Harley married the Daughter & Heir of
S.r Brian de Brompton, by which means it came into that
Noble Family.

S.t & N.t Buck delin. et Sculp. 1731.

To the hawk, whose ground this is, the world is not an anchored place. It is more like a tray, tilting its grass surface this way and that, as he swings it about on his eye-beam. And he is lonely up there above the Welsh hills, which he sees opened out flat beneath him.

It is only my eye, he thinks, tipping the tray of the world, that fixes things. Because he can do that. He can pin the movement which is mouse, despite the horizon see-sawing when he stoops, despite the speed of his fall down the sudden cliff face of these trees, or the world rushing up at him again in three dimensions. Only when he lands does the horizon blink shut and the earth heap itself up around him, in all its strange solidity.

He is so nonchalant, in his fling of feathers, as if gravity didn't exist, as if the ground had no power of its own to hurt him. Because, however fast it slams towards him when he dives, he has never once mis-judged or crashed. He has never felt its hardness against him. He doesn't know its steepness, or its sharpness, or the cold of its earth, or how you labour your weight up it, pulling for the top; like the woman climbing the side of the valley now, who is out of breath and who carries her head slightly forwards as if peering, and who lives, unlike him, in terror of her own sight fading.

There are few people among these hills, so he won't have failed to notice her. He does notice people coming and going, though they live in such a different dimension. She's not food so she's not much more interesting than the sheep, say, or what cars there might be crawling down the steep roads, except that she's wearing a red coat and that is distracting.

Eventually the woman stops to catch her breath. She stands on the steep sward, where it rises up and away from Hopton Castle, and she notices the hawk and admires him turning into the wind and falling. She doesn't realise that his world is a place she wouldn't recognise, his experience of life strange and particular. Because when he lands, switching air for earth so fast, when he stands on the ground, with his cloak around his shoulders and those great arms folded, he must see such a different place.

The woman's world is made of people. She sees swathes of nationality, or time, or social grouping. She sees history and politics and event. She doesn't see that in fact we are all of us living in different worlds – all more or less inaccessible to each other – and that seeing another life, hawk or sheep or human, means nothing, because seeing is nothing like being. She has no understanding of that.

Instead, she stands in the autumn sun and she watches the hawk lift again, listens to him slide his thin cry down the sides of these hills, and she thinks about time, which is a dimension that doesn't exist for him. How different would this valley have looked, in the seventeenth century, for instance?

The black dot of the rising bird. There must always have been hawks here, so that hasn't changed. And indeed the pattern of his life has remained constant, ever since hawks began, so perhaps he doesn't need time. His parents' harsh cries, these sparse fields and the bloody gobbets he ingests have told him only that life is fierce and life is present. Life is right now. That is his point of view and point of view, after all, is everything.

The hawk, on some invisible diagonal, planes away and the woman walks through an open gate and into a field of sheep. And next, she thinks, with some nostalgia, though her father no longer farms, of how you hulk a sheep around at shearing, its fleece greasy, and of the strength of its buck in your grip, the butt of its head. And although she knows a bit about sheep, she thinks about them too from her own experience, or from what she remembers of the nexus of care and predation that animates these high-up, grassy places around England's edges, in which the lives of people and sheep and birds of prey meet, and briefly intersect, and diverge again.

Everything about a sheep is awkward, she says to herself on the side of the hill, starting with its brain and ending with its bolting, stiff-legged run. Maybe that explains her impossible father. Maybe awkwardness is catching. Is that crow on the back of that ewe picking for maggots? Even after a decade and a half of living in a town, as she watches the flock in her town coat, she can't help looking automatically for signs of foot rot or fly strike.

The sheep themselves have eyes only for the grass. They glance up and crop and crop and crop. They splay their feet and plant their weight, hammocking it above the ground, which they know, not so much by sight, as with their knees and with their mouths. The valley is made of food, they think, rolling their marble eyes, half-witted. The grass is everywhere. Why look above the horizon? Only the dog now, running low and open-mouthed at their ankles, galvanises them into some kind of alertness, as they coalesce, skittering in a body at its will. Behind it the farmer comes up slantwise, with long strides.

Come on Tess, the farmer bawls at the dog, all bristles and shite and red hands. Stop faffing around. And the woman, who is labouring across the field once more, sidesteps and apologises and can't tell which way they are headed. I'm sorry. I'm in the way, and the farmer coming level, and appraising her like a bull appraises a cow, says, No, don't worry. It's the dog that's being a prat, not you. And she is reminded that she has a full and feminine figure, which is something he can say without opening his mouth.

I don't know your face, do I – you're not from these parts? He's pretty easy with himself. He has that propensity to talk, which often belongs to people of remote places and which is something else she had forgotten.

5

No, she tells him, she's not from here. Although, she hesitates – she doesn't want to encourage him – her father used to farm sheep and she nods towards the flock. But it's nice to be spoken to on the side of a hill. It's nice to be appreciated.

Whereabouts is that then, he farmed?

Oh, it was Scotland. A little place. You wouldn't know it. She smiles.

Like this then, he says, smiling also. But you won't have a castle, I don't suppose, where you are? I take it you're up having a look at the castle? He nods over at the ruin, where men in hard hats are at work behind wire caging.

She is, and they fall silent, though his eyes say all kinds of things and it is clear that he would dawdle and say more, with his bristles and his shite and his red hands itching no doubt, only the sheep are running and it's a working Wednesday. So he heads away and the woman, whose name is Mia, turns uphill, her weight suddenly an asset.

*

She is no scholar, Mia Morgan, no academic. She has no specialist knowledge, apart from her childhood acquaintance with sheep and her interest in time, to bring to this quiet valley, between England and wild Wales; its stub of a castle, its hanging hawk, its sheep careering now through the narrow gate with the dog behind them. She just has a habit of attentiveness. She knows how to listen and how to look, as if the world were disappearing, as if everything in it mattered. So that is what she does. She sees into the past the way you see through a keyhole, partially and in thin fingers of light.

Reaching a corner, where the wooded top of the hill meets with the field, Mia stops again, leans against the stile and watches the farmer, small in the valley bottom, crawl about his business, with the dog still being a prat. Quiet. The burr of a tractor somewhere and the clank of machinery in the wood behind her, and the hawk repeating its cry, like a blade being sharpened on a whetstone.

From here, the valley appears pleated into feminine tucks and folds, a little stream running clear through its floor. There is everything you could need, she thinks, pasture, clean water. Such softness. And nursed in the middle, the castle, sitting like a navel, in its tender green.

So, what happened here? Backwards and forwards a yellow digger crawls, scooping fallen earth from the castle's middle. I'd show you round, the foreman had said to her earlier on, when she'd tried to gain access, but you don't have an appointment. She'd laughed at him. It seemed ludicrous that you'd need an appointment for a pile of mud and an ash tree leaning crazily out of what had once been indoors. And you'd need a hard hat. Much as I'd like to, he'd added not ungallantly. It's health and safety.

Anyway, she'd thought, looking at the hawk overhead, you need a proper perspective, which is why she had climbed the hill in the first place, to see the castle in its surroundings, to understand why it was there. Not immediately a strategic position. In fact, why would you ever come here at all? On the way to nowhere and so small – 'but one room below and one above' is the recollection of its one-time commander. She has read all the accounts. And a garrison of only sixteen men, until the castle of Brampton Bryan, four and a half miles away, 'lovingly' sent reinforcements.

Round it the hills rear up, Hopton Titterhill, the Black Hill, whose great impassive forms shut the valley so that anything that did happen here, Mia realises now she's looking at it, would happen in secret, out of the eye of the world as it were.

So this is how it is, Mia thinks. This is how a valley is, the hawk, the sheep, the grassy silence of the hills complicit. After a massacre.

Listen. The Devil is abroad in these English lanes, stalking on nightmare legs, with his hocus-pocus and his Hail Marys. Listen for him come back once more, moving about the country by night, looking for a foothold to harry the One True Church, to light fires again and burn the Godly and bring purges and Spanish invasion and lay trails of gunpowder under the Houses of Parliament.

Say it is late February, early March 1644, just barely spring, small daffodils, catkins, buds breaking, though the trees are still bare. A country, like a dog tearing at itself in a fever. Civil War.

Almighty God, our Father, we pray to you for the suppression of popery and Arminianisme. May we ridd popery out of the lande.

And here are the Godly cooped up in their castles, straining their eyes and their ears into the dark. Because it is not life or death, that is at stake, it is eternal damnation.

Armies on the march, back and forth through an England convulsed. Confused alarms in the night and poor communications, and rumour, and waiting.

Now here is the Devil, waggling the legs of five hundred men, down the twisting roads, to Hopton. Five hundred men moving in darkness, into the mud of this little village. The half-timbered houses, the hovels, all sleeping. The godly garrison in the castle, tense against rumour. We humbly beseche that God will enable us in mercy to keepe covenant with him. We give thanks to God in his grate mercy, for our deleverance from the Powder Plott and from the Armada of Spain.

Owls sweep through the valley.

Two hours before dawn, the noise and the smell of an army and the persistence of pioneers with picks working a breach in the castle. May the Good Lord delever us from our enemies. Muddle and makeshift fighting. Dark work.

Dawn, and the enemy looks surprisingly ordinary. Muddy, ignorant men from another county. They have billeted themselves in the village.

Cannon arriving in carts a week later. That was on a Sunday, and in the night, three pieces of ordnance. The valley bulging. Men and horses and cold and little food and the hills rising impassive and the hawk splashing his excrement on a fence post and lifting to the sky as if nothing were happening.

Monday morning waken to drumming.

Inside the little castle, thirty-one men resisting with pikes and muskets and clubs. The cannon shot shaking the hills repeatedly. Nine o'clock till five they shot ninety-six shots at the out-wall and made a breach and inside, the men, working in sweat and smoke, to repair it with branches of trees and with heaped earth. Upwards of a hundred and fifty dead strewn over the spring grass. Blood. Smoke. More smoke. The moans of the wounded mixed with birdsong, rising on the air. Then a truce while the dead are gathered. Bodies heaped onto carts and Colonel Woodhouse picking his way on horseback in a fury. It was such a nothing place.

Quiet all Tuesday till night and then the enemy come to the brick tower and set it on fire.

So another night of turmoil. Of effort in exhaustion, of the flare of shot and firelight and shouting themselves hoarse and running with water. Of wood splintering, of clangour and explosions in darkness. The battle begins to go against the castle. The door breached and the garrison fight to fill the gap with anything to hand, boxes, furniture, but the enemy bring broom faggots to fire the porch.

O Lord, save us in this our hour of peril.

They draw water in buckets to quench it, passing them hand to hand, but for all they can do the porch burns and the door begins to fire. And now, the dull thump of mining underfoot. The castle shakes with the shock of picks and shovels. Cannon shot continuing.

Weary with working all night, and not out of their clothes for a fortnight's time, and the enemy gotten underneath the castle through a house of office on the south side; it is moved they should desire a parley. Above the ramparts the white flag trembling as if exposed.

Surrender granted under no conditions other than Colonel Woodhouse's mercy.

Silence suddenly, and a handful of men and two women emerging shock-witted, haggard, into an ordinary day. With the smoke of the cannon hanging they unblock their port, put their arms on a heap. Stumble into their own valley in the morning. The forgotten sounds of life here, audible again for the first time. Sheep bleating because the lambing has started. Someone's dog. A cockerel. The cots and hovels among the mess the occupying army has made, but the hills familiar, the skyline at least, unchanged.

Samuel Moore, the commander, tied and marched off, for interrogation, over the water by Richard Steward's house, and then he looks back and sees none have followed.

The two women stripped to their smocks and cut about. Watch this. They strip the soldiers naked, tie them back to back.

Afterwards it is hard to know what you've seen. There is muddle and horror. Some say they slit their throats. Some say they killed them with clubs or such things, by beating. Buckling to their knees on their own grass. Many, that they were left in the March cold, tied naked to each other, staring and bleeding, for several hours, until word was given that they be left to the mercy of the common soldiers. Ordinary men, from the outside. Englishmen. Not much difference to look at, between the men of the castle and the enemy; who presently fall upon the prisoners, wounding them grievously, and drive them into a cellar unfinished, wherein lies stinking water, the house being on fire over them.

It is unthinkable what men will do to each other in their own country. This is not a foreign enemy. These are our own countrymen.

Every man of them presently massacred.

*

The hills close round, holding the castle to themselves, as if shushing it to forget. From her vantage point, Mia looks down at the village. Cupped by the hills, its sounds float up to her, people calling companionably back and forth in the plots and gardens below. A car starts up and inches out into the lane. Every noise distinct. The valley is so constructed that anyone standing here by accident, at the joint of the field with the wood, a vagrant maybe, sheltering in this corner, where the blackberries are enormous and grow in globs in the hedgerow, anyone minding their own business, or a boy minding sheep or kine, would hear distinctly all that was going on in the village below. The cannon shot. The appalling screams. You couldn't miss anything.

And then the next morning, or the morning after the massacre say, the castle sunk in silence, its defences gaping. Just the smoke from the ruin still rising on the air, with the hawk winging through and the hills keeping on with their own fecundity, while the bodies were dug into the hard March ground. What happened then? Did the people just go out, stunned, into the fields and carry on with the work of providing?

Now the village has forgotten. The houses have bright plantings. They have cars and tarmac drives and everything neat. The hawk rises and falls and the digger goes on scraping. I think I'll walk up into the wood, Mia says, see if anything suggests itself.

She gets over the stile and enters the wood and climbs. It is warm and it is steep going. Instead of the wide and surfaced path that must circle the shoulder of the hill, she chooses one that goes more or less straight up. She hauls herself, holding whatever offers itself, following what look like channels made by flash floods, but which turn out to be downhill racetracks. Keep clear at all times, a sign reads, mountain bike exit.

So, it would have been sixteen – what? Sixteen forty what? Think of a date, she says to herself. But she can't. It's embarrassing, when it comes down to it, this inability of hers to hold information, as if she were some leaking bucket. A bad workman, her father would have said. A bad workman blames his tools. It doesn't matter, she says by accident, out loud, to drown out the sound of him in her head because he is an exacting man. It doesn't matter. Dates are just a filing system. They're just a way of saying, this happened not now, in a different place from here. I'm writing it all down. I don't need to remember it.

Just round this corner, just up to those trees, where there must be a break and I'll see out. I'll see something.

As if in answer there is the sound of rending from the wood above her, of paths being forced. At great speed, a body of men, urgent and sweat-slicked, in Lycra and coloured helmets come crashing and jolting through the trees. Backs! They shout as they pass. Coming through! And one, towards the rear manages, Thank you! breathlessly, as he hurtles past. Down the track she has just come up, their back wheels slipping sideways. They stand up in the saddle as if at the gallop and at the fence they skid and one falls, pushes his bike limping for a bit and then hops on again behind. She reaches the fence herself, in time to see them shoot out at the bottom, bumping down the fields and over the sward to the castle. Mia watches them dismount, bandy-legged, and drink, heroic, from plastic bottles. They shake their legs out and stretch and stand in coloured knots on the road. She can't tell whether this was a race, or just training. The competition seemed so earnest.

Mia leans on the stile in the sun, eating blackberries. She can hear the men still talking all the way below her, on the road. Then she climbs over, recrosses the sloping fields, dawdling this time, down the brook that runs through the valley floor, to marvel at its stones. It is so clear. They say the waters ran red with blood, as far as the Teme, after the massacre. That's about four miles.

The grass, so short and sweet underfoot and the sun still strong.

Nothing to tell you what once happened here. Only, towards the gate, there is one very ancient hazel, bent and crabbed and with a hole through its middle, which stands, holding its handfuls of wind-stunted sticks like something shocked. It is the first thing Mia has seen in the valley that looks anything like a witness.

All is still as she walks to her car. The hills have settled back to silence. The shouts and the urgency of the mountain bikers and the splash of synthetic colours have seeped into their grassy sides. Just one man remains, by the roadside, as Mia passes, strapping his bicycle onto his car. Afternoon, he says, as he pulls the nylon straps tight. The sheep are quiet and the farmer is nowhere to be seen. Only, as she fishes in her pocket for her keys, an owl calls, hooting in daylight, as though in this valley it doesn't matter. As though there will be no one here to tell you, if you make a mistake, if you confuse, momentarily, dark with light.

Places make people, Mia. That's what her father used to say to her, when she was a child. They were walking back from the sheep sheds in the dawn, the first time, wiping the blood and slime off their hands, with the stars paling and the lines of the hill, in the grey light, like a world cut out of paper before them, and the breath and milk and dung snuggery of the new lambs behind. Places make people. Always remember that. He had a Lowland Scots accent.

Then later, when she wanted to leave Scotland and go elsewhere, places make people again, and this time not in companionship but as a foregone conclusion. As much as to say, you can try, but you'll have to come back. As though the great hill and all the needle rains and the chapped hands and the muck and drudgery and the after-births and the life and the death, and all the things she wanted out of, would get up and follow her into London. Dog her up and down Bond Street and Oxford Circus. Lift her skirts to show that she'd wellington boots and long johns on underneath, and drag her back as unfit for anything but farming.

She has never forgotten it.

But making is making. It isn't possessing, as she'd worried through her teens that it might be. The hill that humped itself through her dreams never came to get her. And now here she is, a visitor to the country these days and doing the brain-work, as her father would call it, that he could so easily have done himself, with his piles of *History Today* by the wing chair and his mind like the flick of a fish's tail, had he not had a farm to inherit.

Sometimes, Mia thinks, places make you so you are only fit for somewhere else, leaning over the gate to the churchyard at Wigmore now. There is a jackdaw, strutting about among the graves, with its hands behind its back, sizing things up. You should have been a crow, Dad. That's the difference between us.

Crows can live anywhere. Anywhere you go in the world you find crows of one kind or another, snatching their living off the surface, as it were, disengaged, adaptable. Because usually birds interlock with a place, or that's how it seems, like a flowering out of particular conditions, like something the landscape produces. Clouds of puffins out of a cliff face, woodcock that bloom out of the forest floor, herons grown on stalk legs out of pools. They bed down, as if the part of themselves that flings constantly skyward were mirrored by a twin somewhere just below the earth's surface.

Only a few people do that. The rest skate about like water boatmen, vacillating, picking and choosing. For the smallest of reasons, they take off and move to somewhere completely different, just as Mia's father did, in the end, when his eyesight went completely and he found himself blind. He just picked up and sold the farm and went to a place called Myddle, in Shropshire, that had nothing whatever to do with him. Because, he joked sourly, it sounded like a safe place to be, if you couldn't see – the middle.

You should have been a crow, Dad, Mia says again, a little out of breath as she leaves the jackdaw and starts the steep climb up from the church to another castle ruin. Walking. Thinking of her father, the first time she'd been to visit after the move, sitting in the little plot at the back of the house, all dandelions and tussocks and rank grass, a place he'd have scorned if he could have seen it; just sitting, just staring with his sightless eyes, a look of puzzlement on his face. A still day, and he sat with the thistledown falling through the air around him. Neither adaptable nor disengaged. Disoriented. Dispossessed.

You look tired Da, Mia had said, to break the silence mostly, to bring him back. Will I make you a cup of tea, slipping back into Scots as if that could comfort him.

There's not a breath of wind here, girl, he said, without turning his head, as though addressing the fence, the poor field behind it. And she'd noticed at the time that his voice was brisk and out of context, the little chips of his consonants and the breeze of his vowels, as if even that was fitted to the climate that had born it, because he'd lived his life so far, under the skin of where he belonged.

A man could suffocate just trying to breathe here.

It's just a warm day Da, she'd said. There's wind everywhere. Then it flashed through her mind and caught in her neck that perhaps he'd lost his place in the world, like you lose your footing and slip; that she was somehow responsible. So now he'll die, she'd thought, because he looked like something blown about, a bundle of dry matter, his cheeks sunk, as though deprived of some lively function. All afternoon he kept raising a hand to his face, to check whether as well as his sight he hadn't lost his sense, some new trick of his body's, to bewilder, to scramble his knowledge of things. Because it wasn't only a breeze he'd lost. It was *the* breeze; the breeze that struck your left cheek as you faced the hill, so you knew it would rain, or the one that scooted you from behind and made everything skip, or the one that flayed at your right, or smacked at your forehead and watered your eyes. It was how your body knew without your head having to bother, how it talked all the time to the place.

And however hard she denies it, even Mia is aware of the parts of herself that her Border childhood has made. Her ability to do without company, her occasional brisk impatience. Something clear, something of coldness and clean stone and water about her.

Now stepping out with purpose she goes, half-conscious of this map that she carries about inside her, through a kissing gate, up the hill, and along the tangled footpath to the castle ruin.

These are the Marches, borders again, and it is intriguing to Mia that her father has, without looking, chosen somewhere to live that is a border, a boundary place. It's on the edge, Da, even if it calls itself Myddle.

It is an outpost, thickly fortified. There are castles everywhere you look. Ludlow, Painscastle, Croft. She can fit the names to her steps. And Wigmore, Montgomery, Chirk. Stokesay and Powis and Hopton and Grossmount. Longtown and Whittington. Brampton Bryan. Skenfrith.

How thick they are, how full of consonants. Wild names for wild places.

Upwards a moment later, under a sunken archway, small curtilage walls either side, surrounding a mossy lawn. Then half a turret and a rowan tree and on again, another rise, another set of walls and towers and shattered ramparts, more and further, she ascends and ascends until the topmost platform, where Mia rests and looks down on the landscape, at last.

Fields hazy with distance. Curve of the horizon. And all the birds wheeling below her this time. Small ferns, moss and wind. Cars like beads on all the roads, silent at this height. You are halfway to the sky here. She runs one hand over the blasted stone.

*

This is how a family of Puritans is born.

Elizabeth I on the throne with her paper face and her hard-as-nails eyes, and her untouched body encased in embroidery. England, with the bitter smoke of Mary Tudor's bonfires still rank in its nostrils, is become a feverishly Protestant country. Small, mud-bogged ways. Carts rocking past. Horses from time to time. The slowness of things, to set against the switchback changes of religion. Take Old John Harley of nearby Brampton Bryan for instance, a Catholic, whose son, Thomas, changing with the times, turns Protestant and marries a Nonconformist.

Wear your hat in church. Don't genuflect. Throw out the altar rails, the incense, images, decoration and all those things that suggest pomp, or mystery, or luxuriance, for they belong to the Devil.

Thomas's wife, Margaret, severe and ardent, lives by these rules. She is from a family of reformed Protestants, not afraid to proclaim the new religion. Clarity is important, to hold to it, to know yourself; ask yourself daily, hourly even, are you one of the elect? Are you saved? Look into your heart, order it, subjugate it. Take care you be not idle, or luxurious, or dark.

For I am a light to lighten the Gentiles.

And lights are made of rush, of tapers, waxed, or floating in oil. There is no such thing as a light that doesn't burn. Thomas Harley's wife, carrying herself into the musky comfort of her recusant father-in-law's Catholicism like a flare. Another woman to burn the country clean. Beating on the doors of the chapel at Brampton Bryan, where the Mass was held illegally. I would speak with my lord. No answer. Just the smell of incense drifting under the closed door and hum of the Latin mumbo-jumbo. I would have my lord Thomas Harley come out to me. Beating with her fist on the locked doors. What if the Queen were to hear of this? Open the doors. Inside, the people listen.

Open! Open, I say. Do you wish to keep your heads?

And the doors open and out comes Thomas, head down, walking quick, because the Act of Supremacy means that Catholic priests are now traitors, and the punishment for treason is beheading.

If Sir John will not change, then the young Harleys will not stay. So Thomas and Margaret, with their possessions on carts, scurry away to Wigmore, where they wind up the hill to the airy castle and set up house and start a family. And old Sir John, who is afraid of nothing, is left behind at Brampton Bryan, shouting in Latin from the popish primer through the long Protestant services, and holding Mass in the castle until he dies.

To this couple, Thomas and Margaret, Robert Harley, the Puritan, was born, here in this eyrie, in 1579. His first sight of the world, this view that Mia is still taking in; the pattern of these fields and lanes, this clean, uninterrupted sky, these wheeling, searching hawks. And from here, as Robert listened to his mother's unadorned truths, fitting them to what he saw laid out below, the world might have looked capable of being ordered.

It is seductive up here. You half-wonder why anyone would leave. If you wanted to just sit and watch people living, Wigmore would be perfect. The burden of involvement lifted, just the sky and the silence. But the moment Sir John Harley died Thomas and Margaret moved back to Brampton.

Mia has stopped thinking and is watching a tiny tractor with a Swiss roll of straw on a spike in front of it trundle across a field. For livestock, no doubt, though she can't see any. Imagine, like leaf drift, the shadows overlapping of how many people, in what kind of clothes, looking out of this ruined window, at the fields and woods and roads to London, watching the world laid out before them and plotting what their place in it might be. Because that is what people do, stand at windows and dream and make decisions. And then, they either stay where they are and do nothing after all, or, like the Harleys, they come down.

*

Down from the castle the landscape is a different place. Narrow roads that were made by feet tracking back and forth through mud between small villages, connecting places that were days away from each other to begin with, half a day if there was a horse, if it didn't go lame, if the ways were good.

And at walking pace these roads would have been places themselves, cupping the noise of their own banks and hedgerows. The chirping, the fluttering, the sound of steps approaching or receding, the cartwheels in and out of the ruts. Long moments of emptiness. I wonder who's coming now. A man's whistle, or a hoof on a stone. Nothing travelling faster than a horse can gallop. Reported news that changes or becomes outdated, often long before it has the chance to arrive, swaying along between the hedges. Just the slow creak of the basket into which letters have been put, paper prayers, carrying messages, hopes, anxieties, the father's repetitive wishes for his daughter's health, married to an older man say, in a shire he has never seen. Please God she is well. While he listens, in the bird-filled silence of elsewhere, to her absence. She hasn't written for a week.

Now the roads are fast with tarmac. So fast they no longer exist except as distance measured and consumed, flexed like cables, between these villages. Onibury, Craven Arms, Church Stretton. And the places they connect are also changed, also uncertain. Houses set down anyhow, in a rush, at odd angles flimsily built, as though infected with impermanence. You can leave a village without even knowing you've been in it.

Mia is at the wheel of her car, heading to her father's for the night. As she turns off the main road and steep down into Myddle, whose jumble of buildings surprises her with the feeling of not belonging, she thinks guiltily that she doesn't visit enough. It doesn't look anything like home. I hope he's not in one of his moods.

Down the main street, brick houses in smart closes. That's new since I came last. Bungalows with red tarmac drives among the old sandstone. Her father's house is in a small modern crescent, off the main street and open to fields at the back; Glebelands, which is what it must once have been, and Mia likes the reminder that its name unfailingly provides.

The house is semi-detatched, so her father and her aunt Ines, who lives with him, have neighbours. This is an awkwardness for them, in particular for her father who is a private man, should anyone choose to have a row. Not that having rows is something that either of them do intentionally, or very often. They go miles round to avoid spoken confrontation. They are expert bottlers and lip tighteners and simmerers and suppressors, Mia and her father. Mostly he manages a quiet life. Mostly Mia's visits, though always brief and far between, are gentle. They communicate by not communicating, by teasing each other and by turning a blind eye, which Mia finds ironic. How much blinder do you need to be Da, she will ask him in her head sometimes, when either the seething or his mildly abrasive manner gets the better of her.

They must have been watching for her because the door opens before Mia has time to knock or to ring the bell. Hello pet. Ines on the doorstep, very neat, very buttons and bosoms, holding out her arms. Come on in Mia, come in, how are you, you look great.

Hello Aunty, and Mia hugs her aunt, who is her mother's sister, though nothing whatever like her, being too small, too soft. And the house, even though it isn't home, smells familiar, of outdoor boots and a certain type of fabric softener and cooking. The radio talking to itself in the kitchen. Looking down the narrow hall Mia can see out through the kitchen window, the cows in the little fields beyond, the sky reddening, the coming dusk. I'm absolutely exhausted, she says without thinking.

Is that you girl?

That's me Da.

Mia's father, tall and still spare, standing in the living room, making his feeling way to the door because he can't wait, shows his pleasure at his daughter's arrival with an embrace that is for a moment almost too tight, a bang on the back that is almost too hard. Well, how does she look, Ines?

She looks well, John. She looks very well.

That's a trim coat you've on girl, Mia's father says because he's seen it with his fingers. Very smart.

Mia laughs. That's my town coat Da. I'll have to borrow something if we go walking tomorrow.

Your town coat. Navy is it? What's the colour Ines?

It's red, Mia says.

Red? John Morgan sits down in his chair. A red coat. That's going some. Are you getting flashy in your old age then?

Mia takes the coat off. It's just a bit of colour, Da. What's wrong with that?

It looks lovely pet, Ines says. It's lovely and bright. It looks very well on you.

Mia stands in the doorway to the living room and looks at her father, sitting now. Bony. Blowing his nose into a shabby handkerchief. Cast up like a shipwreck in his wing chair, all elbow joints and knee joints and thin hair. She isn't bothered by his goading. It comes to her strangely familiar, as though the intervening years have never been. That is what old age and disability do to you, she thinks. Maroon you somewhere before. Because this is how Mia's mother and father used to talk, before he went blind and before she got ill, when Mia's world was still a place of certainty.

What razzamatazz is that? Mia's father would say, when her mother appeared in something new, a bright blue dress, she'd bought once, a yellow jersey, a scarf with patterns, an orange flowered skirt.

It's just a bit of colour, Mia's mother would say. Isn't there enough grey in the sky, for goodness' sake?

The Gypsies'll have you for one of their own if you're not careful. You watch, girl, he'd say to Mia, picking up his newspaper, your mother'll be up behind a cart next thing.

So Mia comes into the room and laughs at her father. She sits down on the chair next to his and her father pockets his handkerchief and turns his sightless eyes to where he can hear she has settled. I'll be up behind a cart next thing, she says to him.

You will, girl. You will.

The stiff little parlour. The tired-looking furnishings, the very few books. Metal-framed windows looking out onto thistly fields. She thinks with a sudden shock, my da is not well off. She'd forgotten. Ines leaves them and slips out to the kitchen. It is quiet.

Mia's father is never in a rush to make conversation. So . . . he'll say, leaning back into his wing chair, his fisted hands symmetrically placed on his knees. So . . . and then he'll leave it hanging for a while. Mia doesn't mind. Most of their communication is done somewhere else, somewhere before, beyond the level of words. On the floor his guide dog sighs and lays his head down on his paws. From the kitchen comes the sound of pans clinking against the sink, crockery and cutlery being gathered, knocking against each other and a brief burst of water. And through the open window the chittering of swallows. Otherwise just silence.

Mia dreams, lost in her own thoughts, so that it takes her by surprise when her father says, So, again, this time more purposefully. Mia and the dog both look up. You're down for a few days. How's life in the city?

There are several questions that Mia's father could, and in some ways would, ask of her, but he doesn't. He just wraps them all up in this one non-specific, as if it were pass-the-parcel. I don't want to go prying, he would have said, if asked. The girl will tell me if she wants to. Only how do you tell someone the things that are bothering at your heart, if an opening is never made. Mia misses her mother.

The city's the city, Da, she says, aware of the unasked questions, answering them in her own way. Everything's pretty much the same. Nothing's changed. The unasked questions fizz briefly like static in the air between them and extinguish.

She holds her hand out to her father's old dog, pets him. Preston's getting on, Da.

I'm sorry to say it but you're right. Ines has put in for another one. He'll do for a while yet. Mia's father puts his hand on the dog's head. He'll do.

Well, Mia, her father says next, after another pause. What is this project you've in hand?

It's just a bit of research, Da. I've been looking at the Marcher castles, or some of them – for a book, you know.

Aha. A book?

A biography of a woman who lived round here, in the Civil War, a Puritan, who held her castle against the Cavaliers.

Aha. Ines didn't tell me you were writing a book. It is the first time he has sounded pleased, really pleased, for a long while. He leans forward, his chin up to listen.

23

Well I'm not, Da. I'm doing the research. Someone else is going to write it. But it's money and it's something different to do.

Mia's voice wavers slightly. She isn't telling the whole story. Her father knows she is withholding something, he can hear it in her voice. He turns his head towards her, but still he doesn't ask outright. I see, he says. Someone else.

Someone else, Mia echoes firmly and another static-filled silence falls between them.

Her father rubs the palms of his hands back and forth along his thighs, in a certain way he has. He changes tack. So who is the woman? he asks. And then before Mia can answer, his impatience and his disappointment getting the better of him, he spits out suddenly, Could you not just write it yourself, girl?

No, I can't write it. Mia laughs at him. Who's going to pay me to write a biography? I can't keep a date in my head.

Don't be so silly. Her father's impatience fully breaks its bounds. You've plenty of brains for it. Just organise yourself. You've to grow up sometime Mia.

Mia lowers her voice. I know what I can and can't do. I can't do it Da. We're in it now, she thinks wearily. It didn't take long. She feels the pull towards their old misunderstandings, as if all their conversations ran on rails, with no chance for manoeuvre or change. She makes a great effort to stop, to keep her resolution. She says, more sprightly, She doesn't think much to me, the woman in question. She's called Brilliana Harley. She lived at Brampton Bryan, the other side of Shrewsbury, near Wigmore, married to an older man called Robert. She disapproves of me.

Don't be ridiculous, Mia's father says.

I'm telling you, Mia says, overriding his impatience with determined good humour, she disapproves of me. Look at her portrait if you don't believe me. Well, you can't, but I can and I'm telling you. You can't write about someone who disapproves of you. It isn't possible.

How can she disapprove of you girl? She's over three hundred years dead.

Well, Mia says, she does, that's all. There are plenty of reasons. Because I don't believe in her old God – all his smitings and election and damnation. Because I am a modern woman. Because I wear a red coat, no doubt.

Ah, Mia's father says, giving in and smiling. His face unclouds. Well, I'm with her on the red coat.

You're a killjoy Da, Mia says as Ines returns to fetch them for supper. You're an old killjoy. You write it. You've nothing else to do. No doubt you and Brilliana would get along fine.

Mia's father's face shadows briefly, the way a cloud will cross a landscape. He rubs his hands back and forth again, considering. Mia doesn't think to look at him. She follows Ines out of the room. She doesn't see the way his mouth is set, so she doesn't need to wonder what might be outlined by its clamped lips, or by the angle of his head to his neck, fixed for a moment, his eyes gazing at nothing.

They eat in the kitchen with the windows pouring with condensation. Open the windows Ines, Mia's father says, touching his familiar landmarks, the frame of the door, the back of the chair, his hands moving as if they were live and separate, like curious animals.

Oh, all the windows are open John, Ines answers, bent double over the warming drawer. Mia looks from her aunt to her father and then at the closed and streaming window.

Open the window girl. She thinks I'm daft. Telling me the windows are open. I'll be growing moss at this rate. Go on, Mia, open that window wide. Unless you want to go back to town with ferns coming out of your ears.

So Mia opens the window with her eyebrows raised at Ines and Ines pulls it closed again while Mia is sitting down. If you want a job doing, her father says, getting up from the table and feeling his way to the counter. He doesn't finish his sentence partly because he is concentrating. His fingers are surprisingly quick and seeing. He throws the window wide, the casement bar swinging free and clattering against the sill. Let it bang, he says, sitting down again. That way I know it's open. With any luck it'll break altogether and then we'll all be able to breathe again.

The kitchen livens with an evening breeze that sweeps in, with a smell of grass and cow on its breath, and the sound of swallows.

Over supper Mia does what she has always done. She describes for her father all the things she has seen that he might have liked or noticed himself, the castles, the roads, the hedges cut high or low, the condition of the fields, and the cows she got stuck behind on the way, swaying home, udders aching, to the milking parlour. She tells him exactly the weather. She makes for him out of words his place in the world, bearing in mind his dislocation, as if to root him, make him feel that he belongs here after all. She soothes him. She answers his questions about the state of the fields round about, reconnects him to the farming year, that otherwise he would sadly miss. And she's good at this. She's observant and she's good at describing.

There's some that are ploughing already Da.

Aha. Who would that be then?

Now how on earth would I know – I live two hundred miles away or something. Ines, who would it be?

Oh goodness, Ines says, I get in a muddle. These farms have been changing hands lately. Where was it exactly?

It's the ground this side of Shrewsbury, Mia answers, using instinctively the farmer's word, 'ground' rather than land or fields. It's on the right-hand side, up the way towards Newton on the Hill.

Aha, her father says, alert. That'll be Robert Black. He's quite a canny one, he is. Was it drilled yet or just ploughed?

It was just stubble ploughed in, Mia answers, just turned over. And her father looks lively, sitting up in his chair at the head of the table. If she stops or pauses he questions her, so she is aware all the time that she must have her wits about her, as he would say, must do his looking for him very closely, in case she misses something that he might ask her about later. Out of habit now, wherever she is, in the streets of London, or out in the country, whether she is with him or not, she keeps in mind his urgent grip, holding her arm when they are together. What's that girl, he'll ask when they are walking. What's over there?

And Mia had better be ready to answer. Well, there's two lots of woods. There's Old Woods away to the right and there's another to the left, follows the road down from Webscott, it must be, I don't know its name.

Aha. And what's close to, now?

Grassland.

Aha. Fenced or walled?

That's fenced, Da.

Is it tidy?

And Mia has to look carefully. Yes, tidy-ish. There's some high-tensile wire could do with tightening, or, there's a paling missing. Or, he's a shoddy farmer, docks everywhere and holes in the sheep netting.

Which way are we facing? And you have to be quick. Come on girl, where's the sun?

South-east. Da, we're facing south-east.

And what's the landmark that way?

That would be Myddle Hill and behind Myddle Hill is the hamlet called Grumpy.

Go on, you're pulling my leg.

I am not Da. You can ask. Ask the postman. It's called Grumpy and it's where you should be living.

We'll sell up, Aunt Ines. We'll sell up, Mia will often say now. We'll buy him a house in Grumpy. What do you think?

So the kitchen window bangs softly and the meal passes, and later, when they go out last thing, arm in arm under the dark masses of the lime trees, while Preston staggers among other people's dustbins, Mia had better know the stars.

Tonight there is a skyful, both the ones that are really there and the ones that burnt out ages ago. All the old patterns still holding, the old arrangements of beasts and hunters pinned to the roof, as if time didn't exist, or memory was visible.

Right girl, her father says, when they reach the end of the crescent and the sky is open. What have we got? The curious combination of his definite voice, its demands, its assumption of hierarchy, with the thin arm she holds. Bone where there used to be warmth and muscle. She holds his arm, which tells her, I am wasting, I am ageing to powder, and listens to the voice and thinks, I used to be afraid of you, Da. I used to be really afraid.

OK, Mia says hesitantly, trying to remember the knack of orienting yourself in the night sky. Find the familiars first, that's what he told her when she was little. Look for what's easy, what you know and then find the others. It's a good clear sky, Da. Wait a minute, Mia says, turning and turning with her head back. Let me get myself sorted. Where's the Plough?

Her father points low and northwards. It should be over there.

OK, I've got it. It is. She is surprised. You don't need me at all. I've forgotten how to do this. There aren't any stars in London. There's a half-moon. Lovely. There's Pegasus, I think it is. The Pleiades. Cassiopeia is right up. Mia cranes back. Almost overhead.

So, her father says, Cassiopeia's up, is it? Winter's on its way then.

While Mia sleeps in the narrow bed of her childhood these Shropshire villages go on through the night, staring at themselves out of modern windows, crouched over the cold egg of their past, forgetful. And in the fields the jaws of the sheep move even in sleep, and the fields hump their backs like they always did. And the moon puts itself to bed and the stars burn through their individual lives and eventually, like it always does, the sun levers itself above the wood and another morning comes.

Mia lies with her eyes shut, partly adjusting to the day, partly preparing, in case she is ever afflicted herself, for blindness. She has done this since she was eleven or twelve, with that mixture of practicality and curiosity, creeping even to the edge of horror, that is so particular to childhood. Now it is habit that makes her do it, habit mixed with sympathy, the need to remind herself forcibly of what it is that her father has suffered. This is her father's world, the world of sound. Car on tarmac. Car again. A chute of birdsong raining from tree and rooftop, and the radio on in the kitchen below. From further away the querulousness of sheep being moved from one field to another. Mia sits up.

Eventually she goes over to the open window and leans out and looks at the morning and wonders what the day will hold. Cows tearing rhythmically at the grass, breathing breath that is as heavy as their udders; a buzzard crying, lying on the air, wings spread as if for an embrace. Not mother earth, its body seems to say. Mother sky.

You don't see so many hawks in London either, Mia thinks, still sleep-dishevelled, looking at him alone in his infinity of sky. Neither hawks nor stars.

The milkman is late. This is, apparently, a problem. Mia leaves the window and dresses quickly. The thin routines of country days on which life is erected each morning. The precise times of the postman, the milkman, the boy with the bag of newspapers slung over his shoulder, earning money for a PlayStation 3, the library van on Wednesdays with Read, Learn, Connect written across its side.

Did you ask him for extra?

I did, John. Now don't get worked up.

I don't need tea Da. I can wait. I'll have coffee later.

You will not. You'll have a cup of tea now like a normal person.

So the day does not start well.

He's disorganised, that milkman.

He's new to the job John. Give him a chance.

He's lucky to have a job. He's disorganised.

Ines goes out to buy a pint at the shop so Mia can have the tea that she doesn't necessarily want. And just as she returns, the milkman arrives, whistling and with earplugs in, oblivious.

Well, what are the chances of that?

Did you give him a piece of your mind?

He wouldn't have heard me, John. He had his music on. It wasn't worth the bother and I'd been and got the extra pint anyway.

Well, you should have done. He's inconvenienced you, Ines. You'll have to take that back now.

What? Ines stands in the doorway holding the plastic milk container by its handle.

Go on, John says staring straight ahead. We don't need it now. It'll go to waste. You'd best take it back so someone else can have it fresh. Food's not for wasting.

I'll go, Ines, Mia offers.

You will not girl. You'll sit right there and drink your tea. Haven't you got work to do? Take it back Ines. I'm not having waste in this house.

Mia and Ines roll their eyes at each other and Ines goes out. He's gone bonkers they say to each other in silence. A pint of milk, for goodness' sake.

After breakfasting and walking with her father in the morning, Mia readies herself to spend the afternoon in Shrewsbury in the County Archive. Just as she is leaving, checking for her bag, her car keys, her laptop, her father appears, as casually as it is possible to appear if you have to grope your way, in the doorway to the hall. Mia is putting on her coat.

You may as well take this, girl.

What's that Da? It is a drab-looking book that he holds out to her.

A local man wrote it, Richard Gough. Lived in the village the other side of the Shrewsbury road, same parish as Myddle. Nothing fancy about him, her da says. He was a farmer, educated type. He wrote a memoir of the place in the Civil War. She might find it interesting. His accent makes four syllables out of 'interesting', rolling the r's in its middle.

Mia takes the book without looking at it. She stares at her father. Thanks Da. She is surprised.

I've read it so I'll not be needing it for now, but I'll have it back in due course, mind. He turns away. Mia sees him sit back in his chair. She looks again at the book in her hand. A farmer. An educated type. She turns it over. Well, well.

In the archive, while she waits for her documents, Mia reads the first few pages. At the front of the book is a diagram of the seating plan in Myddle church, fine, like a skeleton. She looks at this for a long time. North aisle, south aisle. The names of buildings, many of which she knows, written on the pews. Eagle Farm, Church Farm, Meare House. Each pew linked inalienably to a building, as if the church contained the houses of its parish, the way a body contains its organs. Pew by pew the families belonging to each place are named, their small doings, their little flares of vice or corruption, all carefully set down. This is the 'history'.

It is odd, close-horizoned. Like the unknown world of birds, a hedgeful, twittering, fluttering, only partially seen; the precision of their voices, under sharp necessities.

*

A blind century wearing itself to a close. Another blind century. A flurry of men mostly, though sometimes women, writing things down, for there are many now, who feel impelled to write their histories. Organising, ordering, recording events, trying to see clearly, to understand themselves, because it is the 1690s, after great convulsion, blinking to see another king on the throne. Richard Gough, for instance, trying, for himself and for those who will come after, to make sense of things, in case such a horror as war should come again to shake the country by the throat, to turn it upside down and tear its institutions apart. And the population almost amnesiac, the memory of regicide and civil war, dim, like a dream. Only occasionally, in the middle of some task or other, stopping with the shock of disbelief.

Did we do this, really? And how did this fit come upon us, that we killed each other in these soft slow villages? Cutting off our own king's head, as if by violence you could change your very nature.

A fine drizzle now, falling on the open country of the parish of Myddle. Red sandstone houses in the hamlet of Newton on the Hill huddled in mud because it has been a wet season. And here is Gough, in his sixties, recalling his parish, as it was when he was growing up; a diligent local record, the names and characters of the families that lived hereabouts, as a sample, to show what the country was like maybe, in case anything can be learnt from it by those who come after.

I doubt not but some persons will thinke that many things that I have written are altogaether uselesse.

Page sixty-six, the light poor and the weather outside hardening into rain. The people who sat in the sixt Peiw, on the North side of the North Isle of Myddle parish church, were the Jukes family, two sons, Thomas and John, of which Thomas is the more memorable.

Thomas Jukes, a bauling, bould, confident person, for instance, was a great bowler, and often bowled with Sir Humphrey Lea att a Bowling Greene on Haremeare Heath; where he would make noe more account of Sir Humphrey, than if hee had beene a plow-boy.

He would ordinaryly tell him he lyed, and sometimes throw the bowle att his head, and then they parted in wrath. But within few dayes, Sir Humphrey would ride to Newton, and take Jukes with him to the bowles; and if they did not fall out, would take him home and make him drunk.

Then, as always, the road home ran right past the farm. And if Richard Gough loses concentration and looks out at the road, blurred now with rain, he can still see the big man, slumped round the neck of his horse, cursing his way home in the moonlight; still recall the childish terror, what if he falls off here, what if he should roll into the ditch, or come lurching to the door, banging and shouting for help? What violence might he not do?

And once Thomas Jukes did look up and caught the white face of the child in the window watching, but then his eyes were only surprised and unfocused, his body lumped and swaying with the motion of the horse. He looked like a man half-drowned, staring up at the window through water.

And here Gough sighs. His daughters' voices about their business in the house rising and falling, in time with the rain. He still misses his dead wife. Johanna. Who should have been the comfort of his old age.

Put your house in order. And this can apply to a country as well as it can to an individual. If any man shall blame mee for that I have declared the viciouse lives or actions of theire Ancestors, let him take care to avoid such evil courses, that hee leave not a blemish on his name when he is dead, and let him know that I have written nothing out of malice.

Very likely it will rain all day.

* * *

33

When Mia's documents come, they are no more significant than Gough's history. It is hard to maintain interest. They seem obsessive, repetitious. Ornately expressed legalities. Who paid a tax, who didn't. Who failed to keep a fence in order. The tiny, creeping increments by which a country slips into civil war. As if one day, like grandmother's footsteps, just in the middle of all these minute concerns, people got up and took sides and fought each other to the death. She glances up and eases her neck. Where is the mark between the small and the large scale in the life of an individual? How do you know which of the two you are living, so as to stop the horror from happening, if you even can?

She doesn't come out of the archive until the offices close, heading back to where she left her car, blinking her strained eyes in the light of early evening and feeling moth-headed.

I could do with a bit of fresh air. Maybe Da will want another walk before supper.

It is not far from Shrewsbury back to Myddle. Now Mia pulls up and parks further along the crescent, because there is no space in front of her father's house. If she were interested in cars at all, or less fuzzy from her day spent brooding, hunched over documents, Mia might have stopped to think about this. She might have noticed the unnecessarily large Mercedes parked outside her father's house, half on, half off the kerb. She might then have twigged maybe, might have guessed that her father had visitors, and hesitating a moment, she might have turned round and crossed the road to the Red Lion pub, formerly Eagle Farm, to call Ines on the mobile and ask whose is the Mercedes outside.

But her head is full of puzzles and she isn't interested in cars. So she just walks straight up the little path to the door and rings the doorbell.

What a quiet place this is, she has time to think while she waits, glancing across into the soft masses of the lime trees that shade the house, on the other side of the crescent, and watching as a cat steps leisurely across the road towards the shop. Mia is still looking away, her back turned, when Ines opens the door.

Hi Ines. Here I am. She is thinking of what she can tell her father about her day's research. The loan of Richard Gough's memoir is a new bond between them. This is perhaps the opening she's been waiting for. Where's my da?

He's in the living room with the rest of them.

Mia stops as she crosses the threshold. With who? Who's here? I didn't know you were expecting visitors.

Well we weren't. It was a surprise. I tried to call you but you must have had your phone off. And only then, as they reach the doorway to the living room, do Mia's eyes widen with realisation, as the bulk of her uncle by marriage rises to greet her, his wife hovering behind.

Freddy.

And Mia still in her town coat, hesitates, caught. She half puts out a hand, retracts it, as if with her grown-up instincts for accommodation she had said to herself, I can do this, before time dissolves and she is tumbled head over heels, as if a younger self had risen up vivid inside her, throwing her back on her motherless and disoriented twenties as if the decade between had never been. Now that is all I need.

So for one of those elastic silences, they stand, the five of them, because Mia's father is on his feet now and has felt his way to Mia's side. Now girl, he says to her quietly, making two syllables of the word girl. Because this was the risk they took, he and Ines; they both of them knew how things stood. They knew that Mia would not speak with Freddy. They knew her feelings, although they didn't either of them know, or want to know, why. She was young then, they said to each other in the kitchen, discussing the surprise arrival of Ines's sister and brother-in-law in urgent whispers. It was a difficult time for her, they said. Her mam had only just died. It would be different now, living in London, a grown woman. She wasn't wild like she used to be. It would be fine, they said, neither of them entirely believing it.

Now girl, Mia's father says over and over, as though she were one of his sheep, troubled in labour, or caught by the neck in the barbed wire. And while he says it, with his hand firm on Mia's arm – Now girl, be pleasant to your uncle, for your aunt's sake – time stretches enough for Mia to notice, with the mixture of sadness and fury that has filled her and is beating now at her eardrums, that her mother's old curtains, cut to fit, are blowing at the open window. So that she is even able to think to herself, Da's managed to get a bit of a breeze going then, before she turns on her heel, the corners of her mouth down, rejecting the hand that Freddy still holds, sandy-haired, fleshy, towards her.

Freddy just standing looking at her, with a look that he thinks too little of his wife or sister-in-law to hide, a look he knows her father isn't able to see, and the little room fizzing again with tension.

I can't do it, Mia says, half to herself. I'm sorry Da, I can't do it. Then allowing her temper to get the better of her for a moment, whipping round on Ines, angrily as if Freddy couldn't hear, as if his expensive self, his sickening casual dress, his bullish virility, all of which is suddenly so familiar to Mia, was somewhere else altogether, not there, within touching distance across her father's living room. Why didn't you tell me, Aunt? Why didn't you leave a message at the record office?

Let her go, Mia hears, in the little hallway. Let her go. Freddy's pompous voice. And then, as she wrestles with the front door, Shut the window Ines, for goodness' sake. Do we have to sit in a gale indoors?

You should have known better Da, Mia says furiously to her father, knocking against him, as she steps back to open the door. You should have said.

Then out to the car with her father following, deft down his own path. Mia, he says once. Mia, girl, for goodness' sake. What in hell's got into you? Why can't you be civil to the man? I know you don't like him, but this is ridiculous. Then when they are through the little gate and the space widens, he slows, more obviously disoriented.

He feels forward with his hand for the bonnet of her car, for the driver's door. Pull yourself together, he says, leaning in through the window to her. Both of them have a way of lowering their voices to something almost inaudible when they are angry. Pull yourself together girl. He says 'pool'. Will you pool yourself together.

No Da, I will not.

You are acting very selfish, Mia.

Will you just listen to me once and for all? I've told you. I'll not speak to Uncle Freddy.

Her father smacks his hand down on the roof of the car. Mia. You're a grown woman. We had no knowledge they were going to come. His wife's not well. Can you not find it in your heart to do it for your aunt's sake?

No, as it happens, I can't.

Your ma would never have stood for this, Mia. You listen to me. Your ma wouldn't have had this behaviour.

Dad, I'm thirty-nine, and you leave my ma out of it. If my ma was alive things would be very different. Don't you go bringing my ma into this. You don't know what you're talking about. I'm going now Da. I'm leaving. And Mia lets the car jerk forward so her father reels back, looking after her noise with his sightless eyes, angry, miserable.

*

What is it with bloody Freddy Moy? And in the back of his mind Mia's father feels anxious, that he should have asked her at the time. It had been so difficult. Him blind and widowed, bringing up a pettish girl. He'd no knowledge of girls.

It would have been different if she'd been a boy. They'd not have had to leave the farm in the first place. There would have been no gadding off to London. Why is she so ungovernable, he thinks now, groping back, one hand out. Snags his hand against something sharp on the wall. Bugger. Why's she not settled properly? Why's she not raising a family? Gadding about. Not married.

And why won't she come back, look after him, be biddable for one second?

Then, in his upset, Mia's father goes up the wrong path by mistake, finds himself fumbling at the front door of his neighbour, who is delighted to have a drama, who has been watching Mia's departure on the sly, slantwise through the picture window so as not to be noticed. Not much happens of any interest in Myddle, unless the milkman is late or the neighbours have a row.

And Ines has to be called round and finds her brother-in-law, shaky, humiliated, in the neighbour's living room, and takes his arm and leads him home.

Don't worry your head about it John. She'll come round. Ines is gentle and coaxing with him. Look now, you've cut your hand. We'll give it a run under the cold tap. As if he were a little boy. Then she shakes her head. I can't believe she would leave you out there. Just drive off like that.

And Freddy booms at him from the next room. You want to get that girl of yours in order John. She's a middle-aged woman now. It won't be long before there won't be a man that'll take her off your hands.

*

On the road back to Shrewsbury, where she'll have to find somewhere to stay the night now, Mia has to pull over. Oh for goodness' sake. I haven't even got my things. I left my toothbrush. And she bursts into tears.

Mia gets out of the car. She thinks she will take a walk and calm down, climbing a gate and striding out, she doesn't know where. Low fields, very small, very hedged. Through another gate horses canter away, tails up, breaking wind as they run.

If only her ma had been alive. That was the thing that hurt most. He had no idea, her father, when he said that. He had no idea what Mia had protected him from, how alone she'd been. I'm not saying everything's bad. I'm not saying everything's against me. But it's not exactly been a picnic either, she says to herself, reverting to her natural toughness. She wipes her eyes on her sleeve.

I hate crying. Pool yourself together.

The horses turn at the far end of the field, come back at the gallop. Mia heads for a break in the side. There must be a gate there. And there is. Down through a scrubby field to a group of trees and bushes, a glimpse of water. It's an old standing pool.

Mia walks on down towards it feeling calmer. Oh well, back to square one.

In the quiet, the affronted squawk of a heron, as if a maiden aunt had been surprised bathing, all shins and poles and folding angles, pondweed dripping from her knee bones. Rising up from the pool ungainly.

Newton on the Hill again, up to its neck in its narrow lanes. Scandal then, as now. Both good and bad men to be remembered. Many loose women. Bigamy sometimes. Common-law marriage. Richard Gough going on with his recording.

Here is another problem for the historian; so many people sharing the same name in these small places, as if there weren't enough to go round, as if the individual lives were too insignificant to be worth differentiating, or as if you could mask your sin in the character of another.

Thomas Jukes. There were at least four of that name when Richard Gough was growing up; fathers and sons and uncles and cousins. It can hardly be an accident, he thinks drily, that Myddle is so close to muddle.

There is an antient cottage by the side of Houlston Lane, where the Jukeses were tenants for a long time. Here was born another Thomas, who was sett a farm by Richard Gittins. This Thomas kept an inne. Hee married a wife, whose name was Lowry, of the Parish of Llanguedwin. Shee was a handsome woman but he might have had one as honest nearer home. They had three sons and never a good one.

And Gough can remember Thomas Jukes parading his new wife through the village when he first brought her home, sitting up among her boxes, with her eyes rolling. Lifting her down from the cart with those great forearms, something improper in the gesture, even to the child that he was at the time. And the racketing life they set up at the farm.

His youngest son, another Thomas, did use to break his neighbours' houses, but had the fortune to be catched before he had done any mischiefe. At last, his father, in some drunken humour, sett him apprentice to a jugler, a very hopeful employment. Hee only gave with him an old pettycoate of his wife's, which was given to the jugler's wife.

This handsome family of brawlers and thieves, whose boys lounged in church, under the pulpit almost, sitting higher than most of the best people of the parish, which many thought to be unseemly. Eagle Farm, which went by rights with the second pew, was then a noisy place on the road through Myddle, where the Jukes boys did as they liked; smoked pipes like men and talked boldly and goaded the dogs to fight.

And here Richard Gough's youngest daughter Dorothy comes in to call her father to look at a water spaniel found at Shotton, without an owner. The man standing in the yard with the dog a little draggled on a leash. It is the cleverest thing by all accounts. It can shut a door, sit up and beg, stand at table with a plate in its mouth. Richard Gough and the man with the dog look at one another; but will it retrieve? – that is the question.

It'll do most things, the man answers, looking at Dorothy, so I don't doubt it will do that.

In the house in Glebelands John Morgan makes himself tea with feeling fingers and mutters to his old dog and listens, because it is the one sense he can't switch off, half to Ines, back and forth on the floor above, and half to the *Today* programme. Mia, he says to himself, shaking his head, Mia girl. Where in God's name is that daughter of his?

Ines comes into the room, her roundnesses tucked into wool, wearing a cardy despite the promise of autumn heat. I've put the dog harness on the table for you, she says. I'm going to the superstore and then I'll get you your next audios from the library. I'll be back for lunch.

He could ask her. He turns his fine head her way. He could ask her what she thinks to the whole ruddy mess. He could ask her what she thinks happened. Only he isn't the asking type. What is there to ask anyway? Things are as they are. You don't change things by finding out what you don't want to know in the first place. So he has a sip of tea instead, puts his hand on his old dog's head.

Out of the window, in the permanent pasture, the cows are doing what cows have always done, like before the castle was ruined, when the fields were busy and the woods stood round close, the way a person might pull up the bedclothes against the cold. They lie chewing, among brown seed heads of clover and docks, with the thistle puffs drifting by, while overhead the crows row cannily back and forth, pulling on their wings like oars, and a hawk breaks occasionally from the woods, as if flung across the spaces in between.

Did you hear me John? You're miles away there.

Aha. He didn't as a matter of fact, but that doesn't matter either. Out of the radio, on the side, a reporter shouts over helicopter blades, and the cows go on lying in sunlight. Well, it's another lovely day for it, Ines says, looking out.

It was years ago anyway, John Morgan is thinking. Mia was an adult when she took herself off to London. She wasn't a child any more. She wasn't an innocent. She'd not stinted herself on boyfriends he didn't think, though she'd never brought anyone home. He bends his head, his hand still on the dog. He doesn't know if he has failed his daughter. What can you do? He used to be so certain, before he lost his sight.

*

And at the same time Mia, who is sitting in a bed and breakfast in Shrewsbury, sips her tea and reads a newspaper. Concerns have been expressed about the viability of a military mission in the Middle East, she reads. General warns of mission failure.

Two days since she left her father. No communication between them. Just a separate simmering and tightening and a turning separately over. At the same pace but in different places picking up their lives, trying with weary half-attention not to curdle their anger into injury, not to turn sour. And occasionally, though at different times from her father, Mia suffers a pang of sadness and a sudden thought, as she stops whatever she is doing, to ask herself, But why? How silly. And a sharp pricking of tears and an almost reaching for the telephone, before the mood is past and in their separate places Mia and her father pick up again, stirring the tea maybe, lifting it to their lips, going on with whatever their separate business might be, separately.

Yesterday, for instance, she had added to her list of castles, Shrewsbury, Prince Rupert's garrison in the Civil War. If you have a job to do girl, then get on and do it. But she'd had only half her mind on it, so she'd missed the entrance. She'd found herself by mistake above the railway lines, on a covered walkway, with the castle inaccessible below. Coming towards her were crowds of men and women, white shirts and black trousers, on lunch break.

I'm sorry, Mia approached the first of the group to come level. I'm looking for the entrance to the castle. I seem to have walked into a police convention.

We're prison warders, the man had answered. You're going the wrong way – unless you want locking up, that is.

Well now, there's a solution.

But that was yesterday. Today might well be better. Mia goes back to her tea and her paper.

The woman in charge of Mia's bed and breakfast puts her head round the dining-room door. She has been so remiss. There was a call from a gentleman, while Mia was out yesterday. She doesn't know how she could have forgotten. Head like a sieve these days.

And Mia's heart jumps and she looks up suddenly from her newspaper, because it will have been her da ringing. But it wasn't. How could it be when he had no idea where she was? It was her friend Bill from London, whom she'd rung the day before, returning her call. Bill Radic, writer and musician, who is writing the life of Brilliana Harley, and for whom Mia is doing the research. He'd said he couldn't get her to answer her mobile, apparently. He didn't know if there was a problem. And he expected there wasn't and she was probably just avoiding him, and here the bed-and-breakfast woman looks arch at Mia and pauses, just fractionally, in the hope of a confidence. Although long years of experience could have told her that any kind of confidence from this one was unlikely.

Mia says nothing and goes listlessly back to her paper.

So the bed-and-breakfast lady takes up a cloth and does some vigorous swabbing. She only runs the B&B for the company really, and you would be surprised how many people do ask advice, how many let you in on their secrets or their problems, how many cry on your shoulder. She looks across at Mia. She has her down as a hard type now, and hard types make her impatient. And the counter receives a final devastating swipe because looks aren't everything and doesn't Mia know she won't keep those looks for ever.

*

Fathers and daughters. Small echoes, as if life was a song that the world was humming, looping round and back on its own refrain. Richard Gough's daughter Dorothy clanging about the house unnecessarily this morning, as if a wind had got up inside. They have had a difference over the spaniel from Shotton. And he is trying to write.

Old Richard Gough, the historian's great-grandfather, lived to a great age, and was darke twenty yeares beefore he dyed, and yett was very healthfull.

And when Gough was a boy, there were many who remembered this blind man, making his way along his familiar lanes with his stick, for he was vigorous and of an independent mind. Only on market days would he submit to being led around by his daughter Elizabeth, on account of the great crowds.

They are of a persistent stock, the Goughs. There have been eight generations of them in Myddle, including Richard's own son and grandson.

Things change quickly, even in one lifetime, he thinks.

He is remembering the common before enclosure. There were two lytle houses or cottages upon it neare the south-west corner. Towers, a Taylor, dwelt in one of them, and one Edward Grestocke, alias Newton, lived and sold ale in the other, and his wife made cakes, which were accounted the best in this country, soe that two or three of Grestock's cakes made a very acceptable present to a friend. These two famylyes are extinct in this parish.

Only just under two miles, as the crow flies, up to Billmarsh Common to buy cakes of old Mrs Grestock, and mind you touch not a crumb of it on the way home, neither drop it scrambling through hedges or briars. And on a fair day, this was a happy commission for a child, along the stream that came from the spring at the bottom of the valley, past the many standing pools with skaters on their surface.

Mr Osmary Hill, Richard Gough writes, fathers and daughters again, tooke a lease of this common and incloased it; hee pulled downe the cottages, and built a faire house upon itt.

Hee bought a litle meadow called the Partridge Meadow, it lyes att the west end of Sleape Gorse.

He had one son, whose name was Francis, he had severall daughters, who were servants to gentlemen whose sons were his schollers. He had one daughter who was servant to a gentleman who lived neare Wellington, and as this young woman was holding water for her master to wash his hands in the kitchen, he cast a litle water from off his finger into her face, which her mistress, who was present, seeing, and conceiving it too famillier an action, shee in a rage tooke up the cleaver, and gave her such a blow in the head that shee dyed.

Richard Gough doesn't know if this is altogether true but that is what people hearabouts say. It is too good a story to omit, although he does not wish to be accused of invention. *Audita tantum loquor*, he adds at the end of the account. I speak only from hearsay.

*

Later Mia has an appointment with the archive for Brampton Bryan Castle. Brampton is where Brilliana Harley, wife of Robert the Puritan, lived and raised her children and suffered and fought for her beliefs, and died. Mia leaves her car and walks down the main street to get a feel for the place first. It is a village cut in half by the main road, one of the routes to Wales, almost bang on the border and four miles directly south of Hopton. A huddle of red-brick houses with painted porches, some older-looking, half-timbered, a hairdresser's in the Old Forge. Quiet. Mia's feet make an alarming amount of noise. But it feels significant, because of the road maybe.

The castle isn't visible from the village any more. A hedge bulged and huge, like a defensive earthwork, runs the length of the main street on one side, hiding the castle ruins and the house that replaced it, as though to record the embattled status of the family; the only Puritan stronghold in a county of Royalists.

Mia has to remind herself that this is a village that was sacked and burnt, a village at war with itself in the seventeenth century, most of its households for King and one or two for Parliament. Is that anywhere in your memory, Mia asks it as she walks its sleepy centre. The church had to be entirely rebuilt.

The archive is in the estate office. Mia works quietly for most of the morning. She is reasonably productive. Not everything is legible. Some of the documents demand patience, sitting, staring, waiting for the strokes and dashes to resolve themselves into recognisable letters, as if waiting for a fog to lift and reveal a landscape. She doesn't dare ignore anything. Every now and again she sighs.

She spends a long time looking at a nineteenth-century tithe map. It is late in date but she can find nothing earlier that is complete, and Bill had wanted to know some of the field names. This, at least, is interesting to her. My da would like this, she thinks. People's names for their own places. Sharing it out. As if someone had constructed a net and dropped it over the ground, parcelling pieces into little catchments. Tumpy Field. The Plock. The Slang. Crass Moor. Long Fridays. Wet Reels. As if the urge to write, to mark, didn't stop with pen and paper but extended out into the world. How deep do these marks go, Mia wonders. How far back do these names go?

Then she looks at papers of ownership or transfer, at records of sales or accounts, squinting at the past through her keyhole. Who wrote all this down? Did they mean it to be kept this long? But she treats the papers with reverence, because they have survived. Occasionally, looking and listening down the long distances, she is rewarded with a voice that flutters up out of something, like a butterfly seen out of the corner of an eye, an impression of colour rising up from dry grass. A turn of phrase, a particular spelling, an observation, and something briefly alive murmurs, a person talking, though the voice falls again too quickly out of earshot.

Here for instance is a piece of old vellum, torn out of something no longer needed, used as binding for a scruffy-looking book. The Brampton Bryan Parish Register. Brown cobweb of entries, starting in 1598, barely decipherable to the uninitiated. Then, from 1612, kept up by Thomas Pierson, Nonconformist minister and rector, who had the living off the Harley family and whose hand, like his beliefs, is clear and decided. Outside, it is another sunny day.

Mia reads, 1622. Six deaths, six baptisms, no marriages that year. 'Mary the Lady Harley second wife to Sr Robert Harley Knight of the Bath was buryed August 5.'

Sir Robert Harley, the man born at Wigmore, who took the flare-like certainty of his mother Margaret, as if it was a torch passed, hand to hand. Carried it into his own life and became a man not afraid to smash things in the interests of a new order. Hammering the stained glass in Whitehall and Westminster to smithereens. Cleaning out the Episcopacy. Stripping churches of idolatry, pictures, statues, decoration, grinding the old, spooked world of the Catholics to a powder underfoot.

Mary is the second of his wives to die. But there is no record here of Sir Robert's third marriage, in July of 1623, under a year after Mary's death. He would be what? – forty-four years old, his new wife, Brilliana, two decades younger, the daughter of Sir Edward Conway, secretary of state to King Charles I. No record of that.

Mia reads instead, '1623 Ann, wife of John Adderley buryed 6 Jan being the Epiphany

Thomas Griffites of Brompton buryed 16 Jan

Elinor Reece being a poor woman buryed 9 Apr

Richard son of Thomas and Elizabeth Carter baptised 25 Apr

Three marriages in all, that year. Five baptisms. Eight deaths

Alice Cotrel widow buryed 24 Aug'

Mia turns the pages over, looks at the matter-of-fact minimal records; name, date of birth, marriage, date of death. Occasionally a snippet of extra information, otherwise no record that they were different from any generations before or after.

Just people. Just a name and a brief tag, if you are lucky. All the enormous private things that happened, all the stories, gone without trace. 'Poor woman', 'widow', whoever else they might have been along the way, the little child collecting shells and feathers, growing up to be a Puritan possessed by reform. Or the beauty too good for the local boys, with the uncle who made a fool of you. Dreaming yourself some great story. Fighting with your da. How private our real stories are.

The papers on the desk can't answer her questions. They only know about systems of ownership, or legislation, or favour. People are not their business.

The thing that research is most like, Mia says to herself angrily, after a while, glancing at the window and the sky free and flying and the branches bobbing, the thing that research is most like, is sweeping the floor. You have to go into all the tightest corners, under every piece of furniture, no matter how dark, or impenetrable, or awkward the angle. Because you can't afford to miss anything. You have to read all the Census returns, the registers, the court rolls, the notes, the bills, the correspondence, the diaries, the probate records, the wills. You spend your time among the dust and husks of life, gathering them up as though they were precious, making a heap of all the lifeless things, the things that are left behind, the dross, the scurf, the nail clippings. And then when everything is present, for the moment, until more should be dropped or discovered that is, you say to the world, now watch. Now watch me while I reassemble these nail clippings, while I pat all this dust up and stick it back into a living breathing person again.

These are the thoughts that prickle Mia into a fever of irritation among the tin boxes of the Brampton Bryan archive.

They are kind and solicitous, in the estate office, of which the muniments room is part. They come on tiptoes with cups of tea and biscuits, which they put far away from the documents Mia is studying, because you mustn't mix crumbs with crumbs. They don't know how easily Mia gets cross.

*

After her morning in the muniments room, Mia crosses the road fast like someone released. There is no one around. Silent at midday, like so many of these English villages, just cars passing, back and forth over the English–Welsh border at speed, and a brisk wind. She walks the length of the high hedge cut in mounds and bumps and crosses the road again, and climbs a gate to reach the river. She wants to be able to look back at the castle, so she can see it in its setting. It is too shut in now, to be able to see how it once sat, how it fitted itself to its landscape, what use it might have been when it was first designed.

No one in the flat fields, or along the river bank. Mia follows the river, taking her telephone out of her pocket a couple of times and looking at the signal bar. As if her da would ring her. He never would. The little screen continues resolutely blank. There is no signal.

Mia sits down on the long horizontal root of a tree and watches the water.

You can see the castle from here. Dark sandstone towers, still fat, still solid-looking, although ruined.

*

And before, in the obscurity of its interior, a vigorous man, whose movements are quick, as if the winds that whisk continually over the lip of his father's park had somehow collected themselves to make a person. Robert Harley. Aged twenty-five say, his beard pointed, above the high ruff of an Elizabethan courtier, shrewd, careful, full of gusty energy. Not a dreamer. Not a looker out of windows.

Sitting in the bay of the upstairs window, for light, writing letters, long before Brilliana. His hand too is quick, the words a chaos of strokes and coils, as if scattered, blown across the page at speed, crossings out everywhere as he changes his mind. He is impatient. Impatient to be married again because how else to make your position sure, how to else to advance yourself, without a wife, without heirs. Impatient right now, with Sir Thomas Coningsby, whose daughter Anne might have married him, now that his first wife and her child are dead.

He is breaking off the engagement. He doesn't want to be made a fool of. Coningsby's attempt to bargain is insulting. If the dowry is not paid in a lump sum, only as and when the father feels able, then Sir Robert will not take the girl.

Yet remember that you have kept your daughter from an honest man that might have been her husband, whose honesty, for your better knowledge, is so accompanied with discretion, as that it were loth to be censured simplicity.

But then, he is sorry, so he writes to Anne herself, fidgeting the words onto the page with a touch of petulance, blaming her father, whose more than ill usage hath been the strong motive of this fatall breach; wherewith how far you have been of familiarity I know not, but it shall be greater satisfaction to me that I let you know it was his fault.

Look elsewhere for a wife. Choose again. The letters are sealed and handed to a carrier.

*

It is lunchtime. Mia fishes absent-mindedly in her various pockets without taking her eyes off the river. On the way from Shrewsbury she had stopped at a shop in what looked like a Nissen hut. It sold cards mostly and things she'd forgotten existed like Spam and Green Giant sweetcorn and three Mars bars, lined up separately and with spaces in between. It was like something you might imagine from the fifties. What is this place? she had asked herself, looking at its sparse shelves and at its owner, sunk behind an old-fashioned cash register, staring at a newspaper. Pale face, as though made out of window putty. Too much Spam probably. He isn't even reading. His eyes are motionless. Still, for want of anything else she'd bought one of the Mars bars to eat for lunch. Now she finds it, takes it out of her pocket, along with her notebook.

While she chews Mia lets the running water fill up her gaze and take over her mind. She blobs the chocolate onto the page of her open notebook and doesn't notice and does nothing. She goes back, to thinking about the lives lived in these places, to Robert Harley for instance. Brutal bereavements, bowed to as the will of God. The young first wife dead in childbirth. A frustrated pause. Then the second marriage, this time lasting years, two further children, both dead in infancy, the death of a second wife. How would you keep faith under such conditions?

After a while Mia looks down, as if surprised, and sweeps the dropped chocolate off her notebook, so it leaves small streaks behind it. This is all there is on the page. She stares furiously at it for a moment before snapping the book shut.

*

Years pass for Sir Robert. Grey creeping into the hair above the ruff despite the energy. Forty-four now. No children living.

Then comes this small, composed woman in her early twenties, whose expression is most like a bird's. Brilliana. Mia doesn't know how they met. Brilliana has a quickness that must have made her recognisable, familiar to him despite her strangeness. Glimmerings of other qualities that, closeted as a woman must be, are yet untried; a self-possession that will turn into great strength, a shrewdness that will outclass Robert Harley's own, a coolness of head, a certainty.

She speaks French, almost better than English. She reads Latin. Born abroad, brought up at the port of Brill as a child, beloved of her father. A little girl with a sharp mind, watching the wooden ships rolling in under sail. The quaysides full of noise, of drama; the trade, the religious exiles, the foreign dignitaries. Life must have looked so glamorous. Then at close quarters, among others, Lord Herbert of Cherbury, rogue, swaggerer, handsome even to a little girl, with his Court clothes and old Queen Elizabeth's kiss on his lips, dining with her father every night, while he waited for a wind. Religious free thinker. Robert Harley's dear friend, as it happens. Small world.

So she has heard some conversations. She has seen a little of politics. She is of martyred Protestant stock and her father is a courtier, so the connection would be a good and useful one, if it could but be arranged.

Standing in front of Sir Robert those first few times, when they exchanged their ornate courtesies, or first touched formal hands with the spark of something sudden, below speech, did Brilliana know what her life here, in Herefordshire, would be like, Mia thinks. Did anyone tell her? It is incomprehensible, opaque, a woman's life that far back in time, at the limits of England, in the countryside. A Puritan. The hierarchy, the bog of duty and of motherhood, voiceless, anxious, small. The mouse trapped in the wheel. Round she goes and round, it seems. The repetition, of tasks, of prayers. Her life ticks in Mia's neck, like an irritation the more she reads of it. She is unable to understand. How would you tolerate such constraint, such repression, such downright boredom?

Sitting by the river, the weight of a life locked to the land bows Mia briefly, like the pressure of a weather system. No getting out of it, that's what she remembers from her own childhood. The repetitive buying of stock, the putting up of fences and enclosures, the supervising of feeding, penning, breeding, slaughter. Can we have a holiday, Da? My friends are going on holiday. No we can not, girl. Do you think the sheep will lamb themselves? Where does your bread and butter come from? Do you see it growing on trees?

*

Ther was 12 oxen sould at Worcster . . . but the hoorses weare not theare. On Monday Mr Ambler came for the woule and payed his mony.

The new park pale will be ended very neere this week.

Mr Ambler has not keep his bargane in fecthing the wolle, nor I thinke he means it not. The new inclosher is this day made an end of.

Mia glances up. Brilliana's dutiful letters to her husband running in her head. Why didn't you ever once complain?

Walking back later, along the polite banks of the river. This is the Teme. It seems a shallow, biddable stream, grassy-banked. Alders, willows and thorn bend over its waters. It is impossible to imagine it anything except clear, running over these small stones. Mia tries to visualise blood from the Hopton massacre uncurling itself like smoke downstream. At one point, round a bend of the river, among grass and small docks, there is the skeleton of a fish picked clean by something. Mia looks at it for a long time. Dead is so different from alive.

Looking up at Brampton Bryan as she walks on, it is obvious, she realises now, that it sits at the gateway of England and Wales. It is right in the middle of the soft gathering of two ridges of hills, high and woolly with trees, with the road going straight past the castle and on into Wales, guarding the pass, as it were. So this one is strategic at last, Mia thinks, as she winds her way along.

*

The ruins are damp when Mia eventually climbs up from the river bank and walks round the side of the Hall to the castle. They grow a kind of green scum that is not moss, and shreds of undernourished chickweed or nettles. Mia makes her way down the thin central passage, stoops through doorways and looks up at sky.

Dear Mia, Bill's email had read. He belongs to the generation that treats email as a modern version of the letter. Dear Mia, I hope you are having fun in woolly Wales. I'm not in Wales, Mia says to him in her head, still looking at the sky. I'm in Herefordshire. There are so many arched entrances, unimaginably small.

Another husk, another paring, Mia thinks, stepping out of the ruins and into sunlight again. For Bill, writing lives is a pretty straightforward business. You collect the facts, diligently. You order them, chronologically, and then you write them down, as simply and as clearly as possible. You are the servant, as he has told her many times, of the material. Perhaps it is being a musician that makes this so easy. Writing lives is like playing music. You just need a score to interpret.

Brampton holds its dead towers against the sky. It is just standing up now, nothing more. Decay arrested and made safe. From outside, the castle is sunk to the waist in garden planting. It looks very tamed. Ceanothus, a nineteenth-century American import. Mock orange. For all our mania to preserve, things sift and sift through our hands. So much gets lost. What imaginable relation do these castles, for instance, bear to their own past as strongholds, now that even the scale of our lives is different, now that we live in a world of metal ships and skyscrapers and guided missiles and tarmac and reinforced concrete. And even if you manage, through careful reassembly of facts, to name all the rooms again, to put back the towers and the damask hangings, that's not it, is it, Mia thinks. That's not even the half of it.

Mia circles the ruin on its mown lawn. How small you seem, she says to its walls and towers, how fragile. All the same she looks out, despite herself, imagining away the tennis court, which is below the castle mound, and the garden hedges, imagining the unbroken view of the Teme valley and the road out to Ludlow.

The fields open out across the valley bottom, quiet and fertile. This was a good position. It must have been a good place to live. Not as crazily high as Wigmore. Not as swallowed by its hills as Hopton, where terrible things happened and no one noticed. This would have been the perfect place to guard the border, to look out towards London, towards the world of politics and power, and dream of playing your part.

So that's the lie of the land, as her father would have said. That's the place, and places make people, Mia says to herself, under her breath. Places do make people.

The thing about the Harleys, Mia thinks suddenly as she comes down the castle mound and returns to her car, is that they were people who could see out. From the very beginning, she thinks, from Wigmore and then from Brampton, they were a people with a prospect. That's something I can tell Bill.

*

In the car, Mia checks for signal. None. Then driving through Ludlow, she stops on impulse at a phone box. She punches in the numbers for Glebelands, listens to the phone ringing on the table in the little hall, with the kitchen window visible beyond, the cowfield in the afternoon light with the flies buzzing.

Halloo. Pause, long enough to fool Mia, who says with relief in her voice, Halloo Da. But she is interrupted, because it is only the answer-machine after all. This is the number for Ines and John, her father's voice says. Another longer pause. I am sorry we aren't here to take your call but please leave us a message after the tone and we'll return your call as soon as possible. Stiff phrases. Thank you. Pause again. Bye now.

For a moment Mia just leaves the line silent. Her father is probably out walking. That is how he spends his afternoons, with the old Labrador in harness, trusting him down the steep lanes, too proud to have a hand out, stepping with an adjusted stride, only stumbling occasionally and greeting what passers-by there are, through sound rather than sight.

Afternoon John.

Afternoon Billy. Lovely afternoon for it.

It is indeed, though we could do with the rain.

Halloo Dad, Mia says a little tightly into the machine. Hallo

56

Ines. Just ringing to say I have to be back to London now. Sorry things didn't work out this time round. She pauses again. Sorry to miss you. See you both soon. Bye now.

It is an awkward message but it is a message. Mia goes back to the car with a slightly easier heart.

PART II

LONDON

I would have their breeding like to the Dutch woman's clothing tending to profit only and comeliness.

Though she never have a dancing school master, a French tutor nor a Scotch Tailor . . . it makes no matter; for working in curious Italian purls or French borders, it is not worth the while. Let them learn plain wools of all kind; so they take heed of too open seaming. Instead of song and music let them learn cookery and laundry. And instead of reading Sir Philip Sydney's Arcadia, let them read the Grounds of Good Huswifery. I like not a female poetess at any hand. Let greater personages glory their skill in music, the posture of their bodies, their knowledge in languages, the greatness and the freedom of their spirits and their arts in arraigning of men's affections at their fluttering faces. This is not the way to breed a private gentleman's daughter.

From *Tom of All Trades*, William Powell, 1631

The dog, which had got lost in Regent's Park and spent the night staring at rabbits as though they were the product of hallucination, found himself eventually by the roaring Marylebone Road, as the London morning yawned itself into the various sandwich bars and coffee shops round Great Portland Street station. Trotting behind the pedestrians when the lights changed, he managed to cross over and has been unproductively sniffing and urinating back and forth between the pub and the mini-market for some time. No one so far has let anything drop for him. The people have offices and jobs to go to, so they don't notice, or don't want to notice.

Nose up he sets off down Great Portland Street, crosses to the Mexican restaurant on the other side where he comes into the view of Mia, who is sitting, as she so often does, on her bed, looking out of the window.

That's a stray, she thinks, watching him lift his leg for the thirty-fifth time that morning. Poor thing. Several passers-by sidestep him, some of them glancing down to look absently, as they hurry onward to the Tube station. She could grab her coat and her keys, supposing she could find them, run down the stairs of the three floors there are between her and street level, and collar him somehow – she'd need to take a belt or a tie of some kind – and she could bring him up to the flat to keep her company. But he'd be gone by the time she got down there. And then too there is the fact that he probably has a distraught owner somewhere on Primrose Hill, or in Camden, who even now is printing posters saying, 'Missing, Tyro or Benjy or Rob, scruffy-looking, much-loved mongrel, contact x. Reward offered.' She'd just have got fond of him, when she'd have to give him back. So instead she stays sitting at the window and watches him nosing on down the street, alone.

It's not a bad view from up here, although she'd like to be higher. The street is busy, so there's plenty to watch. Pigeons precision-flying, bolt up and down on a network of diagonals that only they can see. Sparrows like airborne grit flit between the window ledges. And endless traffic crawls, under the blinking eye of the one set of traffic lights below her, and breathes its fumes against the sides of the buildings, to coat the windows and the ledges and to creep through cracks and stick to her face, and gather in the corners of her eyes and under the crescents of her nails, and catch in the fine hairs of her nose so that she smells it both day and night. Black grime. That is London for you, grime and the noise of the engines that produce it, the throb of the taxis and buses that even three floors up she can feel reverberating through the building.

It can be pretty disgusting in London.

Also, Mia thinks, there is a chemical thinness to the air, a slight sourness, that you notice most when you've just come from the country. Still, at night, if she can't sleep and sits up like this, with her knees to her chest, there will always be something to watch. The odd rat going door to door, or a drunk, not feeling too clever, who careers down from the pub on the corner, roaring and heaving over the pavement, and the viscous puddle that he leaves behind him, glistening in the street light.

Or there are cats. Maybe a cat would be better than a dog. There are always cats after all. Cats who come out at night to live, like time travellers, in a mediaeval world of rivalry and operatic fights and ferocious coupling in doorways, melting into the modern through catflaps, as the street lights extinguish.

Cats are no kind of companion. Mia thinks fondly of the little dog, who has probably reached Oxford Circus by now. If she'd only gone down when she had the chance. Intermittently, between looking out and thinking, she presses the record button on a small hand-held Dictaphone and speaks into it slowly.

She is trying to send an audio letter to her father but today it is slow going. The memory of Freddy's fat face has made her restless. His skin in the light of her father's living room, sallowing, slacker than she remembered. The ugliness of his small shoes, too shiny, his great bulk too scented, the awful squareness of his crotch, his legs too far apart. How could she ever? As if all these details, which she'd thought forgotten, had simply been overlaid in the jumble store of her mind and now here they are again, because there they always were, and no doubt always will be, making her get up suddenly and pace about the flat. And then she says out loud, For goodness' sake. And in her head she thinks, How could you Da, how could you be so forgetful? How could you put Ines and her sister before me? Although it isn't her father's fault and she knows that.

But for her father to have said nothing, to have accused her like a child of bad behaviour. *You are acting very selfish Mia. If your ma were alive* . . . He hasn't responded to her telephone message. She's had no word.

He doesn't know, she says to herself out loud again. It's not exactly his fault that I made a mess of my own life.

So Mia sits back down, takes up the Dictaphone determined to make another start. They are stubborn people, Mia and her father, as if the granite of the farmhouse in Scotland, where they lived for so long, had entered their bones and fixed them, obdurate, even against their own longing.

Back in London now Da, she says, a little stiffly to begin with, glancing out of the window. Weather is always a safe bet. Weather is his favourite topic of conversation anyway, after farming. It's what you'd call awkward weather, she says, speaking into the Dictaphone. It was good to see you and Ines and Preston. I've just seen a stray dog go past and I was thinking that it would be good to have some company up here. Long pause. She clicks the recorder off.

63

Why do I keep trying, she could ask herself, with a man who is so difficult? Because he is your father. Because it is your duty.

On again, a moment or two later, and spoken more brightly, and with purpose. I thought I'd tell you a bit about my trip for John's book, and how it went. She says John's book, not Bill's, because there are more things than Uncle Freddy between Mia and her father.

But it's hard to go on once she has said John's name. How it bounces back at her off his books and papers and the glass in front of his pictures. Had she said it neutrally enough? She plays it back and her machine-thickened voice says, John's book. Click. John's book. And now she catches John's pale, enquiring eye, as he looks out at her, with his silvered hair and his precise beard, from the photograph she keeps of him on the desk. Well what do I do, she asks him, say nothing? Not mention you?

Erase. Click, I thought I'd tell you a bit about my trip, for the book, how it went. Neither Bill's nor John's.

John Curtesy, the newspaper man, the sometime biographer, whose bed she shared, for how many years? – in whose flat she now lives, and of whom her father sharply disapproves, because he never married her, because of the thirty years or so there was between them in age, because John didn't want children, and because he was no kind of a man. Although none of this had mattered to Mia. Only once, when she'd asked him, agonised by her father's refusal to relent – is it because your first wife hurt you, that you don't want to marry me? – had he put his long fingers together, tip to tip, and looked at her over them. Which would you rather, Mia, he'd said, unflinching, which would you rather, that I be your husband, or that I be your lover? Put like that, it was difficult to opt for marriage.

In the end it was this coolness of John's, this detachment, that held her to him so fast. His aloofness, his adherence to principle. The way that even his skin was dry and smooth like paper, as though there were nothing unruly about him. Like her father he

64

was an exacting man. It made their union in his tiny bedroom, with the traffic rumbling below, among the chaos of the night streets, nothing short of miraculous to her. She never wanted to be without him again, no matter what her father thought.

But he'd had a heart attack in the newspaper offices one day. She'd been told of his death by telephone. Bill Radic, his long-time crony and occasional drinking partner, had cried when he broke the news to her. Can you come down to the Charing Cross Hospital? Then, You'd better sit down my dear, added as an after-thought. Even in shock, as she was, she thought what a bungler. John would never have done that, bungled the telling of some piece of life and death, made such a hash of it as that. She'd driven across London in a blind rage, as though it was all Bill's fault.

There was the cremation, as rushed and severe as John would have liked it, and she felt separate then and ever after, when his friends, out of kindness, asked her for a drink or to their own family suppers. She sat, stricken, at their tables like something made of glass, with all her grief visibly contained, and felt separate. Or she sat in pubs, where the grime got into the beer, which was the same temperature as tears and only slightly less salty, and listened to his colleagues and writing partners and felt separate again, because of her comparative youth perhaps, because of her intimacy with John, which is nothing like friendship. They seemed grey to her, these kind men, very frayed at the edges and dissolving before her eyes. They were nothing to hold on to after all, so she let them all go.

It was different for her, she would think when she got back to John's flat after one of these evenings and found again that he wasn't there although all his things, like her, were waiting for his return. She felt as if she were holding to the walls of a building whose floor had fallen out.

And it is high enough, this flat, which is too big, even a year later. She walks round its T of rooms from time to time, opening doors into rooms she never uses, as though there might be, on the other side, some forgotten person who would look up lost in thought as she entered and gather papers and pens and put a hand to his head in confusion saying, I'm so sorry. I'd completely lost track of time. I should have gone years ago. But of course there never is.

It is the bedroom that is the worst; so small, so dark even in daytime, embracing its loss in silence, as the dust motes fall. She was never his wife so she has no rights here – that is how she feels – except at his invitation and there will be no more invitations now. She stands on the threshold and feels the room's emptiness answer her own and looks at the photograph of John's mother on the chest of drawers, her bird stare three-quarters on and her hair crimped back from her face in a permanent wave. No question of sleeping here. Besides, the bed was the place where John most wasn't, so Mia had gone, after a week of nights spent wakeful on the sofa, and bought herself a modern single bed and had it installed in John's workroom, under the window.

So here she is, in London, in her lover's flat, talking to her father, not mentioning her uncle. And this is what she does most days. She sits or lies on her bed, depending more or less on whether it is day or night. There are many different ways to absent yourself from life. She has found for instance that if you ring no one up, then in the end no one rings you. And in this double absence, of John and now of herself, she has made a space in which to exist almost without noticing; a sort of negative of a life. She sits, or lies, and listens to the silence reverberating around her until absence is really the only thing present.

She makes herself tea and she pores over John's work. If she can't have his body then maybe, at least, she can have his mind. She reads his books, his papers, his meticulous notes and card-index systems, trudging back from bereavement. She has the sense that she is climbing up out of something half-lit and very deep, some underworld that other people cannot see. Watching and reading, she slips back and forth, like the cats. And she waits for time to do what time does, which is mainly to erase.

*

It is another time. Earlier. Another season. Pavements very full. A couple – or are they not a couple? They are not touching – walking up from the busy intersection with Oxford Street. A young pretty woman and an older man. The woman has the stunned look of someone moving through a dream. It is Mia with her lover, ten years before. Their relationship is new, still a secret from his colleagues and from Mia's father.

Towards evening. Street lamps on, although it is not dark, just the early blue-grey of winter dusk. Behind the couple, Oxford Street on late-night shopping, is a solid crowd moving slow and glazed like a snake after feeding, past windows that are filled with Christmas lights. Individual heads turn and look and people go in and come out bag-laden but the overall impression is of a single body easing itself along. Mia and John Curtesy, having extricated themselves, head up at a happier pace, towards the Tube station and John's flat.

You are very formal, Mia says to him, glancing sideways as they walk.

In what way? He is tall and thin and although it is almost Christmas, he is wearing few clothes to protect him from the cold. He has an old-fashioned quality of attentiveness that Mia is in love with. Sometimes she says things for the sake of it, without thinking, just to see that look, just to have him concentrate his attention on her. In what way am I formal?

Well, you are standing very far away for one thing.

John Curtesy looks at the ground between them as though calculating. He makes a gesture with one hand. I think this is an appropriate distance. He smiles. I don't want to walk on top of you.

Mia turns her head and looks into the shop windows. She is trying to hide her elation. I wish you would, she thinks to herself.

I wouldn't care. I wish you would. She can't help gloating. He is so separate, so mysterious to her, this man who is old enough to be her father. He is quiet. She has never been with anyone this quiet. Self-contained. What does he think when he looks like that? What is he looking at?

What now? he asks her, catching her glance. More criticism?

No, Mia says. I was just wondering, seeing you looking, I was wondering what you were thinking, that's all.

He doesn't answer immediately. He goes on walking, with his quick, light, scissoring stride, and he goes on looking. I am thinking about London. I'm always thinking about London. He pauses as if considering, looks across at the synagogue with its blank eyes. Watching it grow, I suppose, he says. I imagine it like an animal, you know, sleeping and fatting, laid out on the ground.

Mia's eyes widen. What an odd thought. Like an animal? How? She looks down at the pavement. I mean, it is the ground, isn't it – that's all London is, surely? It's a place.

No. John has his hands in his pockets, his scarf wound three times round his neck, its ends tucked into his buttoned jacket, crosswise. No, that is not how I see it. He says it mildly though with a focus that, as so often, gives his remarks the tone of remonstrance. The ground is the ground, Mia.

Sorry is on the tip of Mia's tongue, though she has nothing really to apologise for. She can't help feeling half-ashamed. She is a farmer's daughter after all. She should know that. She looks away again at the lit, unthinking shops.

The ground is the ground and the city is the city, John says. The city is only the city because of the ground, because the ground is right. I'll give you that. Because of the river for instance, or the hills, or its position in the land mass as a whole. But you must always be aware of the ground, whatever it's got on top of it. He speaks gently, insistently, otherwise it could be her father talking. You must always feel the ground beneath your feet, Mia, especially in a city. Think about it – Primrose Hill, Maida Vale,

Kensal Rise, Clerkenwell. They weren't always lines of shops and dry cleaners. St John's Wood, the Embankment. They all meant something once.

Of course, Mia says, almost breathless, looking at him. They are standing still outside a Turkish fast-food joint, a doner kebab sweating and revolving behind Mia's head. Leaning on the counter inside, two waiters watch, hoping idly for something to liven the day, a row maybe, a kiss, it doesn't matter which. Of course, Mia says, I hadn't thought of it like that.

It's her dad, one of the waiters says. She's out of line.

The other one dries a glass without looking. That's no way her dad. Look at the look on her. Are you crazy, man? No way is that her dad.

The street side of the window, unaware of his audience, John's face is intent. I see the whole of England as a conversation, he says to Mia, while the waiters watch. A long conversation between a land mass and the people who have lived on it; of what the place is and has to offer and what the people have responded to and looked after, curated maybe, and what they have used, what they have taken, or spoilt, or changed, or broken. He takes one slim hand out of his pocket to gesture at the street before them, the grimy synagogue, the shopfronts for the rag trade, the cafés and newsagents all suddenly included in his vision. It is a small place, relatively, he says. So almost none of it is untouched. It would be wrong, or blind, not to be aware of that.

Mia watches him and listens. Sometimes when he talks he seems to be thinking out loud, to be talking almost to himself.

He stops suddenly. I'm just explaining my own preoccupations to you, he says. And you did ask. He has the grace to smile, a small smile, almost apologetic. I'm vying with the lights for your attention Mia, looking down at her caught between him and the Christmas shops.

If only he knew, Mia thinks, why I look away at the shops. It's only because I daren't believe. I daren't believe my luck, that's why.

She catches at his arm. You have my attention John. You have all my attention. Explain to me.

So he tells her as they walk, arm in arm now, up Great Portland Street, how he sees it; how all these streets around them have people's names, the names of the people who had bought the fields and hedges and lanes and hills, that others had laid out in turn before them, Harley, Cavendish, Conway, Oxford, Portland. Of how they arrived from up and down the country, and built new and splendid estates, with wide streets and little garden plots along the lines of the latest designs, staking their family claims in the oldest act of dominion that we know, naming these places for themselves, and extending the capital. All these streets, John says, the names of them, look – Portland Street, which used to be called Brampton Street, Harley Street, Wigmore Street, Welbeck Street, Vere Street, Oxford Street, Cavendish Place, Mortimer Street – they are one great big extended family.

And Mia holds tight to his arm in the cold, and follows his pointing hand and imagines. As if the bones of a giant had been laid down by the Harleys, whose limbs were made of all the places they lived, or the people they married, and who would be able to rise up, if challenged, and claim this part of London for them, proof after all that they belonged at the heart of things, just as they had always thought.

John looks down at her. All these streets, he says again, are the record of a conversation between people pushing forward for notice and the ground beneath their feet.

So that is why you are working on the Harleys?

They have reached the door to the flats, panelled and imposing, between the RNIB and a travel agent. That is why I'm working on the Harleys, John says, patting his pockets for the key. I'm sitting right in the middle of them. They are talking to me. It would be rude not to listen.

He smiles at Mia. Don't you think?

*   *   *

Up in her window, looking down, Mia lets time telescope back to the great O of the present, shrinking the ghosts of herself and her dead lover to nothing.

Now John is gone. Still, Mia has not forgotten what he said. She treasures the invisible cat's cradle of connections that he showed her. It is a private map, a map made of threads, spooling back and forth, through years of patient marriage-making and fortune-building, stitching England's edge to its centre. Because the Harleys started on the edge, where England tipped into unsubduable Wales, Mia thinks, just as she started in Scotland. Only you couldn't exactly say I'd made anything other than a tangle of my threads. A bugger's muddle, as her father would say.

And the Harleys wouldn't recognise it now; Brilliana's grandson, Robert first Earl of Oxford, Speaker of the House of Commons and bibliophile, after whom the streets are named. Look at the traffic now, Lord Oxford. Look at the filth, Mia says, the tackiness, the litter. And then to herself, Come on then. Get a grip. Get this letter off to Dad, at least. She picks up her Dictaphone again. And because she has the mind to now, she thinks she'll put everything behind her and send her father something cheerful.

You'd have liked the country further down, Da. It's a bit softer than round you, a bit better managed. I met a sheep farmer, looked like he had his head on backwards, as you'd say. Not a very tidy outfit and the dog wasn't much good, nothing to touch your old dog Spey. I've got dogs on the brain today. Click again. Pause.

I'll read you some of the names of the castles. I didn't go to all of them but it'll give you a feel. So she reads the names out loud and the places mist up at her, hang their freshness briefly in the London air. Clearwell, Goodrich, St Briavels, Powis, Stokesay, Hay-on-Wye. He likes detail, her father.

Mia looks out and wonders what to say next. It is difficult to explain to him about London, which she sees only through John's eyes. So instead Mia tells him how she failed to look properly at the map at Hopton, how she got lost and drove round in circles, and how the bed-and-breakfast woman in Shrewsbury was a nosy parker, and had a dog that was fat and made smells under the table.

Dogs again.

Now I'm off to meet with Bill Radic. She says his name firmly this time. She can tell her father that at least, she thinks. He's the man who's writing the book I was researching for – you remember.

Love to you and Aunt Ines. I'll send again soon.

Mia steps over some papers on the floor, gathers up her empty, chocolate-spotted notebook and her red coat and her keys and comes back for her bag and her telephone and steps out into the hum of the streets, late.

At the bottom of Great Portland Street she boards a bus, which she takes in preference to the Tube, because it doesn't involve speed, or darkness, or unnecessary confinement, and because it is red.

Another couple. Another young woman and another older man. Cold weather. Greenwich, where the boats make heavy progress up an oily Thames.

Not Mia this time but Brilliana Harley, writing to a lover, to her betrothed in fact; Robert Harley the Puritan, knight of a shire she has never seen. She is in her father's household, following the King's progress. The glamour and formality of Court.

By the rush light, her pointed features, her neatness, which betray none of her excitement. Because the importance of being betrothed flutters continually in her neck. Her quickness and concentration. She writes in a bold but childish hand. Rhythmic. Brown ink, as always.

Down the centuries her voice is strange and sharp like birdsong.

Sr,

Mr Malle desires me to rwit a very formale letter to let you knowe that my father will not be at dinner to morrow with my La Veere but Thursday must be the day that we shall meet him at Londoun.

My father's not coming tomorrowe is because he hunts with the king and thes lines loose there end if by this information you are not moved to come to Grinwich, for which Mr Malle bids me laye my command on you. And to tell you that he lamints he came not an owirs sounir to a seene you.

This is all the knowne newis from Court which newis Mr Killi-gree has brought out of Spain, we knowe not, but this I knowe, and hope you knowe that none honnors loves and respects you more than your most affectionate

Cosin Brilliana Conway

at seven o cloke at night

It is luxurious to be writing like this, because it is private, because it allows Brilliana to contemplate her betrothed, and because of the surprising fullness of Sir Robert's mouth behind the sharp Elizabethan beard.

On the desk, to one side, lies the drab volume of Brilliana's Commonplace Book, conscientiously dated 1622, the small footprint of one life, if you know how to read it.

Thick, yellowed vellum covers, coarse paper, covered with a spiky hand, quick, full of conscientious intent. It is designed to promote self-examination and contemplation, to guard against luxuries, to offer comfort in the many times of trouble, and to make trial of the central Puritan question of the election of the individual. Am I chosen of God? Is it certain? Am I saved? The product of long hours spent alone in cold chambers, often questioning with a queasy heart, facing down the giddy vertigo of doubt, ordering, hoping, correcting, copying firm answers out of the Bible, with the fingers cramped and the nib scratch, scratch, scratching. She has it always to hand.

This is how a woman like Brilliana lives. This book and its contents are how she pulls herself handhold by handhold, ledge by ledge, up the impossible cliff face of her life. Compiled sometimes in strength, sometimes in weakness, she turns to it continually, like now, to still the beating of blood in her neck, to guard against overexcitement of the body and to realign herself with God's purpose.

Though God be merciful to all his creatures yet he is chefely and most especially is he mercifull to his elect. I am chosen.

God is mercifull to them that keepe his commandements, and to them that heare him, and to them that trust in him. So I believe.

Now none does this but his elect.

God is mercifull to them becaus he in his mercy did chus them before the world was. On this I pin my hope and trust.

God is mercifull to them becaus he reserves for them a crown of glory. I am chosen. I am counted. I have a purpose. Only why would you say it, unless you felt the shiver of its opposite?

And behind the lines, each one carefully annotated with the relevant biblical reference, is the sound of the mind trapped in the body, particularly the female body, hurrying on, with darkness increasingly at its shoulder, the lostness, the insignificance of a woman without a husband – O Lord let me fulfill my purpose – its consciousness of imminent death, from plague, from childbirth, or ague or accident, its constant fear, and its answering resolve. Such a map of anxiety, of thinly veiled need, of courage and self-encouragement.

What use we may make of God's truth, Brilliana's voice reminds herself, firm against future wavering.

The truth of God may sarve to tarify all impertinent men for that which he has threatened he will perform.

God by his eternall and unchangeable counsell haith once apointed whom in time to come he will take to salvation and on the other side whome he would condeme to destruction.

How quaint and alien the phrases sound. How harsh. How would it be possible to inhabit the human body in the shadow of these absolutes?

Only scrawled down the inside cover of the Commonplace Book there is a different, more familiar creed. Four quotations about love that startle and look out of place.

Il ney a rien si devine
   que l'amour sans fine.

O quelle chose est plus triste
Que d'amer est nester point aimee encore.

Knowledge puffeth up
  Love edifieth.

Amour est mon plaisir
  Si j'aime ou je suis aimee.

1622 is the year of Brilliana's engagement. So how can you quiet your blood, how can you school yourself, when you are standing on the threshold of life and love? She puts one small hand on the cover of the Commonplace Book and looks up. She feels constant elation, like passing into light.

On the river outside her window, the lights bob to and fro in the dark and the water glitters. There are occasional calls or sounds of splashing as someone on a boat hails the landing stage. A cormorant flies down towards the sea fast and unseen.

The restaurant where Bill and Mia are to meet is an Italian opposite the British Museum. It's a favourite of Bill's, who lives round the corner in Bloomsbury. He and John used to eat there before Mia had even arrived in London. It serves home-made food out of tins, under framed photographs of the *Mona Lisa* and the Colosseum. Bill likes it for sentimental reasons and because it is busy. He likes the lazy and wheezing patron who polishes glasses at the bar and who welcomes Bill unfailingly with subservience and effusions of spittle. He likes the filthy checked tablecloths, with white paper covers diagonalled across them, and he likes the jaunty bottles of Chianti with rafia bottoms, and the bar and the picture rails dustily garlanded all the way round with vine leaves and fake grapes. He even likes the waiters, of whom there is a constant supply, and most of whom are Polish, rushing backwards through the swing doors to the kitchen, carrying plates of pasta, acting Italian. Cliché Corner, is what he and Mia privately call it. We'll meet at Cliché Corner, at oneish.

Bill is not like John. He is a man like a monument just tending to ruin, a large man who overspills his clothes and who has sad pale eyes that work for most women, though not, it has to be said, for Mia. He is long seated when Mia arrives. The waiters have given them a table for four so that they can spread themselves and Bill has brought with him piles of papers. When the little bell on the door clangs and Mia whisks in, in her red coat, he looks up pleased. My dear, he says, rising with old-fashioned manners.

Mia glances round and smiles. Alone at a table in the corner, an elderly woman with a sad face is eating. Otherwise there is no one, so the waiter makes much of taking Mia's coat and pulling out a chair and shaking her napkin into her lap. And as he does so he eyes a girl who passes outside, her hair and her skirt blowing in the wind. With brisk half-attention he compliments Mia, makes a bow that seamlessly combines theatricality with cynicism, his head still turned to look out of the window. This is what you expect of us, he seems to be saying – a drink for the beautiful lady – so I do it for you, although you know, and although I know you know. Mia turns up her eyes and smiles on autopilot. A bottle of fizzy water, please.

All the rigmarole of eating in a restaurant.

And the head waiter arrives, as if at a denouement, to present the menu which both of them know by heart, and they are left alone.

It is lovely to see you, Bill says with soft gallantry. Mia smiles and raises her glass of fizzy water, because she finds when she sees Bill in the flesh that she is fonder of him than she remembered.

I'm sorry I was so difficult to get hold of. There wasn't a signal anywhere.

Not at all, Bill says. Not at all. It would be very disappointing if you weren't elusive.

Well, that's not what my bed-and-breakfast lady thought. She was very offish. I don't know what you said to her, Bill, but maybe next time, stick to business.

You're so disapproving, Bill says smiling. She was delightful. Carol, I think she was called, a woman after my own heart.

They are all women after your own heart, Bill. Mia is half-exasperated, half-laughing. Aren't they? I thought that was the problem. Have you ever met a single one who wasn't? Have you?

Well, Bill says, there was a traffic warden once who was very uncharming.

Traffic wardens don't count. They aren't human. Think of another.

Lovely Rita, Meter Maid, Bill says wistfully. And Mia says, I give up.

The waiters create a bustle. They shout the order through the swing doors and flick the plastic garlands with white cloths that they keep over one shoulder, though the seats of their black trousers look thin and shiny. Outside, the wind blows and the streets are made of paving stones.

Mia and Bill work round to the question of John's book and how it should be set out. Bill is full of ideas. I've made a timeline, he says, reaching across to pull a couple of sheets from an apparent disorder of papers. He hands the papers across the table. I thought it might give us some bones to put flesh on, if you see what I mean. I'd like to know what you think. I can't write John's book, you see. But I can try to incorporate his view of it, take his line so to speak, and you will have a better idea than me of what that is. You are closer to knowing what John wanted than me, so correct me if you think I'm going wrong.

Mia nods briefly.

I am assuming we will start, Bill says, with Brilliana's childhood, as much as we know of it. And I'd like to preface that with some kind of introductory overview of the religious and political landscape. To establish the time and its conditions, you know?

Mia, who is looking at the timeline, has got as far as Bill's idea of fleshing out. She is remembering the fish skeleton she saw on the banks of the Teme. It's a funny metaphor, she says.

What? Bill asks her, looking up, mid-flow. What is a metaphor? He looks comically baffled.

Sorry, Mia says, 'fleshing something out' – as though you could just pat a life back together again like clay or something. I was thinking this in the Brampton archive. I mean, there's a reason resurrection is thought of as a miracle.

Is that how you see biography? That's a metaphor if you are looking for one.

It's just a current hobby horse. I've been puzzling about the life lost – because, you know Bill, we do say lost for a reason. I'm not being morbid, please don't panic. It's just that resurrection is impossible – I'm not talking about John, I mean resurrection of anything.

We're so partial-sighted. How could you possibly make anything that was more than just two-dimensional guesswork? You'd never get it all. It's a god's job and there's a reason for that.

I'll avoid the obvious remarks about goddesses.

Please do. Mia laughs despite herself.

Shall I tell you about what I've been thinking and then you can tell me it's two-dimensional guesswork?

Tell me, Mia says. You were talking about landscape. Tell me about that. What is the religious and political landscape that you're starting with?

Bill likes to talk. Most of all he likes to talk while eating and despite his slow looks and his large limbs he does both these things with surprising physical energy. He paddles the bread that the waiter has brought them in the olive oil, and then holds it airborne, waving it sometimes as he talks, sometimes jabbing it between them to illustrate this or that point, and not noticing, or not caring, that it spots with oil the papers, his lap, his already-spotted lapels, in its long and erratic journey to his mouth. Mia moves his glass closer to the table's centre.

Sorry, Bill says. Good move.

But whatever else you think about Bill, you can't deny that among his many appetites is a hunger for, and ability to absorb, quantities of information. He is bursting with it. His mind overspills its bounds in much the same way as his body its clothes. A vast untidiness of facts and figures and arcane practices and subtle policies and events and positions and strategies and legalities whirl out of him now and enfold Mia in a blizzard of complexities, as if she were the little figure in the Christmas snowstorm, hands outstretched among the shaken glitter.

And now Bill, having wolfed the bread, moves on to grissini, allowing a fine rain of crumbs to shower over the spots of oil, as he launches without pause into the introduction he has planned. He talks about the port of Brill, where Brilliana was born and brought up and where her father, Lord Conway, was Governor

General for many years. He talks about religious refugees on the Continent, the Catholics and the more extreme Protestants, about Calvin, who was more moderate than you might think, as it turns out, and about the old, colourful Elizabethans whom Brilliana would have met. He talks about seventeenth-century education and about women in general. And he talks about Brilliana in particular, about growing up in the midst of foreign policy as it was practised, about listening to courtiers and diplomats coming and going, and about acquiring, without noticing it, an ear trained to politics and debate.

The door of the restaurant clangs and a pair of shock-headed Japanese boys blow in, along with several leaves, their legs painfully thin in black drainpipe jeans. Home-made tinned soup for the beautiful lady. The boys sit down and something glutinous and orange is put before Mia. And for the good sir most of a tin of tuna, some shreds of over-travelled iceberg and three capers. *Buena appetito*, the waiter says accidentally, in Spanish. He bows and smiles. His smile is made of aspartame.

So Mia, Bill asks, what do you think? You've been very quiet.

You were in full flood, Mia says. It's like being caught in a tsunami – in a good way. She pauses. Bill is not even listening. He is hunched over his plate. He is gobbling. Bill! she can't help herself saying, the tuna is dead. It isn't going to go anywhere.

Bill puts down his fork. I'm so sorry. His pale eyes register remorse. Forgive me. I'm terrible. I am eating and eating and talking. I haven't even asked you how you are. He looks at her anxiously. But you look so much better. It has done you good getting away, I think. You have a bit of colour in your cheeks at last.

You were right, Mia says, now feeling unkind about the tuna. It was good. The weather was lovely and I did a lot of walking. Then she stops and a brief silence falls between them.

Bill waits, watching her. But? he says, at length.

Mia laughs, and looks away, out of the window, where a couple, blown down the street by the same wind as the passing girl and the Japanese, have come to a stop outside the window and are now reading the menu pasted up from the inside. They frown and confer. They are wearing matching Loden coats.

She turns back to Bill. But . . . How does he know there is a but?

Mia, give me some credit. I'm not a block, my dear, and I am concerned for you. And the other thing that Bill has is a lovely voice. I am fond of you. You know that. And he looks at Mia, unintentionally now, with the look that undoes so many women, though never yet Mia. We have already had this conversation I think, he says. So, tell me your but.

There are several buts. Well, there are buts that matter and buts that don't. I can't talk about the buts that do.

Those are the only ones I'm interested in. Bill leans forward. You're not going to waste my time with things that don't matter, so you'd better tell me. Tell me, Mia. You can tell me. I don't like to admit it but I am nearly old enough to be your father.

Well that's the problem, Mia says, looking up at him.

What is? Bill looks temporarily flummoxed. My age?

No, Bill. My father. My father is the problem. Well, he's not a problem, I'm just a bit bothered by it at the moment. I had a row with him. Or not a row exactly, just a disagreement, another disagreement. She looks tired. She looks lonely and embattled. Bill reaches across the table and covers her hand with his own.

So that is why you were staying in the B&B. I did wonder.

Mia withdraws her hand and they sit in silence.

Was it very bad? Bill asks, after a while.

Well, no, not really. I managed to write to him this morning. It's just that it adds up, you see. That he expects so much of me. And that this was about something I thought I'd forgotten. Then Mia says quickly and despite herself, We are all each other has and we can't tell each other anything. It's ridiculous. We just talk about the weather. It's the only thing we don't disagree about. And that's mainly because he can't see it to argue. And then there is this mountain of issues that we can't discuss, that just sits in the room with us. It's so bloody English.

I thought you were Scottish.

We are. That's what makes it even worse. Bill smiles and doesn't say anything and waits. Does Sylvia tell you things? Mia asks at length.

No, she doesn't really confide in me, sadly. Bill shakes his head. I don't think I'm a good enough role model. Anyway, she quite likes making mistakes. It annoys her mother. Mia smiles. Bill's wife is noted for her ambition. What would your father want you to be doing, he asks her. Working freelance for a national newspaper is not enough, I take it?

Oh, Mia says, sounding more indifferent than she feels, being a good wifey somewhere I suppose, bringing up a family, you know, children, motherhood, as well as having a job maybe.

That's reasonably unreconstructed. Did you never consider it? I can't believe you were short of offers.

Thank you, Bill. Mia looks suddenly businesslike. She brushes at something on the table that isn't there. I have inherited blindness to consider, she says. It wasn't an issue with John because he didn't think the world was in a fit state for children. He didn't want any. But tunnel vision can be passed down through women, even if they don't suffer from it themselves. She says it quickly, very matter-of-fact, without looking at Bill.

Well, that is a terrible responsibility to carry. Bill's voice is quiet. But it's your father who is blind, isn't it? If he is wanting you to have children he must think it isn't such a curse.

I watched him go blind, Bill. He didn't. You couldn't inflict that on a child.

But you know, it might not happen, Bill says. We aren't in control of these things. There is Chance. I think you are living too anxiously, Mia, and too much backwards.

What do you mean? Don't say that.

I mean that you are trying to control everything, to contain possible disaster, and meanwhile you just go over and over what is gone, what is already there. How do you know there won't be something better in the future? John was one man and he had one way of living. You are a woman in the middle of your life. You have your life to live, your way. How much time do you have? You should be spending yourself recklessly.

Mia looks surprised. Is that what you're doing? Spending yourself? How?

Anyhow! Bill says with a slowness that belies his message. Anyhow, Mia. It doesn't matter on what. It doesn't matter where you are going. It just matters that you go, you know, with energy, with engagement. Don't let yourself be blocked. It's enough now. Move on, my dear. He stops. Whatever your father wanted, whatever happened in the past – it doesn't matter now. John, of all people, would not like to see you wasted.

They glance at each other. Mia looks overwhelmed.

And in the meantime, Bill says quickly, worried that he has said too much, you can start by helping me with this book. Let's go back to that. He puts his hand briefly on hers again, pats it consolingly. Let's talk about the book, Mia.

And Mia is grateful to him for his gentleness to her, for seeing that she is unhappy. Yes, she says to him, let's talk about that, while her mind asks silently and in capital letters, What does he mean? Is she blocked?

You said you had other buts. Perhaps they were about the Harleys?

Yes, Mia says again, struggling to focus. Pull yourself together girl. Pool yourself together. She clears her throat. OK, well, take your 'overview'. It doesn't mean anything to me. It is too distant, too ordered a way of looking, too much patterning of things that in my experience of life are actually very random, very chaotic. I don't know if I'm living backwards, Bill, but I think I'm living closer to the ground than you are. I have a kind of mouse-eye view.

Bill is still looking at her. Emotion is very bad for perspective you know, he says. Trust me – these things change. I didn't mean to be insulting about the backwardness. We all do it to a certain extent. I just don't like to see you wasted. Now I'm going to sound inconsistent. You look back on your childhood for instance – say, on your upbringing in Scotland, and having an Irish mother, and losing her in your teens – and you pattern that, to explain who you are now. I've heard you do it. It's natural. It's how our minds work. The seventeenth century is just a bit further back and a bit less personal.

It is a lot further back, Mia says, with something of her old argumentativeness. It's several centuries. It's dark back there, Bill, and I can't find any way of seeing into it. It's so foreign to me. And if I look at the events that went into its making then I lose the only thing I can see, which is the individual voice. If you can see a voice. I'm not giving up. I'm just explaining my standpoint, because it feels so different from yours. She pauses. Well, I'm not being totally honest. If I'm honest the detail of it feels insignificant. It doesn't have anything to do with the heat and the quickness and the partial-sightedness of the life lived. Do you see at all what I mean?

Mia talks in little rushes, as the thoughts rise in her mind, not in the long phrases, the loose parentheses natural to Bill. Listen to Bill, John had said when they'd first met. Bill is a man who speaks in paragraphs. And he does.

I mean, Mia says keeping going, patterns assume a degree of sameness, of predictability. They necessarily discard the elements that don't fit. What if life is just wider . . . what if it's more explosively varied . . . more different . . . more whimsical say, than the pattern allows?

The waiter passes with mountains of pasta for the Japanese, both of whom, Mia can't help noticing, are wearing headphones. Each of them is separately engrossed in his handheld device, a telephone or an iPod, she can't tell which. Bill follows her gaze and raises his eyebrows. Fun! he says to her with a smile. What's the point in talking after all?

That's just the point. If you were looking for patterns out of insignificant detail, you might think the whole of the twenty-first century was like those two. You wouldn't realise that there's you playing your trumpet in your flat and eating inedible food in restaurants and me turning into a hermit several storeys up and in altogether dirtier surroundings and this waiter going home to schnitzel and dumplings or whatever he eats in Dagenham or somewhere. You'd get it wrong.

Bill leans back against his chair, watching, half-amused, half-touched at Mia's sudden vehemence. Does it matter? he asks her. I'm the one who's meant to be old and tired. Where's your sense of adventure? Of course we may get it wrong, but what on earth is the point in not trying?

I'm not saying it matters Bill. I'm just saying it's pointless.

OK, Bill says, holding his hands up, it's pointless. Life is pointless, so the recounting of it can't hope to be anything more. But I am a biographer. I happen to think it's worthwhile. It's entertaining. It passes the time. It may even be helpful to some. It's certainly helpful to me. And what if we get it right? Maybe we get it more right than wrong – you don't seem to allow for that.

No, of course I do. I do allow for that. And, she looks up at Bill, John was a biographer too.

John was a biographer. Bill says it softly. John was a very good and a very careful biographer. And the more careful we are and the more detail we gather, the more likely we are to get this more or less right. You don't have to believe in biography. Just give it a chance. The whole point is that it isn't a science. It can't be. You approach it scientifically because it's important that you keep yourself out of it and because that is what the material deserves, but then you bring your instincts and your own humanity and your experience and your sympathetic imagination to bear. It's marvellous actually. He breaks off. Have you ever seen those computer puzzle pictures?

Mia nods in response.

Well, Bill goes on, Sylvia bought me a book of them as a present. It was my birthday, by the way.

Happy birthday, Bill. I'm sorry I missed it.

No. Nonsense, Bill says. That wasn't the point. The point is that biography is like a computer picture. Of course it looks like nothing from the outside but once the 'insignificant' details as you would have it, the squiggles in the computer's case, are assembled and placed correctly, if you simply wait and focus through them, then the real thing, the thing that is beyond them, the scene that those squiggles represent and yet so bafflingly don't show, will just appear, like magic on the other side. And it's in 3D. That, to me, is the point of the detail. You don't look *at* it so much as through it, through the whole of it assembled. So it's important that we be like computers in our assembly. That's all.

Bill, Mia says, pushing her plate away, I have no desire to be a computer.

No, Bill says laughing, I prefer you as you are. But you said you had two buts. So what is the second one then, now that I've failed so signally to dislodge the first?

My second but . . . What is my second but? Thank you, that was delicious, Mia says to the waiter, clearing her almost untouched bowl of soup. My second but is religion, I suppose. I find all the Calvinism, the pre-chosen elect of God – and the sort of fundamentalist ranting – a barrier. Don't you?

Well, elitism of any kind is boring in the end, Bill says. So, to that extent, it's not my cup of tea. But I was brought up in the atheist religion and that can be both fundamentalist and rant-prone. I think I rather like Protestantism. I think it's interesting. Do you believe in God, I can't remember?

Which one? Mia says. There are so many nowadays.

Your mother was Catholic, wasn't she?

Yes, my mother was Catholic, and I was brought up more or less Catholic, although I'm fairly sure she didn't believe. It was just a useful set of rules, if you were trying to bring up an unruly child really.

Which is what you were? Bill smiles.

Which is what I pretty much was.

So that's your mother, what about your dad?

My father used to go to the chapel when I was little. But he stopped when he went blind. I can remember someone from the chapel congregation coming to get him once or twice and my father sending them away with a flea in their ear. He never talked about it. But I don't think it was just the blindness that stopped him going. My parents were a pretty godless pair really. He believed in the stars, if he believed in anything, the stars and the weather. That's what he missed, I think, looking at the stars last thing at night, you know, putting himself in his place against all that vastness, and making predictions about the next day. Rain coming in from the west. All that. Farming stuff. He believed in place. I mean, the specific place he lived in. I thought he was going to die when he first moved, when he couldn't run the farm any more and he had to leave. I really thought he might die.

Mia pauses, remembering her father among the falling thistledown. She looks down at her plate. Liver has appeared. What on earth made her order liver? I thought Protestantism was the same as Catholicism, just sloppier.

Bill glances up, disapproving. It is not at all the same, Mia. You just said you were brought up a Catholic. You should know. People go to war over the differences. Look at Ireland. Look at the Middle East now. Look at England in our period. Didn't your mother tell you – I mean, for heaven's sake, Mia.

Alright Bill, keep calm. I agree. I sounded very dumb. I didn't mean it like that. I know if you're in it, the differences are insurmountable. I just meant for you, as an outsider, why would you like Protestantism in particular? Of all things, when it is so neurotic and so proscriptive and even grovelling sometimes, why is it 'interesting'?

Well, use the computer picture image again. You have to think of religion as a prism, or a filter, through which you look at a bit of society. Protestantism is interesting because it creates autonomy. If you compare the things you don't like, the self-examination, the spiritual hypochondria, with the Catholic practice of confession, for example – for the Catholic there is someone outside the individual, within the church hierarchy, who is in authority. You say sorry and they take it off your hands. They make it all better.

Now take another look at Protestantism, and particularly radical Protestantism – there is just the individual conscience. This is a great freedom, Mia. Just imagine. Individual responsibility, being answerable only to God through your own communion with him – that's the birth of the modern mindset. It means coming of age and taking responsibility, politically, socially. It's grown-up stuff. It means for the first time that people can and should make things better. It may be the beginning of capitalism even. It's certainly the beginning of the work ethic. This is something that relates to the Harleys actually, and we must get back to the Harleys.

Bill's hands are airborne again. See what you make of this. He reaches to his papers, riffling through one pile after another. One or two sheets drift to the floor and the waiters, who are chatting at the bar, rush up to help. Hey *professore*, jokes the one who is really Italian. *Hopla!* he says, catching a paper and winking at Mia. It is the fault of the beautiful lady. She's getting you all excited.

She's getting me excited. You're quite right. You're absolutely right. She and God between them.

She and God! Oh my Lord, the waiter says. That's quite a team.

Aha! Bill has found what he is looking for. Here we are.

Tutto al posto. So I'll take these plates. Do you want some dessert, some coffee?

Bill would like tiramisu, because he doesn't think there has ever been a time when he didn't need picking up, only he daren't. He is afraid of his cholesterol, or his wife, who has recently elided herself with his cholesterol until he can no longer think of one without the other. So he orders a double espresso and goes back to his piece of paper.

So what I am thinking, Mia, is – I looked up the word 'progress', just out of interest, and it seems that until the beginning of the seventeenth century it meant simply moving from A to B. Fine. In 1603, it first started to be used to describe social advancement. You see? Here is the dictionary definition from the moment it changes: 'growth, development; usually in a good sense, continuous improvement'. And the date of the change is 1603.

That is interesting. Mia reaches out for the paper. Can I have a look?

Of course, if you can read my writing. Now the other thing is – it's not really a big deal, but it's a neat tie-in – 1603 was the year the Harleys bought extra land at Wigmore. It's in the Jacqueline Eales book, which I've got somewhere here. Bill pauses again and pulls from the middle of the central pile a blue paperback with a picture of Brilliana Harley in a roundel on the front. Here it is. I must introduce you to Jackie. You haven't met her, have you? Mia shakes her head. He opens the book to one of several page markers. Somewhere here I think. OK, here we go. 'In 1603 Thomas Harley was able to improve the family fortunes by the purchase of the manor and borough of Wigmore', and so on and so on, conveyed it straight to his son Robert along with Brampton Bryan . . . Now, I'm quoting, 'This was the first in a series of carefully planned conveyances between Thomas Harley and his elder son, which were designed to secure an income for Robert and simultaneously to enhance his social standing.'

How about that? He looks across at Mia. So the point about that, this is what I've been thinking, is that as progress comes to be a concept in England, as whatever structures there are – religious, social, political – free up, become things that are no longer fixed but things that can be changed or bettered, as far as the religious radicals are concerned, this family, the Harleys, like so many others no doubt, are caught up – and you have to imagine, this is really a great wave that breaks over England, this wave of progress, that sweeps out the old world and its systems – so they are caught up in it, unconsciously and even against their will at times, but they trust to their own Protestant consciences. They go against their neighbours in the Civil War and then against Parliament when it comes to killing the King, and although they lose materially in the war, they never lose visibility. It's as if they hold to their purpose through everything, hold to the certainties and the independent-mindedness of their faith, these crucial individual freedoms and responsibilities, and they emerge, at the end of it all, tried and tempered and on their way up. So the beginning of the modern world, the beginning of progress, is also their beginning. You see?

Bill downs his espresso and sits back against his chair. He has little spots of colour on his cheekbones and his pale eyes burn.

Well Bill, Mia says, it's an exciting idea. You've done a lot of thinking. She says it almost wistfully. I wish I could be as productive.

Of course you could. Don't be silly, Mia. And like you say, I get carried away with the pattern. It is very likely not watertight. I need your hesitancy and your realism. They are good and useful qualities.

No you don't, Bill. You just think I need something to do.

I do think you need something to do. You are festering in that flat. Bill leans forward. Like I say, you mustn't wall yourself up in a shrine, Mia. But apart from that, I do need you. I need you for lots of reasons and I'm serious – I do need bringing down to earth. John used to think I was very wild, you know.

Did he?

Yes. Very erratic. Did he never tell you?

No. He only said nice things about you. He was a loyal friend, wasn't he?

He was. He was very loyal, and he believed in saying things to people's faces anyway, not behind their backs, which wasn't always such a good habit. Particularly when it came to people's choices of life partners. My wife, for instance.

Mia and Bill both laugh.

Anyway, I thought I'd go to the British Library after this and look at some of the manuscripts again. Why don't you come along? It would be helpful to do it together.

Mia is looking out of the window, briefly lost in thought. I can't now, she says. I'm going to get a dog.

Brilliana's wedding to Sir Robert approaches. Lord Conway, her father, at his writing desk. He is now one of the secretaries of state to James I – although it is not as rewarding a post as might at first appear. There are many niggling matters. The disappearance of the twenty-two-year-old Prince Charles and the Duke of Buckingham incognito, to woo the Spanish Infanta, for instance. This has caused much upset at Court. He doubts very much that it will be successful. As yet there are no signs. He sighs. Besides, there are other graver problems abroad. The King's son-in-law, the Elector Palatine, is ousted and exiled. He is gathering support, fomenting war with the Catholics.

There is no money for war.

Indeed, government seems to be slipping from King James altogether. It appears of little interest to him now. He is ageing, Lord Conway thinks sadly. He is much given to bouts of morbid sentimentality and everything at Court is at the mercy of favourites. The venal and grasping Buckingham, Lord Conway's patron, outrageous in rosettes and ribbons.

It is as though the King's mind, as well as his mouth, had lost its teeth. He drinks too much. The whole Court drinks too much. Sometimes, after a banquet, there are many who vomit, who are insensible with wine.

But it is not in Lord Conway's nature to criticise those set above him. It is easier to put his energy and his faith into something younger, more hopeful, the marriage of Brilliana, his well-beloved daughter, for instance. Please God this may be a good and fruitful match. It is a happy duty to write a letter of congratulation to Sir Robert,

My Goode Sonne – For so methinkes it is your good pleasure that the stile runn, and methinkes it is as rich an embrodery to me as it can be silke lace to you; Although I have tolde you true of my selfe, and coulde find it in my heart to allay my daughter, to raise your valew, yet since she hath a long race to runn with you, and that you have advantages enough over her already, I will not give you this that you may misprise her out of her father's mouth, and therefore I will onely say, that the bargain was equally made, and I pray God much good may it doe to you:

But if it wolde please you to bee as good a sonne as shee wil bee a wife, and as good a husband as I will bee a faithfull friend, I shall take it for a great favour of fortune that I may have the honour to stile myself

your loving father,

Conway.

Brilliana, middle of his five children, is very dear to him. She has such an air of quickness about her. Though there are many things to make a father anxious, foremost among which is the great trial of childbirth. As if unable to close, he begs his new son-in-law particularly, Take care of your own health, and, Make much of my Brill. And as he closes the letter he cannot help a tremor in his hand, the seal, as he sets it, swimming briefly before his eyes.

This is a godforsaken place, Mia can't help thinking as she stands outside the dogs' home, in the noise and the grime of Battersea Park Road. A thin and constant stream of traffic passes. The buildings seem dirty and low-lying, dwarfed by the expanse of railway tracks sprawling away, amongst litter and scrub, under the bridge that rises in front of her. MOT centres, clouds, aeroplanes.

Good afternoon.

Good afternoon. I've come to see about taking a dog.

Certainly, come and have a look. This is Tyro, or Benjy, or Rob.

He looks perfect. I'll take him.

This is pretty much how Mia had assumed it would be, when she arrived at Battersea Dogs and Cats Home. She would walk in, have a look, and come out with a dog.

But there is nothing simple about dog adoption. She has a glimmering of realisation as she stands outside, listening to the barking which rises even above the noise of the traffic, doleful, percussive, painfully continuous. It is unsettling. She hesitates. On the bridge, a fat man sucking on a tiny roll-up lounges and stares. Mia comes to herself. She follows the arrows to a temporary entrance that the building of a new cattery has necessitated. You pay a pound to look round, although the donation is voluntary. Follow the red paw prints to reception.

Mia follows, past the wasteland of railway tracks, now running parallel, past the old wreck of the power station looming above it, all table-leg towers and jagged glass. Staff in scrubs or uniform sweatshirts pass, some walking confidently with dogs on leads.

This is a place of misery.

Up long ramps with shiny railings, where the kennels have the names of London streets, as though the dogs belonged, as though they had an address after all. Leaning on the swing door to the Bow Street kennel, Mia, farmer's daughter though she still is, winces involuntarily. The barking rises like physical assault.

The animals are shut in cages on either side, red-floored, bare except for a bowl or two and sometimes a toy. They fling themselves against the bars as she enters, some with a degree of outrage. One or two sit with their backs turned in attitudes of despair. One has three legs, one an eye complaint. There is a smell, despite the scrupulous cleanliness, and in one or two instances an unavoidable fresh turd.

Mia hurries out again, back to the central ramps, up to another floor, in search of dogs that are quieter, less contagiously distressed. Above her head hang signs which say, 'I hope he loves me as much as I know I'm going to love him.'

O quelle chose plus triste, Mia thinks drily as she mounts. *Que d'amer et nester point aimee encore.*

But the other floors are just the same. All the dogs seem to be of one type. All look like a boxer or Staffordshire cross. They have great bullet heads and slant eyes and wide mouths that would clamp in a fight. Why so many of the same kind? Where are the little dogs, like the one she'd seen pass in the morning? It is as though one breed alone has been selected to be outcasts.

Downstairs again, on her way out, there is another board that asks whether you have seen a dog you would like and, if so, have you spoken to a re-homing officer? You can take a ticket like you would in a crowded shop and wait, if you want an interview.

So dog adoption is not a casual business, conducted whimsically after lunch on the spur of the moment. How shaming, Mia thinks. Dog adoption is a commitment to a life change. There is a queue of people, all of whom understand this better than she does. Mia thinks of their old sheepdog, Spey. Spey had a job.

There are five stages, if she wants to pursue it, to adopting a dog, the first of which is filling in a form and having an interview. After the interview, if you are accepted, there will be a house visit, by one of the home staff, to assess the accommodation you are offering, and only after that do you get to say which dog might suit. It is a long way to come on the off chance, Mia thinks. Then she thinks again, How typical, how stupid of me, not to check, just to assume it would all be so simple. What on earth possessed me?

But the staff at the dogs' home are understanding and kind. They know about loneliness. They have it shut up in scrubbed cages up and down the building, young, old and newly born. So they are good-humoured and apologetic with Mia. She shouldn't give up. They will find her the absolutely perfect companion, one hundred per cent guaranteed, if she will just be patient and go through the system. It will be better and more sure, both for her and for the pet, this way.

Mia is given a leaflet on responsible dog ownership and a form to fill in. The form has small boxes in which she is supposed to write why she wants a dog, how many hours it will be left unaccompanied during the day and why, and what her opinion is on neutering. She is unable to answer any of these questions on the spur of the moment, so she puts the form into her bag and steps back out into Battersea Park Road.

Down the road Mia wanders, feeling aimless now, under bridges for the Underground, running bizarrely overhead, or for the London Brighton and South Coast Railway, 1865, advertising itself with grimy grandeur and booming above her as she passes. In front of it, a wire mesh supports quantities of rubbish and pigeon shit. Dirt. Dirt. Everywhere you look. And even here the barking is still audible, follows her almost accusing, as she approaches a little line of cafés with rickety tables and shiny metal chairs. I need a cup of tea. I really need a cup of tea.

I can't take on one of those dogs. I'd slit my wrists in a month.

Mia chooses a table as a bus careers past before the lights change. No one else is sitting out. Fag butts on the floor, blobs of chewing gum. Why do they put the tables on the street when there's no view and no sun – where do they actually think this is?

In her coat pocket, as if in echo, Mia's phone registers a text. Where R U? the screen asks in capital letters with a series of comical question marks. It is from Bill's daughter, Sylvia. Good question, Mia says out loud, brooding over her cup of tea.

*

Go back again.

Where are you, girl? The blind man's constant question.

Where are you? And to a teenager the sound of it is the sound of a hammer, nailing you to this back of beyond, this endless weather, this grim no-place of your Border childhood. That is how Mia feels, every time he asks it. Moody. Aching for a different life.

Don't you leave me now. Get yourself in here this minute. Fetch my tea. Read me the paper. Homework can wait. Who do you think you are? You are not off out. You are staying right here. You've been out enough this week.

One day he'll ask it, 'Where are you, girl?' and I won't be here. One day.

Arms that used to be whipcord wasting to nothing. Sitting on in the grey light, in the close living room. Her aunt knitting. Always knitting. And what on earth for?

I've got a job, Da.

Aha. Then silence. He flexes his hands into fists and Mia holds her breath and knows that he knows. And where would that be?

The silence between them so thick she could touch it. She is unable to answer immediately. The clock on her father's mantelpiece, tutting at her, as the seconds pass. She's done it now. Uncle Freddy's got me a job on a newspaper, six-month trial. It's someone he knows. Owes him a favour. It's on *The Times* newspaper, Da. Hoping that the name will mollify. It's in London. I'd be living away, Da.

But I'd be back for holidays and the odd weekend, her voice pleading.

Aha.

Should she do this? Can she do it – leave her blind and widowed father? The clock ticks and the needles click, dropping their ordinary sounds into the abyss of time that opens ahead of her if she stays.

So Mia goes. She leaves one April, with Scotland grim, and spring still sleeping it off in a ditch unconscious, and Mia just sitting, just watching through the train windows the ironstone towns and villages of the north, their heads down, clenched against weather of every kind, everything that sky and wind can throw, or spit, or sling at you, ticking them off in her head as they pass. See how hard, how unrelenting Scotland is. All her hopes and expectations rolled tightly like her clothes. When she crosses the border she tells herself she feels lighter. I'm going to London. I'm working on a newspaper.

Where are you, girl?

I'm in London.

Then, as she steps off the train at Euston, crumpled, into the hubbub of the capital, making her way through the streets for the first time and finding the city, for all its filth, lying mild under a drift of blossom and pale leaf tips like an impossible contradiction.

She is nineteen and this is where she wants to be, in the city of her prisoned dreams. Walking through the streets with her bag, and stopping to have a cappuccino in a coffee bar, as though it was the most normal thing in the world. They don't have froth in Scotland.

There are pigeons everywhere. No one says good morning. I've escaped, Mia says to herself. Anything is possible. I'm in London.

But the following day, worrying that she will be late, and unable to read the *A–Z*, she arrives at the office, in confusion and with sweat patches under her arms, twenty minutes before she is expected. I have a Mia Morgan for you, the receptionist at *The Times* says sighing, bored even at nine in the morning. Then to

Mia's shame, as if she were a nobody, as if suddenly and after all her da was right, because even her name doesn't fit in London – I said, Mia Morgan, loudly and slowly into the telephone, with spaces in between. She says she is a Mr Moy's niece. She has a placement apparently. And to Mia in her temporary discomfort, without even looking up, Someone will be down in a moment. Take a seat.

Sitting in the entrance, in the plate-glass window, for what seems like hours, wishing not to be conspicuous, while the doors turn and confident people go in and come out and she goes on waiting for Someone to come down. And Someone, when she finally appears, is Sylvia, the daughter of Bill whom Mia is yet to meet, and who is nonchalant to the point of rudeness.

Christ, you've come a long way to work in this fucking dump. That is what Sylvia says when at last she arrives in the lobby; a greeting as incongruous as the city's blossom, because Sylvia comes out of the lift with an elegant swing to her. She is tall and looks reasonably expensive.

The receptionist mans the telephone in the sing-song voice of her training, and flicks at buttons with manicured nails. Can I put you on hold, caller?

My name is Syl. I'll be showing you round. Wow! Mia thinks admiringly, Clothes! Syl has ladylike features which she tries to disguise and she has cool, pale eyes; eyes that are spatially disorienting to look into, as if to say, Here, have a quantity of sky, or some sea. To Mia, still riding on hope and belief, they seem to open out a world of freedom, like an intake of fresh air. Get a load of this, Syl's eyes seem to say. Mia answers her greeting in confusion, has to remind herself not to stare.

Cool accent, Syl says.

And then, when is it exactly, how soon afterwards, that Mia finds herself sharing Syl's flat in Westbourne Grove, as though that were normal too; staying up pointlessly till the early hours, and drinking vodka and orange, even though it is disgusting, and talking about nothing as if it mattered, and eating takeaways instead of cooking.

Or, after separate nights out, calling in sick with a tea towel wrapped round to muffle the voice. It's unbelievable. We both have food poisoning, Mia says into the handset, looking at Syl who is eating cereal in front of morning telly. They spend the whole day in pyjamas, not getting dressed. So how was last night, Syl asks without looking away from the television.

I think it was great, Mia answers, I can't really remember.

And they both laugh, because really it doesn't matter.

At the crappy little stove, Mia making herself a fry-up. You owe me one for making that call.

Well they take you seriously. Think yourself lucky. Then, after a pause, Christ you eat a lot of grease, Syl says.

Well maybe I'm trying for a heart attack so you have to make your own calls for a change. Do you want some?

Are you joking? I'd vomit. Spooning cereal without looking.

Even through the haze of tiredness, through the drink-induced headaches, Mia feels high; breaking eggs into a pan in a tiny flat in London. Occasionally her father or Ines will ring and the euphoria will vanish for a while and the inescapable life of home will reach out its chill fingers and invade her again like mist. And then Syl has to talk her back to the present, sitting beside her on the sofa. Mia, come on. You're here, not there. You don't have to go back.

But he makes me feel guilty.

You've got a job. You've done really well. What are you going to do, martyr yourself? Don't be ridiculous. Fuck's sake, Syl says, lighting up and offering it to Mia.

Then Mia is comforted and they go back to the round of drinking and partying, to fall in and out of bed with different men, and compare notes, and look out for each other. Going to work together on the Tube in the hungover mornings.

Fuck, Syl will say, most mornings because that is her favourite word, I've smoked all my cigarettes. We have to stop on the way.

And Mia, who has to count her money because there won't be any more, says, Syl you've always smoked all your cigarettes. You've also smoked most of mine. Here – relenting – we can share. And they stop in the street, shielding the lighter, taking puff and puff about, nursing their coughs. And the traffic rattles and the dirt is everywhere and all the people passing look unwell.

How long have you been smoking then?

Since I was fifteen. How about you?

Oh, since Highers, Mia answers.

Highers? What on earth are they?

They're like A levels, only harder.

Didn't you do A levels then, or what?

I was at a Scottish state school, Syl. How was I going to do your poncey English exams?

It makes a change, to feel glamorous for being Scottish. Syl would love to have gone to a state school.

Syl inhales and they cross the road. Oh, there was a guy called you, while you were out last night. I forgot. They walk on together towards the Tube.

What kind of a guy?

He said his name was Freddy.

Freddy?

Yes. Freddy.

Just Freddy, nothing else?

Mia, what's up with you? I'm not a fucking phone exchange. I didn't ask him. I just took the message. Just Freddy. He said, tell her Freddy called and said he'd call later. He didn't want to leave a number.

Sorry. I mean, did he sound old? Did he sound like an uncle, because I don't know anyone called Freddy, except my uncle.

*

At her café table, Mia stares into the middle distance holding her phone, whose screen has long since darkened over Sylvia's message.

Where R U? I'm in Battersea, she types with her thumb, answering Syl in full, old-fashioned sentences. Don't ask. Are you going to be home later? Might call in and see how the other half live.

On the pavement across the road, a small man in a linen suit, who has dyed the hair that circles his head a vivid russet, walks in pigeon steps towards an iron gateway that opens onto a parking space. It is rude to stare. But Mia does. A cancerous-looking church and a series of buildings that must once have served it. Could there ever have been a monastery here? As if in some kind of answer, a metal cross points briefly at an aeroplane from the church's roof. The Cloisters Business Centre, the sign on the gate announces, an indication, if one were needed, thinks Mia, of where we have got to after all this time. There you go, Mia says to Brilliana in her head, look at that.

It is relentlessly noisy. The traffic judders, like the working of some giant machine, and an Underground train eases along on top of the bridge. None of this really makes sense, Mia thinks. Two helicopters, flying low and in sync, menace the gas tower and in the dogs' home the dogs continue to bark. She sips her tea and watches.

Bill's advice about living pools on the floor of her mind like an uneasy leakage. She can feel it slipping back and forwards, coating the surface of her thoughts. *You are living too much backwards. You have your own life to live your own way*, or words to that effect. I know, Bill, she says to him in her head. But how?

What does it matter whose life you are living anyway, she asks impatiently in response, if you can manage it? That is what so many women do, isn't it? – choose someone else's life and then live it. They hurl themselves into it, blind and in white, thrilling at the prospect. Now I am real because now I am someone else.

Later she leaves and walks slowly back along the Queenstown Road and waits for a bus and takes the first one that comes, without looking at its destination and sits, as she always does if she can, on the top deck, at the front, looking out. It is the 452 and it is going to Sloane Square.

The bus stops and starts. Mia's telephone vibrates with another message from Sylvia. Here now. Come 4 drink while boys have T.

Outside, the shoddy little houses that look into their own basements, as if ashamed, are left behind for the wide reaches of the Thames, the great span of the bridge that crosses it, and Mia's bus is swallowed at once, into the streets of a different London, as if the city had stood up and was striding about, its pockets bulging with money, all business schemes and expensive tailoring and success. Now on either side, giant lifestyles are advertised. A boy the size of a building stares, transfixed like Narcissus, in nothing but underwear. And on all other surfaces, perfect people, in perfect clothes, chase each other through fields of pristine cows, or pose in weather, or drive cars down the steps of foreign cities among confetti pigeons. Express yourself, one poster says. Live the dream. Everything looks pretend.

On my way, Mia types into her phone, turning her head to read the billboards as they pass. How perfect life and love could be if you only had the cash. As if a credit card was all it took; the perfectibility of human nature buyable now on the never-never. Is this what we believe?

Not Sylvia, at least. Sylvia has the future of the planet, Mia thinks, that is her creed. Or Brilliana and the white heat of her belief, striving for perfection across the grain of human nature. The voice of the Commonplace Book, so clear, so definite.

Though God be mercifull to all his creatures yet he is chefely and most especially is he mercifull to his elect.

il ney a rien si devine / que l'amour sans fine.

Which did you believe in most? Mia asks. It amuses her to sit Brilliana down, her stiff handmade clothes, her small upright body, on the seat beside her. Which did you believe in most, she asks her – God, or love? Or did you just grow out of love, like we are too childish to do now? Side by side on the plastic seats, the woman who is sure and the woman who is unsure, while the diesel engine judders below and the advertising billboards pass, huge and silent, like a dream.

*

Off the bus, Mia walks up the King's Road, because Syl lives in Chelsea these days, in the quiet streets behind, where if you look down between the painted railings, you can see Filipino women doing other people's ironing in underground basements. Although Syl does not have a Filipino. She has an Irish woman, whom she refers to as 'my friend Shula', with whom she drinks tea a lot and shares smokes and who says 'Mother of God' nearly as much as Syl says 'Fuck'. It seems to Mia, as she walks, a long time since she and Syl were single working girls, out on the town, borrowing each other's clothes and crying on each other's shoulders. He's such a bastard. I thought he meant it. They're all bastards love. They're all bastards.

Syl is married now and John, who was never a bastard, is dead.

Outside the house, when she reaches it, Mia stands in the protected quiet of affluence and listens to the city's muffled striving, traffic dimmed, one siren curiously far away. She rings the doorbell.

Going into Syl's house is another matter. Mia always has the feeling that she is entering something in the middle, like arriving late for a play and finding the action already at tipping point towards murder, or unmasking. Syl has two sons who have long, soft blonde hair and Syl's eyes and whose natures, constantly and vividly expressed, are demonic. They skateboard fast round the island in Syl's surprisingly extensive kitchen and throw anything that is hard and comes to hand and use knives to cut into the furniture. They wear combat trousers and wife-beater vests and their noses run with snot and their tiny mouths are like sewers. Sometimes Mia finds it hard to like either of them, although the elder is her godson. Sometimes she wishes that Syl would cut their hair and put them somewhere else, preferably upstairs.

Fuck's sake Mia, Syl says when she sees her on the doorstep. Don't you know how to use a phone?

Sorry Syl. You said to come by and I was in Sloane Square so I thought . . .

No, come in, come in. I didn't mean that. I meant where have you been? You never answer my calls.

I've been away. I've been in Shropshire, researching for your dad. I had lunch with him today in fact.

Syl closes the door behind her. Oh God, she says, I hope he didn't make another pass at you. Did he make another pass at you? He's such a goat. Honestly. Mia steps over a toy, over a juice cup in the hallway, and then over a series of coats and jerseys dropped at random. Children are like animals, she thinks, looking at Syl's younger child, Gabriel, curled on the floor, as though he too has been discarded, among a spillikin effect of felt-tipped pens. So much is happening in this house, all the time. Shula, whom Mia greets next, grates cheese over the counter, with inappropriate energy, sweeping it up with the great flat of her hand onto pieces of bread for the boys' tea.

Nathan, say hello to your godmother, she says without turning round.

Hey, Nate says, passing Mia at speed.

Mother of God, Shula says, as though Mia and Syl were also her charges, is it any surprise that the children speak the way they do? Will you watch your mouth in front of them, Sylvia? Look at what you're teaching them now. Mia and Syl look at Gabriel, the younger of the two boys, who is five and who is writing with great concentration in red permanent marker on what looks like a placard: fuc ole, Mia reads upside down and in lower-case letters.

Let's have a look, Syl is saying, what are you writing, love? The little boy looks up and Nathan, who is eight, pushes between them and shouts, fuc ole, fuc ole. Vangina, don't you mean? Retard.

No he doesn't. He means fuck oil, don't you Gabe? You're the retard, Nathan. Sometimes Mia wonders if Sylvia is that much older than her children, she enters into their quarrels with such vigour, such partisanship.

Gabriel's face is red with fury. I said it, he shouts, looking at his mother. I wrote it fuck oil.

Nathan is skateboarding fast. Vangina! He whirls past them. You can't even spell, he says. You can't even read, Gabe. He reaches the front door. Gabe rhymes with babe.

Nate! Syl shouts at her son. Will you stop it! Christ's sake!

Nate whispers a worse word as he passes, his eyes lit with challenge.

And here we go again, thinks Mia, watching as the house whirls into chaos. Even so, there is something engaging about this very lived life, rising around her as she stands in Syl's kitchen, the mess, the noise; something that is the healthy antithesis of her own un-life in the flat, with its fixed disorder, its stasis, where the dust falls and where she moves about so quietly, as though it were she, and not John, who was the ghost. Just her own heart beating unstoppably into the silence.

Nathan! Syl shouts, her thin arms braced, hands on her hips, stop it right now! That word is offensive to women. And get off that fucking skateboard.

Bath time! Shula says suddenly and with authority. Standing up, she is a tower of a woman. She picks up Gabriel as if he were a small animal, carrying him with one arm under his waist, face down. He monkeys round until he is on her hip. Say sorry to your mother, she tells Nate by the front door.

Sorry Mum, in a sing-song and without looking. You look like a penis head, Nate says to Gabriel as he goes upstairs. Can we play that game in the bath, Shula?

Yes, pet.

Mia and Syl look at each other. Nice and tidy for Robert's return home. Mia says, smiling, How is he?

I don't know, Syl says. He's invisible. The practice has ballooned. There's no shortage of nutters apparently. Let's take a drink into the garden. She slides open the glass doors, steps outside. He's mmmaking mmmoney, she says in a comic voice, over her shoulder, which is a very important thing to do, so I'm told. She is mocking.

Well, he's in the same practice as your mother, so it's who you are too. And you chose him, Mia says, taking the glass Syl holds out to her and seating herself at a wooden table that looks back at the house.

Did I? I can't remember. I think he chose me. Or maybe my mother chose him. Shit. That's a thought.

Anyway, Mia says, indicating the lit kitchen with its floor covered with slogan-filled placards, you're busy compensating with demonstrations, I take it. What does Robert think of that?

He doesn't like the fact that they are always at the weekend. It's uncivilised.

I see, Mia laughs. I thought that was rather the point, wasn't it – counter-culture?

There is a silence between them for a while. Conversations from other gardens drift over the dividing walls while small birds flit from bush to bush in the last of the light. In the kitchen Shula and the boys come down unbathed. There is a fault with Syl's heat pump and the water was cold. Shula's mouth is set in a line. Your exchanger thingummy's on the blink. You'd better ring your man again.

Syl puts her head in her hands. Her hair stands up in childish spikes. You have to be so rich to be green. In the kitchen, the boys sit down to cheese on toast in their pyjamas.

So what do you make of it then? Syl asks after a while.

Of what?

Of the current situation, of life, you know – everything?

Mia looks blank for a moment, then says in sudden tiredness, Oh God Syl, I haven't thought about life for so long. I've been too busy living.

Or not living, Syl says, looking at her.

Mia starts to answer and then stops, rubs her chin, says nothing. Somewhere distant a siren passes. So somewhere something is happening, Mia thinks, her mind elsewhere. Someone has been driven to rage or to abandon – broken a law or a window, or committed a violence, or grabbed at something they shouldn't, or been hit by a car or a bus or a motorbike and is lying in the street now, wide-eyed with shock, thinking, This is real, this is happening to me, while their blood pools on tarmac and people jostle each other and watch.

Mia sighs and looks at her friend. I just know that life doesn't seem simple to me any more, she says slowly into Syl's darkening garden. It seems to happen all the time and it seems so random. I can't sort the issues out.

Syl softens. She touches Mia's hand. You'll be fine Mia. It takes time. How was lunch with my dad, was he any use?

He was sweet, Syl. He was great actually. He told me to spend myself, however you do that. He told me not to live backwards. I think he told me to have a child. I think that's what he told me.

Oh for God's sake, Syl groans, he's impossible. With him, I suppose? How on earth did that come up in conversation – I thought you were writing a book on the seventeenth century?

Well, we are. Or he is. It was my fault. I told him I'd had a row with my dad. He was just trying to help.

You had a row with your dad this last time you went?

Mia nods.

I didn't realise that. Poor you, Mia. What about?

Freddy was there, if you can believe it.

Oh fuck. Syl says. Fucking Freddy. Isn't he dead yet? What did you say?

I didn't say anything. I just walked out.

Right. Quite right. I hope he looked terrible. Did he look terrible?

He looked the same as ever, just a bit older. Smug, flashy, like I-know-about-you-and-don't-you-forget-it. That kind of look. And of course my da can't see and the aunts just look like rabbits about to be run over. You can't imagine how horrible it is.

Oh God Mia, how awful. I can. I can imagine. I hate Freddy.

And Syl has, she has always hated Freddy, even from the first moment when she and Mia were sharing the flat, when Mia was wild with escaping Scotland, when they were drinking and partying and falling in and out of love.

It had been such a relief to Mia then, not to care, not to think about her father sitting blind and widowed in his chair, his arms softening while another man ran his farm. It was such a relief not to see his eyes blank, or that look of reaching-far-back on his face. Such a relief not to think about her mother's shocking descent, her face fatted with steroids, the thin hands restless, picking, picking at the cloth of her trousers as she tried to articulate and failed.

What is it Ma, what is it you want to say? Nothing. Just the agonised look, the few frustrated animal sounds and dabbing at the lopsided mouth, to get rid of the dribble. At night blocking out the feeling that filled her, like the pressure of electricity, of the brain tumour growing and growing in her mother's beautiful head. Its relentlessness. Its malevolence.

It had seemed to Mia then that the body was just a horrible booby trap. So it didn't much matter who she gave hers to, or what she did with it.

So that was how Freddy had caught her.

Oh and there was a guy called you, Syl's unthinking remark on the way to work one morning. Stooped over cigarettes outside the newsagent, while other people hurried past. The little flaring light of the match in Mia's hand. Smoke and light and hurrying to the Tube and the easy, ordinary morning, which is how life springs its traps on us, always when we are least suspecting.

What kind of a guy?

And then Freddy had appeared, in a sports car with leather seats and pop-up headlights like lizards' eyes. He was checking that his niece was alright in the big smoke. He'd promised her aunt. He was making sure she was getting the odd square meal. Hop in, dreamboat, he'd say to her, holding the door open for her. I thought we'd go to a quiet place I know.

And then Mia would sit back in the leather seats, half-curious, half-numb, because nothing mattered really. She would let Freddy feed her with expensive food. She would let him take her, because he never asked, he just took, with that look of, see me, see what I can do. Time after time she just let it happen, and then she'd let him drive her home, and she'd walk in feeling mauled but still numb, shrugging to herself and thinking, That's what a man is, to find Syl smoking in front of the telly.

Mia, he's no good for you.

I know.

He's a creep.

He's a real creep. I know that too, don't think I don't.

So what are you doing with him? You could have anyone Mia. I mean, you're fucking your uncle. What's going on?

And Mia would turn as if she'd only just realised, a look of surprise in her eyes, of alarm. I don't know Syl. I don't know what I'm doing. But I'm in it now.

Syl was the only person who knew. Mia's aunts knew or guessed at bits, Ines and Freddy's wife, Mary, but they were Catholic. Mia could never have said. So Syl was the only one.

Have you ever thought about telling your dad what happened, Syl asks her now, as they sit together in the darkening garden.

I can't, Syl, Mia sighs. I've thought about it because it would be such a weight off my mind, but I can't. We don't have that kind of relationship. We don't talk.

You must talk about something?

Well, we talk about the weather. We talk about hedges and fields and the other farmers round about. I tell him stuff he can't see. But we don't talk. We've never talked.

I can't imagine that, Syl says. I can't imagine not talking.

Bill says you don't confide in him. I asked him at lunch.

I don't ask his advice, Syl says, but I tell him when I've screwed up. I always do. He's a good person to talk to because he's so unshockable. He doesn't think any of it is important in the end. Maybe you should talk to him.

No I can't do that, Mia says.

Well go on talking to me then, until someone better shows up. And answer my fucking calls while you're about it, Syl says. That's the only important thing.

I have answered, Syl. Mia laughs. You and your dad are about the only people who do call – apart from some of John's more conscientious friends. Those are the calls I don't answer. I always answer yours. Look, I'm here now, aren't I?

You're here, Syl says, and that's great. That's really great. A window opens above them and Nate's head appears.

Are you coming up, Mum?

Give me five, Syl says.

Gabriel's head appears alongside. Are you coming up?

She is coming, Gabe. I already asked her. Get inside, he tells his brother. You're too small.

When are you coming? Gabe calls down.

In a minute. I'm just finishing this glass of wine with Mia. Then I'm coming.

Nate spits. I can spit on you, Mum. Gabe spits. Yeah, I can spit on you. Mia and Syl look up. Little balls of spit fall. They land inaudibly and nowhere near them, on Syl's terrace.

I'd better go up, Syl says, before they do some serious damage. They move to go inside. So what on earth were you doing in Sloane Square? she asks.

I went to the dogs' home. I'm thinking of getting a dog.

Fuck's sake Mia, you are a headcase. What do you want with a dog in a third-floor flat? That flat's enormous anyway. Why don't you get a lodger? You don't have to walk it and it won't shit on the floor.

I like walking. Mia puts on her coat. And I'll get one that's house-trained.

In the King's Road the lamps are on, although it is still dusk rather than fully dark. Mia reaches her bus stop and waits, leaning on the little shelf under the awning. Other passengers gather.

All round her, the life that Mia can't fathom or find a foothold in goes on. The King's Road teems with people going out. Let me show you a quiet place I know. Taxis whisk to the kerb and whisk away again full. The pulse of the streets is quick. In the house Mia has just left, Syl tries and fails to put her sons to bed and wishes their father would come home from his consulting rooms early for once in his life. And Shula sits in her basement and inspects her corn plasters with the telly on, which only her picture of the Queen appears to be watching. The doors in Syl's street open and shut as their inhabitants come home tired and make themselves drinks, or whirl out again dressed up, Bye darlings, I'm late. A man in a suit arrives at Mia's bus stop and puts down his briefcase and twitches his cuffs and studies immaculate fingernails. And now round the corner comes a drinker, creased and bursting, immune to his portable atmosphere and with his clothes caked to a forgotten body.

The doorways are getting colder. There's a snap in the air again. Give us a kiss sweetheart, he says, staggering slightly, to no one. C'mon lady. His hands make a pleading gesture, at the air, at some wraith of his own imagining, weaving and glimmering ahead of him, the spirit of drink herself maybe, or some lost love from before. Mia and the man with the fingernails try not to watch. Reaching the corner, he steadies himself so as not to tip into the traffic; poised now above a grille, legs braced, he stares down into the runnel, gesticulates again. What's a matter, he says to his vision, through the grille in the ground. Why don't you want me? I just can't understand why you don't want me.

Amour est mon plaisir
  Si j'aime ou je suis aimee.

In the park, at Brampton, the trees suffer the wind that comes brawling over the lip of the hill from Wales. This year, 1624, the parish register will record four deaths, nine baptisms, no marriages again, businesslike, without fuss, as if they were routine, these fierce entrances and exits.

The dark rooms, shuttered up for the laying-in, for instance. Women's voices. The queasy anxiety of the first-time mother, shifting her weight around, Brilliana communing helplessly with her God. O Lord, if you see fit. The sudden sickening lurches, what if . . . what if . . . ? And through the cracks at the windows the light of the days that just go on regardless. The trees turning for autumn. Rain for a few days, then wind and sun. And all the time the soft burr of the men, looking at the fitness of this or that piece of ground for stock, talking of timber prices, of fat beefs, of where a horse could be got that would be sound and not expensive, for going about. The little hubbub of their comings and goings rising to this window.

Is it life or death that is being born in this chamber? – because there is no way of knowing. Blind, without either the mind's permission or control, the muscles roll themselves in contraction and the body labours. The woman's eyes are round.

How do you sanctify this – the mystery, the horror of it, the straining and arching, the sinful pain and the livid, animal entrance to the female body? Better to shut it away. The tapers burn down and are quietly replaced.

In between, while her body rests, Brilliana's mind scurries, like something looking for a way out. How much longer? Please. How much longer? Hot water is carried in and out. The women around have their arms bare for work. They are quiet. This is serious business.

O Lord, save this woman thy servant.
Who putteth her trust in thee.

And now, if you were a boy passing outside the closed doors, on some errand or other about the castle, you would hear a cry that would thin your blood. Something wild, too close to uncontrol. Some horror surely that was taking place. Some private witchcraft. So that you'd dally a moment, with your mouth open involuntarily, until the cry came a second time, a third, a long drawn-out fourth. Our Father, which art in heaven. Gabbling the prayers that you know.

Will she die? Now she is surely dying.

A new sound. Frail, high, trembling wail.

The door to the chamber opens suddenly and a woman comes out. What are you standing about here for, you foolish boy? Run and fetch Sir Robert.

It is a boy. God be praised, it is a fine boy.

And the news goes round the castle. A boy. An heir for Brampton Bryan. And there are prayers said and healths drunk and the castle goes back to its business light-hearted, and behind the closed doors the women continue in half-darkness for several weeks more.

Imagine the strong light, when after three weeks, Brilliana and her child emerge. Imagine the air. Like coming back to the world. Like a long time spent underwater, coming back to the surface, exhausted, sodden, breathing again, putting your foot on firm ground. There is earth and grass. There are trees still heavy with leaves. There is the river swollen with rain and the high hills that back the park, scoured with wind, and the bracken on them bronze and dry. The whole energy and business of the physical world turning itself over to the coming of winter. Berries in the hedgerows. Hips and haws. Noise everywhere. How much time has gone by? Noticing suddenly that all the swallows have already gone. Cold.

Forasmuch as it hath pleased Almighty God of his goodness to give you safe deliverance, and hath preserved you in the great danger of Child-birth; you shall therefore give hearty thanks unto God and say . . .

The snares of death compassed me round about: and the pains of hell gat hold upon me . . .

Thou hast delivered my soul from death: mine eyes from tears, and my feet from falling.

I believed, and therefore will I speak; but I was sore troubled: I said in my haste, all men are liars.

And the baby, the little boy – he must be baptised. He must be welcomed into the body of the True Church. So that it can be written down, in a regular hand, matter-of-fact in the Parish Register.

Edward ye sonne of Sr Robert Harley knight of ye Bath and of ye Lady Brilliana his wife was baptysed – Oct 24

And now, writing after the baptism, because that is the way of news in these times, the old father congratulates his son-in-law. His precious daughter has survived her first delivery. She has given her son her own father's name.

My Good Sonne, Our good God be praised who hath in his mercy hearde our prayers and given us a singular blessing which I beseeche him to lend to your family many years and to multiply it by him and by many more such blessings . . .

And it being tru that my comforte and joye is exceeding great in my Brill's safe delivery and with advantage of the sex, I will use no hands to express it but my owne and therefore with a glad harte I do joyfully thank you for the knowledge and thank you for the choice of me to present him to God by the sacrament, for your courteous offer of the name and all your fayre attributes you are pleased to give me, but you shall give me leave to lay two arguments before you and then to give you my advice.

If there be vertue in me worth the imitating, I have begotten Brill so in my best I may, as she will impart enough of me to season her son, if not so much to spoyle his temper. From your father he hath the land, from him through you better things than that, now my advise is that you let him take your father's name that by those two names joyned in him he may remember to keep up in honour that noble family and that house which God hath please to honour him to be a chief beauty of.

If it be possible I will send Brill a blessing in my hand apart, I beseach God to make us thankful for this present blessing and all the rest, commend my love and service to my cossin your father tell Mistris Wryght I give belief to her letter and pray her to take care that Brill catch not cold.

27th October

How considered and courteous, how practical and circumstantial is the world that the men inhabit.

If it is possible, if he has time, he will write a letter to his daughter.

Mia's resolution for the autumn was never again to sit in the dark. But dark is everywhere by the time the bus drops her almost at her door. Coming home at night is always the worst. Even now she has to bustle herself. The lights in her block are on a timer. Having shoved the big entrance door wide enough to slip through, Mia gropes for the switch, which she pushes with the flat of her hand. The long mirrored passage leaps into life and, glancing sideways, Mia meets the gaze of a woman with staring eyes and blown hair, who is herself. Heavens, she thinks briskly, get yourself together.

The block is owned by the Church Commissioners who are too mean, or too full of internal light themselves, to put switches by every door, so having turned the lights on as you come in downstairs, you can be sure that by the time you reach the third floor the lights will turn off as you twist the key in the lock. That is assuming that you can find your key and that your phone doesn't ring, to divert your focus and slow your pace, or that you don't encounter someone coming down and decide to wait for them rather than squeeze past on the narrow stairs. Often Mia mounts the last flight in darkness.

This time, as the lights extinguish and she pushes her door, there is the low burr of a man's voice talking in the empty flat. Burr, burr. Pause. Erm. Burr, burr, burr. Mia stands at the door, mouth a little open, listening down the dark corridor. It is Bill's voice speaking into her answerphone. She snaps on the light.

How silly, she thinks, cross with herself. Who did you think it was?

Even so, when she gets to the kitchen, she can't help herself crossing the passage to put on the lights, in the sitting room, in John's workroom as well. Syl is right. I should get a lodger. She walks back and forth between the rooms in stockinged feet, putting on music, cooking pasta, opening her laptop on the bed in the workroom. Check for emails, listen to the phone messages. When the pasta is cooked she sits on her bed, one leg tucked under, eating and browsing the dogs' home website. It's better than expected. There do seem to be other types of dog on offer, though outside London, it has to be said.

'Jack', she reads, alongside the photo of a Jack Russell. Original. 'Jack is a cracking little pup who enjoys fun and games'. 'Fred', nondescript, not particularly engaging, 'Fred would make an amusing addition to any home'. 'Cuthbert', very small, hairy enough to make it difficult to tell front from back, 'a sweet boy with a sensitive nature, can take a little while to make friends'. 'Suzie', white, neurotic-looking, 'can be vocal'. That's the last thing I need.

After two dispiriting pages of doggish-looking dogs, Mia realises that she has been hoping for the little stray that trotted past that morning. He isn't here. She looks out of the window at the lamplit street. Nothing. No dog. People in and out of the Mexican restaurant, cabs passing, traffic sweeping unending round the corner and on out of sight. It's too soon, Mia thinks, come on, he wouldn't be on the website yet. I only just saw him today. Then with her sensible mind she thinks, How stupid, you don't even know if he was a stray. He could have been reclaimed, or run over, or just taken in. He could have been a she.

I wouldn't want a bitch. That's the farmer's daughter talking.

Mia stares out of the window, at the dark cars, thinking now about Bill and Sylvia, her two friends, so keen to help, so keen to pull her free from the stagnation of bereavement. It is true that so far her interest in John's work has been shamelessly centred on reclaiming her lover, stalking his mind down the tunnels of his own thought. It was the only way that she could think of to cross the divide between them when he died. When she sat at his desk and read through his notes she told herself she could feel him, only just round the corner ahead of her. When, once or twice, she jumped to a conclusion that, turning a page in the notebook she found written out in John's precise hand, almost exactly as she'd thought it, he seemed close enough to touch. As though, if she didn't turn round, he'd walk in through the door again and unwind the long coloured scarf he wore and chafe his fingers and say, Well? in the way that he always used, one fine eyebrow raised.

If only. If only.

But it is two years since John died.

*

Dark round the edges. As if looking into a lit room from somewhere outside. The slow movement of people, their turned backs, drinking and talking but inaudibly. The reel of Mia's memory running. Silent. Spotlit.

Bill, the first time she meets him, in the alien elegance of his upstairs sitting room full of people she doesn't know. Up a long staircase behind Syl and into this room of strangers. His crumpled, soft-collared shirt. His personal untidiness; so unlike any father of Mia's previous experience. And his surprised face when Sylvia introduces them, his undisguised admiration, the frank sensuality of his gaze, which puts Mia on her guard.

Dad, this is Mia. She works at the paper with me.

I am delighted to meet you. And he looks it. His delivery is quaintly chivalrous, a slow voice with the trace of an accent.

She needs rescuing, Syl says, while Mia's face registers surprise and momentary disorientation.

You need rescuing. Bill holds Mia's hand in his. From what?

From herself, Syl says. And not by you, Dad.

The reel jumps from sequence to sequence. It edits. It isn't faithful to an exact order of events, only to its own order of emotional significance. Mia doesn't remember in detail. She remembers Bill saying, Let me introduce you to my friend John. He is looking for a researcher for his book. She sees John's shoulders before she knows they are his. The jacket that is the top half of a suit. She sees him standing in a group of people, listening to a woman talking, and how they turn at Bill's arrival to include her.

I must interrupt you a moment. John, I want to introduce you to my daughter's friend. She is looking for a job as a researcher. And the man holds out his hand. His head is held at an angle of interest and enquiry and his eyes are quiet.

What is your name? Because Bill had referred to her only as Syl's friend.

I'm Mia.

And if she could only go back to there. To the moment when John was luxuriously strange to her, begin it all over again.

Mia sits on her bed, by her night-filled window. She has no desire to move on. Whether or not it is 'enough'. She doesn't care if she is wasted. She sits very still, unaware of herself, her eyes locked on another time.

Dark around the edges. The lit room again, from somewhere outside. Again the slow movement of people, their turned backs, drinking and talking but inaudibly. Silent. Spotlit.

The thin covering of the suit jacket and the man turns, his angled head, his quiet eyes. And again the first time he takes her hand, a stranger.

What is your name?

I'm Mia.

The reel of Mia's memory running. Dark around the edges. The room lit. But weaker, however much she wills it, each time she runs the sequence of their meeting.

And all the while, from the differently lit square of her laptop, Jack and Fred and Cuthbert and Suzie, the Battersea strays, stare out at her with hopeful expressions.

Well, a dog would be a distraction at least, Mia says, looking down at the dogs' faces. Just choose one. Any one. Stop thinking about everything so carefully. Maybe Cuthbert?

Mia takes up the book she has left open and face down on the bed. *Puritans and Roundheads*, it is called, *The Harleys of Brampton Bryan and the Outbreak of the English Civil War*. It has the photograph of Brilliana's portrait on the front. Long almond-shaped eyes, long nose – too long possibly – pursed mouth, prominent chin, with the hint of a cleft, and that severe and alien expanse of forehead that the seventeenth century favoured. Hello, Mia says to the portrait. Who exactly are you?

The woman looks back at Mia, self-contained, very certain. Well, you were a woman, and you married an older man, Mia thinks. So we have some things in common. Did you never make any mistakes? How did you manage? The woman gives nothing back.

You must have been very cold, Mia says, looking at the cut of Brilliana's dress, the expanse of fashionably naked chest. She puts the book down.

Much later, Mia goes down the passage to the bathroom, to clean her teeth before bed. Chavela Vargas is still singing, on a loop, in the sitting room.

And at the same time, in Glebelands, in the village of Myddle, Mia's father opens the door on a thick night. His dog nudges past on old legs, bangs around among the dustbins, barks at the sky and urinates against someone else's car parked at the house front.

Mia's father stands, one knotted hand on the door jamb, and his face upturned to the sky, locked in his own different past. He wonders about Mia. He doesn't yet know she has written to him. He thinks of Mia's face, as he last saw it, when she was nineteen, the year he finally went blind. I wonder if she looks anything like her ma now. He smells the damp on the air and knows there are no stars.

They shall not labour in vaine nor bringe forthe for trubell: for they are the seed of the blessed of the Lord, and their offspringe with them.

Ye have not chosen me but I have chosen you and ordained you that you should goo and bringe forth frute and that your frute should remaine that whatsoever ye shall ask of the Father in my name he may give it you.

From Brilliana Harley's Book of Meditations

Months later. It is winter, which in London means a sky made out of pigeon feathers. The idiocy of January sales. Normally polite people barging each other to reach shoes or sheets, or coloured leather bags, or pots, or pans, staggering between each other with bolts of fabric under their arms. Outside the air is gritty, metallic.

Cuthbert has arrived, small, hairy, very nervous. He and Mia have settled into an uneasy routine of early walks followed by a day on the balcony above the courtyard for Cuthbert, yapping occasionally at the pigeons, crouching under Mia's laundry rack in preference to spending time on his new bed. 'A sweet boy with a sensitive nature', his description had read on the website, 'can take a while to make friends'. You'd better believe it.

Mia, who with Bill's encouragement is knuckling down, walks with her country-bred appetite for exercise, along the Euston Road to spend the days in the manuscript room of the British Library, where the Harley papers are bound into volumes the size of foot-stools. It amuses her, as she passes the shining glass buildings with their outside lifts and their knots of dedicated smokers shivering in the doorways, to say under her breath, East Lamb's Conduit Fields, the burying grounds, Park Farm, Love Lane, Jew's Harp House, Queen's Head. Only scatterings of buildings here. Fields on every side. Just fields and hedges and small lanes.

She breakfasts in the Pret across the road from the library, browsing the banks of sandwiches whose curvature says, Choose me, I am nutritious, I am full of farm-good food; the little bottles of smoothies and juices, the jars of granola and yoghurt and the naughty but nice cakes. She eats at one of the window tables, and drinks two cups of coffee and watches the world on its way to work, and the world in and out of the bar; the people in suits so exhausted and the staff zappy in baseball caps and aprons. How are you today? Enjoy, have a lovely day. Occasionally she reads one of the free newspapers.

What a time to live, Mia thinks, flicking through. Lists of animals going extinct, as though the world were disintegrating, like a Disprin in a glass of water. 'Opposition calls for inquiry' on any or most days. And the same, porcine young man in a suit, pictured every time, squaring his shoulders, his mouth set to look dependable, and his eyes expressing nothing, except the desire not to be found out.

Today, next to the list of animals is the death of an elder statesman, who wore his hair wild and walked his dog and held high ideals. Elder statesmen are also going extinct.

Ideals? How outlandish. In the elder statesman's pictures even the seventies look like a foreign country. Today tastes of money, Mia thinks, and drug companies and celebrity and sport and small scandal and petrol and anti-ageing cream.

Later, up in the reading room Mia makes lists of things from two hundred years ago. She tries, as instructed, to imagine she is a computer and she takes careful notes – the names of the plants that Brilliana would have grown in her garden, for salads for instance. Cowslips, violets, primroses, lungwort, liverwort, purslane she writes, in pencil, because pen is not allowed. Common plants for vegetable gardens included harefoot, blood-wort, penny royal, marigolds, artichokes, cabbage, sea-blite, burnet, catmint, tansy, turnip, broad beans, ronceval peas, pumpkins, skirrets, radishes, carrots, parsnips, onions, leeks, endive, spinach, common sorrel, lettuce, parsley, cress, sage, tarragon, fennel, thyme, mint, savory, rhubarb. She has no idea of what many of them might be. Do you prefer sea-blite or skirrets, she asks herself wryly.

It is exhausting but she is tireless. She copies down the inventory for Brampton Castle, as it must have been when Brilliana arrived there as a bride in 1623. Which room would she have gone into first? Would her husband, who had watched his two previous wives die, have taken her politely into the parlour? Mia writes:

In the parlour:
   One Bible in folio: English
   One horse armour
   One target
   One trumpett flourished with silver the boards and tassells of silke and golde
   Twenty two halberds 4 gilt
   Three French pistolls
   One long table
   One square table
   One corner cupboard
   Fower tables hanging with armes
   Three pittures
   Two long carpette of broadcloth greene
   One square carpett
   One cupboard carpett
   One olde long greene carpett
   Two formes of wainscott
   One wainscott chaire
   One cloth chaire imbroidered with twist crewle
   One cloth chaire yellow and 2 stooles stained with black
   Fower stooles cobered with Turky work
   Two long stooles with Turky work
   Twelve joyn'd stooles
   Six cushions of Arrys work with the arms of the house
   Six Turky cushions with the woodbynd
   Fower Turky cushions with the rose
   Two great andirons of brasse
   One fire fork of iron

An old and strange and handmade world.

On the other side of the desk an American academic and his colleague are having a conversation. They are talking just above a whisper and they are making it, Mia thinks, unnecessarily complicated. I'm going to go down to Rare Books, the woman is saying, but I'll come get you at ten to and we can catch a cab. The man has hair growing out of his ears, which may well be the reason he needs to talk so loudly, in a library, where it is meant to be quiet.

Mia looks across at the help desk to see if anyone will tell them to stop. Then she looks round the reading room. No one else is distracted. Everyone else is working, on books propped on conservation pillows, at boxes spilling over with manuscript ties, tapping, oblivious, at PCs and scribbling pencil notes. Because there is so much to be read here, so many things to be researched and annotated and digested and written up. Trolleys of books and boxes are wheeled up and down. Pale people consume book after book, carry piles of discards back to the help desk, return bowed down with another order, more books, more boxes, more notes to take. So urgent is this search for information that they do not stop, Mia has noticed, for lunch or for tea. They are undistractable it seems. They eat dates and figures and long-forgotten politics and statistics about everything from birth to death to battles and many other things besides and they do not hear even the loudest conversations between others of their species.

Whisper. Have you had a chance to look at the charters? Mia stares, enraged, at the couple. They are oblivious. I'd really value your input on this. Whisper, whisper, mutter. And I'll need to stop by the hotel and just pick up a couple a things. Will we get the chance to stop by the hotel? Oh sure, we can stop. No problem.

Well, thank goodness for that.

Or did Robert Harley take his new wife straight to her room, the place that smells sometimes sour and sometimes of lavender, where she would love him and give birth, and occasionally miscarry; where she would suffer her many indispositions and where, in the end, she would die without him, exhausted and fevered and coughing blood? To the most important room in the castle, in some respects.

So – in the great chamber:
   One bedstead with tester and valence of satten
   Five taffeta curtaines all orange-tawny
   One saten counterpaine
   One large arras coberlett
   One rugge oreng-tawny
   One downe bedd and boulster
   One feather bedd and boulster
   One woollen blanquett
   One fustian blanquett
   Two pillows
   One saten chaire
   One longe cushion of saten
   One little saten chaire
   Two little saten stooles
   One chaire of taffeta embroidered
   One longe cushion of coarse tentwork
   Two square cushions of needlework
   One court cupboard
   One greene carpett
   One paire of large brasse andirons

Mia goes steadily on. She reads accounts of medical practice. She reads accounts of plague in 1625, so bad in London that Parliament had to decamp to Oxford. James I newly dead and Att Henley and att a village neer, called Remenham, in some families both master and mistris and children and servants were all swept away with it, scarce one left of a family. She can't see. She just tries to imagine how it was.

Presumably they had had faith in their medicine, she thinks, however hocus-pocus it seems now. *Aurum potabile*. That is drinkable gold. She stops and looks up at the bent heads all around her. Were they any more fearful then than we are now? In the morning paper, for instance, a river of commuters in Japan wearing masks against infection. *Aurum potabile* – Tamiflu. Which one is worse for you? Was terror of the plague any different from terror of swine flu say, or bird flu, or MRSA?

But it is difficult to tell. The letters are so dry. Lord Conway, for instance, staying away from the capital, at Andover for fear of infection, and thinking, as he always does, of his five children, of his pregnant daughter Brilliana and her husband and her little son.

The Lord of Heaven bless you with his grace and all those comforts and estimations which ryse from that, together with all your brothers and sisters where so ever they may be. I send this bearer of purpose to carry the knowledge of my helthe to you. You are happy if God kepe the plague from aboute you. The doubts and calamities and woeful visitations of it is misery and affliction in abundance.

He shakes the sand across the ink to dry it.

What Mia can't see is the anxiety that clouds Conway's face as he sets his seal. Please God. Will the plague have reached as far as Herefordshire? How can he tell? Worrying. Worrying. Turning the signet ring on his finger in abstraction. What she can't feel are the fragile ties of a family stretched across distant counties, the absolute silence, the lack of news. Such interminable waiting and not knowing. And even now they may all be dead, the precious daughter, the fat little grandson. There is no one going into Herefordshire who could take a letter but Lord Conway cannot wait. He will send a man specially. To reassure. To make contact.

He doesn't ask a secretary. He writes himself. His hand, so angular and diagonal it looks like brown rain. A second letter, passing on a lost enclosure, a very long receipt that is able to cure any tertian ague and is so faire and sure a medicine that may make those sick be so cured. Just in case.

And then a little later, because he still hasn't heard, a third letter, saying just the same as the first and second. I am well. I hope you are too. Despite their similarity Mia patiently deciphers these re-iterated prayers for health, each family member named and brought to mind, passing back and forth along bad roads from London or Greenwich to Brampton, paper charms, as they seem to her, against imagined disaster, written once a month, often less. As though the act of writing itself were enough to ward off evil.

My deare childerne, the Lord of Heaven bless you both and all your boys and wenches, and give you comfort in your selves and in them and all that belongs to you and them and the rest that may concern you.

My children deare, I beseech God to bless you and increase to you all comforts of this life and of that to come.

My children deare, I have thought it very long sence I heard from you and have suspected myself of melancholy for many doubts and feares have presented themselves unto me concerning you and your family, being all very deare to me.

*

On some days, reading accounts of the politics of the Civil War, or lives of this or that person, or meticulous books about marriage or the upbringing of children, or the role of women in society, it is all Mia can do to keep her head from nodding to the desk, the words she is reading swimming before her, landing in her mind as if into deep snow, numb, half-buried, lost already.

It is on one of these days that she gets it into her mind that there is something unseemly, something revolting about the library. The enormity of the communal stifled yawn hanging stale over the bent heads in Humanities 1. The awful hush, or the equally awful whispering. The industry, the boredom, the un-life.

Bill, it's Mia.

Mia, hello. Where are you? She can hear music in the background. Wind instruments. Wait, let me turn this down.

It's very calming. I'm in the British Library. I'm trying not to die.

Bill is solicitous. In his first-floor drawing room in Gordon Square, his shirt half-untucked, he crosses and re-crosses the room on squashed-looking shoes as he talks. He carries the telephone, which is an old-fashioned one with a cord, back and forth as he goes, stopping to flip the line free when it catches on the arm of the chair. The last thing he wants is for her to die. What are you going to die of, Mia?

Boredom. And rage. And pointlessness.

I see. I had no idea the British Library could generate such passions. Bill talks slowly in his deep voice, while he stands at the window to look out. Dark in the square. A couple of people crossing on different diagonals, walking quickly. It must be cold. Are you phoning from outside the library? Don't catch cold. Have you got a coat on Mia?

Mia is sitting hunched with her knees together on one of the stone blocks in the so-called piazza. Don't fuss me, Bill. Of course I'm outside. I told you. I had to get out. She looks at the lights passing behind the huge iron gates. All the concentration of the city readying itself for evening. It is always like this. Faster, more intent than by day. The city's heart rate increasing with the falling of dark. Mia feels the cold, old and un-human, come up through her seat. She huddles over her phone. No, I haven't got my coat on . . . I'm fine, Bill. I'm Scottish . . . It's downstairs. It's in a locker.

People are hurrying home across the piazza now. Not long till the library will be shut.

Bill, will you listen to me? I said, I'm fine.

What are you going to do tonight? Bill asks. Are you going back to that dreadful flat?

It isn't dreadful. It's where I live.

Don't go back there, Mia. Come and have supper with us.

Bill's voice is comforting and very soft.

I can't, Mia says but without conviction. You're very kind but I can't.

Why can't you? Come for supper, Mia. Come straight. Don't go home, just come here.

I can't Bill. I'd have to change my clothes anyway. I need a bath. How about Julia, won't she mind if I come, at such short notice?

Of course she won't. We already have people coming. Jacqueline Eales is coming. It will be good for you to meet her. One more will make no difference. Come, you are always an asset. Julia won't notice. And I want you.

Bill stands by his window and doesn't really look out. He does want her. He has always wanted her, since the first time Syl brought her to be John's researcher. He doesn't know why.

But then he's a quick-blooded man, he can't help it, and there are any number of reasons. Still, even after John, there are any number of reasons. Because of John perhaps, because like all men he's competitive. Because she's warm and alone, and he's alive. Because she always says no. Because she's lovely. Because he's an old goat maybe.

Meanwhile, unaware of Bill's train of thought, Mia clicks her phone off and sits on her cold seat for a moment, thinking Bill is a kind man. I do him wrong.

A little later, having retrieved her coat from the locker and walking stiffly home because, whatever she said to Bill, she did get cold, down the Euston Road in the dark, with the tail lights of the traffic glittering in half-rain now, Mia thinks about her days of working in the library. She is thinking sharply that after all this immersion in detail she is none the wiser. She is thinking about how we experience the historical past as if crossing a dark river, careful, conscientious, on stepping stones. Here is a date, a fact, something solid in the flood. Here is a medical practice, an Act of Parliament, a prayer, a recipe, a letter.

Still, on the cover of the blue book, every time she takes it up,

Brilliana purses her lips and looks self-contained. I know nothing of you, Mia says to her in her head. These facts I've absorbed or forgotten don't make a person after all. I don't know how you talked, how you ate, how you walked, or loved, or sang, or didn't sing. I don't know if you ate skirrets or preferred sea-blite, if you had a sweet tooth, or touched your hair when you were anxious. I don't know if you were brave or phlegmatic when you had your first child. I don't know if your life and loves were like mine, or not. I have no idea who you are.

Late afternoon, at Brampton, with the fist of the new year closed, cold as stone. Brilliana is not yet thirty, a wife and mother, ten years younger than Mia. 1626. A year and a half since the birth of Ned. Sitting alone in her chamber, reading her Bible, praying.

But she is distracted. It is February and the times are uneasy. Charles I, anxious on his dead father's throne. Lord Conway's patron, Buckingham, the inherited favourite, has failed against Cadiz. The country rages against him. There is talk of impeachment.

Now there can be little hope of advancement for Sir Robert and this is a worry. His suit for the Mastery of the Royal Mint will no doubt be forgotten. He must help his father-in-law protect Buckingham from Parliament. And how will he, of all people, rouse himself to act on behalf of one so outrageous? Buckingham's fecklessness. His vanity. His entire expeditionary force slaughtered, too drunk on Spanish wine even to draw their swords. Outside in the dusk someone at the gate. Is there news? Brilliana frets, loses concentration. It is just a boy, idling. She has to will herself back to her devotions.

There are rumours of an English force to be sent against the Protestants at La Rochelle. God forbid.

Then too, it is hard not to dread the onset of labour. She is pregnant with her second child. In her letters to Sir Robert, gone to London for the King's second Parliament, she drops small hints of frustration.

I thanke you for your letter which I reseved this weeke, and you doo or may believe, your linns are next to your self most wellcom to me. I should have binne glad to have hard from your penn that the Parlament has begoun well, for that is my prayers that it may doe all well: and if you have as sharp weather with you as it is here: you finde it could sitting in the howes: but I know you have more witt than a woman and thearfore I need not desire you to keep yourself warme.

Outside, across the snow-filled fields, in the separate world of the animals, the midnight conversations of hares are recorded in long cursive loops; odd meetings and partings and impenetrable communications that it takes a whole hillside to express. Birds wheeling in silence. The last sounds from the forge carry in the stillness. The blacksmith working by the light of the furnace, with the dark coming down outside.

Dark too in the castle. Terrible cold. Approaching the time now and keeping busy. It is only natural to wish for her husband's return. Trying, in the gaps between communications, not to long immoderately for his company, or just for letters. Trying, when at last the carrier brings them in, not to be impatient of the little news they contain, barely a page long sometimes.

Will no one tell her what is done in the world? It is like being forgotten.

Your letters are so wellcome to me that I can not but begine mine with thanks for them: on word from you is exceeding pleasing to me but I should be glad if your biusnes would let you rwit longer letters.

I reioyce you have your health. I pray God continue it. I am sorry my father has had an Ague and I feare he is not so well as you rwite me word he is. All I can do is to praye for him and this is the comfort of prayer that it will healpe when other means faile.

How ill is her father? Please God he may be spared. And if her father is unwell there can be little hope of his prosecuting Sir Robert's advancement. Is there news of his suit on behalf of Sir Robert? A position at the Mint would be a significant advance. If there is no news of Parliament, is there any news of that, at least?

Instead, the endless duties of the good wife, and it is difficult. As yet she takes no decision without her husband's authority. Nowe, that you may not be ignorant of your owane I will give you an account: the payling of the parke is begun according to your derection. She has put two men to the job, Ames and Sibs. Knocking the pales into the ground on days when the weather softens the ground enough to allow it. The old pailes set up with the new, one old paile and another new which they tell me dous very well. The tock, tock of fencing hammers bouncing off the wall of hills behind has been audible all day.

Jhon Walle began the wood saile on Wednesday last and so has appointed evry wensday betwne this and Ester for wood saile.

And the man who looks most like wood himself, Acton, who knows about horses, perswads me that it is to no end to feed the hors you bought at Knighton but would have him rune at grase all this sommer. He is perswaded if you weare asked againe of your pourpose in it you will change your minde but tell I knowe so your first command shall stande.

Your father is well but this coold weather will not let him goo abrode.

Only at the end of her letter, as the comfort of this kind of communication is about to be withdrawn, does Brilliana call her condition to her husband's mind.

I thanke God I have my health well and so has Ned: and nowe
that the time drawes neere that I waite for in our having a fuller
inioying of that bllsing the Lord has given us such hope of, I hope
you will not forget more earnestly to pray for me:

Does he pray for her, as she does daily for him? Does he miss her?

I doo believe I am dayly remebred by you in that kinde: for I am
sure you are better then I and I faile not to doo it for you:
    Does he think of his child? I must beg your bllsing for Ned
whoo makes the pritiest mone for you, and for myselfe I beeg your
deare love or ells you will ill requit your most affectinat wife BH.

On the back, as though she could not bring herself to close the
letter, a series of postscripts.

Martane is nowe heare and tells me Sr Richard Varny has a desire
to selle you a coche mare but I will not entertaine that bargen tell
I knowe your minde. I have sent up by this carrier 3 collers of
brawne 3 turkis and two capons: which and please you I would
present to my La. Vere: and I have sent one chees for my Lord
Vere: and to my sisters I have sent som puddings derected to them:
which if you eate of remember Bromton: but you may doo your
pleasure with these things and I shall be well pleased.

The little boy, in his dresses, sits, sunny, beside her. So she takes
him up and holding his fist in her own, marks out, in scratched
and crooked writing, I pray Ld com home EH.

Amour est mon plaisir
    Si j'aime ou je suis aimee.

Mia reaches home damp and still cold, her hair springy with curl from the rain. Jesus, I need a bath, she says to her reflection, as she stops to collect her mail from the pigeonholes in the long entrance hall. She looks through the letters quickly as she mounts. There is a package from her father. So they are talking again. She is childishly pleased by this. I can listen to it in the bath before I go.

She reaches her floor, juggles the letters and her keys with cold fingers. She fumbles. The lights go out.

God in heaven, what is this place?

When she has found the switch and coaxed Cuthbert in from the balcony and fed him and run a bath and made tea, she carries her Dictaphone into the bathroom and switches on her father's cassette.

Mia, her father's voice says and pauses. Halloo. This is how all his letters start and at this point he falls silent. A silence that lasts sometimes as long as half a minute, as if in acknowledgement of the distance between them, waiting for his voice to reach all the way to London. Or as if he was listening for her reply. Halloo Dad, Mia has got into the habit of saying, in the pause, I'm here. Because it is important to both of them that they are. It is important to announce to each other, I'm still here.

Her father's letters are the only things that Mia approaches instinctively in a methodical, historical manner, as if she were curating an archive. She keeps the little cassettes in orderly boxes, filed, dated, stored in strict chronological order. If she takes one out, which she sometimes does, she puts a marker in its place so as to be able to put it back where it belongs. She knows already how precious these audible traces of a life can be.

She knows because her mother died, leaving behind nothing but a few uninhabited things, a few odd bits of this and that, in which surprisingly quickly, however hard you looked or remembered or imagined, nothing that was real about her mother could be found; the clothes that Mia cried over and pressed to her face at night but that came all too soon to smell only of Mia herself, the knick-knacks, the few photographs. They were nothing to fill the emptiness her mother had left, the hole that Mia felt in herself, through which the world now poured vertiginous and unceasing. So they were parcelled up in the end and sent to the charity shop. As her father said, they might as well go. The piano that neither Mia nor her father could play and which was the only thing of any value, was sold to a local antique dealer, and Mia made a detour every day after school, to look at it in the shop until it sold.

Mam's piano's gone.

Well that's that then, without pausing in his meal, as if he couldn't care. Get on with your homework, girl.

*

Afterwards, in the dark of midnight, creeping about the home of your childhood like a thief.

And if you want the door not to squeak, Mia knows from long experience, you hold it fast towards you and you turn the handle stealthily. That way it makes no noise as it opens. That way your father won't appear on the landing above. Where exactly do you think you're going, girl – this time of night? Get back in your bed this instant. So the teenager that Mia is, with her breath held and her feet bare on the cold lino of the passage, goes into the sitting room after midnight, to get a glass of water from the farm kitchen beyond. She turns the handle, too busy holding her breath to notice the crack of light underneath the door. So she is caught by surprise when, on opening it, she finds the sitting room still lit.

Too late.

Freezing in the open doorway because her da is there, sitting in his chair by the remains of the fire. Should she go back upstairs? But he hasn't noticed. He hasn't heard her. The sharp line of his shoulders unusually bowed, and he is fingering something, a garment, held in his farmer's hands; just turning it, kind of stroking it with his thumbs, and looking at nothing, while the clock drops its seconds and the fire makes the faint and sibilant sound of its opposite element.

Why hasn't he heard her? He never fails to notice an entrance or an exit. He never doesn't hear. He can hear a bat flying; his ears are that good, as if all the energy no longer needed by his eyes had simply transferred itself to his ears. Mia watches him, side on, from the doorway and still he doesn't look up. He just turns and turns whatever it is he is holding in his hands, his head and his shoulders bowed. And then something makes him sense her presence and he looks quickly round with his blind eyes. Is that you girl? And something in his voice is gentle and almost broken and Mia approaches instead of retreating.

It's me Da, in a small voice.

As she approaches, her father scuffles the garment that is in his hands to one side, as if to hide it. Then thinking better of it, he sits forwards, with his elbows on his knees and Mia can see now, it is her mam's green cardigan that he holds, fisted in his two hands. How did he get to keep that, of all her clothes, Mia is thinking. How did he know to keep that back? Because he couldn't see, could he? He would have had to ask Ines for it, and he hated to ask anything of Ines.

Can you see the colour? her father says simply, clearing his throat into the silence and without looking up.

It's green, Da.

It's green. Mia sits, as she often does if her da is in one of his gentle moods, on the arm of his chair and they look, seeing and unseeing, at the cardigan. After a while her father says, as if to himself, That's the colour she wore when I first laid eyes on her.

Where Mia's shoulder touches his, and down the length of her arm Mia can feel her father trembling, a rapid involuntary vibration that possesses him in moments of extreme emotion. Such a pent-up man, so stern with himself, as though he'd corralled all his softnesses like sheep and shut them in. He doesn't say anything more. He just sits unable to stop himself trembling, willing himself to overcome with his mind the unruliness of his body. Shaking. So they sit like that, shoulder to shoulder, and Mia presses herself against him in the hope that the presence of her own body might still him, might comfort him for the loss of that other. Talking to him through the length of her arm. I'm here, Da. I'm still here. After a while, when he has regained control, Mia gets up off the chair-arm and goes quietly out and back upstairs to bed.

They don't mention the incident again. There is no need, in her father's eyes, to discuss or explain, only to get on with it. Things are as they are. You just have to get on with it, girl. That is what he would say, if asked.

But later, when she is leaving for London, Mia's father produces the cardigan again.

Take your mam's cardigan. You've the same colouring as her. You'll look well in it in London. Mia with her mouth open, which he can't see. It is the only compliment he has ever paid her.

*

Well, Mia, her father's voice says out of the Dictaphone as she soaks and sips in her bath. It's been very awkward weather here. Weather of course, Mia thinks in the bath. Don't mention anything important Da, whatever you do.

Very cold going about. Your aunt's been making stews. I've eaten a good many stews. Mia smiles despite herself. She knows Ines's stews. All carrot and neeps and parsnips, as her father would say.

141

Is there no more meat in the world? Have sheep gone extinct then? But he wasn't bad-natured about it. It was just his way. He was grateful to Ines for her care of him. Between them, she and Ines would pile the meat on his plate. You must have half the flock on your plate Da, what are you talking about?

She's put the heating on behind my back but I'm not saying anything about it, her father's voice among the steam. I go down and turn it off when she's out. Pause. Then she'll turn it back on just when the house gets nice and fresh again. Pause. Mia can hear him clear his throat.

I'll bump into her at the thermostat one of these days, no doubt. That'll be a laugh. Then there is a longer pause and Mia can hear something big accelerate away past her father's house, in the road outside, a dustbin lorry maybe. There is clanking coming from somewhere. Ines in her kitchen maybe, or the men outside. Daytime domestic sounds rise in her London bathroom, while the dark of the London evening presses at the window and the street hums below.

So, you've got yourself a dog. Well, a dog's certainly good for company.

The old boy's not so clever. He's a problem with his hind legs now so we're away to the vet's tomorrow.

I don't know how people go on with a dog in the city. I hope you've not gone and got yourself any old mutt, girl. Mind the animal's nature. Mind you get something you know.

Mia swishes the water round the bath. If he could see the dogs' home. If he could see you, Cuthbert, she says to the little dog, who is lying on the bath mat, his head indistinguishable from his tail, under its mop of hair. And her father's voice goes on. Clipped, precise, speaking carefully, close to the microphone.

I hope you're getting something done, Mia. Work is the best way. I'm not saying I'm against the dog, mind.

If you come across anything interesting that Ines could read me, I'd be grateful. I've fairly run through the lending library.

I'll be starting on the romcoms otherwise.

I could get it through the inter-library loan scheme so you've not to bother with sending. Just the title and the author and a publication date. That can be handy if it's tricky to find.

Well, I'd best go now. You'll be wanting to get on. Take care of yourself then.

Bye now.

Bye Dad, Mia says softly.

When she was a child he used to call her sweetheart.

*

If you are lonely, or assailed by fear; if you think it possible that you will die in childbed, without seeing your husband, who remains away; if your spirit should doubt or falter, then there is comfort to be had from spiritual reading. Or from prayer.

Against just this eventuality Brilliana has compiled her Commonplace Book, as something to turn to, something to put mettle in her soul.

What Worship is:

Worship is an inward and outward acte of the body and minde.

In the inward worship is feare, confidence, Hope, Love, Patience, Invocation and Obedience.

In the outward worship theare is hearing the word of God, reseaving the Sacrements, confessing our faith, taking an othe and making a vowe.

Of Predestination:

God doeth by his meare good wille save whom he wille and not rende reward.

God by his eternall and unchangeable counsel haith once appointed whom in time to come he will take to salvation and on the other side whome he would condeme to distruction.

The number of God's elect is infinit and unsartaine. But this semes to condridict many places in the Scriptures wher it is said they are but a littel flock.

This should move us to examen and try ourselves whether we are of this number.

But then, the wheel of doubt, of fearfulness will turn again. Am I one of the chosen? O Lord I am nothing without you. The vertigo. If I die, Lord? The time is almost come, if I should die in childbed, is it certain? Am I saved?

God forgive me for my weakness.

While Mia, whose only certainty is that she has no God, and who is ready now and dressed to go out, goes down the stairs to the little hall and lets the heavy door click itself behind her and feels the old, hard, cold of the street come flaying round the corner at her, unseen and inhuman. It would eat you away like acid if you let it. She hugs herself and hurries on. Past the desperate bundles in the doorways, among bags and cardboard boxes. Think yourself lucky, God's sake, she says to herself, glancing down and shivering past them, on her way to the bus stop. And come on, she thinks, a little further down the road, rubbing her gloveless hands together, it's only an English winter. Because of her small self, out on the hill in all weathers in a skin-thin nylon mac and jeans.

Put a coat on that child before it catches its death.

Wild as the wind. Jumping with life like the lambs. You've gone soft with town living.

And as she goes, the bundles, which have eyes, but which are separated from the world we live in by their own apparent invisibility, may be looking, but don't necessarily see Mia, wrapped in her red coat and her own thoughts, passing. They just hope they have anaesthetised themselves sufficiently and make their own glazed prayers for sleep.

At Brampton the time passes. The Parliament is still sitting so Robert Harley continues to be away. Grudgingly February gives way to March. Across the park the cattle drip and suffer, and the hazels hold out stiff hands and concentrate on the green that waits inside them, while the wind swings down from the hill like a scything blade. There is much to be done about the running of the castle and estate.

Snow yields to rain. The castle sandstone dark with wet. When spring comes, life will be easier. Past the windows that look out up the valley and dream of London, Brilliana goes slowly about her business, gravid, hand occasionally round her belly. Like the green in the hazels, the new life waiting.

She will go to her chamber to pray and to read before dinner, only lately she has felt a great slowness. She is more tired than usual. For many days now she has had a longing for a salad of spinach, to strengthen her. She has her mother's recipe with her to take to the kitchen.

To make an excellent compound boiled sallat: takeof spinach well washed two or three handfuls, and put into fair water, and boil it till it be exceedingly soft, and tender as pap; then put it into a colander and drain the water from it; which done, with the back-side of your chopping knife chop it, and bruise it as small as may be: then put it into a pipkin with a good lump of sweet butter, and boil it over again; then take a good handful of currants clean washed, and put to it, and stir them well together; then put to as

145

much vinegar as will make it reasonable tart, and then with sugar season it according to the taste of the master of the house, and so serve it upon sippets.

Though there is no master of the house at present so it doesn't much matter.

If you knewe howe earnestly I desire to see you; you will easely beleave your letters are very wellcome to me.

Little news from London. Nothing of what is done in the Parliament, just hurried assurances of his own health, God be thanked. And London seems another world away, though the men go up and down as she may not. John Wall now, has been called away to serve Sir Robert. So she must find another, as diligent as John, to be put in charge of the Wednesday wood sales.

Brilliana stops briefly, glances into the castle courtyard. Her father-in-law is in conversation with Thomas Pierson the rector. The two of them used not to agree, though that is not the case any more. Her father-in-law is laughing. He must be on his way out. His dogs trot back and forth on willow legs, sniff, and make water. She should have asked him to look at the drowning of the orchard meadow.

And while Brilliana waits for news and balances her duties with her devotions and tries not to alarm herself, the carrier who is taking her last letter to London dallies in Gloucester, where there are goods to exchange and collect. He has been given a glass of something warming and he is listening to the woman, whose son has found employment at the new pin factory. Her voice is very grating on the ear.

Outside, the spars of the ships great and small, like a forest of pins themselves, tip and sway in the mouth of the Severn, and one of the horses changes its weight in the shafts. A gull lands on the carrier's basket, where the letters for London, urgent with longing, lie staring through latticework at the sky. To my Lord Sr Robert Harley, Kt of the Bathe give these.

Allas my deare Sr, I knowe you do not to the on halfe of my desires, desire to see me, that loves you more than any earthly thinge. I should be glad if you would but write me word, when I should hope to see you.

And then, how many days later, the carrier finally makes his way into London, along Oxford Street, between low hedges, where women dry linen in the fields either side, and into St Giles, where the wastrels and the drinkers go and the driving becomes dangerous and he must look out, must keep his wits about him.

Over the foul and dwindling Fleet Ditch at Holborn Bridge, into the scurry of streets and buildings beyond, spreading westwards from the city. And now the streets are packed. Through the suburb of Holborn he goes, and on, where butchers are crammed against booksellers and where, among the jumbled press of street-sellers, servants, apprentices, clerics, women, children, hubbub and stray dogs, Puritans of differing degrees worry, under the shadows of Christ Church and old St Paul's, up to their ankles in mire sometimes.

Sir Robert's lodgings are outside the city walls, in Little Britain which, despite rapid development, is still airier than the city the other side. His street, wide and quiet and full of booksellers, runs down to the open space of Smithfield, where the fairs and executions are held, and where the carrier is just now arriving, heading for the Ram inn, on the north side, where he will unload. And at the same time, John Wall, who has been in London several weeks now, sets out to meet him.

He walks briskly up the street, towards the pump, the little distance there is to where a knot of people has already gathered, watching, as the first things are handed down. Baskets, kegs, packets, boxes, so easy for something to be snatched away right under your nose if you aren't careful. But at last, among the jumble, the goods from Brampton are unloaded, safe. Several cheeses, a pudding with currants, a jar of something that looks cosmetic. There is no way of checking what has been sent, whether anything is missing. There is noise and jostling. The carrier is not as vigilant as he might be about thieves. John Wall dare not turn his back nor leave the cart.

Overhead, red kites drift like indigents down the length of the street and away, sliding and tumbling, over Smithfield. Once or twice John Wall glances up in irritation. It sickens him to see them everywhere, tearing at the offal for instance, thrown out by the butchers in the shambles, or picking at the corpses of dead dogs in the city's ditches. Coasting at eye level, on ragged wings, one angles its head as it passes, looks right at him. Its stare is insolent, like an apprentice. He would throw a stone at it if he had one to hand. John Wall thinks little of London. He would like to go home.

And Sir Robert, who is sitting over papers in his lodgings, is ill-humoured and headachy. It is increasingly difficult now, to thread a way between the maze of Court politics, and the demands of his religion. Change is very slow to come; the bishops so unshakeably entrenched, so corrupt. Some of the godly, in despair, are looking away already, to the New World. Still, Sir Robert's hopes are on Westminster. It is not impossible, even by increments, that a better order be established. He is newly made Master of the Mint, and there is much on his mind.

What, for instance, is he thinking, when John Wall returns and the letters from Brampton are at last passed into his hands? Looking for a moment, before he breaks it open, at his wife's seal, her clear and purposeful hand, as if recalling himself with effort, from somewhere else.

I should be very glad to heare the Parlement had concluded on some of their waity biusness: for nwes you care not howe ignorant we country peopell be for you will not spare time to informe us:

but this you are sure of that your letters are wellcome: and I must nowe pay my duty to you in letting you knowe how your cuntry biusness goos.

Mr Smith was with me the laste weeke and he has given directions to bringe the water upon parte of the orchard meadowe which will be doun this weeke. I thanke God your father is well but keeps his chamber. He remembers his love to you. On wensday last was a day in the imber weake on which day we did remember to pray for the good sugses of the parlement, and I did not forget to pray for you.

I have sent you up a pote of the powder for the fase: and the resaite heare in closed.

Sir Robert looks out at the street below. 'We country people'. Is there an edge to the way Brilliana styles herself?

Sitting, heavily pregnant, looking out of her own window at the rain-darkened landscape, so remote from London and its concerns, in country that is still so wild, so rude. A soul cramped into practicalities, at the edge of civilisation. The scale of her concerns is now forcibly reduced to her duty of care at Brampton – palings, irrigation, stock – as though her upbringing on the fringes of Court, among diplomats, had never been.

And when he reads his clever wife's letters, does Sir Robert notice? Does he worry that this is not what she is, or does he trust her sense of duty, her work ethic, her obvious efficiency, with or without her interest? The expression of her face comes sharply to his mind, the quickness of her interest. He thinks of his little boy.

Only it all seems so urgent; the teeming and sometimes ungovernable populace of this bursting city, its religious incoherence, the febrility of the new king and his agitated decisions. The rising stock of Catholicism at home.

There is too much to worry about after all. The Devil is everywhere at his work. Sir Robert looks down into the street outside.

There is no corner of England now that doesn't know him, hanging in clouds of incense in the churches great and small, meddling, or silent, or waiting, crackling with heat, flushed scarlet by firesides in country parlours.

Now is no time to be idle. It would be foolish to rest or repine. The letter from Brilliana is scanned restlessly, pushed to one side among the piles of papers on the desk.

Allas my deare Sr, I knowe you do not to the on halfe of my desires, desire to see me, that loves you more than any earthly thinge.

In Bill's house in Gordon Square the lit sitting room is full. Asking for attention, in their dress, in their gestures, his supper guests circulate noisily. The insistent present tense of social engagements. Look at me, they say, with everything but their voices. I am all there is. I am Now. Standing in the doorway Mia hesitates, as if entering a different element. And that is how it feels, this warmth, this wall of sound, the lights after the soft half-dark of the staircase up which she has come, because this room is on the first storey – upstairs from a hall whose chequered floor is stone, a heavy glass-sided lantern hanging on a chain above it, making a dim pool of light.

The hubbub rises to the ceiling. It is a beautiful room, if fading slightly in its decor, elegant like Bill's wife, whose chilly brilliance has gathered a knot of serious-looking people around her at its far end. Julia, who has manners and who is always alert, raises a hand to Mia in greeting, gives a wave and a smile but doesn't rise. Mia smiles in response, takes off her coat and lays it on a pile of others over a chair. She is looking for someone she knows.

Meanwhile at the other end of the room from his wife, one of Bill's musician friends sits at a piano, picking out little runs of jazz while he talks to the inevitable women draped admiring around. Piano notes and a thread of cigarette smoke rise entwined. And on the far wall, behind it all, long sash windows back the room, three of them, almost to the floor, their curtains undrawn so that they make silent black mouths at the people, who flit before them like a roomful of moths.

Hey Mia, long time no see. A journalist who Mia knows from the paper passes quickly. I'm on my way to the kitchen to advise about beans. I'll catch up with you later, she says. And now, to Mia's relief Bill has seen her, and smiles in welcome and crosses the room. Mia, you are here, he says, as though he hadn't been able to be sure that she would come. He has this way when he greets you, of cupping your head lightly in his hand for which Mia is fleetingly grateful. And suddenly as she relaxes into his embrace, she has a longing to be loved, for someone to be tender to her, for a moment, just not to be alone any more.

Are you alright? Bill asks her quietly. What were you thinking about? You looked lost in thought.

I was thinking about the difference between women and men.

Partially true.

A noisy-looking woman with a wide mouth and frizzled grey hair arrives at Bill's elbow. Well, girl, she says in an American drawl. You've come to the right place. There isn't anything we can't tell you about that. That's our special subject. And she jogs Bill with one elbow. Isn't that right?

It isn't immediately clear whether Bill has heard or not. He takes Mia's hand. You're cold. Let me get you a glass of wine. He looks vaguely at the room full of people. I didn't realise I'd asked so many. And only then does he turn to the woman, as if just registering her presence at his elbow.

Mia, do you remember Andrea, who works for the *New York Times*?

Andrea is hard to forget so Mia does remember. Yes, we met here a couple of years ago, I think.

We did indeed, Andrea says. I was on another publicity tour. No rest for the wicked. Her voice is much too loud. You two are working together, am I right? she asks, while Mia waits for Bill to come back with her drink. She talks to Mia with her mouth only. Her eyes are elsewhere, gobbling other faces, widening and winking in recognition of others, as if there were too little time for focusing only on one. You're so lucky, she says to Mia, waving at someone else. William obviously adores you. Are you two an item?

Mia doesn't know what to say to this. It is so sudden, so intrusive. And apart from anything else, she has never heard Bill called William before – only Andrea doesn't say William, she says Wiyam. Let me tell you, Wiyam is a fabulous lover. I know. I've been all round the houses.

This is worse than anything Mia could have expected. You've got completely the wrong end of the stick, she says and turns away.

*

Mia drifts on through the knots of people. Occasionally she bumps into someone she knows. There is a photographer in a leather waistcoat, who has just returned from a war zone and is talking it down in a loud voice, and there is someone's son, very smart, very earnest and in his first year at university. He wants to work for Reuters. Hair smoothed down, eager eyes. Mia finds her attention wandering. She thinks she will talk to an old colleague of John's whom she has seen among the group at the piano. She extricates herself and makes her way down the room again.

As if in all its forms life must obey the same simple requirement, different particles, always moving, combining and re-combining, so that even the most solid things bafflingly contain constant invisible flow; so the people in the room fizz, connect, disengage, as though part of some huge single entity. A bearish-looking man, whose hair, what is left of it, is tousled and whose eyes are like Bill and Sylvia's, gives Mia the once-over, as she tries to pass. You look as though you have lost someone, he says in a version of Bill's voice.

Mia stops, stares at him surprised. No, she says and then after a moment's thought and with a touch of impatience, or I suppose yes, in a way. I've lost all the people that count, she says drily, so it doesn't matter much who I talk to now. The man doesn't move. I've seen someone I know at the piano, Mia says. If you'd let me pass. The man laughs a good-natured laugh and continues to block her passage.

Well, you English women really know how to make a guy feel wanted, he says with evident enjoyment.

I'm not English. I'm Scottish.

OK, he says. I'm not English either. He is Bill's nephew, so he is family, so she ought to be more friendly. Who are you then, Scottish lady? he asks.

I'm Mia Morgan. I'm a friend of Bill's daughter, Mia says.

The man opens his arms. Hey! he says. I knew you were someone. I imagined you different though.

Mia is taken by surprise. What does he mean 'someone'? How different?

Not so tricky. What's the problem? Relax. Spread it around a bit.

This is a pretty strange conversation, Mia says. Do you think we might speak in English? You know – what do you do? Have you come far? – that sort of thing. In England it's customary to wait a year or two before you make intrusive personal remarks. Or do you always talk to strangers like this?

I don't mean to offend you. I wasn't thinking of you as a stranger. He stands directly in front of her. You're Syl's friend and Syl was always my favourite cousin. Come on, he says, she might as well talk to him as anyone else, if she really doesn't care who she talks to. He holds out a hand, which Mia takes briefly. Felipe Radic, he says with a half-bow. He is half-Spanish, half-Croatian, which he tells her with undisguised satisfaction and an air of expectancy. Mia looks at him but says nothing. He lives in New York, so he won't be able to bug her. Although, he adds, he is here to sign a contract with the BBC. So maybe, he shrugs, who knows?

Mia's attention has wandered again. She isn't really listening and besides there is a girl hovering just behind Felipe, who looks as though she has a vested interest and it seems rude to Mia not to acknowledge this. She introduces herself. Hi, the girl says almost too gratefully, I'm a dancer, as if to assert that she is something more than just an appendage. There is a momentary pause. I'm with Felipe, she says next, in a rush, taking it all away again.

We are just back from Papua New Guinea, Felipe tells Mia with nonchalance. I've been making a wildlife film.

Oh, Mia would like to say, suddenly exasperated by his self-assurance. Is that why you wear your shirt buttons open to the navel? Or are you short of opposable thumbs?

Right, she says instead, vaguely.

Andrea, whom Mia thought she had escaped, appears and puts an arm around Felipe's waist.

Wiyam, Andrea shouts, as Bill comes back at last with Mia's drink. You are so remiss. You haven't introduced me to the most attractive man in the room. Are you afraid of the competition?

This is Felipe, Bill says, my nephew. Felipe, this is my old friend Andrea, and have you met Mia?

Mmm. Delicious, Andrea says.

Felipe raises his eyebrows at Mia who feels suddenly sorry for the dancer, striking an agonised pose on the edge of the circle, her eyes round with anxiety.

On balance, Mia thinks, Andrea is the worst person in the room.

Come Mia, Bill says, sensing that she needs to be rescued. I want you to meet someone sensible.

Brilliana Harley in a darkened chamber, the great trial over, resting on pillows. Her women move softly around her and a new baby creases a livid face with crying. The room smells close and the sweat still stands on Brilliana's face. It is important, at this stage, that she does not catch cold.

Paper and ink are brought to her bed so that she can write the news to her husband, still absent. The Parliament is sitting so long.

The writing is spiky and traumatised, chaotic, blotted with Brilliana's fingerprint almost whole on the paper, her hands are shaking so. The map of her own identity, with its little whorls and contours, so distinct, yet left so casually, in haste and inattention, on the paper.

15 April, 1626.

Dr Sr, I make hast to tell you under my owne hand that it has pleased the Lord to blls us with another soon and to morrow being sabath he shall be given to Lord in his ordnance. I pray God make us bothe thankful for all the bllsings and doo you love and long to be with me as I doo you and doo you pray for me.

Let me heare from you.

And scrawled on the back, an afterthought, Ned is well.

The effort of writing is exhausting. She sinks back on her pillows. God be thanked. One of her women reads quietly, a Calvinist text of her own choosing.

The new baby is strong and quiet. Brilliana begins to recover. The women come and go and reports are brought up of the goings-on outside. The vigour of spring. The mares are put to stallions. Stock is bought. All these, in Sir Robert's continued absence, are Brilliana's concern. She has to hold herself to attention in these matters. It is as though she were listening through a long tunnel of remove, so immersed is she in the different state of birth and motherhood.

The new baby is christened.

Dear Sir, – yesterday I received your letter by Smallman and I do wish you give our good God thanks for this great blessing which he has given us of another son and all our care must be not only to speak thanks but to show it in our lives. As you rwit to me, so the child was crisned the last Sabath, and my father stood for my Lord Vere and Sr Andrew Corbet with a great deal of gladnes stood for himself, and Mrs Harbet for my Ante Corbet and because you said nothing of the name I choos that name I love best: it being yours.

I thank God the child is well, and they all say he is as like his father as can be and I pray God make him like his heavenly father:

I thank God Ned has taken his weaining well; but is not admited to see his nurs: Mary Wood has the charge of him and it is all I reqiere of her that she doe that well, he lys in the nursery: he can goo a littel, which I am not a littel glad of, his grandfather will not yeald that any should be loved like him, he must be the finest boy in his eyes.

I thank God I am resnabell well, and this is the first day I have sate up the whoole day;

I thank you for the night gowne and for sending downe the glases but I have not seene them yet. I sent for Witells the last week and I pray you send downe another cradell ruge; it must be reed.

I pray you present my humbell servis to my La: Conway and excuse me to my sisters that I do not rwit to them, for if this letter had not bine to you I should have bine weary before the end of it.

I pray you rwit to me as often as you can.

May comes. Brilliana is still not yet strong enough to leave her room.

This day I have bine so far as the parler to give God thanks with my family. Ned and Robin are well and I will not tell you they are pretty. Ned grows like my father or ells evry on is much mistaken and Robin like you or ells I am. Ned is grown a very very good companion.

The little boy, stolid and burbling, stands holding the leg of a chair, proud of himself but cautious, rocking in his indecision, not daring to strike off alone. Brilliana soothes her loneliness with his company. It is impossible not to dote. Slow transfer of affection and dependence from the husband to the son.

The year unfolds. Ned learns to totter. And in the world of the animals too, children are planned for, conceived and born.

Your mare did foold that night she came to Lemster. The pide mare is taken up and is fatte and the littlel pide nage which you sent for is now fatte. Your father has lent you s20 to bye bease for which I praye you thanke him. He is very kinde to me and I thinke he is the best father in lawe in the world.

I thanke God I am reasnabell well but not abell to goo abrode. And now in your absence, which I think a long time, your fathers kindeness and Gods great bllsing in Ned and Robin is the greatest comfort I have heare.

It does not seme too often to me to rwit to you twis in a day that longes so much to have you with me. I need not say I thinke the time longe that you have binn awaye but it is so in deede. I thinke the time longe betwne Thursday and Thursday thearfore let me intreet you to rwit often.

But this is the last letter that she writes to Sir Robert because in mid-July, after six long months, Brilliana's vigil is ended. The Parliament is dissolved with nothing settled. Sir Robert returns, anxious and exhausted, to his castle and his growing family.

Another room, leading out from the first. Another set of dark windows that line the far wall and open long mouths, as if waiting to swallow, and Bill's guests who are gathering at a table now, dustily displaying their attractions, continue to flutter and settle, and rise again.

Sorry, have I taken your seat? Move up. Tell Margaret to move up one, then we can all sit together.

Soft voices so you would have to lean in to listen, when others here are making so much noise. Two women talking intently.

So, I gather you are working on John Curtesy's book, is that right?

The upward glance that Mia can't help giving. Yes, I am. She is slightly breathless. I am, or rather Bill and I are. Her voice lowered. Strange to hear John spoken of as though he wasn't dead, as though he was still engaged in his writing. On the other side of the table a man watches surreptitiously, craning forward a little to hear Mia's answer, although he is outside the conversation.

Did you know John? Mia can't help asking.

I wouldn't say that I knew him, the other woman answers, but I met him a couple of times. And of course he consulted me about the book. She pauses. She is an academic. She has an attractively cautious way of speaking, as though it was important to say only what was considered, what was provably the case in each instance. I had enormous respect for John, she says. Bill mentioned to me that he was your partner. That must be a very tragic loss.

Hard to hear what is passing between them, these women with

bent heads, Mia and Jackie Eales, the author of the blue book that has Brilliana on its cover. The man trying to listen misses much of what is said. His neighbour is talking to him. There is too much general noise. Fragments of conversation lift occasionally above the general burr. Mia's voice drops below the man's register again. He misses her answer.

And Mia, head bent in concentration, listening to the woman beside her. How are you finding the Harleys? Jackie Eales is asking.

Impenetrable, Mia says. Much deader than John.

They both laugh. And the man watching smiles. And Bill's friends, who missed the whole exchange because they are deep in their own conversations, continue, and the man, who is Felipe, has to turn and acknowledge his neighbour, resigning himself to her company at last.

Are you the wildlife man?

What is it, Jackie asks Mia, that you find most difficult, do you think?

I'm trying, I suppose, Mia says, to get my head around Puritans and what they are, because Puritanism is alien to me – off-putting. I'm trying to see the human bits of Brilliana – I mean the bits that don't change about people over time, so the bits that you can understand or respond to. Across the table Felipe eats with his eyes as well as his mouth. He isn't really interested in the women's conversation. He just wants Mia's attention.

I'm not being honest when I say I find her impenetrable, Mia is saying, unaware of him. I've been looking at her life with some admiration really, some jealousy. She seems so certain. Was she like that already, or did she catch it from her marriage?

My goodness, Jackie says, you make it sound like a disease.

Well it's like that, isn't it? You can live someone else's certainty – I felt like that when I was with John – and then you can wake up one morning maybe and find it's become your own. Mia picks up the spoon from among the cutlery in front of her, turns it over, meditating. I imagine that's how it would have been if John had lived. I mean, she says, looking at herself upside down in the spoon, who are we – the person we are at the beginning, or the one we are at the end? I suppose, in Brilliana's case, I'm looking for how she made herself strong enough to run a siege, to die for what she believed in, how she changed from those longing, dependent letters to someone men took orders from. Is that marriage, or upbringing, or conviction, or what? She looks up at Jackie.

They talk about Brilliana's wedding.

They are considering whether or not it was happy, so they don't necessarily see how she stood, in Greenwich, in her stiff handmade clothes with her new husband's hand in her own. Her pursed mouth, her outward composure and the little pulse ticking in her neck. The great, new weight of purpose. Now my life is starting. They don't feel the cold of the church, the low light of a dim London day filtered through high windows. The steady dry voice intoning the service. Sitting upright through the long sermon. Thomas Gatacker preaching, white face under his cap, against the dark of his vestments.

Yes I remember that, Mia is saying. I remember the wedding sermon – A Wife in Deed – because I always thought it was a bit offensive, having to have a lecture on your wedding day about how to be a good wife. What about a husband in deed – what happened to him?

Well quite, Jackie laughs back, you wouldn't get away with that now of course. But we have to look at these people in the time that they were living in. She says this with absolute certainty. As far as marriage is concerned, for instance, you have to think that in the seventeenth century, a woman who murdered her husband would be tried for petty treason. That's how fixed the hierarchy was. Now that's quite something.

Mia nods. It is quite something. Not that Brilliana would have wanted to murder Sir Robert, Jackie says. Actually, to come back to your point about the sermon, I think Sir Robert was a very good, certainly a very fond, husband.

Do you? Mia is incredulous.

Yes, don't you?

No, I don't. She hesitates and then adds, I think he was a bit of a monster really. I mean, do you like him?

I don't dislike him, she says, and I know one has to maintain a certain amount of distance in order to write about people in the past.

I see, Mia says. I hadn't thought of distance as a good thing. I keep trying to bridge it. She doesn't own up to subjecting Brilliana to London transport. A silence falls between them, as each separately considers the past, its intractable difference from the present, its tiny moments of illumination and its long, dark distances.

Outside and as if to illustrate the point, the stars above the banks of clouds stare with the memory of their single pinpoint eyes across the emptiness between, which is the same thing as time in the end. And a pigeon that has been sitting in the cold branches of a~ tree in the square gardens is startled suddenly from its roost and in panicky confusion between street lamps and the light from the uncurtained windows flies bang into the glass, wings spread.

A woman with her back to the window, inside, jumps in surprise and spills her wine. What on earth was that? Unseen, the pigeon drops away, stunned, before righting itself to swoop upwards at the last minute. A few strong wingbeats, as if to pull itself together and it settles on a branch again, quiet, its miniature heart pulsing.

Oh my goodness, the woman says, mopping at her dress. That gave me a shock. I thought it was someone knocking to get in.

On the first floor? In Bloomsbury? her neighbour laughs.

Then Andrea says in her loud voice, So in London, the giants aren't dead. She makes a theatrical gesture. They're coming to dinner. Many people laugh and join in with the game. Andrea is seen as quite a personality. And someone gets up and goes over to the window and says, Come in, giant. We've started without you but you're welcome.

The table settles again, fragmenting into conversation. Mia and Jackie go back to the Harleys.

So, Jackie says, you think Sir Robert is a monster. Why is that?

I suppose, Mia pauses, gathers her thoughts, I suppose I don't like his push for social advancement – although that's superficial. More really I suppose I'm bothered by the fact that he effectively abandoned Brilliana. I feel those early letters to him are pretty poignant. She's lonely. I see her as a woman under siege – long before she was really under siege – in terms of her literal placing in that castle, you know, in a strange county, with no one, or no one identifiable, to help or confide in, unable to leave. And she's been adored by her father, so she's used to being loved.

I find the letters so fragile, Mia says, so needy, although she doesn't want to be needy – I know you don't have time to write, but if you could just spare a letter here and there – that kind of thing, and she's anxious about running the estate and getting it wrong. And he only writes short letters. And he doesn't come and he doesn't come. Mia breaks off, aware that she has forgotten herself for a moment, spoken with sudden fervour. On the other side of the table Felipe says nothing, but he watches.

And at the same time, while Mia talks, Jackie Eales listens, with her head on one side like a bird and with a bird's focus and alertness, as though listening were vital, in every sense. You have to remember, she says when Mia is done, that what you are looking at is the letters Brilliana wrote when Sir Robert was away. You're hearing only her periodic unhappiness at his absence. We have nothing to set against that, to balance it. He was away very little in fact.

Mia nods. I talk to her all the time in my head.

Oh, that's quite normal, Jackie says.

Is it? That's a relief.

Yes. But in fact, just to go back to their marriage, Robert and Brilliana were not apart very much for the seventeen years of their marriage until 1640 when the Long Parliament met – and the Long

Parliament is unprecedented. She pauses and looks at Mia. No parliament has ever sat that long.

Now Sir Robert didn't know that was going to happen. Brilliana didn't know that was going to happen. And he just had to stay there because he recognised that he'd become a spokesman for the Puritan cause, for the people in the Welsh Marches and in the Midlands. So Puritans there are looking to him to lead them and he couldn't possibly abandon that part that he's suddenly been given, after what must have been a lifetime of hoping for religious reform.

I see, Mia says thoughtfully. You make it so clear. But it doesn't change Brilliana's loneliness.

No it doesn't change that, Jackie says, but it puts it into context and to go back to your initial point, it shows what a close marriage they did have, how fond she and Sir Robert were of each other, doesn't it?

Round the table people are getting up to change places. My turn, Mia hears someone say further down. Go and talk to someone else. Bill arrives, puts a hand on Mia's shoulder, shuffles himself into a space between her and the person on her other side. So, are you succeeding where I failed, he asks Jackie with a smile. Did I hear Mia say everything was clear?

Oh I doubt that, she answers, but we've had a very interesting conversation.

Bill smiles, So have you persuaded her to like Puritanism?

We haven't really got to grips with Puritanism as such, have we? She looks at Mia.

Well, we haven't been slacking, Mia says. We just haven't got round to it.

So you haven't bumped into her prejudices? Bill asks slowly, with his hand still on Mia's shoulder.

Jackie laughs, Well, prejudice is quite a word to choose. Are you prejudiced against the Puritans? she asks Mia.

Bill's had a bad experience, Mia says. He caught me on an off day, didn't you Bill? I'm not really prejudiced. I just don't identify with them, with the introspection, or with what I see as their sort of fundamentalism. It seems a bit extreme, a bit neurotic. She pauses a moment. Do they seem extreme to you? I mean the iconoclasm, the smashing up of pictures and things, and the constant spiritual hypochondria – was that just routine, or were they particularly zealous? I don't know how radical the Harleys really were – what religious reform meant for them.

Jackie nods. The Harleys, I think, were very practical, very cautious. They were responding to the political events around them. Bill has dropped his head to listen. He murmurs in assent.

They weren't radical Puritans, Jackie says. They were Presbyterians. They would have liked to see the restraint of bishops, or even the abolition of bishops, but they weren't a part of a Presbyterian movement before the Civil War because it didn't look an achievable aim. When the Civil War starts, their Presbyterian colours come out because suddenly it looks achievable.

So it was normal, was it, Mia asks, for so much of the day to be taken up with spiritual introspection? It seems odd for someone so evidently practical and political, so outward-looking, to spend so much time navel-gazing.

Well this is very much a Puritan activity, isn't it? Jackie says. Predestination is very much a part of the Christian religion. The Catholics and Protestants both have it but the difference is that it is only the Puritans who elevate it to become the central organising principle of their religion. They must keep checking, writing, monitoring, praying. It is introspection but it is introspection aimed at trying to get a sense of assurance, but also knowing that being too assured would be sinful, because nobody could know the mind of God. So there's this huge and constant tension in what they are trying to do.

It is the tension that makes it sympathetic, Bill says, that makes it dramatic. I think.

Jackie agrees. Have you looked at the diary of Lady Margaret Hoby? she asks Mia suddenly.

No, I don't think I have.

Well, if you are wanting to get a feel for what Brilliana's day-to-day life must have been like, you could do worse than look at that. It's a bit earlier in time but she is a Puritan, so it gives you an idea of how the religious element fitted with the practical.

Lady Margaret Hoby, Mia repeats, thank you, I'll definitely look at that.

And while they talk, listening to one another, considerate, their bodies held upright, their chairs at a decorous distance, Mia and Bill, at least, are part of another altogether darker conversation.

Bill's hand on Mia's shoulder. Felipe watching.

And Felipe's neighbour, who realises that she is failing to engage, makes vivacious conversation and Felipe nods and glances at her occasionally, sometimes with impatience. But all the time, he is alert to Bill, to Bill's hand to be precise, which he doesn't like, generous and pale-skinned on Mia's shoulder. Why doesn't she shrug it off?

You must find that, when you're making your documentaries, Felipe's neighbour is saying, he has no idea what about.

So now behind the dinner-party politeness, along with everything else, there is a hunger in the room, as if between all of them something is lying in wait. Eyes in the grass. Although it is convention, at least with the conscious mind, not to notice. So Mia and Bill go on, listening to Jackie's fluent sentences, holding their speaking bodies dumb and upright, discussing Puritanism. And Felipe goes on watching Mia with animal attention, and his neighbour, with increasing urgency, continues to prattle.

Well, it's getting late, Jackie says after a while. It's been a lovely evening, Bill. Thank you very much.

And Bill, with his old-fashioned manners, rises and takes her hand and thanks her for coming. Thank you also, he says smiling, for helping me with the problem of Mia's prejudice.

Really, Jackie laughs, looking at Mia. How are you going to be able to work with him?

I don't listen, Mia says.

Many people are going home now and the guests who are left, one of whom is Mia, move back into the first room, where the piano is, and regroup themselves and start new conversations, staring into little cups of coffee, or sealing themselves off in the blur of Bill's drink. Bill is occupied saying goodbye so Mia wanders about talking to this or that person, glancing occasionally at the tall windows and the dark pressing to get in, and thinks, I'll just stay a few more minutes. It'll be a cold ride home.

And now the pianist starts up again, louder this time and more continuous. Bill is still saying goodbye but he holds his trumpet loosely in his left hand, so he is obviously going to play. That's worth staying for, Mia thinks, moving past a small group arguing about fiscal stimulus, towards the piano.

You people just don't understand the market, a man is saying angrily as she passes. You're going to screw everything up.

Bill lifts his trumpet and makes one or two little sallies. There is a brief consultation with the pianist, a few false starts. A one, a two. A one two three four, and they reel off together, as if the music were something that already existed somewhere, intact and in full motion, like jumping aboard as a carousel swings past. Django Reinhardt's 'I'se a Muggin''.

Boom, Andrea says, at the appropriate moments. I'se a muggin', Bam. She must have drunk more than she meant. She is shimmying, hands flapping, now that Bill has started up in earnest. Play that horn, Wiyam, she says too loudly with her head thrown back and her grey hair flying, while her partner circles something on the floor that is visible only to him, his arms in chicken wings.

And the trumpet notes rise, clear and light-filled, and float, extending over the room with the same effect as the sun when it breaks from behind a cloud, so people lift their heads and half-slit their eyes and murmur, Mmm, how lovely, as they stop and bask. Only the fiscal stimulus group remains angry and unmoved on its little knot of chairs.

Felipe's dancer is doing her stuff with a thin man whom Mia doesn't know. She is bending herself backwards, her ribs and her child's chest hooped and her short hair almost grazing the floor, and then flipping up again and kicking out and turning, but there is something mechanical and despairing about her dance. Felipe is not watching.

He is with another older woman, who grips him like the Ancient Mariner, her hand clawed round his arm while she talks earnestly and at him about something important. His head is bent to listen although his attention is evidently elsewhere. Mia can't help glancing as she passes and he puts out an arm for her unexpectedly. Come and dance, beautiful, he says looking up at her, his hand at her waist. Will you excuse me? he asks the Mariner as he gets to his feet.

Wasn't that rude? Mia asks, looking back at the woman left sitting on her own. Felipe's arm is tight round her waist. What do you care, he says still looking at her.

I feel sorry for her.

I've been watching you.

I know, Mia says in her driest Scottish tone, it's been very distracting.

*

In the cleared space at the piano end of the room, Mia stands, holding Felipe's hand, almost surprised. And letting herself go, into the stream of the music, she thinks how long it is, how very long that she has been crouched inside herself, holding herself closed like the stone that she sat on earlier outside the library, emanating cold.

Bill plays 'Tiger Rag'. Several people are dancing now, some of them uninhibitedly by themselves. He plays loosely, keeping time with his squashed shoe, shaping even the upbeat tunes so that the music unwinds out of his trumpet's mouth like smoke, so that even while it shakes you, like it is shaking Mia now, while it makes your feet beat and your body whirl, while it spins you, still it fills you up, with all the restlessness of Bill's adolescence by the Adriatic Sea, pulls you inside out, with something that might be an ache or might be an itch, or might just be the weight of the sea itself. Drowns you before you know where you are.

So while Mia dances, Bill's trumpet unfurls for her the small tourist town where Bill and his brother were born, the painted houses and the weary fishing boats and the dusty main drag, and the equally dusty mountains that shut the town in, and all the onus of the pointlessly picturesque, and the desperate girls in cheap make-up and the ache in Bill that nothing could salve, to lose himself, to be out of it all.

He plays the sea rolling in. Day after day, the sea rolling in, with its salt and its pale cold, shifting under different skies, never still. And the jazz that came from elsewhere, that didn't come out of the little nightclubs by the beach, but that spun out of the black vinyl singles played in private, in his room, fusing with the sea, until the two were indistinguishable in Bill's mind; that cool changeability, that pull to elsewhere; the need to be bigger, looser, free, that never stopped until it had dragged him and his brother out of the painted house in the tourist town and halfway across the world, to New York where his brother stayed. And that was where Felipe was born.

And now Bill's trumpet plays England where Bill, who couldn't rest even in all the space of America, got married by mistake and has lived ever since. It plays small fields and slant rain and fog and phlegm spat to the ground by generations of men, who open gates slowly and clear their throats and add their nature to the soil, and it plays things knotted and compromised and subtle and half-understood and quick fish in cold rivers and watchful hawks and the stubborn muck of domestic animals. And Mia just goes on dancing.

She loves to dance, Bill can see that, even while he is playing. She looks easier, freer, dancing.

So now it is Bill's turn to watch. He plays slower smokier songs, without thinking what he is doing. Andrea, who has stopped dancing, leans over the piano and puts her loud voice to use. You're Nobody, she sings, with surprising power. Uh uh, You're Nobody. Great God Almighty, you're No-body until Some-body loves you. And Felipe, who knows how to dance, lets Mia out on the line of his arm, flicks her unthinking, back in again, time and again, holds the flow of her against his moving body, but loosely, as if he could catch not just a fish but a whole river in his close embrace.

And all the while that he is playing, Bill can't take his eyes off them dancing, younger, warmer than he is, unmarried.

God, I feel so sad, Andrea says. Come on, Wiyam, play us Django again. You're killing me.

Bill puts down his trumpet. He shakes his head, while the pianist still plays. No, not now. It's too fast. I'm not in the mood. I'm not playing any more.

So although the pianist keeps going, many people stop dancing, and Mia looking at Bill, still holding his trumpet, with his body sunk into a chair and his tummy slack and his great eyes full of things that are unspoken, leaves Felipe and goes and sits with him for a moment before she leaves.

You play so beautifully, Bill, she says to him, meaning something else, she doesn't quite know what. Meaning perhaps, Don't be sad for me. I'm not worth it. Meaning, Nothing is quite what you think it will be. Or just meaning, Sorry. I'm here. I'm your friend, which is something, if not enough. Nothing is ever enough.

Felipe drinks beer out of a bottle and feels confident, and the door opens and Syl blows in, eyes glittering, with her husband looking exhausted behind.

What on earth time is this? Mia asks her as Syl bends to kiss her father. I'm about to go.

No you're not, Syl says. You're staying for one more drink at least. So Felipe goes to the kitchen and comes back with drinks for everyone and Syl throws herself at him and calls him Phil. How many ages have you been away? And you gave me so little notice you were going to be in town. And Julia greets her son-in-law and goes quietly to bed. Sorry, she says, putting her hand on Robert's arm, I'm exhausted. You look tired yourself. Don't let Sylvia keep you up. And Sylvia says nothing but looks from one to the other in brief irritation, because they are both so grown up. And Mia stays.

And later on, Andrea has to be handed into her coat and found a cab, her hair falling forward over her face and her face flushed. I'm good for two more drinks at least, she keeps saying, even as Felipe pushes her gently into the taxi and closes the door.

Afterwards, Mia can hear him coming back up the stairs two at a time, and the evening wears itself on into the small hours of the next day and the people stand up and sit down and drift and talk, increasingly confusedly, and the windows continue to stare. And outside, in the night air, the real moths bump themselves repeatedly against the divide that they are unable to see, between darkness and light.

Winter morning. Crows and jackdaws in the trees behind the castle at Brampton. Uproar. There is a wind, the birds spouting up every now and then, whirling down towards the park before gathering themselves to turn back. The long lines of the buzzard managing his wingspan among the roost.

People crossing to and fro, but quickly, glance up at the commotion, hurry on. 1629. Lights in the castle because the winter light is thick and sullen. Inside, the rooms almost dark. Damp. Four small children now, five-year-old Ned, then Robert, Thomas and a baby, called after her mother, all swathed against cold, hands and cheeks pink, even inside. Chilblains itching. Brilliana in the trance of motherhood.

In London, Parliament is sitting again. Buckingham, the favourite, is dead, murdered at the docks in August of the year before. The country is strangled for tax. The anti-Calvinist doctrine of Arminianism is taking hold. Everywhere Arminians are preaching the possibility of individually determined salvation. There is ceremony and incense in church services. The King does nothing to curb the slide towards Popery.

Sir Robert is away again, furthering the Puritan cause. He is preparing a speech to Parliament in favour of a declaration of established religion, along the lines laid out by Queen Elizabeth. London seems jumpy and discontented. At the quaysides Puritans stop suddenly, look at the queasy waters of the Thames and wonder about passage abroad. Perhaps Holland. Perhaps the newly granted colony at Massachussetts.

The King is petulant like a child.

A Thursday, say, so the gunners are practising in the yard at Spittle Field. The constant thump of artillery carries west as far as Smithfield. Sir Robert, at his desk as ever, wonders irritably whether to take something for the headache he always seems to have. Letters from home again interrupt him. Little Ned is ill and Brilliana is anxious to have his father's opinion.

Need has bine ever sence Sunday trubled with the rume in his fase very much. I finde that his watter for the most part has a creme upon it. Mr Birde would have me anoint his backe with the same ointment your father uses to his backe, but I will not tell I heare from you, I pray you Sr aske doctor Diodod what is good for him.

And if you remember you did marke some hinderens in his making of water, for befor his water comes from him if you remember the passage of the water does swell bigg.

The swelling of his face made him very dull; but nowe, I thanke God, he is better, and begins to be merry. He inquires for Jhon Walls comeing down for he thinkes he will bringhe him a letter. I must desire you to send me downe a littell Bibell for him. He would not let me be in peace, tell I promised him to send for on. He begings nowe to delight in reading and that is the booke I would have him place his delight in.

Tom has still a greate coold; but he is not, I thanke God, sike with it. Brill and Robin, I thanke God are well and Brill has two teethe. Ned presents his humbell duty to you, and I beeg your bllsing for them all: and I beceach the Allmighty to prosper you in all you doo, and to give you a happy meeting with

Your most faithfull affectinat wife.

At Brampton, Brilliana has been up since five. She rubs cold hands. She will go down to the granary, see how the stores hold up.

*

And in her own morning, Mia wakes to the grainy winter light of slightly later than she would like. Sky made of pigeon feathers again. Her mother's voice is filling the room.

. . . like I said. Anyway, just keeping in touch lovey. You'll have heard the latest from your da but I thought I might catch you before you went off to your day's work.

Mia struggles up to consciousness through layers of time and sleep. Mam, she thinks briefly and some distance below the surface, although it is not her mother. It is her aunt Ines who, despite being such a very different person from Mia's mother, has exactly the same voice. Mia lies on her back while the message finishes and the machine clicks off, her arms still loose at her sides, her mouth still half-open, in that attitude of abandon that is indicative of deep sleep. She must have been dead to the world not to have heard the phone ring.

She is a good sleeper, always has been. Dozy bones, her mother used to call her when she woke her for school, flinging the curtains back so that it was amazing they stayed on the rings. And then later, John, insomniac because he was too conscientious to absent himself even temporarily from his life and who spent much of the night padding round the flat in socks, stoically drinking cup after cup of tea, found her long unconscious hours something to marvel at and would often be sitting on the side of the bed, tea in hand, watching her as she woke. You know, he said to her once, you have an actual talent for sleeping. You do it so well.

How many cups last night, she would ask, putting out her hand to him where he sat, so frayed, on the edge of the bed. Seven was the record. Does it never occur to you that tea is a stimulant? And John would put the cup down and lay his head on her chest so that the sleep that was soaking out of her would sometimes soak into him, for maybe an hour or two, and let him rest.

But now, hearing Ines and remembering her bustling, northern, morning family, Mia can't help a pang of shame at her own luxuriousness.

The farm kitchen with the curtains flapping, as though the window were taking itself literally, as though its name implied a duty, to suck whatever wind there is into its square and to funnel it inside. Her mother banging around, talking to the dogs as if they were human, and the din of the radio, and her father, in his boot socks, blown sideways and in from hours on the hill waiting for breakfast. And now Mia is here, at what time? – five to nine for heaven's sake, wallowing and unwashed. Get up out of that pit, girl, and get some work done.

Oh my goodness. Dancing. What happened to me last night?

*

And at the same time, and in the same city, Bill sits at the kitchen table in his socks, a little haggard after his party, a little sunken, while Julia moves briskly in a blue shirt and a suit, sipping coffee and talking with the telephone wedged between ear and sharp shoulder, putting papers into a leather case. She disregards Bill, like you might disregard the morning slowness of a teenage son, catering for his needs without thinking. A cup of coffee, two Sweetex added, pushed across the table to him.

Bill watches her smooth movements sadly. He would like her full attention, which is unfair because he only erratically gives her his.

I'm feeling lonely, he says to her when she puts down the telephone.

You'll survive, Julia says, smiling at him. She puts his collar down not un-tenderly, as she passes. She is late for work.

And Bill, like Mia, is left alone with the morning. The small square of the kitchen window, which faces in, towards the backs of houses, over yards, roofs, chimney pots, fails to comfort him. It is too full of grey. This cold and watery light of winter that reminds him of his mother, sitting on, in her front room by the Adriatic, watching telly, among small lace mats of her own making, and filtered photographs of her sons. Like Mia now, he sits and remembers. How the grey light came in off the sea and filled up his mother's little room, closed round her heart, congealed it with its damp, and overspread her face. Her patient clammy looks, her wheezing and her heart disease and her silence, until the cold and winter waters won. They took her over altogether and she died, staring at the ceiling, mouth open, among the lace mats and the photographs, with the telly still on.

Ridiculous to blame the sea for her death. His mother never went out. Just he felt the sea wore her away with its inhumanity.

Then Bill and his brother in baggy suits at the funeral, in the cemetery, with the hole in the ground. Felipe's father, her darling, such a man, with his New York life and his New York wife, sobbing uncontrollably as the body was lowered. And the sister, who had stayed at home, with a face as grey as her mother's and a husband to match, furious, jabbing him in the ribs and passing a handkerchief. Making all that noise. You left her. You were the one who went.

Rain rattling on the coffin. A rain made of stiff flowers, forced blooms in strident colours. Even in his grief, Bill thinking, Why do they throw in those ugly things? Is it because they look dead even when they are alive?

And his brother sobbing, though he'd seldom been back to visit. Neither of them had been back much to visit. How to keep going? Bill drinks his coffee. If it could just be sunny.

*

I'd better wash and get going, Mia thinks. But she doesn't. She looks at Cuthbert who is curled on the end of her bed, watching her with one eye but without bothering to move his head. You're lazier than me, she says to him. OK, you lie there. I'm going to make tea. Cuthbert gets up and trots after her into the kitchen. He does a series of stretches, levering himself to his full extent, over back and then front legs, and goes out onto the balcony. Dirty buildings turning their backs. Birds passing like blown grit, too high to differentiate. Mia makes tea for herself and switches on the radio. This too tells her how late it is. The men on the *Today* programme have stopped barking and gone inside, to do whatever it is they do with their days, and Melvyn Bragg is taking over with no time to waste. He is gabbling through the basics of quantum theory before introducing his panel. Lord, Mia thinks, you need to have had a cup or two of coffee before you're ready for that. He's a man that must eat books for breakfast.

She isn't man enough for the library, not today at any rate. Her mobile rings.

Mia, sorry, you sound like I've woken you up. Did I wake you?

No, no. I'm drinking tea. I just haven't used my voice yet. Does it sound bad? I was thinking of ringing my aunt.

It sounds like you've just woken up. Or you're hungover. I'm fucking hungover.

You can't be hungover, Syl. You're just imagining it. You weren't even drunk. Come on. We're too old to be hungover. Stop fantasising.

Syl is mildly put out. Well, it's really bad if my fantasy is just an imaginary hangover. I must be really middle-aged.

You are – we both are.

Well I feel terrible. Maybe it's the cigarettes.

Bound to be. They're much worse than drink. How many did you have?

I don't know. Three packets of twenty? A brick? What are you doing? Don't tell me you're going to the library – I was thinking of inviting myself for breakfast now I've done the school run.

Come. I can't face the library yet. You can meet Cuthbert.

I'll be twenty minutes. Have you got any breakfast? I bet you haven't got anything. I'll bring it. I can go to the muffin shop on the way.

St Martin's Lane, behind the royal mews, in the City of Whitehall. The MPs continue locked out of Westminster. There are chains and bars on the doors, since the King dissolved Parliament in a rage in March. Robert Harley is at home with his wife, in Herefordshire.

Old Lord Conway, in his mid-sixties and broken in health, hauls himself round in the young King's retinue. His legs are by his own account but weake and his feete are lame. Still he writes fondly and regularly to his daughter and son-in-law.

My Deare Children – I can't let this opportunity by of sending a letter with the bearer though I am sorry I have no acceptable news to send you from abroad because I know that you my sonne Harley and you my daughter, borne in a strange land, the daughter of an ambassador and a councillor, will be out of countenance if you be not able to know what the neighbouring princes do and what we think to do.

What to tell them though, when all is uncertain. The war over the Palatinate continues. They speake of a treaty with Spaine but like a thing farr off, not yet declared, nor thoroughly believed.

He takes refuge in domestic matters. He has been to Essex to visit Brilliana's sister, Hellweigh, married to Sir Edward Smith. I was this last week with my daughter Smith where I had cheerful entertainment onely I got a quarrell there against you my sonne Harley that you did not kill all the ratts, for you left one that bitt little Bridget by the nose and the mark remains.

He would like to see Brilliana and Robert, and his grandchildren at Brampton. Tomorrow I look for my wife here. Tonight, His Majesty comes, who I left on Sunday at Theobalds. Tomorrow His Majesty partes hence upon his progression which lasts till the end of August and then he comes to Windsor. When I have spoken to my wife (as all good husbands do) I shall resolve where and how I shall dispose of my family till that tyme. In the meantime I will find every day a tyme to pray for you both, for our Ned, Robin, Tom and sweet Brill and for the babies, Dorothy and Margaret.

He doesn't have many more years to live and the world that he belongs to is also passing. His face wears a look of puzzlement most of the time. At Court the young men pass him over, in unconcern. It isn't rudeness. He just doesn't count any more. It is as if he were slowly being rubbed out, a querulous little man, thinning to nothing.

Also, he doesn't hear. He is often ill and often anxious about the health of his extended family. Long hours of solitude and indisposition give him time that he fills with worry. Sometimes he writes to Brampton twice in a month. Do his letters reach them? There is no way of knowing. Shifting on his bed in discomfort, nothing is certain any more.

I wrote to you lately by a poore neighbour of yours whom my daughter Mary threatens me will never deliver it. This bearer I know well that I need not wryte by him but least you may be continued in your sloth in not writing and for feare of giving ill example I wryte.

Syl arrives at Mia's flat, in a bomber jacket with a fake fur collar and with a quantity of muffins. We need coffee, she says, almost before she is in the door. I hope you've got some. I didn't bring any.

Coffee is about the only thing I have.

Good, and milk?

And milk.

They go down the passage to the kitchen and Cuthbert appears briefly before turning tail at the sight of a stranger and bolting back to the balcony. Syl stops, holding the muffin bag to her chest. Jesus, Mia, what do you call that?

He is called Cuthbert. He's my dog.

They follow Cuthbert to the balcony and Mia coaxes him out. Come on, boy. Come and say hello to my friend. Her bark is much worse than her bite. She's OK, really. Come and say hello. The little dog is too nervous. Mia has to bend down and pick him up.

That's not a dog Mia, Syl says, looking at Cuthbert in Mia's arms. That's a fucking feather duster.

Don't be ridiculous, Syl. You've never seen a feather duster.

I don't care what it is – we have to cut its hair. It can't see anything.

He can see fine. He can see that he doesn't like you at any rate and I don't blame him. Poor boy. Mia puts the dog on the floor again, kneeling down to pet him.

Syl crouches and gently puts out a hand. Sorry, Cuthbert. I'm sorry. How do you do, she says.

Give him a bit of muffin, you've brought enough.

Cuthbert backs against Mia's legs, with his lips pulled back over his teeth.

Is he smiling at me, or snarling? I can't work it out. He's so weird.

Mia feeds him some muffin, which tastes extraordinary to him, overwhelming sweetness and something that he wouldn't know to call chemical. His mouth floods with saliva but he relaxes. He allows himself to be petted.

Is it *In Our Time*? Syl asks, noticing that Mia's radio has been talking to itself on the counter all along. I hate missing that. Have you been listening?

I couldn't understand a word of it. So no, not really.

Are you joking? It's where I get all my enthusiasms from. It's brilliant.

Are you planning to be enthusiastic about quantum theory? Mia asks drily, still in her pyjamas.

Oh. Syl looks crestfallen. Well, I'd give it a go.

I'm not going to give anything a go until I've had coffee, Mia says. And you're right, maybe we should cut Cuthbert's hair.

So Mia and Syl make coffee and find Mia's dressmaking scissors and between them they settle to feeding Cuthbert and cutting his hair. He is surprisingly docile. Their morning is quiet, small-scale, hair-filled. They talk a little about last night. The radio continues to offer information, as though it mattered. They don't really listen.

*

Meanwhile, as if life were a handful of gravel thrown into water, everyone, all over London, living the closed rings of their separate, but similar, days. Across town, for instance, a courier with his CB radio crackling, stands on a doorstep in Harley Street, eyeball to eyeball with a brass dolphin, and feels irritable. He is in a reasonable hurry.

Delivery for Dr Radic. He almost shouts into the intercom, when the receptionist finally answers. Lazy bitch. He wears a helmet, a reinforced, waterproof all-in-one with hi-vis strips on his calves and his wrists. He is older than he would like to be. He feels his life is pointless. It is passing him by, as if it belonged to someone else. He is indignant most of the time.

The door opens and he walks down the hall to reception. Foreign-looking clients on leather sofas. Fat mostly. Two doctors talking by a filing cabinet, Julia and Syl's husband Robert, who share a practice.

Thank you for last night, by the way.

Not at all. You came so late, I don't think there was anything to be thankful for.

Well, there's drink, Robert is saying.

Yes, Julia says, sometimes I wish there wasn't.

The delivery man clumps to the desk. All day delivering things, hand to hand, a modern version of the Brampton carrier, documents, letters, things that are too urgent to post. Delivery for Dr Radic, he says again. You have to sign for it. The receptionist passes the package behind her.

Can I give this straight to you, Julia?

Thanks very much. That's come quickly. This, I'm hoping, she says to Robert, is the proof of the article on surrogacy. You might look it over for me.

The delivery man, in all his outlandish gear, like an astronaut, has to stand at the desk, waiting for his signature. The receptionist suddenly has other things to do. He is very visible but no one in the room acknowledges him. Then he leaves, walking his curious hampered walk, lets the door slam heavy behind him. Thank you for last night, he says simpering as he cocks a leg over his bike, weaves out into the traffic, accelerates, his mood toxic.

Meanwhile in her consulting room, behind a huge desk, Julia holds the proofs of her article in her hand. She has fifteen minutes before she needs to leave for the hospital. She looks quickly through the first paragraph or two but something Robert said earlier that morning is making her impatient. What is Sylvia going to do now Gabe is at school? she had asked him, while they drank their coffee standing up in the little common room at the back.

Exercise her democratic right to protest, was his answer.

Julia holds her proofs but looks at nothing and thinks of Sylvia and clicks her tongue with irritation.

Is it my fault? Where did I go wrong?

Looking back through her motherhood. Trying to remember a moment when Syl swung against her example finally and for good. Was it then?

Or then?

*

Earlier. Say twenty years or so, for instance. Julia younger, making a list, writing a note to the cleaner who will come in while she is at work, putting money into an envelope and watching the clock on the wall with half an eye. All the things she has to remember to do. Ten minutes until she has to leave. And Syl, standing by the sink in Gordon Square, just in from a night's clubbing, watching her mother's efficiency, and smelling ill. Her posture of baby defiance, something glinting in her nose. Vulnerable. Bags under her eyes, turning her head constantly so her nose is always on show.

Her mother looking up with quick notice. Yes, I can see you've had your nose pierced. Her tone is neutral. Checking papers in her briefcase, picking up her keys, her bleeper. I hope it's clean. There's disinfectant in the bathroom cupboard. She knows she is meant to mind but, apart from the fact that it is ugly, she really doesn't have time. It isn't important enough.

It's my nose.

Darling, it's your nose. I have no argument with that.

So what do you have an argument with? You're not exactly radiating approval. My friends? The fact I stayed out?

In exasperation and surprise, glancing at the clock again. I have no argument. I have no argument at all Sylvia. I'm just trying to get organised and go. You're a teenager. I understand your need to express the self that you are only half-aware you have. You're back. You're safe. You look tired. I suggest you get a bit of sleep and then we'll talk tonight. You need to get these exams well if you want to get into a good university.

Maybe I don't.

Well, you will need to do something with your life. You will need to earn a living. Julia is not having this conversation now. She glances at the window. Slant rain on city roofs. Damn. She is thinking of her shoes, which are expensive and not sufficiently weatherproof.

And now Syl's staged explosion. Her mother is ignorant. She knows nothing about her life, about her needs. She doesn't understand. And what Julia hears is, I have chosen my father. He is the one I am following, not you. Although this is not what Sylvia says.

Julia goes down the passage to her bedroom. As though there were no other options for the child than the parent as model, she is thinking, opening her wardrobe to change her shoes. As though the parents were so giant in scale you simply chose one or other, nothing else being visible. And the choice being taken in exasperation, in fury, against the gravitational pull of genetic inheritance. Julia goes back to the kitchen and looks at her daughter, sitting on the counter, scowling now, banging her legs against the cupboard.

Julia has a borderline psychotic to see at nine. She has a conference to attend before lunch on the psychological impact of infertility.

You do not know me, OK? The stud in Syl's nose glinting.

But she does. It is so pointless. Julia does know her. It is so sad. It is so boring, this constant assumption of difference, of defiance, when Syl is what she has always been, what Julia felt her to be, by instinct and by observation, from the very beginning. How the mother watches – because Julia is a mother too; day after day, she watches the baby emerge from dark and speechlessness into consciousness, first of the body, and then of the world. Reading the signs of illness, of unhappiness, of character. Nursing, healing, comforting. As the baby stares in wonder and incomprehension, its limbs jerking uncontrolled, See, the mother says, these are your hands, your arms and legs, and the baby steps into its body. As it copes with the frustrations of communication, of managing movement, thought, society, See, the mother says, this is the world. You can do it. And watching how the child responds, yes, she says, what a miracle, of course, I see that is what you are, recognising the originality of variation and waiting for the child to catch up.

That is all the mother does; watch, and understand.

*

Recently Julia's eyes have gone. These days she has to use glasses for reading, which she wears on a gold chain round her neck. She adjusts them to go back to her proofs. But the words slide off her consciousness, like water on glass. She can't focus. It is painful to her that Sylvia, so bright, as though her hair and her clear eyes reflected the colour of her mind, should deny herself so wilfully. She feels it like something lodged between her throat and her breastbone. Often, as now, she finds herself clearing her throat. Don't let me die with the life I gave you still unexpressed, is what she is thinking. That Syl should have taken her father's muddied, emotional example is nonsensical, infuriating. Clever beautiful Sylvia. She should have been a marine biologist. She could have been anything.

Julia has never been a temperamental person. She is too rational. But over the last few days she has pictured throwing that paperweight on her desk against the far wall. Life is full of frustrations. It must be the onset of old age. She feels weaker than she used to. She is tired. She is still doing too much.

*

And her daughter, busy on Mia's kitchen floor with the scissors, is cutting the hair of a small dog in the daytime.

After a while, when there is hair over everything, when each time

Mia and Syl stop to sip their coffee, or take a bite of muffin themselves, they get hair in their mouths, Syl says, Are you sure there's a dog under here?

I'm sure, I'm sure, Mia says, Oh poor Cuthbert. She sits back on her haunches contemplating her new companion. He is shivering, whether with nerves or cold, who can say?

Then, when Cuthbert is done, Mia pulls on some clothes and Syl sweeps the hair into a pile and puts it in the kitchen bin. She watches the little dog for a while. You know, he looks better Mia, she shouts in the direction of the bedroom, where Mia still keeps her clothes.

Does he? Mia calls back. Does he really, in what way? She comes out.

He looks pretty pleased with himself. Look at him. He thinks he's quite something now. And it is true, Mia looks at her little dog, trotting out onto the balcony again, nose up, sprightly. As if to say, There's a bit more of a sniff about things out here. There's more air. Forgotten energies stir him. He has a body after all, as it turns out, under his rug of hair. He lifts his leg against one of Mia's plant pots in some dim urge towards self-assertion. Trotting across to the other side, another lift, another precious dribble of urine. Then he puts his nose through the railings, watches a woman below beating a rug she has hung over her own balcony, two floors down.

Oh Lord, Mia says, he hasn't been out. What am I thinking of? I'd better take him to the park.

OK, I'll come down with you. I'll walk a bit and then go from there. I have to be back at Dad's for lunch. I want to see Phil before he goes back to NY.

Oh, is all Mia says, OK.

So they find a lead, and a coat for Mia, and keys, and Mia's bag, and Mia mops the balcony quickly with disinfectant from a bucket that she keeps handy and they set off, down the many flights of stairs and into the drab outside, where the sun is still struggling with the sky's opacity and the grime is suspended in acid fog and the people are withdrawn and hurrying.

He's pretty smooth, your cousin, Mia says after a while, remembering. She looks at the sky. There is some feeling that she hasn't yet formulated, a shade of disappointment maybe, or pique because he made such a fuss of her last night, because she had no idea he was leaving. He didn't say anything about that when he followed her everywhere with his light-filled eyes, when he burnt her up with his attention. But then he didn't say much.

He's lovely. Didn't you like him? Syl sounds surprised. God, I used to want to be him so badly, when I was little. He could do anything. He's still pretty cool, I think. We used to sneak off fishing. He could catch anything and we used to nick things from the shop, just sweets and stuff, and he had all these animals he kept, and he was an excellent liar.

Is that a recommendation?

Syl laughs, Well not now, I don't suppose, but it was then. His mother's a nightmare.

Over the Marylebone Road to Regent's Park. No dogs allowed in the Avenue Gardens or in the English Gardens so they have to walk all the way round to Chester Road, tantalising, up the side of the park with Cuthbert in his new old persona, straining in incomprehension at the access to squirrels visible but denied. They go in at the first little gateway off Chester Road and Mia lets Cuthbert off the lead straight away.

Dogs bounding around everywhere. People have enormous dogs in London. Huge great wolfhounds and boxers and lurchers, running their modified and cabined runs, their potential, clinging round them like a smell, just gestured in their bounce, their semi-delinquency in the face of owners' commands. Lulu! a woman shouts repeatedly. Will you come here!

Mia and Syl walk diagonally across, past the rugby posts, to the Broadwalk. Cold trees opening their fingers at the sky, dripping as they walk underneath.

Where are we going? Syl asks after a while.

I don't know. I'm just walking. That's what I usually do. I do a pretty good round inside an hour without thinking about it.

At lunchtime, which comes quicker than expected, on account of their late breakfast, Syl says goodbye and turns away and heads off, with her bag slung over her shoulder and her stride long, like her father's. Mia and Cuthbert watch her go, Mia feeling suddenly lonely.

She sets off at Cuthbert's preferred pace, out across the surprising extent of the park to the north. And all around them, as they go, on the grass, stopping in the middle of the paths, up and down the trunks and branches of the trees as though they were domestic staircases, the almost insulting tameness of the animals.

In the park you can stand right opposite a squirrel, watch it stripping a nut, holding it between over-delicate hands, its housewife's hips planted. Or you can watch the white blink of a crow, like a camera shutter, click, click at close quarters. It makes Mia feel lonelier. It makes her feel almost invisible, this nonchalance of the things that we call wild.

But it isn't even worth miming fear, if you are a squirrel or a crow. All the chains of being are broken. The dogs will chase you, but they have forgotten how to catch or kill. They stop short, baffled, as if peering through mist. The people eat other things.

*

In his kitchen, his shirt tail only half-pushed into the waistband of his trousers and still in his socks, Bill cooks complicated food for Syl and Felipe's lunch.

I'm not that hungry, Syl says, looking into one of his saucepans. I ate too many muffins with Mia.

Don't say that to me now, Bill says, stirring things, padding back and forth.

Sorry. Don't mean to be unappreciative.

Felipe is leaning against the counter. He is wearing aftershave although he is still unshaven. He feels his own physical energy expand and contract in his chest, more like a current than a pulse. He doesn't know what he is thinking about. He looks into the middle distance and is silent.

So, Bill says to him with a note of regret, you liked Mia?

Felipe looks up. Yes. His face registers brief self-consciousness. I think she's gorgeous. He nearly asks if she is coming to lunch, and then doesn't.

Syl turns round. She didn't think much of you. The cousins look at each other. You were too smooth. Nothing personal. She smiles a companionable smile.

Shame, Felipe says. He looks at the floor. He can still feel Mia's body move in his arms. He is piqued by her reported comment, by her composure. He would like to see it broken. He would like to puncture her strangeness, her separation, see her eyes widen, hear her sharp intake of breath. He shrugs. Oh well.

It was just an evening after all.

*

But for Mia it was an evening that showed how lonely she'd become. And now as she walks, the park is grey and cold and crow-filled, as if in painful reflection. She heads Cuthbert back towards the café and they share an organic sausage in a bun and Mia drinks more coffee and reads a book and watches the sudden flight of pigeons, to and fro in their separate and unfathomable social groupings.

The café is more or less empty. One or two scarf-wrapped conversations between students. A pair of middle-aged lovers at one of the outside tables caught in each other's eyes, not feeling the cold. And the pigeons that rise as if flung, as if the grey of the sky had gathered itself in pieces, become corporeal; only with sudden and unaccustomed purpose, given the windless nature of the day, travelling with speed and deftness, as they turn. Because however drab or commonplace pigeons look, there is an artistry to their flight, as though they were of one mind, as though they were conscious of the curlicues they can't help but describe, so pointlessly ornate.

Elsewhere, crows claw the air and find their own space in which to flop down singly, and gather their flitters about them, and jab at things with greedy beaks.

Mia watches the birds and feeds Cuthbert the end of the sausage and stands and shakes the crumbs off her lap. Come on boy. How long has she been sitting without noticing the time? She walks a little stiffly from the cold. We'll go by the water. I need to warm up.

But for Cuthbert, released from the weight of his hair, today is still a new world. Everything is fun. The water-birds on the water, or brooding one-legged among their own shite on the muddied banks, the leafless trees, even the air he sniffs up expectant that only smells of exhaust. Bless you, Mia thinks, looking at him. She doesn't notice the approach of the man with the lazy eye who, coming abreast of her at last, smiles desperately as she crosses the bridge. He waits for a cyclist to pass and falls into step, one arm caressing the air behind her back. Mia looks a dagger at him and takes another way, the long way round that goes along the edge of the pond.

The park is for freaks.

You are the only nice person, Mia tells Cuthbert, as he trots along in excitement, pleased to have this extension to his walk, this whole day in the park. Then, having made their detour, they head back towards the park gates. The day is closing already. It is dark by four these evenings, the lights on now in the streets outside. It is slow going because there are still people passing, occasionally with dogs, all of whom must sniff each other. Cuthbert and these strangers, pirouetting intimately end to end. Mia waits, with half an eye ensuring that no one forgets themselves, or gets too excited. And on the grass the squirrels go on, ignored, and the crows straddle, square-crotched like middle-aged men, one rocking back and forth, hands behind its back, expectorating its croak. Horrible square crotches. Mia knew one like that once.

Diagonally across the sports pitches again, almost at the gate, on a lonely stretch, with the sky laid out for the dark to take it and the street lights strung pretty, like a necklace, Mia glances up involuntarily. There is a man approaching across the grass. Is it just being a woman walking alone that is nervous-making, or is it the encounter with the man on the bridge?

Something has made Mia jumpy.

This man is walking directly towards her. Overcoat. Something familiar about the walk, square-crotched, the blocky head. Maybe she knows him. Does she know him? He heads towards her as though winding her to him on a string. Staring, which is unsettling. Mia looks down. Increases her pace. Then against her instincts, looks up again quickly. Her stomach turns over.

It could be.

And already it is too late to turn another way because the other gate is too far. It is dusk and the park is closing. And as the man comes level Mia's heart is jumping in her neck, she is so sure suddenly that it is Freddy. She is alone, walking very fast. Slicked-back sandy hair, overcoat with velvet facings, and he leans towards her as he passes, says, Good afternoon, insinuatingly. Mia marches on, head down. Her heart is pounding.

It wasn't Freddy. Just an Irish-looking stranger.

It is an animal world, in the park.

*

Back in the flat, Mia turns on all the lights. She makes noise and gathers up the coffee cups from the morning and feeds Cuthbert and washes up and is busy.

What we need is a bit of music, she says to him. He looks up from his bowl obligingly. She picks up clothes. She makes the bed. She checks her messages. Nothing, since Ines. No one has rung.

What to do with the evening. She stands in the middle of John's workroom, briefly at a loss. For the first time since John's death she feels she would like some people in her life. Where is everyone else? What do they all do with their evenings, for goodness' sake?

Felipe, for instance, sitting back as the plane takes off for JFK. He has eased off his shoes so he can sleep through the flight. The seat belt is opened and closed like so. The life jacket is stowed beneath your seat. And the roar of jet engines and the sudden sickening lift and then the whole of London scribbled below in pinpoint light, like a huge doodle. The plane banks, its seat-back screens flickering into life, synthetic air circulating through the cabin. He is thinking only about his next job.

I imagined you different. Not so tricky. Am I too tricky, Mia asks herself, still marooned in the middle of the workroom. Would my life be any different if I wasn't? I don't know how to be. I've been this way so long. She looks across at the picture of John, but John is no help any more.

Come and dance, beautiful.

Or Syl, in Chelsea, who is spending her evening as she spends every evening, sitting on her younger son's bed, nerves fraying, while her children run naked from room to room, whipping each other with towels. Or her husband Robert, unaware that it is evening at all, who bends over a patient's notes, dictating a letter into a Dictaphone, similar to the one that Mia uses for her father, in a voice that is crisp and unhesitating.

. . . on the understanding of patient review at not less than quarterly intervals. If you have any further queries please don't hesitate to contact me. Yours sincerely etc. He clicks off the device, removes another file. In the corner of the window a fly, apparently hysterical, careers about between the double glazing and a flowering orchid.

Mia's flat is silent. She shuts Cuthbert in the kitchen because her father says dogs should not be allowed in bedrooms and perhaps discipline is a good place to start. It is so hard sometimes, to manufacture activity, if you are alone. Then she sits by herself on her own bed with nothing happening around her, the bookshelves standing stuffed, the piles of pointless papers, the dust gathering, the man who is dead – dead. The man who might have been, gone without saying goodbye. How ridiculous, even to have thought of it. Mia tries not to listen to the blank that is her life. Snap out of it, she says to herself. Why can't you just get on and make a life by yourself?

Mia goes and fetches Cuthbert from the kitchen. He is company after all. That is why she got him in the first place. She pats the bed beside her for Cuthbert to jump up, in contravention of all her father's rules, flicks the remote on John's little television. Let's watch the news, boy. Let's see how the rest of the world is coping.

In the lit square of the television, demonstrations in a foreign country appear, urgent and in miniature. There has been an assassination attempt, it seems. And now, on a balcony a president appears flanked by heavies. He muscles forward tearing at his tie. He looks enraged. Pulling open his shirt he beats with one fist at his exposed chest. Here I am, he roars in Spanish, or is it Portuguese? Here I am. Kill me. Is that what you want? Below him the crowd mutters and surges like a sea, the slow booming of many voices merged into a single incoherence. Nothing happens but it is electric. It seems of vital significance. Mia and Cuthbert stare.

Nevertheless it is hard to feel engaged, watching world events like this. Something about the screen makes Mia feel removed.

Just as once, years ago, watching the news with John, when again there were demonstrations and the camera followed or stood against the flow, and boys' faces for the most part, so young, only newly moustached, passed continually either side, shouting, fists raised. And there were banners carried high above the heads of the crowd while something was chanted over and over. John sat very straight with his eyes looking like crying. Then it cut suddenly to footage of a flag being burnt and in the faces of the protesters there was terrible anger. It should have been frightening but Mia had watched with dispassionate curiosity. There were accusations of imperialism and a reporter in shirtsleeves shouting his explanation of events, while behind him flowed, wave after wave, this river made of men, the banners bobbing overhead like sails.

Then, Mia had been safe in John's flat. She had her lover to buffer her against disaster. These televised events had seemed separate, part of a different world. But to John it had been a horror waiting to unfold. He had run his hands through and through his hair until it stood up like a cockatoo's, his eyes swimming. Don't you see what a disaster this is, he kept saying, to the television more than to Mia, to the demonstrators. Don't you see where this is leading? Shaking his head, making his hair stand up. He had predicted war at the time and he had been right, although it wasn't the sort of thing you could take any pleasure in getting right. John detested war.

War is a natural part of a male universe, that was what Mia had thought. Isn't it just what men do?

They had sat up late discussing it, John pacing about distracted. You have no idea of the reality of war. It isn't enough to say that it is natural to men. War is a human solution, he said, to a problem that is, or appears to be, intractable. It isn't either male or female. It was one of the few times she had felt ticked off by him. He looked like a bird of prey, hooked, intent, eyes burning. Parcelling up his thoughts as if they were pellets. He was difficult to argue with. War is most often male in its expression, he said, staring her down, but it is an anger that is shared, if not nursed in the home, by women. Wars only stop when women want them to.

Is that a fact?

But they didn't argue. And later, when Mia was getting ready for bed, John seemed so sad. I find I'm losing hope, Mia. I'm glad you don't want to have children, he said into her hair, when she took him in her arms half-undressed, to comfort him. I don't think I could face it.

I don't not want children, Mia said. I just can't because of the blindness. I've told you that. If I had a boy, he might be blind.

Boys are already blind, John said. What's the difference?

Child after child, after child. 1632. In her early thirties, after eight and a half years of almost unbroken pregnancy and birth, Brilliana has six children. She is finding it hard to regain her strength.

Long periods of weakness that confine her to her chamber. Uncomplaining. Ashen-faced. She holds to the principles of her Commonplace Book, written out against just such eventualities.

What Afflictions are:

Afflictions is all maner of miseries and calamities in this life from the least to the greatest.

OR it is the deprivation of some good things of whiche we are passed as Job who was deprived of all his goods and children.

OR the imposition of some evill thinge on us as the womm which had the bloody flux so many yeares.

Our practice in affliction must be this:

First we must diligently examen our conscience in regard of sinn.

Second we must be silent in the day of affliction our mouths must not open against God.

Thirdly by affliction we must be moved to seek to God.

Foorthly in affliction we must reioyce not that we are afflicted but our sins are pardoned.

Fifly we must pray earnestly for the removal of our affliction but submitting our will to the Lord's.

Sixtly we must give thanks for our affliction for we must prais God for all things.

She is almost too weak at this time to write in her own hand. One of her women must help if she is to write a letter for instance. Also there is often pain.

God hath respect to our strength and will not lay upon us more than we can beare.

Esa. 24:8 In measure in the branches thearof wilt thou contend with it when he bloweth with his rough wind in the day of the Est wind.

But there is always much to do.

Also it is unnecessarily cold for March. The lady's silence, the set of her mouth, in the face of physical affliction. Her almost translucent pallor. Or her halting step when she goes about her duties, and the hand pressed involuntarily sometimes to her stomach, which she thinks that no one sees.

Thomas Pierson, the rector of Brampton, takes a more pragmatic approach. She is frail and he is fearful of the demands that she makes on herself. On the last page of the Parish Register, taken up in haste and written upside down, he makes a note. He is near the end of his own life and he is fond of Lady Brilliana.

Memorandum, he writes, that whereas Dame Brilliana Harley is licensed by Tho: Pierson rector of this church of Brampton Bryan to eate flesh on fish dayes in regard of her great weakness which lycense was made the sixt day of this moneth: and for that her great weaknes dth yet continue, the continuance of the seyd lycense according to the statute of Elizabeth . . . registered till it shall please God to recover her health.

March 14 1632.

The day wears itself away to dusk. Jackdaws settle in the high tops of the trees in the castle ground. Brilliana prays in her chamber. It is not for us to question God's purpose. The nights can be very long sometimes. She holds her mind clenched against hopelessness.

It is night too in Mia's street, and the cats are out, going on tiptoe and turning up their noses at a sheen of rain. They are a disdainful race. Only the insomniac homeless, waking rigid and poisonous, asking themselves why they ever thought this would be better, witness them, tails up, ghosting from doorway to doorway. And the cats jump over the rubbish and the humans alike, as if there were no difference, carrying the cool spirit-level of their lives invisible inside them, balancing it constantly back to horizontal.

At the gate to the park, with its tail curled fastidiously round itself, a tabby sicks up a furball.

Below Mia's flat the traffic lights blink at their own reflection in the puddle at their feet. So few cars pass. The last Tube train trembling the water that holds the green light showing now, so its edges widen and blur, a brief, electric leaf. Amber to red and a taxi pulls up whose driver is on his last fare and whose eyes are sore. The football was a bad result again. His team is looking at relegation.

And Mia is asleep in her clothes, on her bed, curled like a baby. The television is off but she'd been too tired to undress, or to brush her teeth. Cuthbert is asleep in the crook of her knees, one ear cocked to the street outside.

Mia is dreaming her dream. I have a secret, she is trying to say, only she can't make the words come out. She can't move her mouth properly. And it is true. She does.

Before John, it was always Syl who sat up with her at night, on the rare occasions when Mia couldn't manage to go back to sleep, when she dreamed that she gave birth to her uncle's baby, an endless continual labour producing child after child, with Freddy standing over her looking pleased with himself.

Why would we want to sleep? Syl would say. We'll have midnight cocoa. It'll be fun. Come on. Turning Mia's temporary insomnia into a celebration.

Then Mia would relax. She would laugh and forget about it. She would sleep fine for a while, until for no reason her fears would rise to the surface of her sleeping mind and she would see again the flattened stillborn lambs of her childhood, given human faces in her dreams. Blind, the midwife would say brusquely because the dream, which was always the same, played itself out in the sterile spaces of a hospital ward. They were no good, she would say of the corpses. And Freddy would nod, looking down at her. They were all blind. And an attendant in scrubs would come and sweep the stiff bodies into a pile, the legs of the lambs rigid and out-stretched, the fur still matted from birth.

It used to be Syl, always Syl, who was there, who held her hand, who stroked her hair, who said, We'll go out. We'll go on holiday. It's fine. You've finished with Freddy, thank God. It hasn't happened. It isn't going to happen. Come on, we need a new interest. We'll take up dance classes. We'll do the Carnival.

So for Syl, Mia covered the secret of her uncle, and put her parents out of her mind and told herself that motherhood was not for her. She pulled herself together in fact. And later, when Nate was born and Syl wanted Mia to be godmother, Mia stood in the light in the church on the Embankment, with the Thames oily outside, and held the baby that belonged to someone else and said the words required of her and was happy for her friend.

Do you renounce the Devil and all his works, the empty show and false values of the world, and the sinful desires of the flesh, so that you will not follow nor be led by them? The London priest in white robes. Gold embroidery on the altar, lilies, and the roar of the Embankment behind. Julia's hair, as if part of the ceremonial, in a shaft of light from the long window.

I renounce them all, Mia mouths without thinking. Unmarried, living in sin in the eyes of the Church.

So you've squared your conscience, Julia asks lightly, handing Mia a glass of champagne at the reception and Mia flushes. Why? Julia herself doesn't believe. The Catholic service is for Bill's family.

And afterwards there is John to hold her. Don't let her get to you. He makes no secret of his dislike of Julia. She is incapable of belief, except in herself. You've done a lot of renouncing, he says, putting his arms round her in the tiny bedroom, with his mother's picture watching. You must be exhausted.

And later when they are lying in the dark, Are you jealous, sweetheart? Did you wish the baby had been your own? It would be only natural after all.

A little bit, Mia says after a pause, with the lights of a taxi making long fingers across the ceiling. But then it wasn't mine, so I don't know. Not overmuch.

*

Morning.

The cats' shadowy selves, along with all the ghosts, the nightmares that did happen and those, like Mia's, that didn't, evaporate with the coming of light. In baskets or on sofas the cats flop down like cuddly toys, sleek with solidity, petted. Hello gorgeous boy. Eyes slitted to be stroked. Purring.

Outside Euston station the commuters arriving from the provinces, as grey as the streets, pour past the *Big Issue* salesman on the early shift. His eyes are rancid with the hangover behind them. His tongue thick for shouting, Ladies and Gents, your favourite read. Come on darling, get your *Big Issue* from London's only invisible man. The darling clicks past, eyes front, money snug in her purse, her mac swishing.

Dazed after her night of dreaming, Mia is taking Cuthbert back to the park. They walk slowly, fog-swathed inside and out because neither of them slept much in the end. It is reassuringly normal.

The joggers are keeping going, lungs working like bellows, muscles pumping, at the altar of the machine that is the body.

The trees are standing.

Black branches drip a mixture of water and exhaust and tarry grime onto the struggling grass. Mia and Cuthbert make their tour.

Afterwards Mia drops Cuthbert home and walks still fogged, down the Euston Road thinking she will comfort herself with breakfast before she goes to the library. She is going to read the diary of Lady Margaret Hoby, if she can keep her eyes open long enough.

After you.

No, no, after you.

Sorry.

Sorry.

Oops.

Thank you.

Politeness can be confusing, when you are tired. Mia does a clumsy dance with a lady in a suit, coming out of the café. Soup and sandwiches and coffee and brownies and everything you can think of on offer already, even at this hour, waft a de-personalised smell at her as she enters, the smell of no-meal-in-particular. Croissant, Danish pastry, English muffins, sushi, Thai chicken broth, miso, pastrami, houmous, brie, falafel. It isn't about meals. It is about Choice, in little sealed packets.

While she queues, Mia thinks with a pang of the café of her teens.

Purple sandstone street, mottled-looking, ominous, like a drunk. The bell ringing so half the town can hear it. Dinner hour at school in Scotland. Sixth formers only allowed out, headed in a gaggle, to meet the boys in the caf across from the school. Egg and two slices, tea with sugar; beans sometimes and grease in everything, even the Coca-Cola, whatever meal it is you are having, breakfast, lunch, tea. You can smell the grease halfway down the street, very comforting, very insistent. Sitting at the Formica tables, eating chip butties, their new bosoms popping the buttons on their school shirts. I'm on a diet.

You are so not.

I'm not having that anyway. It gives you spots.

Passing round a shared cigarette. Quick, it's your da!

Christ, where?

Had you going there, didn't I – I had you going.

Or it is Michael or Peter or Tommy, lounging in through the door, who they fancy, or don't fancy. Giggling, pushing up their hair every five minutes, dreaming dreams. Peter now; he is a fantastic kisser.

But there was only grease in the caf. There wasn't Choice.

Mia cold, in middle age, standing in the unease of indecision. She takes a newspaper and the little metal tray to a seat by the window that looks out onto a side street.

Did I make the right choice? I don't know if I want this. The newspaper headlines blur in absent-mindedness. Outside there is a small demonstration, she can't make out what about. Twenty or so people standing on the step of the glass building opposite, shouting politely, batting their hands together against the chill that has invaded their fingers. One of them has a megaphone. She watches them for a while, mouthing encouragement to each other, and occasionally shouting in unison, but as she can't hear, her attention soon wanders.

Higher up the building, above the demonstrators, there is a man hanging. He is in a harness and he's moving around in the air, more or less comfortably by the looks of things. He has a hard hat and a yellow bucket and he is hanging, not vertically but at forty-five degrees, his legs open in a V. He is letting himself down in jerky little drops, cleaning windows with a scraper as he goes. Mia watches his progress down the glass face, bouncing with his feet, swinging.

Excuse me, a girl asks, balancing an identical silver tray which supports a similarly global, though different, breakfast from Mia's, is this seat taken?

No. Please, Mia says, gesturing at the chair and wishing her mouth wasn't so full, while on the next-door table, a woman with bowl-cut hair and a northern accent leans forward to tell her companion, I'm telling you, I'm not joking, she had eight terminations because she wanted a girl. The other woman listens, holding a fat sandwich to her face. That's no way to have children, the bowl-cut woman goes on. I'd have killed myself, she says, raising her coffee cup and blowing the foam. That's no way to have children either, Mia thinks as she listens, though the woman's companion tuts in agreement. She'd have killed herself too. But maybe you get used to it by the eighth.

Mia looks out at the glass building again and eats the croissant that might have been granola and drinks the cappuccino that, according to the cup, is the product of a passion for coffee.

And up in the sky, among the flying pigeons, the man in the harness roars to himself, because it doesn't matter and he can, Who-oh, something about halfway there, which seems appropriate. A secretary whose boss is hungover glances up to see him hanging, singing, outside, and laughs.

And now on Mia's other side there is a boy with an eager face, eating an enormous sandwich full of meat and pickles and mayonnaise and tomatoes at nine in the morning. He is thin and dark. He eats with energy and writes in a notebook and now, while Mia watches, he looks up with entranced surprise. Layla! he says and a girl with another identical silver tray sits shyly and impossibly opposite him and they smile.

No one else notices this chance encounter, so electric that it seems, for a moment, to light the café. Mia looks away only partly out of consideration. It is so intense, so different from everything else, the park, her life, the other people, it acts on Mia like a shock. At the table next door, the women, oblivious, move onto other medical matters. Men in suits read papers or talk on mobiles. All around them Nothing happens, while Layla and the hungry boy talk animatedly, with noticeable though different foreign accents, in a language that both of them have had to learn.

She shouldn't look. It is intrusive. But she can't help herself. Life seems to be so vivid to them. She casts little, furtive glances. They are so young. Perhaps that's what it is. They are not yet tired, unlike everyone else. They look like babies.

It is as if they didn't know. Innocently manufacturing lives for themselves in this city, where there are no certainties, only Choice. Where the streets boil with people and the cafés spill out into the boiling streets. Where you can travel underground as well as over and men hang singing in the sky and money never stands still but spins constantly from hand to dirty hand and can you spare a bit of change for a cup of tea or a shot of something? Anything.

Do they have any idea where they are?

Good luck, Mia says to Layla and the boy in her head, as she gets up to leave. Make a better go of it than I have. Good luck and God be with you. If he's there, that is.

Lady Margaret Hoby's diary, through a mist of tiredness.

In the morning after privat praier I reed of the Bible, and then wrought tell 8 a clock, and then I eate my breakfast: after which done, I walked in the feeldes tell 10 a clock, then I praied and not long after, I went to dinner: and about one a clock I geathered my apeles tell 4: then I cam home and wrought tell almost 6, and then I went to privat praier and examenation, in which it pleased the Lord to blesse me: and beseech the Lord, for Christ his sacke, to increase the power of his spirite in me daly Amen, Amen: tell supper time I hard Mr Rhodes read of Cartwright, and sonne after supper I went to praiers, after which I wrote to Mr Hoby and so to bed.

And so the days go:

After privat praier I saw a mans legge dressed, took order for things in the house, and wrought tell dinner time: after dinner I went about the house and read of the Harball.

After dinner I was busie about preserving quinces and a litle before super time I walked about the house: then I examined myself and praied, then I went to supper.

Then the dark comes up and life is suspended in sleep. Or else it is not, and the hours are watched, in pain or trouble, and the bell's toll is counted and the dawn takes a long time to seep into the sky, and at last another day starts.

After privat praiers I did eate my breakfast with Mr Hoby: then

I walked abroad, and took a lector: after I came in and praied, and then went to diner, then I went about and delivered corne: then I cam into my chamber and wrote notes in my testament, and after receved rentes and walked a while.

And again it is night, and then day again.

After privat praiers I did eate my breakfast, then I was busie to dye wooll tell almost diner time; then I praied and dined.

And night. And day.

After privat praiers I did eate my breakfast: then I reed of the Bible, praied, walked a litle abroad, dinned: after, served divers poore people with wheat and beeffe, than was busie in the kitchen untell 5 a clock and then examened myself and praied.

And again.

After I had praied privately I dressed a poore boies legge that came to me, and then brake my fast with Mr Hoby: after I dressed the hand of one of our servants that was verie sore cutte, and after I wrett in my testament notes upon James: then I went about the doinge of some thinges in the house, paiyinge of billes, and after I had talked with Mr Hoby, I went to examenation and praier, after to supper, then to the lector: after that I dressed one of the mens hands that was hurt, lastly praied, so to bed.

And again.

After I was awake and had praised God for my rest, I got up and was lett blood: then I made me readie and went to privat praier and reading of the Bible.
I was busie all the day about mendinge and sortinge linen.

And that is how Lady Margaret lived.

*

Dazed with vicarious devotion, with Lady Hoby's duty and industry, Mia gets into her coat in the bowels of the library. Everyone is going home. The tin doors of the lockers in their primary-school colours click, opening and shutting, spitting out pound coins. Nobody speaking much, or still in library whispers. Bicycle helmets on, straps clipped under chins, clips strapped on trousers, coats, gloves, scarves. So much swathing and readying to be done for the outside, which doesn't care, which has its head down and its head-lights on, at the rush through the cold streets.

Mia walks out through the iron gates and away up the Euston Road to Cuthbert, who is making little forays now, from the kitchen to the balcony and back, because it is getting to be walk time. He is listening for Mia's return, lying with his nose to the bottom of the kitchen door, getting up a moment later and trot-ting back to his bed. Putting his head down on his extended paws, sighing.

In her flat, the telephone is ringing. Bill wants to ask her to a screening of a French film next week. You're such a fucking intel-lectual, Sylvia says to him, lying on a tattered sofa in his workroom, while Nate and Gabe look at a skateboard trick on Bill's computer. What's wrong with Hollywood?

Bill doesn't answer. He is speaking slowly into Mia's answer-machine . . . me and Sylvia and Andrea, he is saying, at the BFI and to have some supper . . .

On the screen, the little boys press the arrow that says play and watch a tiny figure flip in mid-air, a wheeled board glued to its feet. Awesome, they say in unison. They press play again.

Halfway along the Euston Road, while Bill's voice talks into the empty spaces of her flat, Mia is walking fast because of the cold. She is still thinking about Lady Margaret Hoby's life. That is one solution, or was. Only people in religious institutions live like that now; not fitting belief into the odd corners of life, but fitting their life round belief.

Or is that how life is still and always lived? Is it just the belief at its centre that has changed? Each other, say, in the place of God. Mia thinks of Layla and the sandwich boy. Maybe that explains our disorientation; our belief systems are human now, so they can't help but fail. Maybe the whole point of God is that we can't see through him.

And what should I choose? Mia wonders whether she was ever given the chance to believe. It would be easier to blame someone else. She thinks of her hard-worked parents, who tried, who taught her, at least, to say her prayers. Our Father. God bless Mummy and Daddy. Gabbling through them before she fell asleep. GodblessauntyInesuncleFreddyauntyMary pleasegodmakeme a goodgirlamen. As if goodness were beyond our control. Why did you draw on the wall? I don't know, ask God, he didn't make me good today; although she hadn't seen the inconsistency at the time.

She can't imagine her father praying, or her mother for that matter, who never sat down but who did go to Mass every Sunday. She can't imagine either of them locked in daily contemplation.

Except once, when the door handle to her mother's room was still at Mia's eye level, did she open the door with difficulty, to see her mother with her forehead in her hands, sitting quiet at her dressing table. Still. Posed, almost. Until she looked up startled to see Mia, still holding the handle of the door and the door ajar.

What are you doing? Mia's baby self asked, the look of elsewhere on her mother's face making her aware of intrusion.

Mia's mother had pursed her lips, brisked the brushes on the table into position. Praying, was her curt answer, without looking at Mia. As if to say, Never you mind. I'm Praying to God.

Once upon a time, Mia says tartly, remembering the religion of her childhood. She can't remember ever really believing in it, so it can't have been an option. Once upon a time, there was a princess called me, and I was special. I was saved. It's the oldest story in the book.

At the pedestrian crossing, Mia finds herself wedged against a string of girls who talk animatedly while they wait for the lights to change. I'm not in a position to pass judgement on anyone, one of the girls is saying in a tone of voice that is sanctimonious, and the others respond with a chorus of pious, Oh no's. Definitely not. Everyone is entitled to their opinion.

Mia purses her lips, as if she were her mother. On the other hand, why would you want to live like that? Nothing sacred, nothing real at stake, in the lukewarm complacency of non-judgement. The vigour, the purpose, the commitment of life through the prism of belief shrunk to accommodation, to a sort of negative, not mattering.

Only, how do you tell the difference, Mia thinks as she walks round the corner into her own street, between belief and opinion in a liberal society?

They say that in London the trial has taken place of William Prynne, the lawyer. They say he has been most harshly convicted.

From one family member to another, the urgent letters go, jogging up the mucky ways to the capital. From houses where the February fog sits on furniture indoors. Where, outside, its thick and impenetrable white is just a proof, an outward manifestation of the country dweller's isolation.

What is happening?

No one knows.

Wee country clowns heare various reports of Mr Prinn's censure. Some say hee is to loose his hand and eares, others his hand only; a third sort there are that say neither hand nor ears, but hee must pay 6,000l, and endure perpetuall imprisonment.

Wait for the answer. Go out and come in again wet from sudden rain. Guard against the onset of a cold or an ague. Take physic. Listen to the rumours that continue to circulate. Pray and eat salted meat in dark rooms and at all events keep moving, so that the cold may be kept from entering your bones.

Then at last, the authoritative voice of a letter from London. Prynne is to be degraded in the Universitie, disbarred at the Innes of Court. He was fined I believe it was 4,000l. He was withall condemned to the losse of his eares, whereof he is to parte with one at Westminster, with the other at Cheapside, where, whilest an officer doeth execution on himself, the hangman is to doe it on his booke and burne it before his face. He is to suffer perpetuall imprisonment. His booke was, you may remember, against playes.

Because Prynne took it upon himself to write a book arguing that popular stage-playes are sinfull, heathenish, lewde, ungodly spectacles, and most pernicious corruptions. Because he said that profane and poisonous stage-plays which are the common idol and prevailing evil of our dissolute and degenerous Age, had their rise from hell, yea, their birth, and pedigree from the very Devil himself, to whose honour and service they were at first devoted.

Then, a month or two after publication, the Queen took part in a play with her ladies, so that Prynne's accusations now looked treasonable. It is a dangerous time to have opinions.

Mia and Cuthbert walk again, this time in the dark and the damp, round the edge of the park by the railings, which are a satisfactory challenge to the size of Cuthbert's bladder. Mia is patient partly because she doesn't have anywhere particular to go and this is Cuthbert's time, and partly because she is still worrying about belief. Runners in Lycra work their arms, their breath furling briefly in the street-lamp light. Perfectibility. Nose down and possessed with the need to distribute urine evenly across the city, more than once Cuthbert threatens to trip one with his lead. Sorry, Mia says, as the jogger jigs and sidesteps. She watches the little dog, leg cocked, intent. He's drawing his own map, she says next but to herself. He's naming his own places.

They cross over, past the strange college buildings that Mia can never decipher, that look from the gold insignia on all the boards as though they offer something arcane and independent, possibly for foreign students. She looks at the lit windows and watches people passing to and fro inside. Today, remembering lunch, she wonders if Layla and the sandwich boy are among them, with their notebooks and their wide, everything-for-the-first-time looks. But if they are, she doesn't see them.

Then on a little further there is a small iron gate that always seems to be open and a patch of grass that leads down to the water and a bandstand. Here Mia lets Cuthbert off the lead so he can properly enjoy himself in the shrubberies and attend, conscientiously, to the boles of the trees and to every pillar on the bandstand. Mia loops the lead round her own neck, pushes her hands as far into her pockets as they will go and walks down to the edge of the water.

Birds in crowds bobbing, work their necks back occasionally to preen, burble to themselves their inscrutable watery dreams. How many. How many different types and breeds and sizes there are, non-natives and immigrants some of them, all alongside; while above them, the lights of the city tremble on the air, as if it were water, and the towers and buildings, old and new, shoulder above each other, their profiles dark against the night sky. And every now and then a late one arrives on the wing, descends beating, legs extended, to land on the water among a soft cacophony of birds briefly woken, and the lake rocks, shivering the reflected lights, and settles itself back to what short-lived stillness water can manage.

Mia waits for Cuthbert and thinks, This is a whole city. This is London. Old London and new London and future London dreaming itself up, all piled on top of each other. Like John said, something that can't stop growing, a giant organism. With its systems of opinion or belief and its furious people, flying in and out like the birds, whirled along roads, jiggling and pushing and trying to make sense of themselves, judging and not judging.

It wasn't ever fixed.

Meanwhile, too newly dead to have dissolved altogether, the ghost of orthodoxy, like the cats and the homeless, shifts from door to door, wondering why it no longer belongs; here where only moments before, people hurried in passionate conviction, raising armies in whispers, where they were arrested, or burnt, or imprisoned or beheaded, or had their ears or their tongues slit, or were cut down from the gibbet half-dead, to be killed by disembowelling. Just because they believed.

Crazy. Now, where the ghost passes, it leaves behind it only a feeling of unease. This is what Mia feels. Just the illusion, glimpsed or imagined, the possibility of one animating, patterning system that might shrink death to nothing. Just the urge to commit to something, to each other maybe, or to one shaky conviction or another, to a religion, anything, that would order and subordinate, that would light all things from the inside out, so there would never need to be this coldness, this dark, this lonely and fearful disparity.

Is this how everywhere feels, or is it just the city?

Because while London teems and jostles and is so blind, at the ends of the roads that lead out of it and away, where the roads thin themselves to single track and get lost in the villages of deep countryside, there is space that opens out between people's lives. There is room just to be. Like Mia's father and her aunt, who sit not speaking, just clearing their throats now and then in their living room – and who knows what they are thinking – while the clock on the mantelpiece busies itself spilling out time, marks the silence with its small and audible marks, with authority, as if measuring were system enough.

Will you have a cup of tea, John?

Aha. I might as well. If you're making. There's some time to kill before bed.

And while Ines goes through to the kitchen to kill time, in London people are hurled through contiguous lives, almost overlapping, on top of each other, all at once, searching for definition, for differentiation, for something to hold onto, as if they had no control, as if time didn't so much tick into the silence as whirl itself at them like a wind spout.

All around Mia, on this night, in the houses and the offices and the restaurants, and spilling out of the pubs, the wine bars and the clubs, and on odd benches in dark squares, or on street corners, or road crossings, everywhere, in all places, there are people looking for meaning, rummaging through each other's assorted articles of faith, picking them over as if they were bric-a-brac. Everywhere, people bravely or desperately turning over each other's creeds, taking them home on loan, trying them for size in the empty rooms of their souls.

I believe, they say to each other, clutching at straws, trying to make sense of it all, I believe in You, in Universal Tolerance, Disarmament, the Environment. I believe in Self-help. I believe in Work.

Because with so many other lives right under your nose, there is still the worry that someone else might have cracked it, that there would be room to breathe, that there would be solace, or significance, or more time, that life might finally make sense from some other angle, if only – if only – one could find that angle out.

Be sober, be vigilant because your adversary the devill as a roaring lyon walketh about seeking whom he may devoure.

For we wrestle not against flesh and blood but against principalities, against powers, against the rulers of the darkness of this world, against spirituall wickednesse in high places.

In that day the Lord with his sore and great and strong sword shall punish Leviathan the piercing serpent even Leviathan that crooked serpent and he shall slay the dragon that is in the sea.

From Brilliana Harley's Book of Meditations

Brilliana's eldest son and soulmate sits in Magdalen Hall at Oxford. He is fourteen. He smooths the legs of his suit with his hands because although his hands are cold his palms are continually moist. He is anxious. His tutor is being long about the organisation of supper and this is a strange place. It is said there is a Proctor for every house. The chiefest thing they will amend, it is said, is the wearing of long haire. Ned puts a hand to his hair at the back. He swallows. The principal protested that after this day he would turn out of his house whomsoever he found with haire longer than the tips of his ears.

It is 1638. His mother is a long way away.

And at Brampton, many days' riding, by long and muddy roads, from Oxford, Brilliana endures the nothing that is happening and has no idea whether Ned has arrived safe or not. She counts the days and calculates the journey that her son is making. She forces herself to be conservative in her estimation, so as not to be unduly disappointed by the absence of news. Now they will be att Ludlow, now att Gloucester. She prays for his safety and his well-being and she suffers the hollow that his loss has made in the centre of herself, as if it were a second parturition. What am I now, her mind asks occasionally, in unguarded moments. I am empty. I am nothing.

That it may please thee to preserve all that travel by land or by water; We beseech thee to hear us, good Lord.

Then too there is worry. What kind of company might he not fall into at Oxford? Oxford is a city. There will be so many of corrupt nature, so much temptation. And he is only a child. Sometimes she will share her worries with her eldest daughter Brilliana who is nine. Remember your brother in your prayers. The Devil is always at work seeking out whom he may devour. The girl's eyes round with terror for her childhood companion, her adored eldest brother.

Might I write my brother a letter?

She may send with her mother's letters, once a week, if there is paper to spare. Paper is an import so it is never in plentiful supply.

So that is something to hold onto, the possibility that she may write her own letter to him some day. The little girl has no experience of the world outside Brampton. Is Oxford like to Shrewsbury at all? It must be bigger. It must be higher in its towers and spires and it must have many more people.

Would you know the Devil if you saw him? To her, as she goes about the castle, in her many miniature duties, the rooms and passages seem empty and cold for the loss of her companion. Often she stops and shivers involuntarily.

It is important not to allow oneself to sink. Brilliana bustles her daughter with gentle severity. Trust to God, in whose hand we are held. Be sure of your own election. Out of the window the tipping year suspends itself in unexpected sun. Perhaps by now they will have come to Oxford.

By now surely they will be there.

Oct 25th

Good Need – I hope thease lines will finde you well at Oxford. I longe to reseave the ashurance of your comeing well to your iourneys end. We have had faire weather sence you went, and I hope it was so with you, which made it more pleaseing to me.

You are now in a place of more varietyes then when you weare at home; thearefore take heede it take not up your thoughtes so much as to neglect that constant sarvis you owe to your God. When I lived abroade, I tasted something of thos wiles: thearefore I may the more experimentally give you warneing.

Another week, another day and it is difficult to hold patience. Surely by now there will be news.

Another day.

A further day; now drawing slowly to a close. Lights are lit in the castle. Difficult to see the small stitches, your fingers doing it by memory, creeping the linen along by tiny increments, rolling the hem between finger and thumb as you go. One of the women reading from Calvin's Commentaries as they work.

For the ungodly prayseth himself in the desyre of his own soule and the boystrowse man blesseth himself and despiseth the Lord. The ungodly in the hight of his nosetrils, regardeth not: al his crafts show that he thinks there is no God.

And a shout goes up that there are horses seen on the darkening road. William Childs saw them. Like as not it was Sir Robert come back from Oxford. Although it was hard to tell exactly. So a boy runs along the stone passages, I beg your pardon My Lady, it is thought that Sir Robert is come home.

Into the castle yard, the metal shoes ringing on cobbles, and the rooks that have newly roosted fly up again and circle cawing at the disturbance, and someone holds the horse's head so Sir Robert can swing exhausted off his mount. His coat is caked with mud spattered up from wet roads. At the back of the park a moon gets up unnoticed.

Days go by, then, as they do now. More nights. Brilliana, rising in cold rooms, dressing by rush- or candlelight while the dawn gropes its way to the horizon. Quick movements. The low voices of her women, and praying no doubt, and order, and discipline. One of the children has a cough that has kept it wakeful. The castle stirring but deep in cold and dark and quiet still, just the occasional shout or call from outside as animals are moved, or as the forge lights its fires, or the carpenter's shop or the wheelwright gets going, with the sky showing its first threads of light.

And here, in London, another day opening.

Oh Lord, Cuthbert, nine again. This is becoming a habit. At least three hours, maybe four hours late for privat praier, Mia thinks lying on her back, with Cuthbert shifting and sighing on her feet. Let alone reading of the Bible or examenation or wool-dying. Mia sits up, pushes back her hair. Cuthbert gives a couple of conversational half-grunts, half-whines without taking his chin off his paws.

But today there is sun, as if the city too had stirred and lifted itself free of its blanket of mist and stretched itself and opened. Mia makes tea and brings it back to bed. For this first, waking-up part of the morning, she and Cuthbert sit side by side, Mia cradling a cup of tea, and look out at a newly lit world of rooftops and sky where more things than yesterday seem suddenly possible. Cuthbert's head tilts, angling itself to watch the pigeons, which are still his greatest fantasy. His ears are cocked right forward and sometimes when a pigeon passes particularly close, he can't help himself and makes a short exclamatory bark and looks at Mia.

OK, Mia says drily, after about three of these exclamations, you have to accept you're never going to catch one. They can fly, in case you hadn't noticed. We will go for a walk and you might have better luck with the squirrels. Let me get dressed.

But Mia has made the mistake of saying the word walk, so now she has to dress with Cuthbert bolting back and forth between the bed and the front door, yapping, hysterical with anticipation. Sometimes, out of exuberance or the muddled desire to hurry the process along, he carries something with him, Mia's bedsock, for instance, or her shirt.

Cuthbert, for Pete's sake. Mia watches as her shirt goes without her to the front door. She has one foot in her tights. The telephone rings.

Mia hesitates. It is insistent the noise that a telephone makes, bursting in on things, bouncing off walls and books with an almost delinquent urgency. She'll never get out if she picks it up. The answerphone comes on and Mia hears her own voice, machine-thickened, apologising stiffly.

Hallo pet, another voice is saying now. It is Ines. Ines never rings twice in one week. There must be something wrong.

I'm here, Mia says picking up. I'm here Aunt. What's the matter? Is something wrong with my da?

No lovey, your da's fine. Everything is OK. He's out on one of his wanders with Preston.

Oh thank God, Mia says, putting a hand to her heart as she stands in her undress, looking back at Cuthbert. Preston's OK, is he? I mean, is he safe to be guiding? I thought Da was thinking of getting him put down.

No, he's alright. We've a new trained dog coming so Preston can retire but we'll not put him down unless he's in pain. Don't you worry Mia. Everything is fine. I just thought I'd ask you while your da's out. Ines is sounding tentative, anxious.

What is it?

You know how your da is about needing help.

Does he need help? You said he was fine.

No, he's fine. He's fine.

So what is it, Ines? What does he need?

Well, it's not your da, so much – well, it is your da, but it's just . . . But Ines is unable to get any further.

Mia stands with her mouth slightly open, increasingly baffled, increasingly anxious. Ines, for goodness' sake. What is it?

It's my sister Mary. It's your aunt Mary, Ines says in a rush. Mia is quiet. But Ines goes on, almost gabbling now she has got started. Well Mia, you know Mary has the cancer. She has cancer of the breast now. Quite bad, I'm told. She's an operation booked for the summer and I would love to be there to help her out. I don't want to impose on you with the . . . And then Ines runs out for a moment. I don't want to put you out. With your views, I mean. I know you have your views. About Freddy, I mean.

There is a brief pause, during which Mia tries to understand what exactly it is that Ines is asking of her, before Ines, having said the name she dreaded, rushes on with the rest of her matter. I just want to spend a week or so giving her a hand, she says, while she recovers, you know. Freddy won't be any use to her. I want to go over to stay with her a while. Your da thinks he'll be fine by himself but I thought you might be able to come down for a visit.

So that is what she is asking. Of course, Ines, Mia says with relief in her voice. Of course I'll do that. No problem, Mia says. Give me the dates when you know and I'll put them down. Thank goodness, she thinks. Thank goodness that was all it was. And it will be good. She'd wanted to make time for her father and now it's done for her.

On the other end of the line Ines's voice is also registering relief, relief and surprise and gratitude. Oh, that's lovely, pet. Thanks ever so much. You're a good girl.

Mia feels faintly ashamed. It's nothing Aunt. I meant to find a time for a proper visit. Tell Da I'm looking forward. And I'm sorry about Mary. Are you worried for her?

Well sure I am, Ines says briskly. I am worried for her but she's in good hands. Freddy's paid for everthing private, so we'll see.

Mia doesn't know what to say, other than, Well that's the least that old cockroach could do, which would be unproductive in this instance. Poor Ines. This little round soft woman, who never married, who looks after her dead sister's husband selflessly, afraid now, for the loss of another sister, for herself, for her own death probably, genetically prefigured in that of these two. So, I'm sorry Aunt, is all Mia says in the end. I'm sorry to hear it.

In the little hallway in the house in Glebelands, Ines replaces the handset. She has no idea what Mia's life is like. She can't picture the flat. She has been to London once but that was long ago. She saw a show. She ate an ice cream. The Post Office Tower had just been built. She doesn't know it is called the BT Tower now.

*

Mia goes on with her dressing. Outside, in sun and wind, London has been busy for hours. Cheapside, in the City, a scurry of suits and slick hair and pallor under suntan, may not have slept at all, for instance, because Cheapside's god is money, and money never sleeps.

I'm up for it. I've got a ten o'clock. I can one hundred per cent guarantee. I wouldn't lie to you.

In the place where cattle were sold and where those whose religion was out of fashion were burnt, there is an underground car park.

And here, round the corner from Robert Harley's one-time lodgings, is St Paul's behind a screen of branches. Sudden sun after rain. So that the water-laden twigs catch the light, spin it into a haze, until all that bulk of stone behind looks uncertain, like a mirage. It might be there. Or it might not. It might be just the ghost of its old self, massy and crouching, the stub of its thunder-struck spire instead of a dome, behind the trees.

Light at its tricks everywhere, on this day of sudden sun. A long and angular shopping mall that looks like it is made of clouds or smoke, disappearing up the street before your eyes, as if nothing here was substantial, nothing permanent. So you might see among the hurrying backs that pass, holding mobiles to their ears and gabbling to themselves, one in particular. One man, say, with a long stride, who tips himself forward slightly as he walks, quick, his sword swinging at his left leg all the time. Robert Harley, whose god is God, on his way to the Tower, to visit Prynne. Sidestepping a horse turd so that three orange flies, who have left it to the last minute, zip upwards briefly before settling again once he is passed.

Past the memory of the fishmongers trading in Friday Street, where the black cab swoops round the corner. Past the memory of the Eleanor Cross, of the pillory where Prynne hung for three days and was clipped. Over the faint suggestion of blood spilt on the ground, of the half-ear that landed among dung and mire, to be snatched up and fought over by kites. Skyed suddenly, over yellow brick and chimney pots, and then dropped again, somewhere else, to someone's surprise, because this is a city where anything, at any moment, might fall from the sky, before being swooped on, retrieved again and consumed. Swallowed like so much else. Forgotten.

*

Here one minute and gone the next which, even miles away, on the same day, amongst the blossom-covered tarmac of Surrey, is exactly what is worrying Freddy's wife, Mia's aunt Mary, until she has become just a huge pair of dark eyes, open unreasonably wide on a terror that won't go away. She has the cancer.

The doctor has said so. I had it from her last week. It's the boob. She's out of her wits with fear, poor thing. We must all bring her out of it. Get her mind off it. That is what her friends say in an ecstasy of telephoning, at length and at all hours, because life is suddenly real once more.

So here is Mary, sitting in front of a giant gin and tonic, in the window of the golf club before lunch. Freddy is out on the green bullying his way to another win. Get your hair done, he's told her. Smarten up a bit. That'll make you feel better. Pull yourself together. You're not dead yet. That was Freddy's idea of a joke. He'd laughed when he'd said it, and he repeats it now to his friends. You've got to get their minds off it, he tells his golfing cronies. They can't put these things in perspective, he says. She's not dead yet. I've booked her a private operation. The meals are fabulous. It's more like a hotel than a hospital. Try to loosen up in the elbow, he says loudly then, to one who is having a better day than usual, retrieving his ball from the hole. You'll find your swing improves, Freddy says, standing over him as he comes upright again, a little red and straining. Mark my words.

Mary has had her hair done and she's come out for lunch, but she feels terrible. She keeps glancing down at the blue angora swell of her bosom. What is it doing, the cancer? Is it growing now? Is it eating her now, inside out? She sits very still as if it was something dangerous that she was afraid to wake. She just looks nervously down. Looks down. Her eyes round and terrified. Looks down again.

Out on the green the golfers pass, trundling their bags about, climbing in and out of buggies. There is much jocularity. The wind is blowing. Someone's hat bowls away at speed, bouncing along towards the rough. It's a nice day for a change. Can't complain.

*

It is also the day for the French film with Bill and Sylvia. A session in the manuscript room, working on the Harley letters together and then a trip to the cinema. But it seems a shame to sit in a library. Having finally managed to dress and to walk Cuthbert, Mia dawdles down the Euston Road. The trees, arms raised as if in praise, hold leaf-tips and buds, antiphonal to the appearance of the sun, the sudden blueing of the sky; though the road is rushing as always, traffic careering round the corner as the lights change. People dashing across side streets in little absent-minded flurries. Hurry, hurry all the cars say while the trees go on singing.

On the other side of the road the heavy church of St Pancras sails against the traffic like a ship, its soot-blackened caryatids swathed today in polythene that flutters as Mia passes. And all along, round the endless half-finished buildings, builders' barricades stand crooked, sandbags made of plastic hessian slumped over them in exhaustion. New London growing out of the roots of the old again, like coppicing. Someone has remade the steps to the Elizabeth Garrett Anderson Hospital out of pristine polystyrene, and there is a shiny river of damp course newly painted at its feet. Lolling against the wall and raising their eyebrows, the builders take time out of their busy schedule to watch Mia on her way.

Morning darling. It could well be ironic.

When she was younger she would have cheeked them right back but she hasn't done that for a while now. She just gets past as best she can, scrabbling her body parts back together as if the builders just by looking could disassemble her. Their fingering eyes.

There are builders everywhere, come to think of it, though they are not all the same. Further on, where the protective boarding comes right out onto the pavement so the passage is narrowed to single file, Mia fails to notice that a workman carrying a battered Hoover stands waiting by a tree for her to pass. Looking up and lost in thought as always, she starts as she sees him standing there, covered in dust, his quiet patient looks.

Oh! Her hand to her chest in surprise. I'm so sorry. Thank you.

The builder nods slightly and when he answers his accent is foreign, Polish possibly, and his face looks thin under his cheap beanie hat and his eyes so tired, because of the grinding nature of his work perhaps, or because London is impersonal, or just because he is miles from childhood.

Mother-tongue-less. Disconnected. On pavements full of people speaking foreign. Every day he handles material that is hard, corrosive, abrasive, cold. He bangs things and hauls things and lifts things, all of which will outlast him. Brick and stone and concrete and dust and metal which must be worked with hard sparks that fly at your eyes. In his country there is a culture of respect for older women, so it is natural to him to wait for Mia. He doesn't even think about it. It isn't a big deal.

Chastened, Mia stops to buy a *Big Issue*, as though she could put something right for herself that way, as though she could reverse time so that it was she who waited respectfully while the builder passed. The salesman is loud and apparently unbeaten by life.

Ladies and Gentlemen, he bawls his usual patter into a flood of people coming over the crossing, Your favourite read. Get your *Big Issue* from London's only invisible man! Come on darling. You know you want to. And again the darlings pass him by. No one can see him. So no one stops. Then when Mia reaches for her purse, Thank you, lovely. You must have gone to Specsavers. Mia laughs. His irrepressibility is admirable after all. What's your name, lovely? I'm Peter.

My name is Mia.

Peter bows to her, his face florid with weather and with drink, his eyes blazing. You can't imagine how many people walk past me every day. It makes a difference if someone stops. He becomes expansive in this moment of gratitude. She's got a nice smile. It's nice to see a nice smile every now and then. These grumpy sods. Excuse his language. And the sun is shining. It is spring. Peter throws his arms wide. How about she comes down to the pub on the corner later, to watch the football. Does she like football?

I used to support Celtic, Mia says hesitating.

Well, Celtic are shite, darling, but you'll learn.

Right, Mia says, half-wishing to get on now. These encounters only ever go in one direction. Then, Who do you support? she asks, feeling bad again. You have got the time, she tells herself. Just give him the bloody time.

Tottenham, darling. Peter bows again. Tottenham's the club.

OK, Mia says, maybe. She bows back. Well goodbye then, she says.

The pub on the corner, Peter says as she moves on. She turns round, looks at him over her shoulder. It's an Invitation! He spreads his arms again and the people flood past him and Mia smiles.

OK, she says. Maybe.

He looks after her and he puts his hands to his chest, his fingers long, meeting on his breastbone. The name's Peter, he shouts. You take care now. Then Mia walks quickly on and he goes on standing with the people flowing round him, as if he were an obstruction lodged in a flood of water.

Entering the library courtyard, Mia looks up. Against the sky, there is the tracery of a construction crane, jaunty, blue and yellow like a sci-fi toy, an alien on one leg with its one glass eye looking out over the map of the world. Mia can just make out a tiny man in the cab, lonely like a god. I wonder if it makes more sense from up there, she thinks briefly. On the jib it says FALCON in giant blue letters.

Inside the library, Mia leaves her red coat in the basement and crosses the library's airy hall. She stands on the little escalator that ascends, under the modern lights and the strange sail-like constructions hanging from the ceiling, towards the library of George III. Golden, glass-fronted, a wall of books from another world, there is something almost sacred about it, as though these moving files of students were being offered up in continual oblation.

Strange, Mia thinks, that we could go so easily back to this, having cut the head off our king. As if the Civil War had been nothing; a brief illness, from which we recovered only to go on as before, picking up where we left off, plodding steadily down centuries of subservience. King after king. And now here are these books, with the touch of those pampered hands, or their greasy prints after eating, the skin, or stray hairs, preserved between their closed pages, all alarmed and kept safe behind glass. How inconsistent of us.

In the middle of her trance of amazement, Mia notices Bill, who has come out of the reading room and is leaning on the gallery stair-rail, to Mia's dismay deep in conversation with Andrea. Behind them, the portrait of Brilliana's grandson, Robert Harley, first Earl of Oxford, eyes Mia as she ascends.

Here she is, Andrea says, the Lady in Red.

Why is this so irritating? Mia's eyes follow the gold-tooled spines of the books from floor to ceiling before she turns to acknowledge Andrea's greeting.

Mia! Bill looks round at her with his usual slow delight. This is perfect timing. We are going to the restaurant to have a cup of coffee.

Well, is no one going to do any work today?

Robert Harley, whose manuscript collection helped start the library, watches them as they go awkwardly, in a three, down the stairs to the café.

Little Brilliana has a barking cough. For several nights she has slept with a poultice on her chest. She feels a constant anxiety about her brother Ned. The Devil is very real to her. And also, it is cold. Shivering about the castle through several punishing days of frost. Getting up in the dark. Everything stone hard and if you knock your hand by accident, when fetching something, water for washing, say, or carrying a dish or a pan, it is enough to bring the tears to your eyes. The world seems a sullen place of angles and corners, of cold that shrinks you to your skeleton, your shoulders strung tight in defence, every muscle tensed to preserve warmth.

Her brother's departure, which marked the end of his childhood, marks also the end of hers, although she doesn't think in these terms. Like her mother she waits till the carrier be returned with a letter. It is long, waiting.

Then on a thick day, the carrier is here again. Snorting like his horse in the castle yard. Plumes of steam coming from his nostrils, banging his hands in huge leather gloves and watching the unloading of various baskets and boxes. He has one letter for little Brilliana alone. This is more than could have been expected or even hoped for.

Deare Brother,

I take this as a very great faver from you as that you would be so much plesed as to grace me with on of your letters wich is more than every I did dedserve. I humbly thank you for it.

At night now, the little girl sleeps with the letter under her shared pillow. She doesn't tell anyone this for fear of being thought superstitious, but it is a comfort.

Christmas passes. It is mid-January and the castle is full of anxious talk. The Scottish Assembly has abolished bishops. There has been war between the Scots and the English since November. The Harleys are watchful. Changes are afoot at last. The abolition of bishops in England would be a thing much to be desired.

William Prynne has been fetched from the Tower and arraigned again for writing a pamphlet against the Bishop of Norwich. He has had the stumps of his ears cut off this time and the initials S L, for seditious libeller, branded on his cheeks. Then he was taken by boat back to the Tower. He will never be released. Idolatry is everywhere.

Deare Brother

I very much longe for to heare form you for it is a very longe time sinc that I hard form you.

My father had lately broutght him a most horrible picture of the Great God of heaven earth, the wich he brok all to pices.

I pray God all to keepe all our hartes upright unto him. Good brother labour for to keepe your harte upright unto your God for you ar in a place were is much vanity.

My Robert hath not his tethe. Thank God my sisters remember there love to you. I thank God my father and mother ar both well.

And in his rooms in Magdalen, in his newly adult life, Ned Harley's eyes widen as he reads of his father's iconoclasm. This is news that his mother's letters did not tell him. What was the terrible picture that had to be broken and where was it found? God be thanked that his father is so vigilant.

So Brilliana tells her brother, how the picture was brought up to the castle and the wrappings removed and there it lay, evil with colour, on the stones of the castle courtyard. And her father and

Mr Gower in terrible silent destruction, as if an exorcism were taking place. The waters of the Teme carrying away the sinful dust, the flakes of paint, the pieces that wouldn't break any smaller, so that one of the angel's faces swirled and bobbed on the surface, eyes fixed upward as if in prayer, until it was lost to sight in the race.

Thou shalt not make unto thee any graven image, or any likeness of any thing that is in heaven above, or that is in the earth beneath, or that is in the water under the earth:

God incline our hearts always unto you for these are trying times.

Deare Brother

The imag that I writ you word of it was found in Buckton in on Robert Matthies house. He pulkkin up a plank in his stable he found it their and he keepe it a quarter of a year in his hous and it should a been sould for 7 pounds then somebody told my father of it and then my father sent for it and broke it in pices and flung the dust of it upon the water. Good brother keepe your heart upright unto God. Watch over your heart. Wee had all need to doe so for the Dvell is ready still to tempt is. My sisters remember there love to you.

It is a soft night. The sandwich boy has just taken Layla's hand for the first time. Both of them are electric with saying nothing. Neither of them knows what the other is thinking so it is better to pretend that nothing has happened; in case he has done it by mistake. Above their heads the blossom on the trees that line the road is yellowish and luminescent, as though it were not just the lamplight's reflection but its source. It looks manmade.

The sandwich boy thinks, I'm in London, England. I'm in love. His body says to him, It is spring. Between the next two street lamps he kisses Layla on the cheek, in a questioning way. She is so young she smells of apples.

*

It is after the French film now and after supper. Mia arrives home not tired enough to sleep, although it is already late. Cuthbert has put himself to bed and raises his head at her arrival only to put it straight down again, though his eyes swivel lazily, following her around the kitchen.

I'm sorry to disturb you, Mia says with dry formality. I need tea. She sifts through her mail while she waits for the kettle. A letter from her father. She slots it into the mouth of the Dictaphone.

Halloo Mia.

Cuthbert barks at this disembodied male voice. Shush! Mia tells him, in the inevitable pause. It's only my da.

There's been rain. Sheep prices have fallen. Sheep farming is no longer profitable. Donnie Mackay has been on the phone. He's selling up. There's no money in it and his son is into the bikes, as she knows. Scottish consonants falling like a dry precipitate, but soft, in the electric late-night light of Mia's kitchen.

Mia listens, dreaming into the middle distance.

Ines is into the decorating. Spring cleaning with a difference. I hope she's not putting up any silly colours. She says you're coming down in the summer.

Mia waits through a pause that is longer than usual. That's good, her father says with a mixture of precision and caution. The new dog should be here and you can give me a hand. You were always great for the animals. Though don't come if you're busy. I can manage things fine so there's no need.

Thanks for the book recommendations.

If there's anything you want especially, for your birthday, let your aunt know. She's on at me to send something nice but I don't know what you need. Are you doing alright for cash, girl?

He believes in work. He doesn't like the idea of her living on a dead man's money. Mia makes a sound of impatience in the back of her throat.

Ines read me your piece in the paper, which was interesting anyway. You don't seem to write much since you gave up the full-time job. He pronounces it 'fool' time. Mia clicks her throat again. Let us know if you write anything else. There's often a fair few verbs missing. You're writing very loose these days girl, or am I behind the times?

Thanks Da. Cheers. The kettle is boiling urgently. Mia sighs. She listens to the silence of her kitchen. It has the same sound as static, a kind of dark fizzing, which is less the passing of time than its simple presence; the thickness of its existence.

Her fortieth birthday. So now Ines is onto it. Mia had hoped to keep it quiet. And today Bill had wanted to have a party for her.

I don't want a party.

But you are going to be forty, Mia, he had said as they drank their third cup of coffee in the gloom of the library café, in the lee of the King's gilded books. We must celebrate. I like birthdays.

Celebrate what, Mia had said tetchily, the end of possibility? The death of potential?

Come on honey, Andrea had said, her grey hair falling into the coffee. You've survived, for God's sake. You don't need to be so tight-assed about it. Look at me. I'm about to be sixty. What's wrong with forty? You're a spring chicken. You're gorgeous. Isn't she gorgeous, Wiyam?

She's gorgeous.

*

And Peter the *Big Issue* salesman, who had thought so too, at the time, but who has already forgotten Mia, lost her down the toxic labyrinth of his own mind, lies on his bed in the doss-house, slammed after the football, the exact result of which he has also lost. He is bipolar and when he reaches the top of his swing he is unable not just to sleep but even to close his eyes. Even drunk, as he is now, it is as if the world were made of blinding light. He lies on his back as if electrified, very still, his eyes seared open, with the blanket up under his chin. He breathes fast as if he'd been running. He feels a terrifying elation.

Under the luminous blossom Layla and the sandwich boy sway and nearly lose balance.

April, and there is news they are pressing for men to be soldiers. Two hundred have been asked for to fight the Scots in the Bishops' War. The strong men hide themselves for fear of being taken. All the ministers round about have been asked to contribute monies. It is a sorry problem. In Spain and in Germany there are reforms afoot. Let me upon this put you in minde, Lady Brilliana tells Ned, that this year 1639 is the yeare in which maney are of the opinion that Antichrist must begine to falle. The Lord say Amen to it: if this be not the year, yet shure it shall be, in due time.

Otherwise, the Harley family busies itself with the little concerns of ordinary life. The country is softening towards spring now and the ways have improved. The quicker pulse of a different season. Everything clean and new, and on either side of the road that the carrier travels, and in all the fields, the impossible stained-glass green of the hedges.

But in Oxford Ned is ill. For a while he tried to hide it from his family lest they worry. And it is true that hearing at last, Lady Brilliana is anxious enough to write every other day, for heatherto you have bine the great comfort of my life. In her chamber she prays alternately for his health and for strength, should the worst happen, to submit willingly to the hand of God.

My deare Ned, I hope this is but an ague, which are very much every weare; be careful of yourself, keepe a spare dyet; and my deare Ned, O that I weare with you.

Little Brilliana sees her mother's distracted looks from time to time, in moments when she is off guard. This morning she had twice to tell her there was a man come from Hereford, for she did not hear.

At last news comes that Ned is fully recovered, although when the letter arrives Lady Brilliana is ill enough herself to be unable to write by her own hand. She lies in her darkened chamber and dictates a letter. Be careful of your health for my sake, she pleads with him. I believe the sneezing powder did you noe good, and let it teach you that wisdome not to take medicines out of a strange hand. His tutor has said that he may not go home at Whitsuntide.

Almost a whole year since he left to go to Oxford. When may he return? In mid-July Brilliana sends Ned up a hat and stokens for his ride home. But still no word comes of when he will be released. My deare Ned, I longe to see you, and without your tutor seet doune the day when your father should send horses for you, your father will say the time is not yet this 3 weekes that he and your tutor agreed upon, but I was not then bye.

Another month. August, and at last he is coming.

Long before it is possible little Brilliana scans the road for a horse and its youthful rider, for the fluttering black garments of his companion. What if he is changed? Will he be changed? And how long till he will actually come? How long till Ned Harley be returned home?

The road continues empty. Its hedges either side thick in full leaf, the little birds hopping and criss-crossing, fatting themselves against winter.

Then unexpectedly they are here, materialising out of the haze of dust and distance, hooves audible on the dry compacted road, occasionally ringing on stone. He is taller than when he left and high in energy despite the journey, his cloak hung over the horse's crupper because of the heat, his travel clothes caked and the light fuzz of hair on his upper lip. God be thanked for his safe passage. It is an inexpressible delight to see him.

So the castle settles into its routine again and both mother and daughter are able to unburden themselves of all they have thought and felt since his departure. For two full months the family is complete.

But with the air sharpening into autumn, Ned leaves again for the Michaelmas term. The horses that only recently were so impatiently awaited, retreat between the hedges until once more it is just the little birds that hop and criss-cross, alighting this time among berries.

Again letters pass between Oxford and Brampton once a week. Peaceful concerns, whatever happens abroad.

Deare Ned, your letter was very welcome to me, for, my deare Ned, I cannot but say that I injoy meself with more comfort when you are with me, and next to seeing you, to heare from you is most pleasing to me. It is October. I thanke God your father is well, Lady Brilliana writes, and this day is gone ahunting, and your brothers with him, it being procured with much dificullty from Mr Simons.

Brilliana's watch needs mending. The younger boys need a schoolmaster. The fruit dishes are broken and need replacing. Little Brilliana has lost her hood and dare not tell her mother.

Deare Brother
I pray you doe me the favor as to send me a black crape hood. I praye you send me on as soone as you can for my mother will be very anger with me if shee see mee without on. Therefore pray brother send me on and send that way I pray you that my mother may not know of it.

I hop brother that you will com home at Crismas. Deare Brother I would very fain send you a token.

November comes and with it a black hood for Brilliana. Despite her care, Brilliana's mother cannot fail to notice for it looks very new. She says nothing to the child but to her son she observes, I see your sister has a new hude; it semes she lost hers and durst not tell, and so, as I gees, rwit to you for one, which I will pay you for. She is not inclined to reprove her daughter for it is nearly Christmas and Ned is again expected home.

Out of the doss-house and after his morning shift outside Euston, Peter the *Big Issue* salesman, with his eyes red from insomnia, moves through streets that to him are ablaze with white light. The light makes him giddy, so that, even sober, he sways slightly, as he walks. He goes into the pub on the corner, where he orders a drink and sits down and looks into his pint, only to find that now even the beer is on fire. The intensity of his world has him strung to the point of insanity. Today a constant humming has begun in his ears.

Meanwhile, the other side of Hammersmith, in a snake of traffic, Syl is at the wheel of a rented van. She is a good driver. The music is on loud and she is smoking with one elbow out of the window. After a while she says suddenly and a little sadly, Who are you kidding? She says it out loud. Fuck's sake.

Stop start. Stop start. Traffic lights. Roundabout. Over the flyover and up past Chiswick to the M4. Hogarth's house on a brown sign with a little picture of a building on it. She has bought a skate tunnel for the boys, off eBay, and she is driving to collect it. Mia is covering for her because there is only one of Shula, and Gabe has swimming. Mia will pick Nate up from school and give him tea for a treat in a café. She is his godmother after all.

These are the first days that spring has appeared to be even a consideration. So as Syl gets onto the motorway and puts her foot down, London, behind her, is dusty and blinking in this third consecutive day of gentle sunlight and Mia and Cuthbert are standing in the playground of a red-brick school building waiting for Nate. It is a Catholic school, which is inappropriate given Syl's own position – less lapsed than abandoned. A full and conscious collapse into atheism, Mia thinks as she waits; that's what it looks like. But Syl likes to tell people that her children are being state-educated and she is nothing if not persuasive.

So here Nate is, cocky, with a little rucksack on his back and his skateboard in his left hand, swaggering about with two boys whose mother is on a mobile phone.

Hi Mia, he says when he sees her, cool, unsurprised. When he smiles he looks like Syl. Where's my mum? Are you picking me up? He doesn't wait for Mia to answer because Cuthbert trots round suddenly from behind Mia's legs. Nate's face lights up. Is this your dog? Hey! He calls to his friends, come and see my godmother's dog. The children crowd round.

What's his name?

Can I touch him?

He's so furry. Is he a boy or a girl?

Can he have a crisp?

Does he like Haribos?

Cuthbert backs away from so many outstretched hands, from the crowding faces and the high voices raised in excitement. He stands at bay against Mia's legs.

Guys, guys, Nate says with his arms out, suddenly proprietorial. I think he's scared. Leave him. I'll talk to him. His girl's hair flopping forward as he kneels down next to Cuthbert.

The mother on the mobile phone finishes her conversation. She calls her boys without acknowledging Mia. Apple, Taylor, come on. We're going to be late.

Why did you call him Cuthbert? Nate asks Mia as they head off together, away from the crowd of slow-moving parents and children, to the bus stop. That is a geeky name.

Well you can talk, Mia says. Look at what your friends are called.

How do you mean, Nate says, looking up at her, like Apple?

Mia looks to see that Apple and his mother are out of earshot.

Well, Apple is a pretty weird name for a guy, you have to admit, she says, watching for a moment to cross. Now! she says, and they skitter over.

Well, we don't call him Apple, Nate answers when they are safely on the other side. Because that's a name for cunts and he's like my best friend.

There is challenge in his voice. He is expecting a reaction so it is tempting not to give it. Mia pauses. How old is he anyway, this little boy swinging along as if the world owed him, eight or nine or something, the same age as little Brilliana? Mia didn't know that word until she was fifteen. My ma used to say it was worth saving some things for when you're grown up, she says drily. I'm worried you'll have run out of swear words.

Nate smiles unexpectedly. They'll make some more. Probably. I'm at middle school anyway now.

Of course, Mia says. Middle school makes all the difference. They get on the bus and Nate chooses the seats. So what do you call your friend then? she asks when they are settled.

We call him Mac.

So Mac is not a cunt's name, I take it?

Nate is looking out of the window. It's the name of a computer.

The bus makes a meal of its routine journey, pulling away from each stop with the urgent slowness of dreams, idling at traffic lights with a vibration that amounts almost to a ship's rolling. The driver is chewing. In the mirror angled towards the passengers he looks unconcerned.

What about your name? Mia says to Nate after a while.

What about my name? Nate says, still looking out of the window.

I mean, do they give you a nickname?

My name's Skate Nate. Nate is a cool name. My mum chose it.

Of course, Mia says, I forgot.

Nate looks round. It's already a pro's name.

I see.

In Syl's van, the phone has rung. She picks it up without taking her eyes off the road. It is her mother wanting to know if she would like a lift to the British Association for Pharmacology dinner.

I'm not going.

There is a measured pause. All Julia's pauses are measured. That is how she never loses her cool. Robert is doing very important work on bipolar disorder. Perhaps Syl doesn't realise? He is giving a talk. The voice is clipped, brisk. Only to those who know her is the knife edge of irritation apparent. Syl might actually find it interesting. Pause. What is she interested in at the moment?

My children, Syl snaps. And the state of the planet. Her mother had used the word support. Syl grips the wheel with both hands. She hates the word support. It itches in the back of her neck. Small trees with delicate green leaves process towards a vanishing point across the flat fields either side. Syl feels herself spitting out answers as if she were a cat. Support your fucking self.

Where are you? her mother asks. You sound strange.

I'm in a van. I'm going to collect a skate tunnel for the boys so I can't go anyway, I won't be back in time.

She is driving to collect a skate tunnel? Her mother's tone is lightly incredulous. There is silence between them.

On the bus, a different conversation. So that's what you're going to be is it, a pro skateboarder?

It is as if Mia has dislodged the critical stone from a dammed pool. Nate's eyes widen and flood with excitement. She hasn't ever seen this side of him before. He talks fluently, feverishly. He uses his hands to gesticulate. Hey, he can show her, if she'll come to the skate park on the way home. Can they go to the skate park? It's near. Can they go, because he can show her if they go? It'll be quick. He has already got most of the moves. Well, not most of them because there are literally like thousands but he can do loads of the flip tricks and kick tricks, the slides and grinds and soon he thinks he will be able to do the Ollie over a chair. Well one day, he thinks. Does she know what an Ollie is?

Mia shakes her head, no, she doesn't know, unless he is another of Nate's friends. She is touched by the child's enthusiasm. She would very much like to see an Ollie. There is plenty of time.

Off the bus they head for the skate park, under Nate's direction. It turns out to be just a series of concrete surfaces colonised by a collection of low-slung, cap-wearing, mainly silent skaters. It's not exactly a park, Mia says. They watch for a moment. There is one terrifying long, half-oval slide that the skaters take it in turns to mount and then roll down, flipping their boards in the air at the top. There is not much camaraderie, or so it seems to Mia, just an almost introverted concentration on performing the trick. The only obvious rule is to stay cool, whatever falls or scrapes or mistakes you make. They shake back their hair and shrug when they come off their boards. Occasionally someone lets out a muffled exclamation, or a swear word. Otherwise nothing. Otherwise just the percussive sounds of the board rolling, the wheels smacking down, the back of the board being kicked.

Nate puts his schoolbag down. You stay here, he tells Mia.

The other boys are in their teens. Nate looks tiny. Are you sure this is OK, Nate? Mia asks. Does your mum let you come here?

Course.

Mia finds a bench and watches as Nate queues for the slide. She can't help feeling anxious and when she isn't feeling anxious she can't help feeling mildly bored. She listens to the roll, thwack, roll of the boards, the syncopated shuffle of the boarders punting themselves along to get up speed before a trick, the quiet exhalations, the rare exchange of words. She watches Nate. Every now and then she gives him an awkward thumbs-up, just to show she is still paying attention.

After a while Mia gets distracted. She watches instead the birds, the starlings that at a distance seem to be London's grime made flesh, if flesh is really what this grainy gathering together of fluff, of bits of wire and black dust could be called. Then she watches the people passing and she watches the cars, and she watches the people inside the cars, who think they are invisible and who sing and bang their hands on the steering wheel and look in the rearview mirror to check for bits in their teeth and illegally read texts on their mobile phones.

Every now and then she looks discreetly at her watch.

So when Nate comes off his board, she only catches it out of the corner of her eye, the misjudged turn and flip and the crumpled landing which scrapes his shin on the side of the slide. He slithers quickly off carrying his board, limping. He cries into the crook of his free arm. Mia can see he doesn't want to, but he can't help himself. When he reaches her bench, feeling himself far enough away from the other skaters, he rolls back his trousers to look at his leg, which is bleeding. He sits beside her, hunched over his leg, looking at the blood which clearly horrifies him. And for once, he doesn't swear. He just says, Ow! Ow! Ow! over and over, like the child he is.

Mia thinks he is brave with his skinny little shoulders in his oversized skate shirt and his baggy trousers, his trainers with the enormous soles and the laces looped, not tied. She sees how careful it all is and she tries to put an arm around him and to look in a proper and motherly way at his injury, only Nate holds himself separate in his misery. There is only ever one mother. How well Mia knows that.

Do you think you can manage to hobble over to there, look, to that café? We could have hot chocolate and marshmallows, Mia tells him. I know Cuthbert would like a bit of something. He's a great man for tea. You could give him a bit of cake if you had some.

Nate wipes his eyes on his sleeve. He puts a hand out to the little dog, looking at him, head cocked, at Mia's feet. What kind of cake does he like?

Well actually, Mia says, putting an arm out for Nate to lean on, he prefers a sausage roll. He'll eat a whole one of those if they have them. But if they don't he hasn't ever been known to turn down carrot cake, if you're offering.

They go into the nearby café and Mia orders. Where is my mum, Nate asks? What time is she coming back?

Would you like to phone her? She's been out to Reading to collect something she bought on eBay. I think it might be a surprise so maybe you weren't supposed to know but this is kind of an emergency, isn't it?

It is.

Mia watches him while he talks to his mother. He has put his foot up on the chair so as to look at the blood again. It's really bad, Mum. It's bleed down all the way to my sock. He pauses and Mia can hear Syl reduced to something so unlike herself, a tiny reedy presence coming out of the phone. I was doing a flip trick, he says. You've seen me do them, Mum. I've done it loads of times.

We are having cake and hot chocolate, he says. I've made friends with Cuthbert. Mia looks out of the window while he talks. There is a group of older children in school uniform, reminds her of herself, sitting round a table, drinking Cokes and milkshakes, their school files balanced on a spare chair. Biro'd love hearts. Me 4 eva.

What are you fetching, Mum? Nate asks. Mia says it's a surprise. The reedy voice giving an indistinct answer. Mia's here. OK. He looks up. She wants to talk to you. Bye Mum. I love you.

By the time Mia finishes talking to Syl, Cuthbert and Nate are already sharing cake, although when Nate is too slow about dividing portions Cuthbert takes decisive action and helps himself.

Hit him on the nose if he does that. That's very bad manners.

I can't, Nate says. He's too cute.

He's not cute, Mia says. He's just greedy. Go on, just give him a tap. He has to learn. Get down! she says, with her father's severity.

Can I borrow him when you don't need him?

Mia laughs. I need him all the time. You've got Gabriel and your mum and dad. What do you want to borrow him for anyway? He wouldn't be much good at skateboarding.

I could take him for a run with me, or we could watch telly? Everyone's really dumb at my house.

Afterwards they cross the square, bravely hobbling. Mia thinks it is getting colder. She should get Nate back for supper.

I won't be able to have a bath, Nate says.

No, Mia agrees, no way.

They take a taxi home, because of the injury. Mia flagging one down as they reach the far side of the square, although if she were by herself she would walk. Nate can hardly contain himself with delight. I never get to go in one of these. Mum says they are a rip-off and they aren't green.

Well she's right, Mia says, but we agreed didn't we, this is a kind of emergency.

He sits on the tip-up seat. Puts Cuthbert on the other seat.

I think he's better on the floor. He might fall off, Mia says. Also I expect the driver would prefer not to have dogs on the seats.

It's not that, darling, the driver says, watching them settle. It's road safety would be bellyaching if anyone saw. You know what I mean?

The taxi brings back Nate's swagger. He examines the buttons on the doors and talks to the driver over his shoulder. Shall I put the heating on, he says after he has pressed one with a fan design on it. The cab fills with a feeble blowing.

Tell you what, the driver says, you just sit tight chappie and leave the controls to Mum.

*

In the pub across town, Peter is bleeding from his nose. He is fighting with his best friend. He doesn't know what about, or why. Just that all that light and tension has concentrated itself into something wild, a murderous energy. He will kill something. Maybe even himself.

Wearily the police break it up. It isn't hard. Neither of the men is in good condition. Come on Peter, as if he was a child. Pack it in. How many times already? The police are heavy with kit, bleepers, coshes slung round their waists, beefy, stab-vested. Handcuffs.

247

Peter is manhandled into the back of the van alongside his mate. Shoulder to shoulder. He stumbles, partly the drink no doubt, partly the light which for the moment is still blinding. Trading incoherent insults. When are you going to give it a rest Peter? the officer asks, not unfriendly. And the other policeman turns round. Still full of piss and vinegar then? Who's your friend? Go on, introduce us.

Driving through London, to be spilt out at the station again. Put in the cooler for the night, where Peter's light switches off without warning and he feels himself staring, plunged vertiginous, into the horrors of his own darkness, down which he will fall now for many days to come.

1640. The castle at Brampton is wrapped in quiet. Lady Brilliana is unwell. Sir Robert writes to Ned, putting as good a complexion on it as he can, so that the boy does not worry.

Your good mother hath still continued in her bed since you went hence and yesterday in ye evening shee had an abortion whch ye women about her discovered to be a male. Dr Wright of Hariford had been with her but was gone before this befell her. I have also sent for Dr Deodate but shee is (I prayse God for it) now in very cheerful state. Shee sends you her blessinge and I mine.

Down the passages past Brilliana's chamber the servants move quickly, whispering instructions to each other, carrying linen often for there is much blood, carrying Dr Deodat's prescribed remedies, or cordials, or trays of broth to strengthen. And in the darkened chamber Brilliana is strengthening slowly, though she has been very weak.

Today a boy hurries out to the courtyard with two letters for the carrier to take to Ned at Oxford. The first, although written in the hand of another, is from his mother, dictated slowly in a whisper, Brilliana being too weak to sit up. The signature alone is hers, propped on the arm of one of her women, to scratch it in a shaking hand before lying back again, eyes closed.

Deare Ned

It hath pleased God that I have beene ill euer since you went; but yet I reioyce in Gods mercy to me, that you enioy your health, wch your letters haue assured me of. I thanke you for them, for they haue been sweet refreshments to me. Your letter this weeke by the carrier I receiued last night, and I blesse God that I receiue such childlike expressions of loue from you.

And here Brilliana had paused, unable in her weakness to prevent a catch in her voice, a few tears squeezing sideways out of her eyes. It didn't matter. Her women are kind and quiet. Leaning forward a moment later to hear when she began to dictate once more.

I hope I receiue the fruit of your praiers, for the Lord hath beene pleased to show His strength in my weakenesse, to enable me to undergoe such a fit of weakenesse, wch hath made stronger bodies then mine to stoope.

This day seuen night it pleased God I did miscarrie, wch I did desire to have preuented; but the Lord wch brought His owne worke to passe, and I desired to submit to it. Your father out of his tender care ouer me sent for doctor Dayodet, who gaue me some directions, and is now gone. I thanke God I am prity well, and I hope that as the Lord hath strenghened me to beare my weakenesse in my bed, so I trust He will enable me to rise out of my bed.

I was so desirous that you should know how I was that I entreated your father to let you know in what condition I was.

My deare Ned, since I cannot see you, let me heare from you as often as you can. I thanke God your father is well, and so are your brothers and sisters.

Remember me to your tutor, who I desire to remember me in his prayers. I pray God blesse you with those eternall riches of the sauing graces of His spirit. So I rest

Your affectionate mother

Here enclosed I haue sent you two letters, by wch you may know Mr Hibbons tooke a vomit contrary to all cousell, and thereupon died.

The second letter that the boy is carrying downstairs is from little Brilliana. All Ned's anxiety has turned itself into finding fault in his sister. She has been accused of not passing on the news of her mother's illness fast enough. He has written her a furious letter. How should she have kept this from him? Did she have no care for her mother? Ned can be powerfully angry. He adores his mother. What could his sister have been doing that she thought her mother's health unimportant?

Her response is a letter of anguish, full of crossings and blots, wept over.

Deare Brother

I thought that news would come fast enough to you therefore I would not send you that news but I fain to bee the mesenger of that wiche I am now of that is that my mother is better then shee was.

You say that I was busy at play and so could not find in my herte to go to see my mother. If shee has been very ille while you were at home if you can say you ever saw mee at play and could not find in my heart to come to see my mother then indeed you might a thaught so now but I am sure you nevery saw mee doe it.

You say your parents be the greatest joy you have under heaven. I would have you to know Brother that they bee as much ioy to mee as posibel they can bee to you and the greatest grive I have when they are not well. You say I shew myselv most un sister-likly to wards you that I could not have done so to the worst friend I have.

Ned doesn't respond. Going about the castle, lonely for her mother's company and care, anxious, the child carries out her grown-up duties. Once when no one is looking, she sits down on the step to the stillroom and cries into her hands in despair. She feels so lost. Three more days pass. Ned's angry letter is still much in his sister's mind. Her father is sending again so as to stop Ned from worrying. The letter is beautiful, in a secretary's hand.

Having the oppertunity of this bearer and being this morning early in my bed I rather choose to make use of R Sankie his plume than not let you know how the state of your good mother is. Dr Deodat went hence on wednesday and though shee bee not out of her bed (which is not to bee expected) yet I prayse God shee is much better than shee was.

Then at last letters arrive from Oxford, two letters, containing tender expressions of anxiety, for his mother and a stiff unbending one for little Brilliana. She hastens to reply.

Deare Brother

I am exseeding gald that I am now the mesenger for this good news that my mother is resnabel well and that my mother has rose out of her bede. I being the mesenger of this I hop it will make amens for the formore falure. Sence that you have writ mee such anger letter not having the lest spark of love in it I would bee very gald of a letter with more love in it then this last had. I hop it shall be buried in the grave of obilvone and so I rest your deare sister tell death.

And in her chamber Lady Brilliana is well enough for the moment to write a letter to Ned in her own hand.

My deare Ned, I thanke you for your earnest desire for my health. I am, I think, better for your prayers. I thanke God I am now abell to site up a littell. This day I sate up out of my beed allmost an ower. I should be glad to have you with me, since I can let your thoughts be with me. I did not thinke I had bine with child when you weare with me. The Lord bless you and make you still a comfort to

Your most affectionate mother.

*

But whatever dramas are taking place on a small scale at Brampton, like a great vat put to boil, elsewhere the country seethes and spits and bubbles. Almost a month after she miscarries, Brilliana's brother, now Lord Conway, who has only just heard, writes to Sir Robert with an anxiety that mixes the national with the domestic, because that is how things are going now. The one is so continually spilling over into the other, that soon no one will be able to differentiate between them any more, and these tight-knit families, so careful in their correspondence, will turn on each other, almost by accident, tear each other to shreds across hair-thin lines of religion or politics.

Sir

I was very sorry for the advertisement you gave me of my sisters sickness and the cause of it. Your servant tells me that you doe not enioy your health. To heare of the recovery of yours and my sisters will be very welcome newes to me therefore I pray let me have the contentment soe soone as it is possibly convenient for you.

A second war over the abolition of bishops in Scotland is planned and Conway is raising troops and money.

We have bin here very busy in the Concell of Warre, and you will shortly heare of the effects of our consultations. Five troopes are now immediately to be levied to be put into Barwicke and Carlisle, and two thousand more are forthwith to be raised, with whom I shall have some command. Sir Thomas Coniers will be Lieutenant Generall, and Mr Willmot shall be Commissary Generall.

If you think your sonne olde enough if you send him to me I will take care of him. If there be any about you that will bring theire owne horses they shall have very good pay. If they bring servants mounted upon serviceable horses fit to serve in the troop, a servant may looke to his own horse and his masters and the master shall receive five shillings the day for himself and his man.

If there be any good strong trotting geldings in your partes I pray let me know theire number and their prizes. If there were any one that were extraordinary fine I would gladly buy him for my selfe and would put him to the great saddle. I would do the like if he did pace.

Lord Conway stops writing, scratches himself. His heart isn't really in it. He is a comfortable and indolent man, a voluptuous man in eating and drinking and of great licence in all other excesses. A goose with garlick, now that is a fine thing, or for that matter, a dish of broiled woodcocks. He is not at all like his sister. He had better send what news he knows. News after all is the great commodity.

The Prince Elector is still in prison. His two younger brothers are coming from France into Holland by sea. A ship of the Kings doth goe for them. The Queen of France is again with child. That King is troubled with the gout. My Lord Lieutenant of Ireland is within ten days to goe into Ireland there to holde the Parliament. The Parliament here will holde at the time appointed. If there be anything within my knowledge that you would be informed in let me know it and you shall receive an answeare. And now I pray excuse me to my sister for my not writing and assure yourself that I am your most faythfull, loving brother to serve you.

And as Conway says, now at last, after eleven years, the Personal Rule is to come to an end. In April the locks and bolts are undone at Westminster and King Charles calls his Parliament.

Sir Robert is returned for Herefordshire and although the King's business is the raising of revenue for war, for all those who have been barred from Parliament, this is the moment to address the many terrible ills of the last decade and more. There is no appetite among the Puritans for war with Scotland. Old enough or not, Sir Robert doesn't think of sending Ned to fight with his uncle. Ship money must be withdrawn immediately. Arminianism must be put down. MPs mustn't again be imprisoned without trial. These are the matters at the front of Sir Robert's mind. He prepares to speak to the house on behalf of Prynne and his fellow authors Burton and Bastwick. He will argue for their immediate release.

But Parliament sits for under a month before the King in anger dissolves it once more. In May there are riots in London. A mob of apprentices attempts to storm Lambeth Palace in search of Archbishop Laud. In August Brilliana's brother and his forces are routed by the Scots at Newburn. It is a humiliating defeat. There was not enough money granted the army to prosecute a war effectively. This is the truth of the matter in his eyes. I would that they that spake ill of me had been there that I might have spoken ill of them, he observes in a letter to a friend. He is preparing now for a different kind of battle, for the King's fifth Parliament, in which there will be strong debate. Blood is running high in London. Sides are beginning to be clearly drawn. Bankrupt, in November the King calls Parliament again.

At Brampton Brilliana is still struggling with her own health. For barely a fortnight she will be out of her bed, before the bleeding starts again. This illness which I have makes me very weake, for as soune as I am pretty well I am ill againe. Nevertheless, her interest in Parliament and its doings remains vigorous. At last changes seem to be afoot. By December the King's two most hated and most powerful supporters, Laud and Strafford, have been impeached and imprisoned. Now Sir Robert has his way at last. Brilliana writes to Ned that his father has seen the triumphant return of the Star Chamber prisoners.

He saw Mr Prine and Mr Bourton come into Loundoun; they weare met with 2000 hoors and 150 scochess, and the men wore rosemary that meet them.

I have heare sent you the 7 articells against my Lord Straford; your father sent them me. The parlement goos on happily.

Cheapside crammed and seething. The scarred men in dark clothes riding slowly through, pressing a way through the throng. The air electric. And the mutinous cheers that greet them, and the sprigs of rosemary cast before them in remembrance. We have not forgotten. There is too much anger in this celebration.

Great events and small. Along what strange lines or paths are we drawn towards or away from each other. The chance encounters that we tell ourselves are fate. The coincidence of arrival or departure, the rhythmic loops and intersections of our meetings, and all the journeys made to land ourselves in the right place at the right time; are they governed by design, as we want them to be, or are they just chance, doodling its boredom across our lives?

Several nights pass. The hood of the sky, with all its stars attached, has slipped round and is looking half at something else with its winter face. Nate and Gabriel dream separate dreams, great uncontrollable worlds that rise differently from their sleeping minds in the same small bedroom. Peter is locked in his own dark. Layla and the sandwich boy lie whispering in each other's arms.

Overhead, there are planes flying in over England's dark patchwork of fields, the air hostesses in make-up and exhaustion clipped into seats for landing, looking out at the prickwork of lights that gather, concentrated, like a grounded galaxy, into this neon blaze, which must be London. Here are the outlying fields around the city's inflated suburbs, in the sodium night of suburban, early, spring. And here are the roads with traffic still pulsing, despite the lateness of the hour, black cabs ferrying travellers, no matter how many people are sleeping, from town to airport, or airport to town.

Here, from above, is Bill's house, much the same as others in the street, birds roosting in one of its chimney stacks, and its roof, with its tiles grimed, dotted with bird droppings. Here are its roof timbers, pocked with nails, carrying out their duty of quiet load-bearing, centuries old, and below that, the dark attic with the dust falling on cardboard boxes and broken coffee machines, and downstairs here are bedrooms, with clothes slumped over chairs, and beds not yet inhabited, because all the people are on the first floor, denying sleep in rooms that are frantic with light and music.

It is just before two in the morning and a woman is going soft down the carpeted stairs, struggling into a coat as she goes and with the furtive look of someone slipping away early, although in fact it is so late. It is Mia, following the doodle of her own life unwitting. Her shoes that were silent on the stairs, click like a clock across the stone floor of the hall and she is in a hurry to open the door and get out, before someone calls her back. She doesn't bother with the lights for the same reason.

Is this 'tight-assed' of me, she asks herself, walking a quick tiptoe now and swinging her bag which insists on sliding down her arm, back over her shoulder. It is way after midnight so it can't be ungrateful, surely? She struggles with the lock and the oversized door handle, which stick and which turn different ways, while her bag descends again down her arm and has to be slung back, before she can get the door wide enough to pass out into the dark street outside.

And there on the doorstep, in the yellow pool made by the lantern overhead, is Felipe.

Happy birthday, Felipe says. Am I too late? He doesn't seem as surprised to see Mia as she is to see him. She is, in fact, unable to do anything for a moment. Caught with the door still wide, still standing only on its threshold, she waits for her composure to return, for something to say to arrive either in her head or on her tongue.

You're not, she says when it occurs to her. It's in full swing. I just thought, she pauses and then goes on inconsequentially, I had no idea you were in England. She is flustered. It's a bit of a low thing to do, isn't it – leave your own party early. I didn't expect to be caught.

It's OK, Felipe says easily. I mean, you don't need to feel low about it. It's after midnight. I'm just sorry I'm so late.

Well, I wasn't exactly waiting for you.

I didn't really suppose you were, he says, smiling and standing aside slightly to allow Mia to pass. Mia doesn't move. She just stands with one hand still on the door and the door open. So, Felipe says, I see the marking of another year hasn't mellowed you.

You saw me last under a month ago. Mia looks into the dark of the street. It feels as though it is a long way home. Why would I have changed? She shrugs, then she stops, Sorry Felipe, she says. It is the first time she has used his name. I'm so tired suddenly.

Under the pavement a Tube train rumbles like the workings of a giant digestive system and the plane trees in the square catch the vibration, the hanging pompoms of their seed heads trembling invisibly.

Why don't you shut the door? Felipe says to Mia. Come and have a drink with me. He says it with surprising authority, reaching behind her, when she still doesn't move, and pulling the door shut himself. He has a kind of force to him that is difficult to resist, certainly tired as Mia is, and at two in the morning.

I've already had a drink, Mia says, hesitating. I've had enough drinks – too many probably. I'm going home. Then she looks at him. Aren't you going to go up? They'll be expecting you. I really don't want a drink.

What do you want then?

Mia struggles with a head fuzzed with tiredness and with Bill's wine, with the recent bright light and noise, now changed for darkness and this deserted street, and she struggles with Felipe's presence, so unexpected and so insistent. He stands close and he waits for her to answer.

She leans her body back against the door, partly to win for herself a little space. I want a cup of tea and my dog and to be able to go to bed quietly, she says.

OK, then let me walk you home.

Mia's eyes are round. It's miles! Are you crazy? It's two in the morning or something. She looks about her, as if for corroboration, for help from some unseen quarter. What about Bill's party?

It isn't miles. It's round the corner. Come on, a walk will do you good. He takes her arm. Come on honey. Let me walk you. It'll shake down all those drinks. I only got in a couple of hours ago. He looks at his watch. It's still early for me.

But you should go in, Mia says as Felipe steers her towards the street. They will be expecting you.

Felipe glances up at the lit windows of Bill's house, where every now and then a figure crosses. Mia follows his gaze and down from above the sound of music floats like a benediction. They stand listening. They'll live, he says.

So Mia lets herself be walked. I didn't have that much to drink. I'm not drunk. Do I seem drunk to you?

Felipe laughs. No, you don't actually. Not drunk enough maybe.

They pass out of the square, into a wider street where the traffic lights, like all of their tribe, are conscientious about changing, even in the periodic absence of cars, and where the black mass of a Victorian church squats on the corner with its gargoyles staring. Come in and be saved, a poster says in capital letters on a board outside. Mia walks mechanically, not thinking, just watching her own feet.

Maybe, Mia says.

To her relief, Felipe doesn't make conversation. They walk the quiet streets of Bloomsbury, their own footfalls and the occasional car the only sounds. Sirens in the distance. After what seems to Mia a long time, they join Oxford Street where the pavements are still busy. Knots of people are wandering in search of drink, or dancing, or just in search of each other, some loud, some sadly shambling and incoherent; all of them watched through glass shopfronts by the still and silent mannequins, dressed for every eventuality. Mia glances through the windows at them as she passes, their sphinx smiles and nylon hairstyles and their hands posed in 1920s gestures.

What are you looking at, Felipe asks, the clothes?

No, Mia says, startled back to herself. I'm looking at the faces of the dummies.

The dummies! What's so great about them? Look at me, Felipe says in Bill's soft voice, I'm alive. I can talk.

So Mia laughs because she can't help herself. OK. What do you want to talk about?

Myself obviously, Felipe says.

Well at least that's honest, I suppose. Which aspect of yourself in particular?

I'm kidding.

They pass a Lebanese fast-food joint, which is acid yellow and has strip lighting and high stools with chrome legs and plastic seats. Hey! How about we have your tea here, Felipe suggests. Come on. Do you still want tea?

Mia looks at him. He is crazy. You sounded just like Syl when you said that, she says, because it is true; he did. Well, it's not a bad idea, if you like. And it's so late it must be just about breakfast time. She considers the poisonous-looking interior. It looks nearly as dodgy as the cafés at home, she says. OK, why not?

They sit on the stools and order English Breakfast tea. God, Mia says, squinting in the brightness and as though she has only just thought of it. This light is murderous. I'm forty. I must look terrible.

I think you're lovely, he tells her.

Mia pushes back her hair with the flat of her hand, just the way her mother used to, in an inherited gesture of exhaustion. Don't be smooth with me Felipe, she says. I'm too tired.

You're nearly home, honey. I'm not being smooth. I mean it.

If she hadn't been tired, and if it hadn't been two in the morning, Mia would have thought about men. She would have thought about men who find it easy to say what they don't mean, and men who are tongue-tied, and who can't say even those things that they mean most, and men who say nothing at all just for fear of seeming weak. Because men, she thinks, fall broadly into these three types.

Besides, she is wary by nature and compliments come so readily to Felipe's lips. He is brimming with them.

Or is he just foreign?

But it is late and she is tired, so she can't be bothered.

By the way, she says instead, looking into the tea that she holds with both hands, how do you know where I live?

I asked Syl.

God, Mia says, are you a stalker?

After their tea, they plod up Great Portland Street in silence, Felipe holding Mia's arm lightly, because he feels her tiredness. It is a long street. I'll watch you in, just in case, he says when they reach Mia's door.

Mia looks at him, how stocky he is, how sure of himself with his shirt open to his chest and no scarf to keep out the night cold. You'll catch your death with all your buttons undone like that, is what she thinks, only for once she doesn't say it. She doesn't have the energy to be tart. There is no one else in sight. What do you think is going to happen to me while I look for my keys, she asks him, half-laughing, half in exasperation. In an empty street? Or have I missed an axe murderer in the shadows? She nods towards the end of the road, where it goes up to the Euston Road, the ghost of the turnpike in the dark.

Aren't you tired after your journey? Do you not get jet lag?

Felipe says nothing. He just stands there, looking at her with his head tilted like Cuthbert. He is stubbornly gallant.

So Mia swings her bag forward to find her keys, rummaging among lipsalve and loose change, and as she bends her head to see in the little light there is, Felipe leans forward and kisses the side of her neck. With the touch of his lips Mia stops, her hand still in her bag, her keys still un-extracted.

For Mia it is as if everything had come to a sudden standstill, as if all the traffic, the late-night taxis and cars, all the wandering people, and the unseen rats and the cats silking in and out of the shadows, had frozen, as if everything in the city had held its breath, because of a man's mouth brushing the skin of her neck. And Mia feels something inside her give a sickening lurch, something long forgotten that melts like spring. And at the same time something old and cold and made of Scottish granite says sourly and in her head, Oh OK. So here we go again. And with that the city spins into life once more.

Such complex and conflicting reactions to a simple kiss. Only with John had Mia found thought and feeling to be indistinguishable from each other, so intermixed and so in agreement that she hadn't been able to tell where one ended and the other began. But it is too late now for disentangling which voice she should listen to this time. It is already tomorrow, after all. So who's to say whether it is through complexity, or inattention, or exhaustion, or even all three, that she finds herself later, inside her flat and in Felipe's arms.

*

Afterwards, in the night, Mia gets up. She thinks she will go into the bathroom to wash maybe, to get a drink of water. But when she turns on the light into the passage and sees ahead of her the door at the other end, she goes there instead, miserable and confused, and gets into John's bed. The coldness of it, under his mother's bird stare that she can't see but that she knows is there on the chest of drawers. The mustiness. The sheets, unused for two years. She turns her head to the window where the open curtains let in the thin light of the city night. Greyish, sodium sour. She feels, as she hasn't felt for a long time, the sudden hopelessness of loss. Because there are only his hands in the end, she thinks. There is only once and briefly that one mind, his mind incarnate, expressed in that one body.

She lies flat, as if under a great weight, and lets the tears run sideways and into her hair. Come back, John. Just please come back.

Across the ceiling the long fingers of the cars' headlights sweep and sweep and Mia lies lost in the bigness of this bed, watching them and asking herself, Now what have I done? Now what have I let myself in for?

Later, dazed and unsure whether she is sleeping or waking, she sees Felipe standing in the doorway. He is looking for her. In the half-dark he comes forward and picks her up the way you might pick up a child to move it into its own bed. Mia is too tired to say anything. She just allows her head to fall forward, into Felipe's neck, allows herself to be carried. So in silence Felipe cradles her, turning sideways through the door and taking her back down the long passage to John's workroom, to her single bed under the window. And whether he knows it or not, picking a woman up and carrying her like that is a quick enough way to her heart. That is the language women speak after all, cradling. That is what they know. Down the passage, without speaking, he carries her, and lays her gently back on her own bed.

Only then, when he lays her down, does he say once and softly, He's gone baby. I am here now. Be with me. And it is as if something dislodged finally, as if in Mia something squeezed itself free at last through an impossible constriction, like a freshet bursts through a narrows, the obstruction that blocked it tumbling and rolling in the sudden turmoil of water.

1642. Brilliana is again alone. All of a sudden England is losing balance. As if it were a tray, just as the hawk would have it, the country is tipping. People are sliding pell-mell, clutching at certainties, wondering which way to turn for the best. Terrible Chinese whispers pass up and down the narrow lanes.

The King is fled out of London, to York. Sides are being drawn up. Families wake to find fault lines running crazily through their midst, a brother, a son, gone to join the opposing side. Brilliana's brother-in-law Sir William Pelham has declared as a Royalist. Almost all of Herefordshire is for the King, including the Harleys' kinsmen, the Crofts of Croft castle and the Scudamores of Holme Lacy. Brilliana in her isolation is now under constant threat. Letters are no longer carried safe to and from London. Rumour travels faster than dependable news. She doesn't know from one minute to the next what to do for the best. Should she flee, with her younger children, to London? Should she stay and arm the castle?

There is no one to advise.

16th May 1642
My Deare Sr
I am glad I have such a hand to send by as Mr Broughtons. How this cuntry stands I beleeve he will let you knowe to the full.

I much long to see you and I hope the Lord will in his good time give me that greate comfort.

I should be glad if you thought it might best stand with your estate that you would dispose of your estate so in the country that it might be to your best advantage and that I might come to Loundoun to you. I think Robine and Tom are now fite for Oxford.

You are the greate comfort of my life and therefore I can not but longe to inioye it. I doo not say this out of any discontent of being in the country for what you shall say is best I shall most gladly doo. I thanke God the chillderen are well only Doll has bine very ill and in such paine that I was faine to send for Doctor Wright. He went away this morning. I thanke God she is better. Shee had the wormes and has voided a bundance. I longe to hear from you. This day I heard from my brother Pelham. He and all his are well but I am not of his judgment. He is now going to the Kinge to Yorke.

But even as the country tips towards Civil War, still the days have to be lived through somehow. So there is rain for almost a week, and the trees darken into the heavy green of summer, and up and down the country landowners make anxious calculations about the condition of the new crop, whether it is advanced enough, about the hay, whether to cut early or late. So life goes on with the curious business of being ordinary, see-sawing in that mix of blindness and concern that people moving towards crisis always exhibit.

It is time for Little Brilliana to finish her education. She is sent to London, to her aunt Vere's household. White-faced, making her preparations, packing up her clothes, the little adult dresses, the Bible, the Book of Meditations with the beautiful embroidered cover, made for her by her mother. She has never been away from Brampton before and London is extremely far away. She is thirteen.

Now Brilliana has two children, abroad in the world, to worry over.

Deare Ned send me word whether your sister lookes as pale as shee did. I have not bine well theas 3 days, but it is as I use to be.

I hope to send you your shirts shortly. I pray God blles you and presarve you in all safety: and deare Ned, let me heare the truth of thinges, tho it be bade. We heare that the kinge will sommon all that will be for him, to come to him.

I pray God compos thinges to His glory and his chruches advantage.

It is difficult to feel safe at Brampton. When any from the castle go into Ludlow or Shrewsbury they are reviled. Brilliana writes again to Sir Robert.

Sence you thinke I neede not be afraide wheare I am I will bee of your minde and as willingly stay wheare I am as remove to any other place only I should be very glad to see you.

They are growne exceeding rude in theas parts. Every Thursday some of Ludlow as they goo through the towne wish all the Puritans at Brompton hanged and as I was walking a day in the garden, one of the maids being with me they looked upon me and wished all the Puretains and Rounde heads at Brompton hanged and when they were goone a littell further they cursed you and all your children and this they say they doo every weake as they goo through the towne.

On the faire day an unruly fellow was brought before Mr Broughton and he a bused Mr Broughton exceedingly. He sent him to the stokes but he so resisted that they weare faine to take the halbards and to watch the stokes a long time and the next morning he rane away. All night he swore against the Rounde heads.

I have not bine very well this day.

Summer unfolds. It is easier to speak frankly to Ned. He has more time than his father. She writes to him constantly, easing her anxiety.

My deare Ned – Now I thanke you for your letter by Mr Braughton, whoo brought it this day somethinge late, so that I am shortned in time to rwite to you.

I acknowledg I doo not thinke meself safe wheare I am. I loose the comfort of your fathers company, and am in but littell safety, but that my trust is in God; and what is doun in your fathers estate pleases him not, so that I wisch meselfe, with all my hart, at Loundoun, and then your father might be a wittnes of what is spent; but if your father thinke it best for me to be in the country, I am every well pleased with what he shall thinke beest.

I have sent you by this carryer, in a box, 3 shirts; theare is another, but it was not quite made; on of them is not wasched; I will, and pleas God, send you another the next weake, and some handchersher.

Your sister Doll is not well, shee has a great weakenes upon her.

And a week later; beleve me I longe to see you, and I wisch you were with me to morrow on the faire day. I hope they will be quiet, tho I somethinge feare it.

I am sorry you finde that paine in your head. I beseach the Lord to free you from it, and to blles the phisecke to you, which you have taken. I shall extremely longe to heare how you are affter it; and pray, deare Ned, send me word particularly how you doo, or elles I shall not have much contentment.

Mr Braughton is now come that he may keepe the faire quiet, and Mr Floyd has mustered up his fors.

The fair passes without incident though the Harleys' horses do not sell.

Alone in her chamber, strained, writing by a taper. I have defered rwiteing tell it be late, that I might let you know howe the faire went. I thanke God heatherto it has past quietly, but I was somethinge afraide, because they are growne so insolent.

I hope this night will be as quiet as the day has bine. I pray God blles your phiseke to you; and, deare Ned, let me know how you doo in every particular. I hope to send you your other shirt by Martaine, when he bringes up the horses.

I have sent your father a box of Shrewsbury cakes.

Just as I am rwiteing theare is a quarrel begoun.

Alarm. Raised voices in the dark, the sound of violence. Out of the window lights jog past as others gather to settle the dispute. Running feet. The nights now are seldom quiet.

For five days after Bill's party, Mia stays with Felipe in the lodgings he has behind the Tate Gallery, a one-bedroom flat at the top of a town house. She says very little. Sometimes she feels she has switched off her head and is living only in her body. At night when she lies in Felipe's wide bed, there is different traffic in the streets outside and different rain taps cold on the windowpane, or slides down the roof tiles to glug in the gutters. In the mornings, waking early because Felipe has no curtains, she is disoriented by different light, different birds flying and a view of different sky.

They eat a picnic breakfast, as if they are teenagers, of coffee and whatever they can find in the fridge; yesterday's sliced ham, or banana cake or half a fruit yoghurt each and some crackers. Cuthbert sits between them, on a double ration of titbits.

You'll get fat, Mia says looking down at him.

Felipe is negotiating a contract with the BBC, a year's filming in the Gabon, so he goes out during the day, to meet the producer, or his agent, or to plan with the camera crew. Mia spends her days walking Cuthbert through the wide quiet streets of Pimlico or looking at the sliding river. She buys odd bits of food when it occurs to her, in shops that are unfamiliar. Occasionally she looks at messages on the little screen of her mobile phone, from Syl maybe, or from someone enquiring about freelance research. Currently unwell, she types in. Sorry. Will call back in a few days. Afterwards she thinks how much her da would disapprove. To Syl she says nothing. She doesn't know what to say.

What am I doing? she asks herself at intervals, still incredulous.

Otherwise Mia watches the enormous television that Felipe has in the sitting room. She works her way through the DVD collection of wildlife films that line his shelves, his own and those of others. Distractedly and without looking, she eats yoghurt-coated peanuts or Bombay mix while the screen fills with places that show in sharp and alien light. Here are mountains that she has never seen, or shade-striped groves full of feeding deer or the slow movements of giant pandas. Here are barren places inhabited by communities of meerkats, in attitudes of attention and responsibility. Here are penguins standing sentinel over a single egg in wastes as white as lunacy.

She has the vague feeling of going back to some kind of beginning. So this is how life is, is it? I see, she says. It's fiercer, it's much more physical than I'd thought. She watches animal after animal hunted and killed; unrelenting things that drop out of the sky with the weight of stones, talons outstretched and eyes terribly focused. She watches things that spring and pounce, whose babies roll with pleading eyes, in puppy fat and fur, but who grow up with spines that flex double-jointed, at speed, and a silhouette like a flick knife. She is dimly aware of her jaws moving slowly like the jaws of the grazing animals and of her body waiting for Felipe to return. Am I hunter, or hunted?

At around tea-time, she watches strange mating procedures and wobbly births. She watches heat rise visibly from terrain that is uncompromisingly inhospitable, under fierce skies. She watches the patient progress of people who have nothing, across wastelands of sand, or rock, or snow, or tree-dotted prairie, following food or moving towards water. It is a wider world and there is so much more to survival than she had ever imagined, so many strategies, so many different ways to adapt.

What did I ever think I was doing, like a mouse, in this tiny corner? And in the end, why did I ever worry? What does it really matter after all?

In the evening, if Felipe is not back, Mia and Cuthbert turn off the telly and venture out again to walk by the Thames. Slow river, gold sometimes as if made of honey, and a nearly full moon risen early, while coloured kayaks bob and jostle, upended from time to time, like ducks. At low tide there are long mudflats, where the gulls pick at the water's edge and cry their holiday cries. And alongside, adaptably copying, pigeons tiptoe getting their pink feet wet.

Then later there is Felipe's tread on the stairs and whatever takeout he has picked up on his way home and the three of them picnic again. Mia looks at him in silence and thinks he has seen all those places, all those animals and people, all that urgency and uncompromise. She looks into his eyes as if hoping to find some trace or reflection. He is very accepting, that is all. He is more boyish than he had looked to her at first. He doesn't appear to question or to puzzle.

Is that why you don't have much? she asks him once.

Much what? he asks, fitting a whole kebab into his mouth.

Much in the way of possessions.

Well, I'm always on the move, he answers with his mouth understandably full. And I'm always broke.

Now and then, when it is mild enough, they climb out of the window onto the flat roof, to eat where they can look out over a jumble of gardens penned in by walls, with houses on every side, grown leggy like plants, as if reaching for light. They spy into lit windows at other lives, as if they were watching telly.

In the days, they are separately tranced by this discovery, this new strangeness, the compulsion of another. And at night, they spend the long and feverish hours fighting each other's bodies for union beyond the corporeal, for something that will dissolve at last this lonely singularity. They sleep damp and only fitfully.

Mia has no idea what she is doing. She hasn't told anyone where she is, so nor does anyone else.

I don't even know you, she says to him once, locked in his arms, breathing his breath. Who are you?

I'm me, he answers.

Evidently.

On the sixth day Felipe flies home. They leave his flat together in the early morning, just as it is getting light. They walk as far as the taxi rank in the Vauxhall Bridge Road, where Felipe puts down his bag to kiss Mia goodbye. He puts his hand behind her head, the same way as Bill. I'll be back, is what he says, although he doesn't say when.

OK, Mia says in return and she watches the cab edging slow into the gathering flow of traffic. He waves once and then there is just the street, full of nothing, of ordinary cars and buses, starting another ordinary day. There is nothing to do so Mia walks back towards the river and on towards Chelsea Bridge.

She goes along the quieter streets where no one is up and the pizza delivery bikes lean companionably together in crowds, the Domino bikes blue and the Pizza Hut ones red. Cuthbert meanders happily, sniffing and urinating. A flock of pigeons, strutting in the road, flash upwards with the passing of a single car, then switch undecided and steer like traffic flow round the side of a tall building. Watching them, Mia copes with the disorientation of a sudden wave of emptiness, as though someone has turned her inside out.

At every tree or post Cuthbert must stop and Mia is patient because she has nothing better to do. She stares at the ground. And all along, the streets are marked by people's nightly incontinence, as if by acid, shadow streams of urine and of vomit in star splashes across the pavement. Everything that people allow to splurge out of them in the night, like something dreamed, reduced to the merest suggestion, in the morning.

Gone, Mia says by accident and out loud. Cuthbert looks up.

Then, in Turpentine Lane, a small woman in flowered pyjamas and a battered overcoat, emerging from a basement. She is heading to the shop on the corner, for milk and a newspaper no doubt, to read the doings of the world. She wears house slippers on her feet and a bobble hat against the cold. But when Mia says good morning, she just stares back, jaw clamped, and says nothing. They walk on along the river, down past the lock at Chelsea Bridge, where a heron stands on the mudflats and a single duck paddles, self-absorbed, on the puddle the river has left behind. Mia stops again and sighs.

Then on and right at the bridge, with Cuthbert patient now. She is walking towards Sloane Square, towards Syl who won't be expecting her.

It is Robert who answers the door. Mia had forgotten that it is a Saturday. He only looks surprised for a moment. He recovers and is immediately welcoming. Come in! Come in! Come and join us. You're just in time for muffins. He doesn't ask whether or not she is expected. He is a psychiatrist after all.

Mia! Syl says, as Mia comes into the kitchen looking dazed and with Cuthbert still on the lead. Warm smell of a family not yet dressed, at breakfast; the little boys' long hair fuzzed from bed. Nate swivels on his chair. He sees only the little dog. Oh wow! It's Cuthbert. That's so cool. Cuthbert's come for breakfast. Here boy, here boy! He and Gabriel jump down from the table. See Gabe, I told you, Nate says. He's really cute and he likes cake. Leave him. I know him. Leave him Gabe, I said.

I'm looking, Gabe says, with his hand on the dog's head.

I'll feed him, not you.

For the second time in his life Cuthbert tastes muffin.

Syl too is up from the table. Mia, are you OK? I tried you but you never answered. What's up? Where have you been?

I've been with Felipe.

PART III

THE WELSH MARCHES

My heart Ned

I haue bine so longe in puting
vp the plate to send your father
that I haue no time to write
any more then that I longe so ser
you

I am Confident you are not
troubled to see the plate goo
this way for I trust in our
gratious God you will haue the
frute of it

Pray God Bless you

your
most Affectionat Mother

BRILLIANA HARLEY

I doo long allmost to
be from Brampton

I pray you
send me word
whuether my
lord Clare
be Come to
Seendain

July 9
1642
Brampton Castell

In the hampir which the Plate
is I haue sent your father a Cake
it tikes sent me Most Monday

Hiatus. Months have passed since Mia and Syl stood face to face in Syl's kitchen, in the silence after Mia told her, I've been with Felipe. How her life has accelerated into change. Sometimes it feels as though her mind is suffering a kind of emotional jet lag, an amnesia. When she wakes, for instance, and lies watching, in the light, the endlessly raining dust fall on John's books, on the silver-framed photograph that looks back at her from the shelves, as she climbs slowly upwards to consciousness again, she is aware often of her mind's settling itself, like a latecomer, into the circumstances of her present condition. Oh yes, I remember now. I'm different, though the world looks the same.

Or, when she washes her face in the green-tiled bathroom, she will stop suddenly and stare at herself, the cleanser only half rinsed off, and ask, Is this me? Is this who I am now? Though she looks unchanged. It is as if, after all this time, after all the questions that Mia's mind had asked and failed to answer, her body had simply taken upon itself the business of solving life's puzzle, as if it had shrugged its shoulders and taken the plunge and said, as it did so, The answer to life is – just life.

Now it is summer. Mia is driving and she is happy. She has the radio on and is singing loudly to the songs that she recognises, keeping time on the steering wheel, and looking out, as she passes, at the green that is everywhere. She feels like someone drinking after a long thirst. Someone drunk, in fact. Look at all these leaves, Cuthbert. For goodness' sake. Look at these fields and woods.

It is so good to be free of the city for a while.

She is going to her da's to look after him, while Ines is away at her sister's, and despite the fact that Cuthbert has been sick twice, she has made good time. She took the longer route, round the bottom of Birmingham, thinking to stop along the way, to prolong the happiness of the journey, and to enjoy these first sips of summer in fields for a change, to walk Cuthbert. She knows she needs to gather her thoughts, brace herself because it's her da's she's going to after all, and now there is another obstacle between them, something else that she will have to own up to, something else to be judged by. So, after Ludlow, she heads briefly off the A49 into the hills. I'll take you to Hopton, she tells Cuthbert, who is glooming in the passenger well, next to a small heap of sick.

Sticky weather, when they eventually leave the car and set off up the hill. Close. The ground wet with recent rain, and more to come, by the looks of things. Mia and Cuthbert walk slowly up behind the castle ruin, look at the turned backs of the hills, humped, silent, under a weight of sky. All the sounds are muffled. A soft bleating-under-blankets of sated sheep. There is a great tit hopping in the hedge when they stop to rest on the stile, where Mia finds to her surprise that time has passed. Change, only visible on the return, like a private game of grandmother's footsteps. Maybe that is why we go back to places. There were delicious blackberries here, she tells Cuthbert who is looking out at the high line of the horizon. They are setting off down the hill again to the car, when a shout from below stops them roughly halfway.

Hoi! The same sheep farmer as before comes lumbering up the field towards them. He is red in the face even at this distance, one arm flinging up in a gesture of riddance. Get that dog on a bloody lead will you! There's livestock here. Can't you see?

Mia waits till he comes level, steaming like a bullock, his hair plastered to his forehead with the closeness of the day. She feels composed. Cuthbert, unnerved by the size of the place he has found himself in, and anyway afraid of sheep, sits at Mia's feet, curled like a cat. His stillness makes no difference to the farmer, who looks at him, head thrust forward, meaty hands on his hips. I've seen a dog like that tear the neck out of a sheep before now.

Yes, Mia says, but not this one. She is unable not to laugh, at the farmer, at the idea of Cuthbert tearing at anything, let alone a sheep's throat. She should have been apologetic. She is a sheep farmer's daughter, after all. Her da would have a fit. Only the rules seem suddenly not to matter any more. Cuthbert is a dope. He's not going to do your sheep any damage, she says gently, as if to make up for laughing. I'm sorry to have worried you.

You haven't worried me, duck, the farmer answers, sleeves rolled to the elbow, red hands dangling at his sides now. It's your friend there'll be worried, and he nods at Cuthbert, if I have to take a shotgun at him. Blow his brains out. Then he leans forward, looks again at Mia. Haven't I seen you someplace before?

You have. You've seen me here, looking at the castle. Just under a year ago.

Oh, aye. He looks her over, appraising again, I thought I recognised you. A shrewd look, taking it all in, getting the picture. So you've come back then.

I've come back, Mia says, and I've brought a dog.

The farmer continues to look Mia over. You're keeping well at any rate? It is half-question, half-statement. He has a pretty good idea. He's seen them like that, the ewes, when they've taken. They get a kind of gloss on them. You can usually tell more or less.

Yes thank you, Mia answers, laughing again, because of the farmer's red and swelling physical presence, his animal frankness. She feels thoroughly sniffed over, like one of Cuthbert's meetings in the park. Well, we'll be off. Get ourselves away from your sheep before you blow our brains out.

I didn't mean to shout. Mia has to lean back. He is standing too close and there is a fair tang of the yard coming off him; checked farmer's shirt rolled to the elbow, grimy over the belly where he's been hefting sheep no doubt. He falls into step with her, as they turn to go. Only you never know, he says. Can't be too careful with walkers nowadays. You know. One minute all's peace and quiet, he says, and the next you've got a bloody riot on your hands and a dying ewe to dispatch and whatnot. It's too late for sorry, then. You know. You've got to be careful.

I know, Mia says, watching her feet on the tussocks. My father used to farm sheep.

Oh yes, I remember now, the farmer says. His great feet, in mucked-over boots, clump-clump beside her, punishing the ground with every step. You said before. Is it hereabouts he farms then, or what?

No, he's long given up. He's blind. He lives the other side of Shrewsbury. I'm just down for a visit.

They stop when they reach the gate. Mia goes on and back to her car and the farmer swings open the gate to the yard, going back to the job he'd been about to start before he saw Cuthbert gambolling, off the lead. See you again maybe, he calls over the gate as Mia walks away. Have to come by for a drink one evening, he says and he watches her walk, all the way until she gets into the car.

*

And in the car Mia is suddenly amazed, sits motionless, both hands on the wheel with the engine running, asks herself, Now what on earth came over me then? I would never have walked a dog off a lead in a stock field. A private act of rebellion maybe, against her father, a last piece of defiance before she has to sit down and take the bullying she knows she is going to get. She shrugs, pulls out, heading off on her way again. Cuthbert jumps down into the foot-well.

Mia goes back to singing, to enjoying the look of everything as they pass. The rain that had promised at Hopton, a light June rain, is now falling. Trees hang over the road in full leaf, hedges thick themselves with growth, and grass and green tangle rise to mid-calf along the verges. Even so, Mia has the window open. Coming to the turning for Myddle she descends and, as she shifts gear down the hill, she sees the spare frame of her father trudging ahead of her on the road, shoulders bent in the wet, walking with a new guide dog.

Halloo, Da. She has to lean across the passenger seat because her windows are old-fashioned enough not to be automatic, struggling with the winder.

Is that you, girl? You're well ahead of yourself. His sightless eyes, that are always a slight surprise, no matter how many times you see them, turned a bit askance because it is difficult to judge exactly where someone is, just from the sound of their voice.

That's me, Mia says. Then Mia gets out herself, to greet her father and to help with unharnessing his dog, putting it into the boot of the car. You're soaked to the skin, she tells him. What were you thinking of? His cheek is a little more sunken, cold and wet when she kisses it, unevenly bristled where he's missed in his shaving. He seems older than when she saw him last and she feels the little, familiar pang that she always feels when she sees her father after a time of absence. His hands gripping her shoulders in a momentary excess of emotion.

There you are, he says, confirming her presence with his touch. Are you properly dressed, girl? This isn't the town here. You're thin enough. Have you been eating?

She is not thin, Mia thinks, though he can't tell just from her shoulders. Mind Cuthbert, she tells him evenly, opening the door to the passenger side for him. He's in the well there, where you'll put your feet.

Cuthbert, aha. So this is Cuthbert.

A tractor passes them half on the verge the other side, toots as it passes. The driver jouncing about in his seat gives a nonchalant wave. Everyone knows blind John Morgan and his dog. John raises his hand. Who's that in the tractor? he asks.

I wouldn't know, Da.

He looks less old, sitting in the front of her car, big and spare and soaking wet. Mia pulls out behind the tractor and they make slow progress down to the village. Cuthbert, perhaps because his space is invaded by the legs of Mia's father, perhaps because human warmth is preferable to the vibrating floor of the car, jumps up to sit on his lap, which is surprising to everyone. And at the same time, because there is another dog in the boot and because he can see now out of the rushing windows and because what he can see is a place unknown to him, he sets up a steady barking.

Good grief, girl, John Morgan says, you've gone and got yourself a lapdog.

Cuthbert! Mia says in exasperation. Will you quieten down!

Cuthbert continues to bark. Well, you've a good control of him, Mia's father says drily. Then he puts one of his great hands over Cuthbert's muzzle. Hssst! he says. That'll do. Cuthbert reduces his output to a whine. What on earth did you want with a lapdog, Mia?

I live in a flat, Da. I'm three floors up. I couldn't have had a big dog.

Aha.

Luckily they do not have far to go. Here already is Glebelands, with its limes in heady flower and its houses backing onto the modest fields. Swallows skimming through the wet, and cats at windows in disgust, and the cows coping, dimly registering their brief holiday from flies. In the neighbours' window a shadow crosses. It's that daughter of John Morgan's come back again. Not before time. Poor man.

Thank God for that, Mia says, switching the engine off with Cuthbert barking again.

Give them a chance to get acquainted outside, where there's a bit of space, Mia's father says, as they let the guide dog out of the boot. So they stand in the falling rain, for what seems a ridiculous time to Mia who has forgotten how to be in weather, while Cuthbert and Saba, the new guide, go nose to tail turn and turn about. In a soft voice, his eyes looking straight ahead, John Morgan talks to his dog.

That's a girl, he says. Good girl, the O's stretched and Scottish. Good girl. His voice has great tenderness in it, when he talks to animals.

Right, he says after a while. That all seems to be OK. In we go then.

Ines is there when Mia and her father open the door to the little hall. Goodness me, you're soaked, she says when she sees them. She is bustling with lists, with plastic bags to be taken to her sister, with food in careful containers to be left for Mia and John. Soup for lunch tomorrow, under cling film in the fridge. There's a pie for tomorrow supper. There's a chicken for cooking and for eating cold after. There's sliced ham, which your da likes for tea. There's a fish pie and a cottage pie in the freezer. There's stewed fruit similarly for afters. Mia is still holding her case.

Let us get in the door, woman, John says, before you start with the instructions. Get the kettle on, Ines. First things first. He rolls his R's, very crisp, very Scots.

John Morgan makes his way through to the kitchen, sits down at the table. The window wide to the rain and the radio on. He likes to listen to the news, the shouted reports from wars that are being fought elsewhere. War is important to understand. He had a better feel for things on the farm, when death was more present. Where you've got livestock, you've got deadstock. That was one of his sayings. Hard not to feel at a loose end when life isn't urgent any more.

*

All that first evening of Mia's arrival, Ines is in a flurry. No sooner has she sat down than she jumps up again, plump hand to her chest. Oh my Lord. I almost forgot. Even while they are eating she is up and down averting disaster, remembering a shirt or a sheet that must be put to dry, moving food from one container to another.

Can you not sit still, woman? John Morgan says more than once, in exasperation. And, Aunt, I can see to it, Mia says repeatedly. I can do my da's laundry. Don't worry yourself.

But Ines is unable to stop. I'll just pop this onto the clothes rack.

Eat, don't mind me. I'll just put these last apples to stew for crumble. I'll just make that topping for you and put it in a Tupperware.

For a while Mia jumps up too, stands next to her, pleading. Leave it Aunt. Please, I can manage. Come and eat with us. In the end she gives up. She sits down with her da and they eat and Ines goes on bustling and talking, half to herself, half to Mia. How's life in the city, Mia? You look well. If I just hang this over the cooker rail now, it'll be dry for the morning.

Mia's father eats in silence. Looks like a mood's in the offing, Mia thinks to herself, looking at him at the end of the table. He dabs at his mouth sourly between each mouthful, the blind man's anxiety that he might spill something, might eat less than perfectly. It makes Mia want to dribble. She chews with her mouth open as she thinks it. Close your mouth when you're eating, girl. Or am I eating in the cowshed? Ines, give Mia a napkin.

She's got a napkin, John. Leave her alone.

Well, give her another one. She doesn't know how to use it.

Oh yes, Mia thinks, it's a mood alright. Ines has gone back to her twittering. For all the years she has lived with John, Ines has never noticed that a woman fussing is the one thing he can't stand. Mia's mother never fussed. Whatever it was that there was to do, birthing a lamb, your arm in up to the elbow, feeding extras when help arrived suddenly, for shearing, or dipping, coping if John had to be away for some reason or other, no matter what, she just did it. Well someone's got to do it, she'd say matter-of-fact, instructing Mia, Quick girl, fetch your da's vet bucket. Get these potatoes scrubbed. Get your bike out and pop to the shop for me. And if Mia sighed, or made a fuss, Well it isn't going to be done any faster for you sighing over it. Get on with it, girl.

She's a miracle that woman, Mia's father would say, though never in his wife's hearing. You'd better follow her example, was what he meant. You'd better live up to that.

Now he pushes his plate towards the middle of the table, gives his mouth a final savage dab. What we need in this house is a few less women. And Mia can see him thinking, If I'd had a son now . . . if I'd had a son.

If you'd had a son, she thinks grimly, he'd have been blind too by now, most likely, and then there'd be two of you to look after. But as usual she doesn't say it.

After supper they go and sit in the living room with the two dogs and to stop her father from finding Ines too troublesome, Mia offers to read to him. What'll it be, Da? Do you still get *History Today*? I could read you a bit of that? But her father is not easy to placate. He's read everything. He wouldn't be able to concentrate anyway with that clanking going on in the kitchen. All that clucking and flapping. Good grief, what would there be left for her to do in a real crisis, he wants to know. Just a bit of peace and quiet, that's all he asks. Just a few less women in my life.

Right, Mia says, undaunted and speaking sharply to him at last, well without Ines you'd have a pretty uncomfortable time of it, Da. You should be a deal more grateful. There is silence between them for a moment, while Mia holds her breath. It is always dicey, speaking your mind to your father. But Mia really doesn't want to argue. I've an idea, Da, she says next, more coaxingly. Why don't I read you some of the life of Brilliana I've been helping with? Would that maybe interest you? I have it in my bag in manuscript. It would be helpful to know what you think.

Well, he says, one way of wasting time is as good as another.

So Mia fetches the manuscript, held together with elastic bands, and she settles on the sofa opposite his chair. I'll read you the introduction Da, and you just stop me if you think of something better to do.

Mia has a good reading voice, low and strong, and she's done this on and off for years now, reading to her father what he can't any longer read to himself. Outside the rain lets up at last and the day slowly closes.

Well, aha, is her father's comment as Mia finishes Bill's introduction. He blows his nose.

Is that all, Da? Mia says. Just, Well, aha?

John Morgan looks with his sightless eyes down at the long hands spread on his knees. He nods his head from side to side in a grudging little movement as if weighing something up. It's a slow start. He's not got anywhere near the matter. He clears his throat as though something sour has filled it. You may as well go on.

Ines has taken her fussing upstairs so it is quiet, just the carriage clock that measured Mia's childhood, going on with its work, ticking its small brass tick into the room, second after second after second.

*

Across the middle of England to its off-centre heart, Bill, unaware that Mia is reading out the words he has spent the last year or so writing, sits in sandals with the long windows open to the city's night. He has music playing and he is trying to read. He hates to be alone. He picks up the phone on the desk, dials, waits.

Hello, he says simply. Then he says nothing more.

Hi Dad.

What are you doing? he asks Syl slowly after a while. She is not doing anything much, watching telly with Shula because Robert's back late. Is Mum back?

No.

Then after another while he says, I miss Mia you know.

Dad! Syl says, but it's too complicated to go into. Fuck's sake. Then she says, Well it's not for long. I miss her too but she'll be back soon, and she does have her own family. You aren't her dad. She has a father, you know. She has a dad already.

I know, Bill says. I just hope she's OK. I feel protective. She's vulnerable.

She's fine, Syl says firmly. She's absolutely fine.

I know, Bill says and his voice is sad. You're right. Then after a while he says, But I don't think Felipe is going to look after her. Pause. Do you think he will look after her?

286

No, Dad, I don't. Syl is not at her most patient. That's not the point though, is it? Mia doesn't need looking after. She's fine. Like I said. I know her, Dad.

I'm thinking of offering her the ground floor here, Bill says, very slowly, as though he hasn't heard. Sylvia's message doesn't suit him. Do you think she'd like that? To live in, I mean? I think she should sell that flat. It's too lonely. What do you think?

I think it's Mia's life, Dad. If she's lonely then that's what she's chosen. Syl sighs. It's a sweet offer, Dad. I just don't know if it's practical. You haven't asked Mia. Mia's a loner. She's fucking contrary. She seems OK to me. And I mean – she ruffles her hand back and forth through her hair, one eye on the telly – I mean, what about Mum? She's not going to want someone downstairs. You know what she's like.

Bill says nothing but he stays on the line. He looks at his feet under the desk. His toenails need cutting. OK Syl, I'll think about it.

OK, Syl says. Just make sure you get it straight about who it suits. Is it Mia who needs company or is it you?

In the square outside Bill's window, the big plane trees are heavy with leaf. Another summer under way. Maybe it suits us both, Bill says, unable to bear the trees' renewal. It could be convenient. Two birds with one stone, you know. She could be quite separate. He is silent again. She could pay rent.

Dad! Syl says, in exasperation. I am not talking about this now, OK? Just think it over and talk to Mum first.

OK OK, Bill says. He pauses. What are you doing now?

I'm watching telly with Shula. I told you. Watch some telly Dad, or read a book. Mum will be back soon.

OK, Bill says, defeated. He hangs up and just sits in his sandals, looking at the unusually clear surface of his desk. He is always depressed when he finishes a book.

*

And in the house in Myddle, Mia has finished reading Bill's first chapter. Brilliana has been born in the garrison at Brill. James I is on the throne in England. The clock continues its job of measuring.

Well, Mia's father says, clearing the sourness at the back of his throat again. You could have done it just as well. If you'd been bothered to get off your backside, he says. Cuthbert, who seems annoyingly to have taken to her father, has jumped into his lap and is curled with his chin on John's knees, watching.

So that's what this is about is it, Mia says, sparking briefly into irritation, because she's tired, because she could be in her own flat in London, or out among people who actually like her. You think I should have done it myself? Is that it? Well that's a load of rubbish, Da. And what's that dog doing on your lap?

He's your dog, her father says. You tell me. I don't know what you wanted with a lapdog at all, Mia. I've no idea. His great hand curls soft round the little dog's tummy, although his head is held forwards, in an attitude of attention and uncompromise, concentrating on the middle distance, as though his mind was made up. You tell me, girl. There's no dogs on laps in this house.

Mia laughs at him. She can't help herself. And you're pretending you don't like that dog, she says to him. You've been wanting a lapdog yourself to pet all this time. You miserable old hypocrite, she adds, only in her head. Look at you. Daft bugger, she would like to say to him, in the language of her childhood, because that is what her father would have said in her position. Or, you're soft. Only she'd better not swear in front of her father. Wash your mouth out, young lady. If you're wanting a clip round the earhole you're going the right way about it. So she keeps it to herself and instead she just asks him, Will I read you another chapter since you're enjoying yourself so much?

Aha, he says. Let's hear it then. What's he called, this writer fellow, did you say?

He's called Bill Radic.

That's a foreign-sounding name. Foreign, is he?

He's Croatian. He came to England in his early twenties.

John Morgan rubs his chin, considering.

Croatian, you say? He makes it sound like he is hawking. And what is going through his head is, What side was he on in the war, and he knows the answer. And although he doesn't ask the question out loud Mia feels it, because she knows her father, his xenophobia, his set judgements of other nations because of something that happened when even he was a child. She feels stubbornly loyal to Bill. He's very clever, Da, she says defensively, her eyes pricking. And he can play the trumpet. I'll read something else.

This is going to be a hard week.

No, you won't. You'll read that. Read away, girl.

So Mia lowers her head and lets herself be bullied. She reads the manuscript of Bill's book to her father, just as Bill had laid it out to her over lunch at Cliché Corner. She reads about the England of the early 1600s, about the diplomatic comings and goings, boats going fearlessly back and forth to the port of Brill, about the court of James I, about Puritanism and the hope invested in this new king, about Brilliana's early childhood and about the Harleys setting themselves up in Herefordshire, through marriage, through local politics. And although she knows the book, although she has read it before, been over it and over it with Bill, still his careless elegance, his flowing sentences, catch her up as if they were music and she reads with absorbtion, forgetting her father and his prejudices, losing herself for a moment in Bill's telling of the story she has lived with so long.

From time to time Mia looks up from her reading to see how her father is taking it.

He listens with his head on one side, shaking it every now and then, when there is something he doesn't like, nodding and murmuring agreement occasionally, sometimes just giving an audible intake of breath. He listens, as he always does, with extraordinary attention, head cocked, one hand limp on Cuthbert's tummy.

When Mia finishes for the evening he is silent in contemplation.

Quite interesting, he says at length, leaning his head back against the chair and making a mouthful of the R's in interesting. I grant you that.

Mia has the sense not to react. They sit in silence for a while. At ten, Ines comes in to say goodnight and to turn on the news for John, and when the news is over, he clears his throat and asks, So, who is this Bill? How did you come to meet him?

Mia waits for what seems like a long time, the clock's brass seconds falling into the silence. He is my friend, she says. He's Sylvia's father, you know? Who I told you about. Then she says bravely, because for goodness' sake and there's nothing to lose – And he was John's best friend. The single syllable of John's name, which is the same as her father's, dropping between them like a stone.

I know him through John.

Even to herself her voice sounds high and defiant. She looks at her father. It was going to be John's book, she goes on, more quietly and as much as anything just to stave off the moment of her father's response. It was going to be John's book, only he died before he could write it. Bill took up where he left off. So the research wouldn't be wasted and to get over his loss. She doesn't say anything about her own loss. Even so, this is more than she has ever said to her father about John.

Aha, her father says softly and bends his head and there is another silence. Nothing. After another long while he leans forward to turn off the radio. I'm sorry about your John, he says quickly and very matter-of-fact. He clears his throat again.

Your John.

Mia's eyes fill. So little and so late, but still, so much more than she expected. She says nothing at all. She could say, It's alright, Da. She could say, I'm OK with it now. Because she is, she thinks. She has survived. She has more than survived. But she says nothing. The way her father is, saying nothing is always best.

But he is so many years behind. This absurd game of catch-up that she and her father are playing; it would be natural to tell him about now. She ought to tell him about now. She would like to. He is all the family she has. She looks at him, sitting in his chair, trying in his cussed way to make his peace with her, trying to understand, in his doubly dark world. I don't want to risk it, Mia thinks. Now will have to wait. There's still time.

Would you like to take the dogs out? she suggests instead.

They walk out arm in arm, the sky still clouded, so no stars and a thick dark, like a blanket. A solitary car goes up the main street. In the village houses the lights are on. It is quiet and it smells so fresh. Mia breathes. It smells lovely, she says. You have no idea, Da. The town is terrible. It really stinks.

I can believe it, girl.

*

Later, when Mia is alone in her room, thinking about readying herself for bed and feeling physically tired and yet not ready to sleep, she stands and looks at herself in the mirror over the basin. The challenge of being with her da; why they do this to each other, tussle, tear each other apart. Just as she had done when she'd been a child, always pushing it, she never knew why. To make her da angry maybe. Driven to antagonise him because her mother never would. Driven to rebel. Even if she got a smacking.

Like a bottle of pop. What'll I do now, she used to ask herself, to test him. What'll I do to use it up, all this fizz, this energy to annoy? And then she would think of dares for herself. She would go out with Spey down to the illegal river say, which was death itself, to puddle the edges into places for tempting loach, to wade along, bending under branches trailing flood-wrack, or to chuck stones and slip by accident, heart beating, in the dusk, and get a soaking to the waist. Oh my God. I was nearly drowned, Spey. I might have got swept away. Now I'll be for it.

How did you get so wet?

I slipped in a puddle.

That's a very big puddle. Do you think I was born yesterday?

Don't you ever lie to me, young lady. There's no such thing as a secret. Her mam tight-lipped. Good grief, you're going the right way about it and no mistake. Do. You. Want. Your. Da. To. Hear? with a space between every single word. Yes. I. Do. Let him give me a smacking till kingdom come. See if I care. But then her teeth would be chattering with cold and her mother's hissed reproaches were on the whole a better option than smacking so she'd shake her head. No Mam. Sorry. Not that her mother wasn't capable of administering a sound smacking if the mood took her, only that her punishments didn't carry either the formality, or the moral terror, of her da's.

So now she feels unstrung by her father's sudden apology. He has never, in living memory, ever, apologised before. Well Da, she says to her reflection, maybe it's a start. She leans her forehead against the cold of the mirror for a moment. Maybe now everything will be different, and she feels, oddly mixed and like a bubble in her throat, elation, apprehension. Mia turns away from the basin and checks her phone for messages because the signal is so uncertain here, intermittent, if at all. Feels the pull of this new gravity, which is Felipe, tugging at her inside out. Two messages from the paper. A new research job. One from Syl. Nothing from Felipe.

And what do you want, she asks herself in irritation. Do you want to go getting yourself dependent on another man? Is that what you want? And a yearning part of her says, yes, oh yes, that is all I want. That's the only thing there is, after all. And the rest of her thinks, oh for goodness, sake, and for how long? In the washbasin mirror, she looks into her own eyes, as if they were the eyes of someone else. Mia. Get yourself together.

The words to an old song come back to her suddenly, she doesn't know why. When she was still a child, about the time of the expeditions to the river. Her mam at the upright piano, head turned to look at Mia, little, maybe six or seven in a pilled jersey, delighted. I'll sing you three oh. Green grow the rushes oh. And Mia would thrust her tummy forward, shout out, What is your three oh? The piano banging and her mother singing.

Three, three, the ri-vals. That was the three of them, antagonistic, independent, bound together. Her father in his chair in his farming clothes, legs stretched to the hearth. Cut that racket out. Haven't you got something useful to do? And the piano would be closed because they always did what he said, though not until her mother had finished the song. Slower and slower to the last line and with emphatic enunciation.

Two, two, the lily-white boys. Clothed all in green i oh. One is one and all alone and evermore shall be so.

She always sang the song to the end. Then she would get up from the piano with dignity, as though a flag had been placed, a piece of ground claimed. One is one, Mia remembers now. All alone. Evermore shall be so. She sang it triumphant, hammering out the notes in defiance of her husband's wishes, to keep herself going no doubt, however many chores there were to do unquestioning, however many lambs to birth, however much she was ordered to stop singing, to get on with it, to pool herself together. And suddenly it comes to Mia that this was a declaration, her private assertion of the irreducibility of the individual. That was what her mother had been expressing. Her creed, wrapped up in a nonsense song, sung to her little daughter and her exacting husband; a hymn to freedom.

Mia looks out at the night. Well, well. And I always thought that song was about loneliness.

How could you possibly sleep with your brain whirling like that? So Mia takes a leaf out of her own book as a child and decides to go out. Downstairs she and Cuthbert go, stealing so as not to wake anyone, hoping that Saba will not bark. Like when Mia would dare herself to go out, with Spey for protection, to face the hill in the dark with all its host of horrors. Then she'd walk her small self over the stiles in the dry-stone walls, with the wind in her face, and the playground stories jumping in her neck. There's a murdered man gets up and walks around, all covered with blood. There's a beast. There's a ghost that if you see it you die. There's a dead baby with no eyes that cries. And she'd walk with her hand on Spey's collar, till she found in the end, each time, just the hump of the hill, rising stubborn and empty against her, solid, always itself. Just turf and tick-filled bracken after all, and the wind passing over. So she could go back to bed in triumph. I did it. I did it. I walked the hill at night. You lied. There was nothing.

Mia finds her father's key and clicks the door as softly as can be managed behind her and heads up the road towards the church and the stump of the castle. Some childish, fear-facing, remnant makes her go through the lychgate and up the gravel path, yews bulking alongside and the church tower looming. She walks round, past the little walled graveyard overflow and on to the stile, which she knows is at the back, and up and over and into the field beyond, all tussocks and thistle, where sheep have replaced the cows of last year. And here she thinks she will just walk until her brain stops whirling and tiredness overtakes her, or until she hits the road that runs on the far side to loop back to the village. It is easier walking home on a road when you are tired.

Thick, thick like a blanket. Even her feet on the road muffled to nothing. The rain has left everything swamped in itself, inturned, as if the heaviness of the sky kept every sound dumb. Just this thickness, this closeness, and occasionally a bird or animal surprised. Where she walks by the wall, for instance, a pigeon rises heavily from its roost with the sound of its opposite, something falling uncontrolled through leaves and branches. Mia strikes out, across the open field.

She walks as fast as she can, given the dark, and rhythmically, to lull herself. What a so-and-so her da can be when he wants. How will she ever survive this week? And then it comes to her suddenly that maybe even he is not as certain as he'd like to be. Maybe he would have been something other than a farmer if things had been different for him. She doesn't know what thwarted ambitions he might have had, to be something else, to live another way.

He hasn't let her know him. He's able enough. A teacher maybe, or a doctor, an engineer, or a writer, a historian himself, if he hadn't had a farm to inherit. Mia has no idea. She lifts her face to the starless sky and thinks how unfair life can be, equipping people for paths that they'll never be able to follow, disappointing them as often as not, locking them into these lives they didn't choose.

Am I choosing? Or is life just happening?

And next Mia thinks of Syl in her pyjamas, her hair standing on end, shorter than her children's, of her pleasure and her generosity, that morning when Mia arrived unannounced at breakfast. How Syl had thrown her arms round her, had hugged her. I knew that was going to happen, she'd said. I'm even jealous. It's so great, Mia. It's fantastic. Now you're properly family.

But I'm not anything, Mia had said, pleased despite herself but so dazed at the speed with which her life had changed, struggling to be realistic. I mean, we aren't even together.

Syl had made coffee, shambling round her kitchen. Of course you are, she'd said, so matter-of-fact. I can tell. It's perfect. I know both of you so I can tell. You're both fuck-ups. You don't want convention. It's perfect. This is so great. We have to celebrate. What can we have, she kept saying. And the little boys and Cuthbert got under everyone's feet until Robert took them upstairs to dress, with the promise of a trip, so that Mia and Syl could have breakfast in peace.

The point is, Mia had said when they were gone, he's gone back to New York and I don't even know him. It was just . . . I don't know. It was just five days.

Well, it wasn't just five days to Phil.

How do you know?

I know. That's how. He's my cousin, don't forget. He asked to be invited to your birthday, Mia. He organised his meetings round it. Dad loves you. I love you. And now Phil loves you. Of course you're family.

But he doesn't know me.

Mia, will you shut the fuck up? What is wrong with you? What does he need to know – your favourite colour? He really likes you. He told me. Stop putting obstacles in the way of your own happiness, will you?

Dawn for Mia comes, very slow, from behind the wood on the rise above Myddle; thin, as if someone had simply diluted the night until it was nothing more than a grey wash. One or two birds, hesitant, in the tops of the trees and then a little later, a rush of birdsong tipping itself out over the morning like water, and the light comes up properly and in the farm kitchens the lights are on and people are nursing quick cups of tea in their working clothes, standing up with one eye on the fields.

Mia is sleeping deeply, her eyelids flickering with dreams, her body doing what bodies do without the help of a mind, breathing, circulating, decaying and renewing, building bone, breeding cells. Cuthbert lies on her feet, his consciousness closer to the surface, one ear responding to the sound of a tractor in the lane outside.

In the kitchen downstairs, John Morgan, who is unable to break the habits of a lifetime's farming and who anyway enjoys this, his only few moments of independence in the day, is drinking tea that he has made for himself. These are the hours when he talks to his dead wife. Well, she's home, love, he says in his mind. She seems happier. Because he's not a fool and he is aware of what Mia has been through, even though he found himself unable to help, unbending in his judgement of her various choices. She's got herself a dog, he says, a silly little thing. Then he relents a little. Reasonably companionable.

Sooner than he would like, Ines appears. She has got what he would call a bit of a flap on. There are suddenly a quantity of her own garments to be ironed before she leaves. Isn't it always the way, she asks no one in particular. You always leave your own things till the last. John doesn't answer because now that he is no longer farming he would gladly do his own things at any time, if he could, only he can't, so it is a stupid question. Ines puts the ironing board up in the corner of the kitchen and gets to work still in her dressing gown because she knows that her brother-in-law can't see that she is not yet dressed.

It is over an hour later that Mia, risen early for her, having set an alarm, appears dazed with sleep despite a bath and fully dressed, Cuthbert trotting at her heels.

Morning Mia. Morning Cuthbert, her father says in his hours-awake voice. And Ines says, Look at you all dressed and ready to go, as if Mia were six years old and needing a packed lunch for school. Complicated responses to both these greetings move in slow procession through Mia's mind, too slow to articulate. Morning, she just says and concentrates on making it across the kitchen to the kettle. She is feeling ill.

What will you have to eat, Mia? Ines asks, dashing away at a blouse with the steam iron.

Oh nothing, thanks, Mia says. It's too early yet.

Her father is sitting over eggs and bacon and toast and tomatoes and several other oddments from the night before, re-hashed potato, mushrooms. Get something sensible down you, girl. You are getting fussy in your ways. You're up too late these days, that's what.

I'm up in plenty of time, for what I have to do Da, Mia answers calmly. Would you have me up two hours earlier just to sit and twiddle my thumbs? I go to bed later than you anyway.

Were you out for a walk last night, her father asks, or was I hearing things?

We went out for a late-night breather, Cuthbert and I, Mia says evenly. That's all. We'd done too much travelling. She looks down at Cuthbert who is eyeing John's new guide dog on her bed in the corner and giving a little whine every now and again. Has Saba been spayed, Mia asks her father.

She has. Is your man interested?

He seems to be. What's up, Cuthbert? Will you just settle? Will you settle down?

They drink their tea for a while in silence. On the eight o'clock news, politicians shuffle and sidestep, their voices smooth, over policy fudge and U-turn. Look, they say, when they particularly need to obfuscate, and, With all due respect.

Mia dreams out of the window and listens to the news with only half an ear. She gets up to make herself more tea. When is she going to tell her father about Felipe? Maybe she should say something before Ines goes, get it out of the way. You'd as well eat something, her father tells her. Put yourself some bacon on while you're up. What do you want to go getting thin for? Is she thin, Ines? he asks his sister-in-law.

She's just so, Ines says with her customary reflex for conciliation and without looking.

The telephone rings in the little hall outside. Shall I get it for you, Aunt? Mia asks because Ines has walled herself in with the ironing board.

Bless you, Ines says, flustering with the iron and the board and the unfolded shirt. I'll be right there. She is easily made breathless.

Mia goes out to the hall with Cuthbert in attendance. Picking up the telephone, she glances back at the kitchen window and the fields beyond, at the slow business of grazing they contain, and giving her father's number in the rising tone of 'can I help you?' she hears, uncharacteristically hesitant, because he wasn't expecting it to be Mia who answered, the voice of her uncle Freddy.

He sounds caught. Is that you, Mia? he asks, his voice halting and needing clearing. Mia holds the phone and stares at the window and waits without replying. This is her uncle Freddy, after all, with his hands and his car and his springy body hair. You'd better face it, dreamboat. You don't have a lot of options, with his fingers probing. Your genes aren't clean, dreamboat. Who's going to want you to have their baby? And Mia feels the bubble of elation in her throat again and as she looks out of the window she says very slowly, Hello, Freddy.

And now Ines has come to the doorway into the hall and is looking anxious. She makes nervous movements with her hands, rubbing them together as if she were washing.

I am fine, thank you, Mia is saying almost primly into the telephone. She pauses just fractionally. I am expecting a baby.

It is as if the little house, turning on some invisible axis, has caught itself and swung to a stop, as if it held breathless, counting seconds in limbo, before setting off spinning again, only faster this time, whirling, almost giddy, and in the opposite direction. Mia stands holding the telephone to her ear with the sound of her own sentences fizzing in the air around her. She looks at her aunt who is still in the doorway, swaying very slightly, with her mouth open. She looks at her father who is sitting at the table, his hands either side of his empty plate, his blind eyes turned towards her and it is to him that she says, in answer to Freddy's question, He's a wildlife film director. He lives in New York. He's younger than me. He's delighted.

No, we aren't married.

I don't know, Freddy. I will be a single parent. I have a dog now. Mia looks down at Cuthbert. It is a mad conversation but she feels very sane. She feels light enough to float. She feels as though something huge and weighty has slid off her back, something that before had bowed her to ground-staring immobility. It is my life, she is thinking, and I am living it. She has a moment of wishing that Bill were here to see her. Look Bill, I am doing what you said. I am living just like you told me to.

I will pass you over to Ines to talk about travel arrangements, Mia says out loud. Give my love to Aunt Mary. Tell her I am sorry for her trouble, and even as she holds the telephone out to Ines she finds herself thinking, in surprise and as if she were an observer, How composed I am. And she walks back into the kitchen. She puts her hand on her father's rigid shoulder. Will I make you a cup of tea, Da?

They hear Ines say very quietly into the telephone, Good Lord, Freddy, I know as little as you. Mia is my family now and I'm not about to start with the judging. Freddy, it is clear, has found the words that were not available to him when he was talking to Mia. She's a grown woman, Ines says. A child is a child, Freddy. Then she puts the phone down and goes upstairs.

For a long time Mia and her father sit opposite each other drinking their cups of tea in intense silence. Mia wonders whether her aunt is crying, wonders in this new position of strength and composure whether she should go up to her, which of the two of them, her father or her aunt, needs her presence most. Then her father clears his throat. He looks small and very old. Your mam was expecting you before we got married, he says, in a wondering voice, as if to himself.

We're not getting married, Da.

Aha. Well, that's as maybe.

A while later, the morning of her revelation, Mia leaves her father readying himself for his walk and goes upstairs to her aunt. She knocks softly at her door and, without waiting for an answer, goes in. She pauses fractionally on the threshold because the room is so much her aunt's, so light, so coloured compared to her father's. It has Irish linen cloths on the chest of drawers and the bedside table and an armchair in bright blue flowers and cushions on the bed to match, and there are photographs of Ines and her sisters everywhere. There are no photographs anywhere else in the house. There is no point in photographs now her father can't see. He has one in a frame by his bed that he fingers on occasion, a snapshot of Mia as a little girl leaning against her mother's side on holiday, on a beach, but that is the only one.

As Mia had suspected, Ines is crying.

Are you crying because I've shamed you, Aunt? Mia asks her, sitting down on the bed at her side. I'm sorry if I've shamed you.

Ines reaches for her hand. Oh no, pet, she says, her crying if anything increasing. I don't know what you know, but your ma came to me when she was in the same position. I'm remembering your ma that's all, and now Mary's dying. It can't be helped and Freddy won't have it but you know, she is all the same. I'm just crying for my sisters. I'm not crying for you. I'm crying for them.

And Mia has to take Ines into her arms as if she were a child. There isn't anything you can say. She knows that well enough. So she just sits with her, rocking her a little, instinctively and without noticing, and looks over her head at the tops of the trees in the sun. And she too thinks of her mother, because this is a new bond between them, ever since she has known she was pregnant, since standing with her back to the bathroom door, holding the plastic indicator, that worked like the magic painting book she had as a child, where you washed water over a picture and the colours came up, pale and miraculous. She had waited, staring at the little window as the blue line innocently materialised and she had leant her head against the cold tiles and looked at it and looked at it, unable to stop the sick excitement that rose from somewhere deep below consciousness, that beat its wild pulse, and coursed through her body. I'm pregnant.

It's done. It's too late for thinking about it any more. I'm having a baby.

Ever since then, she has wished more than ever that her mother had survived to be with her now. I feel so sick Ma, she will say to her in her head, as she gets up in the reeling mornings, or I feel so sleepy, in the heavy evenings. Now she misses her fiercely, feels again the unfairness of her loss. Was it like this for you, she would ask if she could, when you were expecting me?

She had thought with relief sometimes, Well, this is something that I spared my mam at least, the shame of a bastard in the family. Because her mother's family was so Catholic. She had expected disapproval. She had awarded herself disgrace.

So when Ines wipes her eyes at last and blows vigorously into the handkerchief that she keeps always up one sleeve, Mia sitting at her side says, So tell me how it was when my ma came to you, if you can, I mean. I don't want to upset you, Aunt. I'd just really like to know.

Oh well, Ines says, still holding Mia's hand, she was so like you, you know. She was proud and she was very headstrong but she was frightened, because the times were different. She was in a lot of trouble but she just kept saying how pleased she was. I know I should be ashamed, Ines, she'd say to me, but I just feel excited. I just can't think of it as a bad thing.

That's how I feel, Mia says. I feel so excited.

Well, it is exciting. A baby. And there's all this death. And now a baby. Ines shakes her head. It's wonderful news, whatever anyone says. But for your ma, well, our father wasn't having any of it. He threw her out. He didn't even want to know John when they were married and then your other aunts wouldn't speak to him. They cut him off, until your ma died.

Oh them, Mia says in disgust. They're terrible. They used to ring me up, you know, just to disapprove I think. I got a phone that shows the numbers on it when a call comes in, so I wouldn't need to pick up. They never have anything good to say about anyone.

They're a pair of old crows. You don't need to listen to them, Ines says with her tiny mouth pursed. They were no use to John when Kath died. No use at all.

So you aren't disgusted at me, then? Mia asks her aunt.

And Ines takes Mia's hand again, in both of her own this time. I'm not the least disgusted, Mia. On the contrary. I'm delighted. Oh I'm delighted.

Mia thinks, not for the first time, how big-hearted her aunt is, her dedication to her sisters, to her blind brother-in-law, to Mia herself.

And what about Aunt Mary and Freddy? I gather Freddy wasn't best pleased, Mia says.

Well, who gives a blind tinker's cuss for what Freddy Moy thinks? Ines says, using an expression that Mia hasn't heard since her mother died. Freddy's not worth the consideration.

This is outspoken of Ines, who is always so moderate, always conciliatory, to a fault. I wonder what you do know, Mia finds herself thinking, although the whole question of Freddy is suddenly of no importance to her any more, his dry, caught-off-guard voice on the telephone, so sneaking, so underhand. That's done with now, she thinks. That's finished.

So tell me about the baby's father, Ines says. It will be tough on you, pet, if you're doing it on your own. How is the father? Is he pleased himself, and will he help?

Mia looks at a picture of her mother, young, smiling, in her teens maybe, that sits on Ines's chest of drawers. I don't know, she says slowly.

One is one and all alone and evermore shall be so.

*

In the afternoon Mia drives Ines to the station in Shrewsbury, leaving time enough for Ines to get a few bits and bobs before the train. Shrewsbury is soft and cried-out after yesterday's rain and they walk, because the streets are steep and Ines is afraid her good shoes will slip in the wet, arm in arm between the newsagent's and the chemist and the little gift shops, looking for things to cheer Mary.

It's a treacherous place this, Ines says, looking down at the sheen of wet on the pavement.

Would you say so, Aunt? Mia says, smiling.

I would. A starling scoots rudely in front of them to land over the door of the shop they are passing, flirts its tail, makes a splash on the threshold. Its wings almost brush Ines's face. See, her eyes say to Mia as she startles, her mouth clamped shut, what did I tell you? All around Mia the snippets of conversation that are either absent from a London street, or else subsumed in the volume of life, the roar of traffic, the many, many, hurrying feet.

Bit of an improvement.

What's that?

I say it's a bit of an improvement, on yesterday.

Oh yes. A woman wheeling a basket stops, a little breathless, in the middle of the pavement. It's an improvement, she says to the man who has accosted her, but I'm not that impressed. Mind you, it's meant to get better. The wet doesn't do me any favours.

Mia and Ines have to separate, as does everyone else, to get round them. No one seems to mind. Morning. Morning. After you. Well Else, the man is saying as they pass, don't go getting your bikini out. There's more to come at the end of the week, so they say. I'm not complaining. We need it. We do need it.

Oh we always need it, Else says. It's what we want we don't get.

A dog tied up, waits for its owner to buy a paper. Next to it a pre-school child with a lollipop shoots passers-by, while his mum reads the notices in the window. Nearly new, collapsible stroller. No job too big, too small. Wanted: caring homes for spaniel/collie crosses. An old man with a stick inches past the child, raises his stick as he goes, shoots back. Time was. I remember when. Hallo Charlie, he says to the dog.

Did you say you were over the twelve weeks, Mia? Ines asks.

I'm over the twelve weeks.

Well then, I'd better start knitting.

So they stop at the knitting shop. A female prison warder, in uniform, is coming out, inspecting a newly purchased ball of multi-stripe wool. Well, Mia thinks, you need something to do while you're imprisoning people, I suppose.

What will it be, a hat, a jacket, a blanket? Yellow, because we don't know the sex yet, do we?

Oh Aunt, Mia says, please, anything so long as it isn't one of those insipid baby colours. Red or green maybe. I don't know.

Well, green is good and Irish.

Or orange, Mia says, picking up a ball that looks like it's on fire. What about this orange? That's a beautiful colour.

Good grief, Ines says, well that's a gypsy colour and a half. What on earth will your da say?

My da's blind.

Mia! What a thing to say, her aunt says, taking the orange wool out of her hand. Shaking her head, looking at it. That's not one bit the colour for a baby. And Ines might have tried to talk her round, to the primrose yellow she is holding in her other hand, only there's a train to catch so instead she just gives her head another shake. You're so like your mam. Oh dear. You're just so like Kath. She looks again at the ball of wool. Well, if that's what you want, pet.

So they buy the wool and the needles required and a pattern for a jacket and then they walk arm in arm again, downhill to the station, where Mia fetches the bags and settles Ines into her reserved seat and watches, from the platform, the small round figure of her aunt carried, waving, away.

Well, that's that.

*

Later, at about tea-time, Mia looks out inadvertently, as she busies herself in her father's kitchen, sees a mottled sky above the field and the far wood. The sun, which is still too dilute to break through, has patterned the cloud with channels of watery light and the cows, as if sap-stoned, just chew with their eyes glazed and stare at nothing. Mia stands, looking. This sky is unbearable. She's heard nothing from Felipe for a while now. She puts both her hands on the counter, her arms straight, her head bowed between her shoulders, reeling suddenly with – what? Loss, apprehension, loneliness, longing? Or maybe just the cocktail that pregnancy is infusing in her system.

Deare Sir

I should have bine glad of a letter by the carrier but it semes your biusnes would not give you leave to rwit.

It is enough for me to thinke how much I desire to see you. It is too much for me to tell it. Every on thinkes theare paine most and thearfor I thinke you can not desire it so much as I doo.

Minutes pass and Mia lets her head hang. She is just waiting for the weakness to subside, that's all. She can't even picture where Felipe is. She has never been to the Gabon.

I can not so often as I desire inquire after you in this kinde and that makes me laye holt on every opertunity to tell you I longe to heare howe you doo and more to see you.

*   *   *

307

She lifts her head, puts one hand across her belly, an involuntary gesture of protection. His emails to her are hurried. They can't get the shots they want. A whole lot of equipment fell in water. They are in danger of going over budget. One or two lines, late at night. And she has nothing to tell him in return. Long-range communication loses its point after a while.

Pool yourself together. Mia looks again at the sky, wipes her eyes with a tea towel. Bastard, she says under her breath and puts on the kettle. Her da feels his way in from the sitting room. Is that the kettle I hear?

It is, Da.

Are you singing, girl? What's that you're singing? He stands with one hand on the door frame.

Sorry, Mia says, looking up again, I didn't realise I was doing it. She is chopping carrots. Cut. Cut. Cut. It's Green Grow the Rushes Oh. I've had it on the brain this last day.

Aha, her father says. Eight for the April Rainers. And Mia puts down her knife and turns to him and laughs out loud. Now what's got into you, he says in genuine surprise. Mad, this daughter of his. Where to goodness is Ines when he wants her? He can't have this, singing and laughing at nothing, going on for a week, although he doesn't say so.

Nothing, Da. I'll make your tea. It's just, trust you to notice the line with the weather in it.

Starve to death without the weather, girl. And don't you forget it. He goes out again, groping his way along the passage.

One is one, Mia who is now two, sings loudly while she makes the tea. She bangs the cups and cupboards about, thinking of her mother, who has sent, unbidden, this small comfort from beyond the grave, passing it on as it were, for her to sing to her own baby, to the other One inside her. If she's a girl I'll call her Kath.

How women find their strength. While Mia makes the pigeon steps her peace-bound position requires and thinks them big enough, elsewhere, women in war zones, or in extremity, or under oppression, take a stand, in gas or in bullets, speak, with their own voices, their own convictions, shoulder their lives.

Slowly and by imperceptible degrees Brilliana readies herself for sacrifice. Her physical strength gathers and with it her determination and her self-reliance. All her decisions are her own now. One is one. There is no one to help. The whole of Herefordshire is for the King. Brampton, alone, is for Parliament.

Lately, Sir Robert, who is gone to London, has written requesting that plate be sent up without delay, to raise cash for an army, but Brilliana is reluctant to comply. Should she, or shouldn't she? She has a cautious practicality about her now. She wishes instead to arrange to borrow money, for we doo not know what straits we may be put to, and therefore I thinke it is better to borrow whillst one may, and keepe the plate for a time of neede. Deare Ned, she asks, tell your father this, for I have not rwite to him aboute it.

Daily, Brilliana battles with a queasy fear, strengthening herself for what is clearly to come.

Since your father thinkes Heareforsheare as safe as any other country, I will thinke so too; but when I considered how long I had bine from him, and how this country was affected, my desire to see your father, and my care to be in a place of safety, made

309

me earnestly desire to come up to Loundoun; but since it is not your father's will, I will lay aside that desire. But deare Ned, as you have promised me, so let me desire you to let me know how thinges goo.

I thanke God I have bine very well, and so well, that I am abell to goo abroode.

I have sent you a shirt and hafe a dusen handcherchers and some powder for your hair.

I had no letter from your sister this weake. I hop the horsess are com well to your father: and by this carrier I purpos, and pleas God, to send the 2 pistolls you rwite me word your father would have, and the gillt plate which he has sent for.

Your brother Tom has bine extreme ill, and it pleased God, that doctor Wright was with Mrs Litellton, and so came to see me as he went home, which I thought fell out happily for your brother. Yesterday I was exceeding fraid of him, but this day, I thanke God, he is better, so that I hope Docter Wright may leave him to-morrow. He fell sike on tusday last; so that, deare Ned, I finde that on trubele foolows another.

None of the Castle can go to town now without there being a fight.

Mr William Littellton being at Loudlow last weake, as he came out of the church, a man came to him and looked him in the fase and cryed, 'roundhead'; he gave the fellow a good box of the eare and steep to one that had a shuvell and tooke it from him and beat him soundly. They say, they are now more quiet in Loudlow.

And on another day Brilliana's kinsman Sir William Croft pays a courtesy call, but he is the enemy now. He is stiff, withholding. He never asked how your father did; spoke slightly, and stayed but a littele. I never hard of a man so changed as they say Sir William Croft is. He gave me a slight visit.

I feare your father dous much neglect himself. Deare Ned, put him in minde of eating in the morning.

I pray God derect your father and the parlament what to doo. Your father they are growne to hate. I pray God forgive them. My deare Ned, I am not afraide, but sure I am we are a dispised company.

I doo long almost to be from Brompton.

I am not afraide.

I have often toold you, I thought you would see trubellsome times; but my deare Ned, keepe your hart above the world, and then you will not be trubelled at the changes in it.

By the enclose paper to your father, you will knowe how poore Hearifordsheare is affected; but, deare Ned, I hope you and meself will remember for whous caus your father and we are hated. It is for the caus of our God.

I sent Samuell to Heariford to obsarve theaire ways. He had come home last night, but that he had a fall from his hors and put out his shoulder. He tells me that they all at Heariford cried out against your father, and not one said any thinge for him, but one man, Mr Phillips of Ledbury.

Who to trust? I could wisch that my cosen Adams weare out of the howes, for I am perswaded he will give the other side what assistance he can.

And if Brilliana is to stay at Brampton, the castle must be armed. Shot for cannon must be made, a force must be equipped. They need muskets, gunpowder and match. She doesn't wait for instruction any more. She makes her own enquiries.

My cosen Davis tells me that none can make shot but thos whous trade it is, so I have made the plumer rwite to Woster for 50 waight of shot. I sent to Woster, becaus I would not have it known. If your father thinke that is not enoufg, I will send for more.

I must needs thanke you for your two letters this weake; for, beleeve me, in this trubellsome time and your fathers absence and yours, your letters are of much comfort to me. My deare Ned, at first when I sawe how outrageously this cuntry carried themselfes aganst your father, my anger was so up, and my sorrow, that I had hardly patience to stay; but now, I purpos to stay as long as it is poscibell, if I live; and that is my resolution without your father contradict it.

I cannot make better use of my life, next to sarving my God, than doo what good I can for you.

You're like a man with a thirst on you, Mia says to her da, as she makes them tea on the third day. She is referring not so much to the tea as to his compulsion for the talk radio. Its voice endlessly monologuing in the small kitchen. This is Mia's father's world, a world entirely made out of sound, where the confines of a room, or a country, or nation state, the evidence of this time or that, are all notions, just compartments he has made in his mind, differentiated from each other by a patchwork of conditions, remembered, or imagined, from programmes he has heard over years of blindness. He has the ability to listen that only comes from deprivation. While it talks they drink tea, sometimes together, sometimes apart, all day until they are awash. Her father is listening.

What's that, girl?

I say you're like a man with a thirst on you, the way you listen to that radio, Da.

I've eyes in my ears, he answers, head held up, shoulders still square, like a coat hanger, as Mia hands him his electric razor. He shaves himself by feel, at the kitchen table. There's a world out there, Mia. A man needs to keep himself informed. Oh yes, a man, Mia can't help herself thinking.

My deare Ned, I can not thinke I am safe at Brompton, and by no means I would have you come downe.

I wisch you with me, but dear Ned, I am glad you are at Loundoun, becaus that is a safer place.

I have receved the box with the 20 bandeleres, but the boxes with the muskets and rests the carrier has left to come in a waggon to Woster; he promises I shall have them shortly.

Turn it up a bit will you, her father says. The buzz of the razor setting up competition with the news. Then when he has finished shaving and is sitting stroking his chin for places he might have missed, he mutters to himself more honestly and with a hint of bitterness, It's my freedom.

And Mia, who is too sharp ever to miss anything, stops, holding the cups in her hands, and looks at him. She sees him there, upright, his back not touching the old kitchen chair, sightless, everything about him alert, critical. Sure, he wasn't this sour when Mam was alive. She sees suddenly the man that circumstance has made him, how prisoned, still feeding himself the world, still considering and taking positions. He's very self-respecting all the same, she thinks with admiration, almost as though she were seeing him for the first time, very undaunted. She just stands looking at him, while he listens and passes his hand back and forth over his face, round his mouth, over his neck against the direction of the hair growth, looking, looking with his fingers. It's always good to have an opinion, he says as if to compensate for a moment's weakness, his voice distorted by stretching the skin on his chin to check for stubble.

Haven't you enough opinions to last you the rest of your time? she says briskly, banging the cups like her mother used to. Talking their language.

There's nothing wrong with opinions. They don't cost anything and they keep you a foothold in the times.

Here I have sent you a coppy of the sommons was sent me; that if I doo not give them my howes I shall be proseeded against as a traytor. I heare theare are 600 soulders apointed to come against me.

Where's that tea, girl? Are you growing it yourself?
So the radio stays on, day and night, for the whole of Mia's stay.

314

It informs the kitchen about the world even when there is no one there to listen. It tells the cupboards and the sink and the electric kettle about how we live, about the smallest and most trivial of our ways as well as our moments of tragedy or drama. It is her father's only extravagance, a combination of proof that there is still a world even though he can't see it, and distraction from his condition, insurance against resentment. In her room above, all through the night, Mia can hear it talking into the dark below. Shipping forecasts in a voice from the 1950s. Discussion. Opinion. Radio drama. *Book at Bedtime.*

And then again and again, more or less hourly, news is relayed in neutral tones, and people are called to account in interview, and global crises are endlessly debated. Strained reporters shout into the kitchen from areas of conflict or natural disaster, revolution, hurricane, earthquake or landslide. The collapse of mines or of systems of banking. Explosions. Pandemics. We can't know for sure what will happen from here, the reporter will answer at the top of his voice, to the silent arc of the mixer tap, gleaming in moonlight, a drip gathering in suspension on its lip. He has to shout to be heard over the crackle of gunshot, or of forest fire, over chanting, or dull explosion. We still don't know what the outcome will be, but one thing is becoming certain. We are looking at the unfolding of a humanitarian crisis here, in wherever.

Here at the house of a Roundhead gentleman the Cavaliers had their whores, they spent and consumed in one night 100 load of corne and hey, made great fires in the closets and threatned to burne his servant William Cooke, divers books, and writings of consequence which were left in his study, they tore and burned, and lighted tobacco with them, and some they carried away.

They brake downe his parke pale, killed most of his deere.

For the first few nights the radio keeps Mia awake. She can't make out what is being said, just the importance of it all. The reporters' voices at full pitch demanding her attention, crafting their bulletins because this is their art. The rolling cadences of devastation. As if through words, through exaggeration and the sounding phrase, we could somehow get our heads round it better. This is me, they say, closing with urgent solemnity, so-and-so, reporting from the front line, anywhere in the world.

Every now and then, in the small hours, Mia will hear her father go downstairs, hear the scrape of a chair as he sits down to listen, or the wheeze of the tap if he turns it on for a glass of water, re-assuring himself that the world is still out there. Like her own John, he drinks tea through the night. When he was farming he never had trouble sleeping. He was too dog-tired at the end of the day to keep awake but since going blind, he can't get enough exercise to make his nights unbroken. Mia lies, pregnancy making her wakeful too, listening to the sounds in the kitchen below. I must take him on a long walk while I'm here, she thinks, rolling over and willing herself to sleep.

Always, when she arrives down in the morning, her father is there at the table ahead of her. She comes in dazed, a little cross sometimes that Cuthbert trots straight to her father, jumps into his lap even at the table.

Why is that dog on your lap, at table?

You tell me, girl. He's your dog.

Cuthbert and her father have an understanding. For several days the sun shines unbroken. The cows in the field beyond gather at the fence and look over into the poor little garden, as if they too wanted to hear what the radio has to say. Mia spends most of her time in the kitchen. There isn't a great deal to do because Ines did everything before she went, but the kitchen is where her da expects a woman to be, and somehow it is easier than brazening it out in the little parlour.

Slack time. Making tea again. Listening to the radio. Now, curi-ously, although it is Felipe she misses, the man she talks to is John.

I'm pregnant, John. I'm sorry to say. Although I'm not sorry.

He leans in her imagination against the counter, in his thin clothes, in his socks, his face held forward, listening, in that way he had. His hair no doubt standing up. Because he ran his hands over it, back and forth, when he was thinking, and he will always have been thinking. How strange that he should be here, after all this time – having searched so long for him elsewhere. How strange to find him now, in this kitchen where he never came, where he was never welcome. Sleeves rolled, slim arms crossed. She doesn't put words into his mouth. She just sees him. Just tells him things. We're at war again, John. For no better reasons. As she shakes the tomatoes for lunch out of their box in the fridge, unwraps the pork pie. I'm remembering what you said before, about the women nursing its causes in the home. I'm wondering. You have the same name as my da. I know you know that. He's no easier but I'm getting to care less. It doesn't matter any more.

The radio gives another report of a guided missile strike that has gone wrong and Mia's father comes in for lunch. He doesn't wait to be called. Lunch is at quarter to one and it better be on the table. More often than not, they eat in silence, the radio doing their talking for them. Often, as Mia can't help noticing, the voice coming out of it is Scottish.

Have you noticed that Da, how many of the presenters are Scots?

Why do you think I have it on? her father answers. Very capable people, the Scots. Reminds me of home.

Then they will eat in silence again. I don't know how Ines stands it, Mia tells John as she washes up.

From time to time, the doorbell will ring, or someone will rat-tat-tat with the letter box and a neighbour will be standing, partly out of curiosity, because life can be unrelieved sometimes in small villages, partly no doubt out of kindness.

I'm Robyn, from over the way. I said to Ines I'd look in and see how you were doing. And then Mia has to ask them in and more tea has to be drunk and the weather or the news, or most likely both, must be alluded to, though neither ever really discussed. It is a fine line between conversation and discussion. After a day or so of this Mia's natural impatience gets the better of her.

How about we get out of the house for a day or so, Da? It's great weather for it. We could take a long walk.

To her surprise her father seems pleased. They spend whole days making planned explorations of the countryside, consulting the walkers' Ordnance Survey beforehand, trying out footpaths and bridleways. This is grand, John Morgan says once, as they pull, arm in arm, up the road to Newton on the Hill, where Richard Gough lived once and wrote his history, I'm just about getting the lie of the land now.

I should have done this with you years ago, Da. I feel that bad, I didn't.

As usual and all the time, Mia describes the land on either side to her father as they go. At his request she assesses numbers of livestock, proportion of clover to grass in the grazing meadows, picks hedgerow flowers and offers them to him for identification. They stand in the sun on the single-lane roads and Mia gets her breath back, watching him looking at the flower with his fingers, scenting it, considering. No, he'll say often in frustration. I can't do it.

Yellow rattle.

Yellow rattle, aha. Then he'll feel it again, try to find some identifier, smell it more thoroughly. Often though, he will know. He says the names matter-of-fact, in as scientific a way as possible. A vetch of some sort. Ragged robin. Knapweed.

These little roads, these quiet places. It's a strange thing to think of civil war here, Mia says when they reach the hamlet of Newton on the Hill. Don't you think?

Although Richard Gough's war was a quiet affair, like his place. There were twenty men went to the war from these villages, Myddle, Marton and Newton. Thirteen of whom were killed.

Thomas Formeston of Marton, Nathaniel Owen of Myddle, Richard Chaloner of Myddle the blacksmith's son, killed at Edgehill, Reece Vaughan a weaver from Myddle and John Arthur, servant to Richard Gough's father, both killed at Hopton, cutt in pieces after the siege, Richard Jukes and Thomas Jukes, one of the many, and on and on.

Now the village is silent, heavy with summer. No one around as Mia and her father stand and picture it before, in the war, out of the way, the last to hear what was happening in the country at large. There was only one skirmish that Gough recalled, more a village argument than a battle, while he was a schoolboy at Myddle, under Richard Roderick.

But the schoolmaster was conscientious, so the boys saw almost nothing. He commanded us boys to come into the church, soe that we could not see the whoale action.

Straining their ears to hear, in the church's cold interior.

A regular looter, it is told, an Irish cornet, Collins, a garrison soldier for the King, came as he often did into the parish to take away cattle, provision and bedding and what he pleased. He threw the blacksmith's best bed into the pond, thinking it not good enough and later, having his horse shod, was taken for someone else and a brisk young fellow shott him throw the body with a carbine shott, and hee fell downe in the same pond as he had previously cast the looted bed.

So the only death in the village was a muddled accident, just a village grudge between cheats and thieves played out under the title of Civil War. No echo now, not even the water-ring ripples of the lives lived here, of the people who knew these buildings, who must have gone daily in and out under these stone archways and small doors, or who trod these lanes and fields, homeward in dumb exhaustion.

Or of Gough himself, when his time came, walking slowly back, stopping and putting out a hand, as if in intimation, before something happened. Standing in the stone archway with his heart squeezing in his chest, as if the Devil himself had hold of it. God forgive me. Lamb of God that takest away. Our Father. And Richard Gough had fallen then, on the cobbles of his own yard, where Dorothy, who will never marry now, found him later, stone dead and with a look of puzzlement on his face.

Mia and her father go on again. Just this lazy-making sun and a single cat sleeping in the middle of the road.

*

In the evenings, pleasantly tired at last, Mia reads to her father from Bill's manuscript. It's rough Da, it's only a first draft, but it's something to read and it's about these parts.

It is indeed, her father says. Read away, girl. I'm all ears.

They sit in the parlour after they have eaten, with the windows wider than Ines will ever allow and Mia, having known Brilliana so long, goes back to the beginning, reading through the early years of dependence and uncertainty, through pregnancy and childbirth, under siege in the home that is too new, long before she is truly so, at the mercy of fear, or baffled by business, or just incapable of escape from this life she could never have imagined or adequately prepared for.

She reads Brilliana's loneliness in her husband's long absences, and her father listens, the passionate phrases of her letters raining down on his blind head.

Allas my deare Sr, I knowe you do not to the on halfe of my desires, desire to see me, that loves you more than any earthly thinge.

She does a deal of complaining, is all he says.

Is that right?

And on another occasion, later, after a competent description of stock managed and rents taken, of a horse rejected – he is hansom but has no pace and thearfore I bye him not – Well, I take my hat off to her, Mia's father says. She's shaping up. He shakes his head as he reconsiders. She'll do all right yet.

320

Right you are Da, Mia says. Will I read on?

One night, the telephone rings while Mia is reading, too late for it to be Ines. Her father stands and feels his way out to answer it. This is something she lets him do for himself in Ines's absence. Let it alone, girl. That woman thinks I'm incapable, he'd said the first time it rang. Mia can see he likes doing it and besides she is too tired to get up after her day of walking. This time it is someone her father doesn't know. It takes her a while before she realises, to her surprise, that it is Bill.

Aha, indeed, her father is saying in a polite voice, well it's nice to meet you, so to speak. There is a pause and Mia can't hear what Bill is saying. She holds her breath wondering whether her father will give Bill a piece of his mind over some small thing. But no, he seems almost deferential. She's here, he says. She's well. She's walking me off my feet. I'll hand you over. Then, while Mia gets up, she hears her father clear his voice and say almost shyly, We've been reading your book. Another pause. Oh no. Not at all. It's very interesting. The Scottish R's rolling. Pause. Aha. Longer pause. Mia stands at her father's elbow. Aha. Is that so? Well, we'd be delighted to have you down here sometime, if you think of visiting Shropshire. Aha. Well let us offer you a bed, at the very least.

Mia takes the receiver. Bill's familiar voice at the other end of the line. She forgets to be surprised that he should ring her here, that these separate ends of her life should be so casually, so smoothly joined. But Bill is family now. Her baby's great-uncle. And he is taking Mia's pregnancy as though it were his own daughter's. Mia, your father says you are walking? You're not getting tired?

I'm fine. It's good for me.

London seems so far away, such another life from the quiet routine of her week with her father. I'm resting Bill, and I'm getting some air. I feel well.

As usual Bill is in no hurry. Mia watches the cows and listens to his familiar voice. He just wanted to check that everything was alright, he says. He is thinking of coming to see Brampton for himself. Her father has asked him to stay.

Mia looks back into the sitting room at her father. I think my da would like to meet you, she says with amazement in her voice.

Well I'd like to meet him, Bill says back.

But this is their only interruption. Otherwise Mia reads on, through Ned's early years, his quickness and cheerfulness, Brilliana's growing absorption with him in particular, though with all of her children, her growing in strength and stature, her example to her family and to the community, her certainty.

My deare Ned, I thanke God I am not afraide. It is the Lord's cause that we have stood for.

Until they come at last to the moment of crisis, to her shouldering, even in failing health, the captaining of the castle. The discovery at last of her full authority, her diplomacy, her skill in managing the little force at Brampton with the enemy shelling the castle and its officers, her head cool, under threat of her life.

Mr Phillips is full of corage and so is all in my house, with good Doctor Wright and Mr Moore, who is much comfort to me. The Lord direct me what to do; and, deare Ned, pray for me that the Lord in mercy may presarve me from my cruell and blood thirsty enemies.

Periodically Mia's father will interrupt. Have you your feet up?

I'm fine, Da.

Her father takes to sitting not in his usual chair but on the small sofa beside her, mainly, Mia thinks, so he can check whether or not her feet are up. He reaches out every now and then, pats his hand down her legs to where they bend at the knee. Put your feet up when I tell you to, girl. Mia laughs.

They're my own feet, Da.

You'll be glad of the rest when the baby comes. I can tell you. It's a good deal of work raising a baby. You'll be wanting help.

OK, Da.

Then in exhaustion once and suddenly afraid of what she has unwittingly taken on, Mia lets her head sink on her father's shoulder. Alright, sweetheart, he says under his breath, or is she hearing things? With her feet up and a day's walking behind her, it gets harder and harder to keep her eyes open. Twice, in these evening sessions, the words on the paper start to slide and what she reads loses connection with what is actually written and her head sinks in sleep.

John Morgan just sits, a woman's head, his daughter's this time and after all these years, on his shoulder again. He doesn't move. He just sits as the evening lengthens, listening to Mia breathing.

Well, he says in his head, to his dead wife, the cart is well before the horse, but we are having a grandchild. We are having a grandchild.

In the kitchen a man is closing his report on a terrorist attack somewhere on the other side of the world.

August comes with its heavy trees and its roads breathing permanent clouds of their own dust. It is as if the ground itself is unsettled. The King has raised his standard and now the country is at war with itself. Parties of horsemen move with urgency between the hedges.

At Newcastle, the King's German nephew, twenty-three-year-old Prince Rupert, arrives by boat from prison in Linz. He brings with him his brother Maurice, and the companion of his years in prison, a white hunting poodle called Boye. With their own band of trained soldiers they ride across country to join their uncle at Leicester, where Rupert is immediately made General of Horse.

News filters back along the roads and ways of England of his victories, his foreign fighting methods. He becomes a terrible symbol to the Puritans of all that they most fear, his cold glamour, his armour and his bedroom curls.

He is rumoured to have burnt Birmingham to the ground.

Slowly the King makes his way south. Prince Rupert is impatient and easily frustrated. There begins to be division about strategy. Should they descend on London like a whirlwind, or should they act more cautiously, consolidate? There is a stand-off at Turnham Green and London is not taken.

News is sporadic and often conflicting. It is impossible to know exactly what is happening. Brilliana trusts only her husband and her son. Any information she has that she can be certain of she sends on. There is much rumour and superstition.

It is said the Antichrist walks abroad. Now are God's elect to be truly tested.

In a meadow just north of Hereford, for example, two standing stones, used as flood marks for the water meadows, are said to have been removed to about twelve score paces distance, and nobody knows how. The common opinion is that they were carried thither by the Devil.

Even the educated believe this. William Westfalling, a gentleman, rides to the meadow to see the stones for himself before writing to let his friend know of the horrors afoot in Herefordshire.

My kind love and service remembred to you and your good wife, these are to let you understand of a strange thing which happened upon Wednesday was sennight in the daytime about 12 of the clock, a mighty wind did drive a stone as much as 6 oxen could well draw six-score yards, and ploughed a furrow a foote and a halfe deepe all the way it went, and another stone which 12 oxen did draw many yeares since, was carried the same time a quarter of a myle and made no impression at all in the ground.

The serving man of a local gentleman, James Seaborne, riding to Hereford with his head full of the Antichrist, saw one of the stones, while he was a great distance off. He swore he saw it. Whirling across the valley bottom with deadly intensity, and a black dog going before.

Because I would write the truth to you, I ridde this morning to see the stones. Thus praying to God to mend these miserable times, I cease.

Your loving friend, Wm Westfaling.

And there are rumours too about Prince Rupert, as he makes his way south and west, clearing the country for the King. His dog Boye that goes into battle with him has been heard to utter accurate prophecy. He has been seen to catch bullets in his mouth, that were shot at his master. Some say on good authority that the dog is the Devil in disguise.

*

Boys of fifteen and sixteen, who have never seen anything but the town of their birth, armed and with no instruction, tramp exhausted through thick country. Always the news filtering back to Brampton is mixed. Whatever they hear from further up the country about the King's success, in October of 1642 Royalist Hereford falls easily to a division of the Parliamentary army. This is good news at last for the Harleys.

A former apprentice, among the force that takes Hereford for the Parliamentarians, writes to his master in London, in the lull between action. He sits in travel-caked clothes, bent over a leather writing scrip, his legs crossed underneath him.

Dear Master,

We were commanded to draw out fifteen out of every company in our regiments, in all about nine hundred, with three troopes of horse and two peeces of ordinance, with which we marched towards Hereford. After we had marched ten miles we came to Bromyard, the wether wet, and the way very fowle: here we got a little refreshment, and from hence marched ten miles further to Hereford, but very late before we got thither, and by reason of the raine and snow, and extremity of cold, one of our soldiers died by the way; and it is wonderfull wee did not all perish, for the cowardly Cavalleers were within few miles of us.

The boy's hair is matted with road dust. He is exhausted but he writes on. He doesn't ask himself why, only that it seems bigger than human exigence, bigger than exhaustion, the need to record in detail how they came to Hereford, barely able to stand with hunger and cold, legs shaking with fatigue. How they stood in front of the shut gates of the town for two houres, up to mid-calf in dirt and water, denied entry. And can it be necessary to take this out-of-the-way place? His scorn for the city, whose inmates were all malignants, save three, which were Roundheads. The foolish slanders used by the Marquesse of Hertford to fright the towns-people.

The Roundheads are coming. In no wise open your gates or let them in. If you do they will plunder your houses, murder your children, burne your Bibles, and utterly ruinate all.

So the citizens were resolved to oppose us unto the death, he writes, and having in the city three peeces of ordinance, charged them with neyles, stones &c, and placed them against us, and wee against them, resolvinge either to enter the city or dye before it.

Rain of makeshift artillery falling among puddles.

But the Roundheads in the city, one of them an alderman, surnamed Lane, persuaded the mayor that his Excellency the Marquess and all his forces were at hand, whereupon he opened unto us, and we entered the city at Bysters Gate, but found the dores shut, many of the people with their children fled, and had enuffe to do to get a little quarter. This night, though weet and weary, wee were faine to guard the city.

His letter is several pages of careful hand. News is everything.

*

Barely a couple of months pass and Hereford falls to the Royalists again. Lord Stamford is driven out by the Marquess of Hertford's forces and Fitzwilliam Conningsby is made governor. Brilliana is once more in great alarm. Should she fly the castle now, while she can? Should she stay? No one to advise. In the storeroom, or in the castle pantry, she stops and stares, panic rising in her throat. We could starve. Looking at the carefully laid-up provisions, counting in her mind, the cheeses, corn, malt, salt-meat. She tries to calculate but the numbers jumble in her head. We could starve to death. We could starve.

The country around so hostile that almost nothing gets through. Her letters now are written on linen to make them easier to hide about the carrier's person, a tiny square, folded flat and tucked into the lining of the sleeve for instance.

My deare Ned – My hart has bine in no rest sence you went. I confes I was never so full of sorrow. I feare the provicion of corne and malt will not hold out, if this continue; and they say they will burne my barns; and my feare is that they will place soulders so neare me that theare will be no going out. My comfort is that you are not with me, least they should take you: but I doo most dearly mis you. I wisch, if it pleased God, that I weare with your father. I would have rwite to him, but I durst not rwite upon papaper.

Thears a 1000 dragonears came into Harford 5 hours affther my lord Harferd.

Strange to be at war with men personally known to you.

On the soboth day affter I receved the letter from the Markis of Harferd, we sett that day apart to speeke to our God, and then on munday we prepared for a seege; but our good God called them another way; and the markis sent me word he remembered him to me, and that I need not feare him, for he was going away, but bide me feare him that came affter him.

Mr Connisbe is the governor of Heariford and he sent to me a letter by Mr Wigmore. I did not let him come into my howes, but I went into the garden to him. Your father will sheawe you the letter: they are in a mighty violence against me; they reveng all that was doune, upon me.

My deare Ned, I pray you advis with your father wheather he thinkes it best that I should put away most of the men that are in my howes, and wheather it be best for me to goo from Brompton, or by Gods healp to stand it out. I will be willing to doo what he would have me doo. I never was in such sorrows, as I have bine since you left me; but I hope the Lord will delever me; but they are most cruely beent against me. I thanke you for your counsel, not to take theair words.

Nine days past theare was held a counsel of ware, what was the beest way to take Brompton; it was concluded to blow it up, and which counsell pleased them all.

Now they say they will starve me out of my howes; and they have taken away all your father's rents, and they say they will drive away the cattell, and then I shall have nothing to live upon; for all theare aim is to enfors me to let thos men I have goo, that then they might seas upon my howes and cute our throughts by a feawe rouges, and then say, they knewe not whoo did it.

On both sides accounts filter back of barbarities committed, of plundering and looting and destruction. Scudamore, Brilliana's kinsman, has suffered both at Llanthony and at Holme Lacy. Llanthony in particular has been ravaged. The hangings, linen, pewter, brass and all moveables have been carried away. The glass of the windows all broken; the barrs of the windows, locks, bolts, hinges of doors carried away, the ceelings broken down, the flooring of boards broken up and burnt or sold, nay the very stayres taken down and burnt together with the vessels which after the beer was drunk up were thrown into the fire, though there were wood and cole in good plenty. In fine not so much as a beame left in the house onely the rafters remaine which hold up the tiles.

Lady Scudamore taken prisoner in her own chamber, lying weeping, because if the Roundheads should come in what violence might they not do? And the horror of the sound of wrecking elsewhere in the house. Furniture and crockery smashed, and raised voices, and, is that cracking the sound of fire? Surely that is fire. Because fire is, next to violence, the greatest terror.

Then released at last, led shaking through corridors made unfamiliar with destruction, hangings torn and trampled and the windows out. And everywhere the roughness of strangers, their coarseness and the devastation. In the yard, hoisted on horseback though sickly and unfit for travel, and a hard adventure of a night journey at Christmas, up behind one of Scudamore's men.

But in their turn, the Cavaliers behave no better. One of the King's regiments under Sir John Byron quartered themselves at Bulstrode Whitelocke's house. Bulstrode's tenant, William Cooke, hearing that they were to be made a billet for the Cavaliers, hurried out with armfuls of possessions. He threw into the moat much of Whitelocke's pewter, brass, and iron things, and removed to some of his tenants houses and into the woods, some of his bookes, linen and household stuffe, as much as the short warning would permit. Despite Byron's orders that no damage or plunder be done, the thousand or so men garrisoned in and about the house did just as they wished.

They eate and dranke up all that the house could afforde, brake up all trunks, chests, and places, any goods, linen, or houshold stuffe that they could find, they carried away, cutt the beddes, lett out the feather, and tooke away the coutains, covers of chayres and stooles, his coach and 4 good coach horses and all his saddle horses, and whatsoever they could lay their hands on.

A family can be reduced to physical and financial ruin in a matter of a few days. The new moat at Brampton is flooded with water for protection. The castle is in constant expectation of being besieged.

Brilliana now sends her letters in two halves. Separately the sheets make no sense at all, Deare Ned, imagin to all strength and go all to geather. If she pretends to be writing rubbish to entertain her son then the letters will get past, even if intercepted. When you have laughed at the nonsense, please yourself with this, that is reson; I thanke God we are well, though all would not have it so. Intermittently there are gaps cut in the text of one sheet, as though the letter had been censored. Only when the sheets are placed on top of each other does the message appear in the cut spaces.

I desire you   would pray   your father   to send me   word what
he would have   me doo: if I put   away the   men I shall   be plundered
and if I   have no   rents, I know   not what   cours to   take
If I leave   Brompton   all will be   ruened   Mr Coningsby   swore he
would be   in Brompton   within five days

One of the Brampton men is surprised and captured.

To my greefe I must tell you that honest Petter is taken. 6 set upon him; 3 shot at him as he was opening a gate not fare from Mortimers Cros. He fought with them valiantly and aquited himself with corage: he hurt 2 of them, and if theare had not bine 6 to on, he had escaped: he is wounded in the head and sholder, but not mortally; he is in prison at Loudlow. I doun all that is poscibell to get him out, but it cannot be.

Ned Harley is old enough to fight. He is to be given his own troop of horse. He writes to ask that his brother Robert be sent to join him. On a little scrap of paper Brilliana writes requesting a sword for my sonne. He must at all costs be properly equipped. And I think you will find him a very good soulder.

Samuel Moore and Nathaniel Wright, the doctor, have settled at Brampton and intend to stay and assist Brilliana until her troubles be past.

In time, Honest Petter is released from prison. He was greeviously used in Loudlow. Turkes could have used him no wors; a lefftenant coronell Marrow would come every day and kicke him up and downe, and they laied him in a dungon upon foule straw.

Meanwhile Ned rides out of London with his company, to join Sir William Waller's forces, on his way to his first engagement in battle. He is nineteen years old. He has asked his mother that Robert, his brother, to be sent to join him.

My hart is with you, and I know you beleeve it; for my life is bound up with yours. My deare Ned, sence you desire your brother to come to you, I cannot be unwilling he should goo to you, to home I pray God make him a comfort.

I am confident you will hate all plundering and unmercifullness.

Waller's forces join battle with Sir Ralph Hopton's Cornish army at Lansdowne. In a furious charge, Ned Harley's horse is shot underneath him as he rides into the attack at the gallop. Mercifully neither Ned nor his brother are hurt. Brilliana writes to Sir Robert thanking God for the boys' survival.

July 14th 1643

My Deare Sir

By the carrier I receved your letter which was exceeding well come to me. On Tuesday last one that I sent Ned Harley returned. He was theare where the fight was. I had a letter from Ned Harley and one from Robin. They weare then both very well though thay had laine 4 nights in the field. The Lord was exceeding merciful to us in preserving of them both and especially Ned Harley whoos hors was killed. I hope the Lord will still be gratious of me and them in sparing of them.

Deare Sr you may believe that my hart is full and I trust the Lord will be so gratious to me as still to support me, and deare Sr pray for me for I have great neede of it. This cuntry begins to be reenforsed againe and I heere I must look for more summons, but

I knowe Him I have trusted.

No rents will be payed me.

Waller's forces are routed at their next battle, at Roundway Down. Ned and Robert go with the survivors back to London via Bristol. Meanwhile Prince Rupert, who is sweeping the south-west, has taken Cirencester and reaches Bristol himself, at the end of July, just as Waller's exhausted troop leave. On 25 July he storms Bristol and takes it with ease.

A day later, Sir William Vavasour, the latest governor of Hereford, still under Royalist control, moves with seven hundred men and sits down in siege in front of Brampton Bryan. He has his own gain in mind, along with his loyalty to the King. Were Brampton to go unchallenged, the only remaining Parliamentarian stronghold, in an area so largely Royalist, it would reflect badly on Vavasour's command. He writes to let Prince Rupert know of his position.

I found that I had been lost in the opinion of these counties, neither should I get half the contribution promised me, unless I made an attempt upon Brampton Castle, Sir Robert Harley's house, which I ventured upon. It is a strong place, but I am lodged very near it, three pikes length from the port.

Privately he is sure that with only a lady in charge it will quickly fall.

SIEGE

THE SOUTH EAST VIEW OF BROMPTON BRIAN CASTLE, IN THE COUNTY OF HEREFORD.

To the R.t Hon.ble EDWARD Earl of Oxford and Mortimer, and Baron Harley of Wigmore. Owner of these Remains. This Prospect is humbly Inscrib'd. by My Lord Y.r Lords.ps most Obed.t & Oblig.d Serv.ts Sam.l & Nath.l Buck.

THIS CASTLE belonged for some Ages to a Family of Distinction call'd Brian de Brompton. In the days of K. Edw.III.d Robert de Harley married the Daughter & Heir of S.r Brian de Brompton, by which means it came into that Noble Family.

We, the Lords and Commons, have for the just and necessary defence of the Protestant religion, of his Majesty's person, crown and dignity, of the laws and liberties of the kingdom, and the privileges and powers of Parliaments taken up arms, appointed and authorised Robert, Earl of Essex, to be Captain-General of all the forces by us raised, to bring to condign punishment all rebels and traitors. And we do humbly beseech His Majesty to withdraw his royal presence from those wicked rebellious attempts, that His Majesty will leave them to be suppressed by that power which we have sent against them. And that His Majesty will not mix his own dangers with theirs, but in peace and safety, without his forces, forthwith return to his Parliament, and by their faithfull advice compose the present distempers and confusions abounding in both your kingdoms, and provide for the security and honour of yourself and royal posterity and the prosperous estate of all your subjects.

The Parliamentary Declaration

This is how it happens.

Up from Ludlow, along the flat banks of the Teme, two or three hundred foot soldiers marching. Early afternoon. And in the fields and the woods, all carries on as though it might be any July day, then or now. The fat hares lie with their ears flat, starting away only at the last minute, to flee on a zigzag, leaning into the corners like riders.

Sound of tramping feet. Too warm for speech, only just into the afternoon. Two o'clock. The Teme bubbling quietly by and the alders leaning into their own shade. In the open fields the wood-pecker's rude laughter and the little bore-holes his beak has made pillaging the anthills repeatedly. And on a smaller than human scale, the ants in crisis, carrying things that are tiny and precious to safety. The ground shakes under the passage of feet. A child looks over the hedge, eyes round.

The soldiers have been seen. Shouts from the guard on the castle walls.

At the same time, on the brow of a little hill to the south, two or three troops of horse stand up on the crest and divide. No messengers now can get in or out of the castle. All are stopped.

Frantic calculations take place. How many are they? How best to prepare, because now our hour is nigh. Now it is high time to wake out of sleep: The night is far spent, the day is at hand: let us therefore cast off the works of darkness, and let us put on the armour of light.

This is a public fast day. It is entirely in keeping with the enemy that they approach the castle on one of the Lord's days.

There must be seven hundred, or thereabouts. Men swarming through the little village. Food to be demanded, billets found for some. Towards evening, a blind man called John Powntney making his way up the village street and there is a hand on his shoulder stopping him. Who are you for, King or Parliament? Quick! Speak up!

The panic on the man's face is comical to the soldiers. He cannot see who has stopped him, nor how many they are, but he answers wisely, only hesitating a little. I pray you. I cannot see. I am for King and Parliament.

And those few who are watching see him butchered, unarmed and sightless, and kicked dead, out to the side of the road. So as not to be a let to the ordnance when it is brought through on the carts. There is a great gun coming to be brought to play on the castle. That will reduce it quick enough.

It is rumoured the King himself is to come down. There is only Gloucester that remains Parliament-held in these parts. The King is to lead the army against Gloucester. Now for a moment Brilliana gives way to terror. She has her three youngest children in the castle with her and the enemy looks so very many. They set about killing the sheep and lambs, driving away the rest. And what will the castle do for provisions? In these first hours of siege going up and down the corridors, consulting with Nathaniel Wright and Mr Moore, with Captain Priam Davis, who is a tried soldier, keeping the inhabitants of the castle, fifty-odd musketeers and fifty civilians, in a state of calm. And yet sometimes a weakness rises up from the pit of the stomach. The stories are so bad, of how others in a like case have been used. Although she would not show it, fear curdles in her chamber in the moments she is alone, until it seems a solid presence that waits till her back is turned, to put its cold hand at her neck. Somehow she gets a letter out to Sir Robert. A scrap of paper, written in a loose and terrified hand, quick large writing.

My Dearest Sr

I believe you heare the King is to come into theas parts. I desire you would derect me what I should doo whether stay at Brompton or remove. I beceach the Lord derect us and keepe us safe. I thanke God the chillderen are well. I am in very greate haste I rest but no haste must shute out this that I beceach the Lord to give us a comfortabell meeting begging your love and prayers for your most affectionat wife.

But there is little time for anything. Events unfold so fast. In the evening a trumpeter approaches the castle walls with a summons for Lady Brilliana to give up the castle to the force gathered at its gates without delay.

Madam,

Our relations to your Ladyship makes us careful to prevent if we can any further inconveniences to you and therefore to that end we think fitt to acquaint you that Sir W Vavasour by his Majesty's command hath drawn his forces before you castle with resolution to reduce it before he stirs from thence.

Your Ladyship may do well to take into your consideration the posture you are in. Bristol taken by Prince Rupert and he is now before Glocester, his Majesties forces successful everywhere, so that Yr Ladyship cannot hope for any reliefe. And upon those terms if yr Ladyship should be obstinate we cannot promise and expect those conditions for you that are fit for your quality. Neither any quarter for those that are with you, who further must look for all extremity upon their families and substance forthwith.

Madam we wish you would take this seriously into your thoughts and we expect a speedy answer being your Ladyship's humble servants

Henry Lingen

Walter Pye

William Smalman.

All these men are known to Brilliana. Walter Pye is her husband's kinsman. She sits to write an immediate answer to their summons, schooling herself to calm, to clarity. But continually, as she writes, her heart beats up into her neck, so great is her outrage.

My own family, my neighbours come against me, a woman alone with her little children, in her own home.

Sir

Your relations to me which you are pleased to make mention of might have invited you to another piece of service than this that you are now come upon.

Vavasour's drawing his forces before my house by the King's command I dare not, I cannot, I must not believe it. Since it hath pleased our most gracious King to make many solemn promises that he would maintain the laws and liberties of this kingdome, I cannot then think he would give a command to take away any thinge from his loyal subjects and much less to take away my house.

If Sir W Vavasour will do so, I must endeavour to keep what is mine as well as I can, in which I have the law of nature, of reason and of the land on my side, and you none to take it from me.

For Bristol and Glocester it is no precident to me if they are taken, that I should give away what is mine.

Your servant, Brilliana Harley.

The men of the county baffle over her answer. She does not plead like a woman alone. She talks legalities. How is this?

She will scare soon enough. She will gather up her skirts and run like any other, weeping, crying mercy.

Thursday morning, the enemy approaches close enough to the castle for those inside to be able to see their faces. An evil-looking crew. They revile the castle with jibes, with rude gestures.

Waller's bastards! You! Roundheads! Look to yourselves. We will rip you. We will hang you all for traitors.

So the castle opens fire. Among the Cavaliers' party, a boy is hit and killed. The shooting goes on all that afternoon and through the night.

Friday the 28th the same. Smoke from the exchange of fire hangs in the stillness. It is hot.

Brilliana settles into quiet leadership. There is no help for her. Now she must keep her head. In her few spare moments she turns in on herself as is her wont, calms herself with prayer, with reading brief extracts from those writers she finds to offer most comfort. Calvin's Commentaries on the Psalms of David.

And thou O Lord art a shield for mee, my worshippe and the lifter up of my head.

With my voyce have I cryed unto the Lorde, and he hath herd mee from the hill of his holynesse.

I layd mee downe and tooke my rest; and I awaked, bycaus the Lorde upholdeth mee.

I will not bee afraid of thousand of thousands of people which have pitched their tents on every side against mee.

Outside, there is firelight from the enemy's encampment. The continued thud of shot. It seems, looking out, as though they that walk back and forth in front of the fires are demons. Black forms lit by flames. Smoke hanging. Night noises, the bleating of the odd remaining sheep. Owl calls. These are comforting sounds.

The wavering light of the taper in Brilliana's chamber, where she sits holding the book in a steady hand.

David uttereth a woonderfull and almost incredible constancie of minde, in that among many deathes he slept as soundly as if he had bin out of all daunger. And surely though he were tossed among the cruell waves of cares: yet is it certain that they were assuaged by fayth, so as he rested in God, were he never so much disquieted.

Even so the godly do always escape conquerours out of all feare, like as despayre overwhelmeth the ungodly which rest not upon God.

For like as the power of God is unmeasurable: so beleeve they that yt shall continue invincible against all manner of assauts, outrages, practices and powers of the whole world.

Wherefore in daungers let us lerne, not to mesure God's helpe after the maner of man: but to despise whatsoever terrour trumpeth in our way: even in this respect, for they are but trifles whatsoever things man do practice against God.

Shooting all day on Friday, till the sound did ring in the ears of those kept close in the castle. The heat continuing and the stretched nerves. In the evening another trumpeter steps up with a letter for Lady Brilliana, the same roundabout language, the same chilling combination of ornate compliments veiling threats of unnamed violence, this time from Sir William Vavasour himself, then garrisoned at Wigmore.

Madam,

I took notice of your Ladyship's letter and denial upon Wednsday night with much regrett for I thought the demands made to you by those gentlemen were so reasonable that they ought not have found contradiction from anybody, much less from a person of your wisdom and vertue. How your Ladyship can term yourself one of the king's loyal subjects when either by yr command or connivance at least the rebels in yr house have committed so many thefts, murders, and taken so many prisoners for no other cause but for being good subjects.

Truly madam I comprehend only those who acknowledge his power and obey his commands, which if it please your Ladyship to do by delivering up those rebels in your house which you now endeavour to protect (and truly Madam I must be plain with you) much in vain, for we will never suffer the King's power to be affronted by so small a part of the county, the dispute will end. I shall deal fairly with you.

Madam I am your servant and to one so noble and vertuous am

desirous to keep off all insolences that the liberty of the souldiers provoked to it by your obstinacies may throw you upon. Yet if you remain still willfull what you may suffer is brought you by your self, I having by this timely notice discharged those respects due to your sex and honour.

It is as well to encourage her to call to mind the barbarities that soldiers are capable of in battle. There is rape and murder. No need to spell it out. Better not in fact. There are women who have seen their children killed before them. Often it is impossible for even the noblest of captains to restrain the brutality of their fighting men. She has been warned.

Brilliana is not to be frighted, though her hand shakes a little when she reads the paper. This could be anger. She is stung by the accusations of murder and theft. None in my house tolerated by me did ever commit murder or theft, things which I abhor as much as any can. But these men must be played at their own game, and it is not for nothing that she is the daughter of a diplomat. Now without noticing it, when she makes her capital I's, they stand large and flowing, as though even in writing her strength of identity would out, an unconscious figure for her loneliness, the only lately discovered scale of her personality.

Sir

Those gentlemen you write of seemed in their letter so farr to befriend me as to let me know you had sent souldiers before my house to reduce it. I wrote the gentlemen word I would endeavour to keep what was mine as long as I could and I know that does not make me an ill subject nor give any one warrant to take it from me.

Sir I have heard such a fair report of you that it possessed me with a belief that so noble a soldier as your self would rather have put forth your power to have rescued me from injuries than to have poured them upon me, and I think it exceeding strange that so ingenious a mind should take up such false reports as it seemes you have of me.

She is angry enough to write a long letter, refuting each of his charges and closing with the observation, you and all the world is deceived if you think there is any drop of disloyal blood in my heart, and none can less cherish our gracious King's enemies than myself. She is also the daughter of a courtier.

Why you are pleased to term me obstinate I know not, my endeavour is to have my will stoop to my reason and not do any thing because I will do it. And indeed this she has always demonstrably done.

Sir I need not tell you your soldiers have taken my beasts and all else they can and shott at my house these two days and nights but for what cause I am ignorant, and therefore I believe you will by these lines see your mistake in me and so be sorry for what injuries you have done me and recall your soldiers that I may not be further wronged by them.

*

In his own chamber Nathaniel Wright, the doctor, stands at the window, only half-aware of his wife's comings and goings behind him. It is a miracle that Lady Brilliana has the strength both of mind and body to run the siege, to write these long letters of negotiation with the enemy. Their wicked demands, their letters of threat and cajolement held in her small hand as she reads, and today, about the castle, her upright carriage, her certainty. The men do respect her authority. God be thanked.

Though she is very much alone.

Outside there is commotion as the dusk falls, dark shapes moving. They are taking the castle horses, even out of the stables, under our very eyes.

And much later, waking in alarm to the noise of bellowing, of animals running in panic. Sticks, shouts, hooves in the night. The Cavaliers are plundering the cattle.

Saturday dawning, with the noise of shot continuing. Two more troops of horse appear on the horizon and clatter into the village to disperse themselves around the castle. Breathless news from the ramparts. My lady they are reinforcing. Then in the evening, the cavalry drawn up before the castle, in battle array, and the heartbeat sound of a drum. Approach of a messenger. And the drum. And the silent horses facing. And the drum. And the drum. And again, a letter.

I shall not trouble your Ladyship with much or often writing to you. Colonel Vavasour is losing patience with this game of toing and froing. The problem of chivalry, taking arms against a defence-less lady. If only she were defenceless.

If only she weren't a lady.

Then indeed they might rubble this little castle, fire the village and be gone. Diplomatic tiptoeing in this out-of-the-way place.

Truly I gave strict command that your cattle be safely preserved. If your Ladyship shall approve yourself loyall they may be restored. I make no pretences my self to them. I have ever abhorred the thing plundering.

For my soldiers shooting these two days it was directly against my order, for indeed I was not in a present condition my cannon being not then come and I do not love to spend my shott in vain, nor do I believe they had given fire against your house had they not been provoked to it by your first and often shooting from thence who have killed a little boy, which truely Madam if not timely prevented by a treaty must be revenged by your Ladyship's humble servant, W Vavasour.

Unearthly silence while the letter is handed over, in the shadow of the castle walls. Jingle of harness and the men's faces. Summer evening.

In under the barbican and Brilliana is left to consider her reply.

And so it continues, the letters back and forth and the men camped in the heat, increasingly restive and the small bombardment. Brilliana plays for time. She pretends to contemplate flight. She asks for her brother-in-law, Sir William Pelham, who is with the King, to be fetched to give them safe convoy out of the castle. This will make it harder for Vavasour to act against her.

My rents have been stopped for these 12 months now and my cattle and horses taken by your soldiers. I cannot tell how to think that of your self you would so injure one that had no way deserved it.

I believe my condition cannot be paralleled that one of my condition, who have my husband from me and so wanting much comfort, should be besieged and so my life and the life of my little children sought after with that of my whole family without any cause given.

Sir you have been pleased to be the instrument to take away that upon which I and my children must live, which was the stock upon my ground, and which being gone and my rents not paid I must bethink myself of another place to be in, of more safety than my own house.

This letter earns a few days' ceasefire, for it seems the lady has weakened in her obstinacy at last, although the slights to his honour sting Vavasour. When he has done everything in his power to proceed with chivalry. Quickly, let those in the castle lay down their arms and a garrison be installed in their place and we can secure the castle and be shot of the whole affair. There is still Gloucester to be taken. There are more important and more manly battles afoot. In his garrison headquarters Vavasour paces in frustration. Why has this commission fallen to him? He is waging war on a woman.

The cannon arrives. The church, which faces the castle gate at a distance of sixty or seventy paces, is taken by the Cavaliers. This is too close for comfort and it is necessary now to block up the double portcullis against them. And now, just when she is most threatened, the lady turns about again and seems to wish to stay.

Sir, for me to yield that you should place a garrison in my house I cannot find out any reason for it. By this I conceive I should become a prisoner in my own house which I cannot yield to, for so I should speak my self guilty, and thus much more I must say, My dear Husband hath entrusted me with his house and children and therefore I cannot dispose of his house but according to his pleasure and I do not know it is his pleasure that I should entertain souldiers in his house, and surely sir I will never voluntarily betray the trust my husband reposeth in me.

Now the enemy comes close under the battlements and begins to set up breastworks and batteries. Battle is properly engaged and the castle gives fire and beats them back. God be praised. In return the Cavaliers fire a house in the village. An hour later and the castle outhouses are on fire. Heat and smoke. And again the thin noise of the trumpet heralding another letter. To and fro, this stalemate of chilly gallantry, the exasperation thinly veiled, the restrained animosity. Sir. Madam. Your humble servant, to serve you.

Barely dawn and there are shouts. The Cavaliers are firing the castle mills. They burn furiously all the early morning, smoke hanging heavy over the castle, and at ten o'clock much of the village catches fire and burns almost to nothing. This is a terrible day. In the afternoon they place a saker, a siege cannon, in the window of the church steeple, hauling it up on ropes in heat and blinding sweat. In the castle, yet unaware of what is happening, they just hear the rhythmic shouts, the Heave! Heave! Heave! as it makes its progress.

Quiet. Birdsong.

Then ten great shots from the cannon in the steeple, with balls of six or seven pounds. The castle battlements are shattered, but no harm done. On the hills round about the castle, the malignants

347

of the county stand to watch. They give great roars of approval each time the cannon plays.

This night the enemy cast up siege works at the parsonage on the east side of the castle. This cannot be prevented on account of the dark. Then from the west side, with the advantage of a wind sprung up, they fire a bomb. Again, God be thanked, no harm is done.

Now because it is summer and there is fire about and also a wind to fan the embers not yet out, the parsonage house and its barns catch light and burn to a cinder. This is to the castle's advantage because it has been the enemy's chief quarters and the place where they began to raise batteries and breastworks. It is difficult to stop fire once it has started.

Twenty-six shots this day, which strike down a chimney as well as battlements and shattering tylestones from the roof. Bullets rain into the house through the breaks but the castle inhabitants take shelter where the roof is whole and none is hurt. The roar sent up by the Cavaliers when the chimneys are toppled.

What fools.

And godless, for even on Sunday there are eight cannon shots before morning sermon. Praying despite the continued musket shots. Nathaniel Wright gives private thanks that among a hundred men, women and children shut up in a close house, in the dog days of summer, still there is not one sick or feeble person amongst us. This is ever his fear, that they be brought low by the spread of disease.

Into the third week of the siege and the heat continues and the constant rain of cinders, that drift and settle, and cover surfaces, and stick to the skin. The smell of charred wood and stone and the endless headache gunfire. Always there is smoke in the back of your throat.

Anxiously examining the well in the castle. Looking again at the stocks of food. Is there two months' supply? Or less?

Brilliana's unruffled presence. And the worry at night, over her children, over all those in the castle. Under cover of darkness she manages to get letters in and out occasionally but it is a risky thing.

There is never enough information, on how the country stands, whether the King's forces or those of Parliament are uppermost.

What to do for the best?

And in her fitful rest fear will put its cold hand on her sometimes, so she starts up out of sleep, heart beating wildly, over she knows not what. Silence. So she lies back down again. It is nothing. Nothing at all. Just my weakness.

A new gun arrives, a monstrous thing, that they place at the west side of the castle. It fires with a splitting roar, leaping backwards as it does so, as if alive. Dangerous even to the men who work it, if they are not quick and watchful. And they shout and ram it with powder and cover their ears for the report and wipe the sweat and smoke from their faces and start again. Hot metal smell.

In the summer sky a hawk making lazy circles, jinks sideways at the explosion, sees below it the black body of the cannon jump, like a fighting dog springs back on its haunches the better to hurl itself forward again. The plumes of smoke curl up and disperse.

At the third firing, the ball bursts a window in the castle, shatters the wall by the clock and breaks the bell. Splinters of wood and glass, stone flying. In the roar and disorder it is indeed as if something wild and raging is amongst them at last. Crash and shatter and the women in the parlour knocked off their feet. Lady Colebourne is hit as she stands by the parlour door. Screaming. Mrs Wright, the doctor's wife, too is hit.

Feet running. Fetch the doctor. And the shouts go round the castle. Fetch Dr Wright.

Lady Colebourne laid out, blood pouring from her eye. It is your wife and Lady Colebourne, Dr Wright. Lady Colebourne has lost an eye.

Dr Wright in shirtsleeves, his mouth drawn tight in concentration. Hold the lady still. And a man has to hold her down. His instruments of surgery quickly applied. The speculum, the duckbill. Is there foreign matter in the wound? How much splintering is there to the bone? A cauterising iron to control the bleeding.

Stitching and poultice and bandage. And his own, his precious wife to be ministered to. Propping her on his arm, his heart beating despite his calling. Soothing, looking for the source of the injury. How bad is it? God save my sweet wife. And his wife's eyes dark with panic, like a horse's in terror. A gentlewoman. They would shoot at a gentlewoman.

But both ladies are alive.

*

Now there is no let-up in the firing of cannon. Two more great guns are brought against the west wall, the day after. The noise becomes hellish. Twenty-nine shots in all and cannonballs falling, nine pounds in weight, though miraculously the castle holds. In the evening of this day the trained bands of Ludlow, two troops of foot, are added to the enemy's number.

It is hard not to despair, looking out at them massed and swarming, hearing their rude shouts. Roundheads! Traitors!

Lord, how are they encreased that trouble me: Many are they that rise up against me.

Many there be that saye unto my soule, there is no helpe for him in God. Brilliana strains for the sound of a messenger who might have made it safe through the enemy and the darkness. If she could but hear news of help from outside. If she could but hear that Ned and Robin are safe.

By this lesson David teacheth, that though the whole world with one voice should move us to despair: we must rather give eare to God alone and evermore feede ourselves inwardly with hope of the helpe that he hath promised: and bycaus the ungodly go about to murder our soules, we must fence them by prayer.

Easiest now to pray the first prayers, the prayers of most habit.

Lighten our darkness we beseech thee O Lord; and by thy great mercy defend us from all perils and dangers of this night.

Lighten our darkness we beseech thee O Lord. Lighten our darkness.

*

In the morning it is apparent that the enemy now have five more great guns in position, as if this were the day appointed by them to beat the castle to dust. Two to the east, two to the west and one on the south. Heavy bombardment. Now the enemy is in good earnest. Brilliana urges those in the castle to bear up and play the man.

And when the day is over at last and no great harm done, Captain Priam Davis writes his diary of the siege, as he does every day. He records the numbers of shot from the great cannon. 48 this day. He pauses. The noble lady was this day more courageous than ever, he writes.

And while he writes he is aware of whispered commotion, of hurried unblocking of ports, of a figure tense and cloaked for travel smuggled in. A messenger.

A messenger has made it through hostile country, through all the enemy courts of guard. Letters are come at last. In this Brilliana's wisdom is great, for she continues to hold intelligence with those outside the castle. By this they hear that all is not lost, that Sir William Brereton for Parliament has routed Lord Capel and that Vavasour is on the point of being called west.

The next day, as though undecided or in deliberation, the enemy is so quiet until evening that they are scarcely noticeable. In the evening, more intelligence. Their greatest gun is broken. And this is great news. Moreover the cannoneer, not being careful enough, was killed when it misfired. The castle mason, who has gone over to the King, was killed – and this too must be a sign. He was shot through the hand as he stood, pointing out the castle's weakest part to the enemy, and the shot went on into his belly and so he died.

However the next day the firing starts up again as if to make up

351

for lost time, shooting continuously for two days, sometimes battering at chimneys, sometimes at the walls, sometimes at windows or tiles, now from the west, now from the south, so that it is hard to know where to hide the most vulnerable in the castle. Running along corridors between bombardments, the castle children with some of the women.

To the still room, for safety. Now! Go!

Between the shots the Cavaliers curse. Thieves! Rogues! they shout. Harley's bastards!

After this it is necessary to work even through the Lord's day to repair the damage to the castle. The wall in the west is battered almost to a breach. So they line the walls with earth and make strong barricades.

News still coming in and out of the castle. Now it is heard that two more of the great guns are broken and their cannoneers wounded out of the battle. It is rumoured that Prince Rupert has given orders to fire the castle and come away.

It is rumoured they are preparing fireballs.

*

The weather breaks and becomes very foul. Rain coming in through the many rents in the castle roof and now the castle cannon misfires and the cannoneer is hurt. It is God's great mercy that not more of the castle inmates are injured.

The cook is shot through the arm with a poisoned bullet and looks as though he cannot be saved. There is no news of relief. Fireball grenades are truly a terrible threat. Sunday is spent in fasting and praying for deliverance out of the hands of this bloody enemy. Mercifully there is little shooting.

Monday and Brilliana, frayed but determined, holds a council with her captains, Priam Davis, Samuel More and Nathaniel Wright. It is imperative that those quarters the enemy is using to prepare grenades be fired. It is decided a party will leave the castle and engage the enemy on the side where the grenades are being made.

This they do bravely, in a very small number. They make a surprise sally and with rockets they fire the house where the tinder and all materials for the grenades is kept, and kill many of the enemy without any loss to themselves. This causes brief panic amongst the Cavaliers.

The next day the enemy moves closer under the castle walls, casts up breastworks and trenches in the castle gardens and walks. They are close enough for their poisonous language to be a constant annoyance. In the evening a drum beating. A letter from His Majesty for Lady Brilliana by hand of Sir John Scudamore.

*

And later, in secret, sad news from London of the bad case of the Parliamentary army throughout the country, so that some in the castle weaken and advise surrender.

Brilliana settled and pale. Her voice so low as to be almost inaudible. I had rather choose, she speaks slowly, with emphasis, an honourable death. God will own his cause. The men around her drop their heads in shame. What could they have been thinking? They follow her lead. Surely this is a noble lady.

The parley continues for seven days with a cessation of arms.

Brilliana finds time to write to Ned at last.

I cannot but venture these lines, but wheather you are at Loundoun or no, I know not. Now, my deare Ned, the gentillmen of this country have affected theair desires in bringing an army against me. What spoyls has bine doun, this barer will tell you.

The Lord in mercy presarve me, that I fall not unto theair hands. My deare Ned I believe you wisch yourself with me, whoo are my great comfort in this life. The Lord in mercy blles you and give me the comfort of seeing you and your brother.

The writing is minute. The paper measures no more than two and a half inches in length.

In the evening Sir John Scudamore is let into the castle by a ladder and a rope to speak with Lady Brilliana. He urges her surrender.

The cook dies at last, despite all Nathaniel Wright's ministrations.

*

Brilliana addresses a letter of appeal to Charles I, that he might move the enemy from her gates, or else give her safe passage elsewhere. She protests her loyalty. Her father was a courtier after all; her brother is a Royalist. Your poor subject did never offend your Majesty, or ever take up arms against your Majesty, or any man of mine, or any by my appointment was in actual rebellion against your sacred Majesty.

They wait for answer.

News comes and goes about the state of Gloucester. It is fallen. It holds out. Sir William Brereton is coming to relieve us. The enemy are bringing hoggs from Lingen park, with which they will mine the castle and so blow us out. It is said the Scots are in England. Nothing is certain, and the King does not answer.

Then, on 5 September, a knight comes with an answer that is supposedly from the King, signed by secretary Falkland. No one believes it to be genuine.

But at night now there is the rumble of great ordnance being moved out. Lord God, is it possible they may lift the siege at last? But in the morning, shots continue and the number of enemy looks to be no less. On the 8th, a party of Cavaliers attempts to leave, taking with them the church bells. For this they are killed as they go through the village. On the 9th, the enemy fires their own barricades and then it is certain they are going indeed.

In the evening, secret intelligence arrives that the King is calling his forces from Exeter, from Shrewsbury, raising the siege in order to engage with Lord Essex, who is marching to relieve Gloucester at the head of a great army.

Priam Davis closes his diary. The Lord was this day pleased to take away these bloody villains and to return them with shame, which had vexed us almost these seven weeks for which we desire to be humbly thankful to our good God that delivered our poor family out of the hands of fifteen malignant countys set against us even to our extirpation and ruin.

Brilliana, in her chamber, mutters fervent prayers, O Lord who has seen fit, this day . . . But within moments, black exhaustion claims her. When her woman comes in, she finds Brilliana asleep in her clothes.

*

Look out of the windows now. There is nothing. The village is burnt. The stock is gone. The castle itself in tatters.

How weary, weary, is Lady Brilliana. When she wakes sometimes, the day and her duties are like the light at the top of a well shaft. How to haul herself up with so little strength.

Approaching Michaelmas. Round Brampton the country still swarms with men of the King's party. If any leave the castle they must be armed and prepared for skirmish, although Brilliana insists no revenge of any kind must be enacted on her disloyal tenants. No one will help with repairs to the castle except they are first captured and made to do so.

Foraging parties leave daily. There is little doubt that this is nothing more than a brief reprieve. Brilliana plans and orders and shifts as shrewdly as any captain. What food can be found. Ammunition. Repairs to the castle walls. There will be a second siege, she knows it full well. And winter is coming. This will be hard.

God, if it please you, give her strength. This is the prayer of all who pass her in the castle's passages. There is no one who could do what she has done, and those who counselled surrender, scuttle past, head down a little, because how did she hold her nerve? This is shaming, if you are a man.

And Nathaniel Wright, the doctor, sucks his teeth when he passes. Her eye has an unwholesome glitter. Won't you rest, my lady? Let me see to the foraging party. He would like her to sleep, to eat a little. Her eyes so hollow, so fevered-looking.

Nothing shakes Brilliana's purpose, not even her husband's request for her removal.

A letter has come from Sir Robert at last, urging Brilliana to leave and come to safety in London. He instructs her to hand Brampton's safekeeping over to one of his men.

Sept 24 1643

My Deare Sr

I hop before this you have hard by Proser that the Lord has bine gratious to us, and has sent our enimys away from before Brompton.

On labour day last the 23 of this month I received your letter by Fischer in which you advis me to come away from Brompton. Deare Sr heatherto God has made me (though an unworthy one) an instrument to keepe possession of your howes that it has not fallen into the hands of spoilers, and to keepe to geather a handful of whom so such as feared the Lord to geather so that his word has yet an abiding in theas parts, which if the Lord remoufe Hearifordschire is misrabell.

In this worke I have not thought my life deare, neather shall I.

Sir could Ned Harley come downe I should think meself to have much comfort and I thinke he would doo his cuntry sarvis and himselfe good in healping to keepe what I hope shall be his, and in maintaining the Ghospell in this place. O lett me begg of you to take poore Hearifordscheere into consideration and commiseration.

Sir the man you write of to intrust your howse with, if I should have followed his counsel it had bine goon. Therefore I doo not thinke he would keep it. Mr Baughton is of an opinion that if pleas God I goo away it will not be longe keept, not that I dod any great matter but I have something more aughtority and I should have more care than any other.

My deare Sir I pray you consider all things and doo not looke upon me as if I weare afraid but what you would have me doo in that which may be best for you, and that I shall most gladly doo. All my pleasures are in you and then I must be moost pleased when you are pleased and therefore deare Sir thinke what you would have me doo and let me know it and I shal be best pleased to doo that.

I sent to you a greate while agoo for a gowne I pray you will you send me one. I desire it may be silke, chepe, made up plaine. I beleeve my Lady Veere's measure will sarve me and my cosin Davis man may bringe it downe.

Brilliana closes her reply. She sends a party of forty men down the road to Knighton, four miles away, to engage with Colonel Lingen's troop who are quartered there. The mission is a success. The men return without injury or loss of life, bringing horses, arms and even prisoners back with them. This frightens the enemy enough to quiet them for six weeks.

Could my son Ned come to me.

*

Could I just see my son again.

Sometimes she feels such a weakening. Of spirit. Of body. The weather is unseasonably cold. They have been ferrying earth into the castle to shore up the broken walls. The chill that comes out of it, like the grave. Brilliana shivers constantly. She has taken a fever. Perhaps she should do as Sir Robert suggests. Perhaps she should leave.

I am exceeding glad of this opertunity by which I may say something of that great deale which I would fain say to you.

I very much longe to heare from you and weather you would have me come from Brampton and how I would come. On sabath day last Sir William Vavasour sent me a letter from my brother by

357

a trumpeter and writ me one from him selfe. His letter was after his usuall straine that he must present against me as an enimye.

A second siege is coming.

Deare Sir pray for me for I have greate neede of it that the Lord would never leave me to myselfe but so guide me by his wisdome that I may be abell to deale with the sutile and malicious enimyes that are against me. Mr Moore is a great healp to me that I may more cheerefully undergo the greate burden that lyes upon me. I thank God all the children are well but I have taken an exceeding greate coold which much trubells me.

I have scarce time to write which has made me scribell.

On 9 October Brilliana writes to her son Ned. His troop is to be made into a regiment, promotion for him. As it has pleased God to intrust you with a greater charge, so the Lord in mercy blles you with a dubell measure of abillitys, and the Lord of Hosts be your protector and make you victorious.

My deare Ned, how much I longe to see you I cannot expres.

Oh my son. At her desk, she covers her face briefly with trembling hands. My son. My darling son, if you could have come.

I am now again threatened; there are some souldiers come to Lemster and 3 troops of hors to Heariford with Sr William Vavasor, and they say they meane to viset Brompton again. My trust is only in my God.

I have taken a very greate coold, which has made me very ill thees 2 or 3 days, but I hope the Lord will be mercifull to me, in giving me my health, for it is an ill time to be sike in.

*

Samuel Moore in a hushed house, writing with a shaking hand, a letter that is incoherent, full of mistakes, abbreviations, corrections.

News for Sir Robert that must be sent via a third party, so it can be broken gently, so his health is not unseated with shock.

Sir this bearer is despatched away being my Lady Harley is ill.

About a week since she had a fit of the stone which by great blessing and the Drs great care it dissolved and she became so well as she was purposed to come among us to meals.

Her pale face. Her halting step, disguised that no one should be unduly concerned.

But Friday night she had such a cough that hindered her sleepe. Yet after taking something to help it she rested well. About 11 a clock yesterday she had a fitt of a mixed disease of apoplexy lethargy with some convulsion. The doctor was firstly called who hastened and found her without sense but his industry was such with God's blessing by 4 of the clock she became pretty well recovered and putt us into good hopes of a recovery.

In the taper-lit chamber, the horrors of fever in a body already overstrained. Coughing blood. Liquid-looking eyes that barely recognise those around her, and the sweat standing on her forehead.

This morning aabout 3 in the morning she fell ill again but speakes and is sensible yet the carefull Dr that is not a minute from her adviseth to send to Sir Robert and I desire you carefully to acquaint him lest a sudden apprehension should do him hurt.

The Dr is not without hope, yet he feares her. He is as careful and vigilant as a man can be.

If alteration to health (which our good God grant) or death happen there shall come other messengers.

If the Lord take this sweet Lady it were necessary there should be a head of the family. In my judgement the Coll. Ned Harley were best come but we must leave to better judgement to determine.

Our greefes are more than agrees with reason. The letter becomes fragmented. To give her . . . knowing her goodness, let us be borne with, we are men of naturall affection.

Then another message, hot on its heels.

This messenger was purposed to follow the other immediately but after we thought to stay him till we saw an alteration, so at 6 of the clocke this Sabbath day the sweet ladyes soule went to keepe the eternall Sabbath in heaven, where she can never be besieged.

*

Brilliana Harley is dead.
Wrap the body in lead, as requested, until her beloved son and husband be returned, to lift her down, to take her out into the air of these border hills for the last time, to lay her in the ground she made her own.

For I am a stranger with thee: and a sojourner, as all my fathers were.
O spare me a little that I may recover my strength: before I go hence, and be no more seen.

Pause.

Christmas passes. There is still not a dry room in the castle. The constant chink chink chink of hammer and chisel. Francis Nixon, William Parkes, Richard Price, the castle masons and carpenters at work on repairs.

But now there is a bigger hole to fill than any in the castle's roof. In a high tower, for safekeeping, there is the body of its female captain, coffined and wrapped in lead. It is waiting for the honourable funeral it deserves.

How long, when she breathed her final requests, did Brilliana think it would be, before someone came back to take over the care of the castle that she had guarded with her life, to have her carried out, to have the right words said over her body?

Almighty God . . . we give thee hearty thanks for that it hath pleased thee to deliver this our sister out of the miseries of this sinful world; beseeching thee, of thy gracious goodness, shortly to accomplish the number of thine elect, and to hasten thy kingdom . . .

Until peace perhaps.

And now, how to replace her? Nathaniel Wright, the family doctor who has charge of the garrison, stopping in the middle of some task, shivering with a chill of alarm. How to keep these people to their purpose now. Upwards of a hundred in the castle, under his command. Captain Priam Davis, Captain John Hackluit, Captain Henry Archibald. These he can be sure of. Various prisoners.

There is a small body of soldiers, otherwise just servants and villagers, and the fifteen-year-old Thomas Harley, armed with a sword, playing the man to his grieving sisters.

Such a shifting, uneasy county. Slipping. Backsliding and a siege is a hard thing to withstand. Sometimes he catches their eye as he passes, in a passage, or at meals or household prayers. Thomas Child for instance, John Collier, a sullen look, an insolence about them. William Child also. Many of the soldiers. It takes strength to turn them round, to make them stick. It takes a forcefulness he doesn't think he has.

Nothing is secure. John Cotar, long-time servant of the family, creeping out of the castle at night by secret arrangement. Listen and I'll tell you all the castle's weaknesses. I know it. I was newly made Quartermaster before I left. They have provision enough for twelve months.

And again, a few nights later, two more leave the castle for the King's party, under cover of darkness. Then fifteen soldiers of the garrison. So now there are only fifty fighting men.

Nathaniel Wright stiffens his resolve. He must keep the garrison whole, that is his task. And he has the Harley children, the castle children in his care. *I would have my children and my nephew Smith guided by your counsels.* He must honour the request of their absent father.

But every time he looks, he can find no fire in himself equal to this task, of igniting purpose in uncertain men, of burning out dissent or of lighting the way.

If it snows, and the little Harley girls look out of the castle windows and hope for horsemen, how black the burnt buildings look against the white world outside.

Brampton again, same time as before. Waiting. Waiting. Up all night on the battlements straining into the distance. What's that – that light? What's that noise – is that an army coming through the dark?

Nothing. Just night sounds making the watch jump.

Then the day comes when, out of nowhere, he's here. The Bloody Butcher Woodhouse with a great army, demanding the castle by summons. Nathaniel Wright spits it away as if a maggot was in his mouth. He won't even read it. He refuses to treat with tyrants – didn't Woodhouse massacre all at Hopton? Firing of muskets at random into the enemy massed before them.

But then they are gone again just as suddenly. Up and left. Four days' grace, not knowing whether or no they will return. Frantic preparations. Are we in readiness for a second siege? Do we have enough food, munitions, bandages? Is it right for the children to stay here? Is there no word from Sir Robert?

What would Lady Brilliana have done?

Second week in Lent, 1644, a cloud of dust and the sound of drumming. What is this multitude coming up the road from Shrewsbury? Calling up and down the castle to come and look. Running feet. Women and children in the passages. Up the steep spirals to the rooftops, jostling one another to see out. What is it? What is it? Please God it might be reinforcements from Gloucester. Nathaniel Wright on the battlements looking out.

One by one they are gathering to see. They come out of the little doors in the tops of the towers, bent and blinking in the light.

Crowding on the battlements in silence. Just the dust cloud and the sound of the advance.

It is Woodhouse come back at the head of most of Prince Rupert's army, from Shrewsbury. The Red, the Green, the Blue regiments and rumbling with each their great ordnance. Little birds start up sideways out of the hedges as they pass. Horses straining. Men pushing the heavy cannon in and out of the ruts in the road. Are there indeed this many? Or do they look more because of the narrowness of the road?

It is the Serpent himself winding between our familiar fields.

For the moment there is nothing to do except watch. A crow caught in a cross-current jinks away sideways over the trees.

The enemy bring up their ordnance. There are so many men, set down in close siege, dug into trenches. So many guns. So many miners and colliers already breaking the ground, losing no time to dig a way under the castle.

Fall on! Fall on! And the shock of cannon.

Eighty-seven shots that first day, with a twenty-and twenty-four-pound ball. The castle walls reeling. The stones already loose and giving way. There are breaches in the walls already and the towers tottering. Chains of men barrow earth to shore them up from the inside. It is the earth the Lady Brilliana had brought into the castle for its protection. God rest her soul.

On the next day the enemy cannoneer is shot, with a musket ball, through the porthole. This cheers the garrison briefly, though the breach in the walls is now fair and big enough to enter. Still the Cavaliers are afraid to try. For five days they come forward and look to follow but their hearts fail. They have no stomach for hand-to-hand fighting.

News from Gloucester, God be praised – and even through such a host – that we will be relieved in three days' time. Now will we die in the breach rather than give it up.

But when night falls and some throw themselves down on pallets, armed as they are, and lose themselves instantly in black sleep, the enemy come and fire the breach, and there are shouts again, so the men start up in confusion. Waking to this hell of flames in darkness, and the cannon pounding.

Eight or nine times during that night the breach is fired and burns fiercely. There is so much dead wood and matter lying around. The children lie rigid in their shared beds, eyes wide to the flickering light cast on ceiling and wall, listening to the shouts outside. Help us. Their minds shape their dead mother. Help us, as if in prayer.

The men's heads spinning with the repeated alarms. Dumb. Running with water. And all the time the great and small cannon playing furiously, though by a miracle none is hit.

Still the roads from Gloucester are empty. There is no sign of the promised relief. No message comes. The watches relieve each other in silence.

Three more days the garrison holds and each night there are dreadful alarms. Twice in one night the whole of the enemy rises up, with a roar of Fall on! Fall on! so loud it is as if Hell itself were broke loose. Volleys of shot and the sky flashing with explosion and the clouds of sulphurous smoke rolling over the ruined towers by moonlight.

But when the alarm is over the men of the castle, ragged with exhaustion, mock the enemy in the breach, laughing loud. The voice of one man clear across the battlefield, calling in a strong voice that barking dogs will seldom bite. So there is laughter and cheers and one or two more call out in defiance. And across the field in response carry the voices of the enemy.

Trading insults across the dark between, in a shared mother tongue. This goes on all night and into the days that follow. The miners have now come so close under the walls that the garrison is afraid. How far are they? Scraping, scraping. Picks and shovels muffled underground. Ho there! Do you hear us, Roundheads – we will blow you up to the Devil.

Even if the cannon were to give them rest no one would sleep now, the threat of the enemy underneath is so horrible. But they hold up. Don't you know, you moles, the Devil is down there with you. Come into the breach, the men of the castle call. Come into the breach and fight like men.

Oh God let me sleep, they say under their breath, to themselves, after. Let me sleep.

A storm of great shot from the enemy, and in the lull after it, a parley sent over. Would the castle receive a letter from one of their friends – Captain Samuel Moore, of Hopton? The answer goes back; they will, on condition that all hostilities on both sides cease until the parley is over.

Agreed.

Moore urges the treating of conditions for surrender, to avoid the effusion of blood. Nathaniel Wright holds the letter and considers.

Strange silence for a while, just the continual ringing in your own ears, until some of the castle men appear on the battlements to look out. The Cavaliers forget their word of honour and give fire.

Messengers running back and forth.

No surrender. Because of Hopton, because of the bloody deeds of that army when quarter had been given under hand and seal. So what is the point of treating for conditions that will only be ignored?

The truce holds. The parley continues. There was no quarter given at Hopton. This is a false report. It was surrender under no conditions other than Colonel Woodhouse's mercy. Nothing under hand and seal.

Another letter is sent for, to verify this. If Samuel Moore agrees that no quarter was given then we will reconsider.

The messenger posts to Ludlow to wait on Samuel Moore. The reply doesn't reach the castle until midnight, meanwhile the bombardment has begun again. There is no question of letting down the castle ports in the night, to receive the letter. The enemy storms. Fierce fighting.

Wednesday before Easter, spring morning. The letter is received and the enemy's account verified. No quarter had been given at Hopton. So, finally, there is talk of conditions for surrender. The castle and its arms will be presently given up, and the garrison yield itself as prisoners. The lives of all of the garrison will this way be preserved and no violence offered to anyone. If these conditions be not accepted then the castle should expect extremity. No quarter will be given.

So Brampton is delivered up and the Harley children greet their neighbour, Sir William Croft, who is now their enemy. And Sir William Vavasour, the governor of Hereford, and the bloody butcher Woodhouse walk about the castle rooms as if they were their own.

Two hours later and a messenger slides off his horse from Prince Rupert. The Prince has ordered that all in the castle be put to the sword, most particularly Dr Nathaniel Wright, the garrison's commander-in-chief. There is a council of war while the matter is argued out. All are agreed. Put them to death – for their treasonable defiance, for resisting so long, for their proud Puritanism. Hand them over to the soldiers, as we did at Hopton. Nathaniel Wright, most of all, has something too much of haughtiness about him. Strip them. Let them be killed.

Only Sir William Vavasour puts up his hand to silence the company. This is the household of a gentleman, Sir William Croft's cousin. How shall Sir Robert Harley's children be put to the sword? Who wishes to see the throats of those little girls cut, who wants to see Sir Robert's servants, his divines, his doctor, hacked down with their hands tied, chopped about like cattle? Uneasy silence round the table. Is this what you want? Are we made brutes of at last?

Take them to Ludlow and keep them all prisoner.

*

So they go as captives to Ludlow castle and Brampton, which is too battered for use, is fired at a second order from Prince Rupert.

Sacked and burnt like the rest of the village, the roar of the fire carrying down the valley, sparks spouting upwards and travelling out on the breeze. Beams crash to the ground as the castle falls in on itself. The high tower catches, flames sucking at the windows. In time the floor gives way and the coffin that was waiting for burial spirals through the blazing storeys to the ground. The lead casing melts and the body of Brilliana Harley is consumed to ashes.

CODA

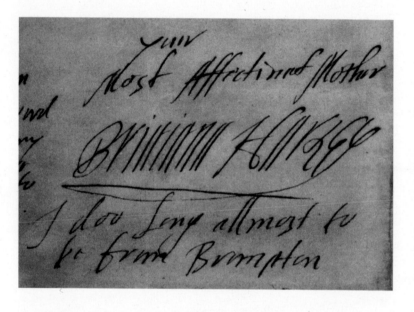

Somebody say this was England? These precious green fields. The sun on our faces, the mist rolling in from the hills. Somebody say this was England?

From 'England', Trevor Moss & Hannah-Lou

The unchanging hawk hangs in his loneliness of sky; then, or now, it doesn't matter which. His presence above these hills is such a constant and he is so little affected by time as to seem somehow outside it altogether. As if he could rise from one century and stoop on another.

All our great changes, all our vicissitudes are no more than background to him, like weather, or a changing season. If he chooses, spiralling upwards on a thermal he can make us into insects, just with the power of perspective. He can rise from a post, or the branch of a tree, the only time he looks effortful, and lying himself across the wind and letting himself be carried, he can shrink us to pin men, little dry-looking things that scrape about or scuttle across the ground, everything about us negligible; like Mia's father, for example, with Saba in harness bumping between high hedges like a daddy-long-legs. Or like the farmer at Hopton, whose dog is so small it has become a seed head.

If he goes higher, as high as he can, he can make us vanish altogether.

Now, in the park at Brampton, the tiny beetle, which is Mia, walking and the hawk falling. It is three months on from her last visit to her father, towards the end of a wild September, so she is visibly pregnant, blooming, though swaying slightly and making sure of her steps, across the bowl of the park bottom. She is no longer working on the Harleys. Bill's book is with the publisher. Felipe is still away. But here she is, visiting the castle and grounds one more time. She is looking, although she hasn't admitted it to herself, for Brilliana.

Mia walks slowly up the wind-backed hills, towards Wales. She is hoping despite herself that there will be something. There must be something, some trace, some memory. If only just to salute it and say goodbye. Because the fervour, the poignancy of this one life, caught in the press of time, seems to Mia too vivid just to disappear.

As she walks she thinks of what she knows of this woman, nonsensically looking for her walking this way maybe, also pregnant, stepping down from inspecting the new park pale for her absent husband. Her small face, its mouth compressed in certainty, the composure in its gaze, her wind-blown garments.

In this work I have not thought my life deare.

Such a sacrifice to make. Where are you? Mia asks. And what happened to your work? Has it survived into this culture of trash and compromise, or did it never come to be? And your God of elections and smiting, did he care, was he there in the end? Or did you lay down your life for a story?

But nothing answers. There is no evidence of Brilliana in the fields, or along the roads, nothing of her in the wind-scoured park. Dead and gone.

I doo long almost to be from Brompton.

You are, Mia thinks, conjuring, for her own satisfaction, the frail ghost of Brilliana leaving at last, as she never did in life. Putting down her duty in death and walking out down these old lanes, through rain as pale as herself, and colder. Because rain and cold don't matter any more. Place is nothing after all. For I am a stranger with thee: and a sojourner, as all my fathers were. It's just a thought. Maybe it was too late. Maybe she stayed.

Places make people but they don't necessarily hold them. Mia should know. Generation after generation we are wiped off the surface of the earth, as if we had never been. Here one minute, gone the next, as the hawk would have it.

We don't matter, Mia says to herself out loud and in a tone of surprise. And then, in silence but with sudden clarity, she thinks, We don't matter at all, to the world, to anything, except to each other. She puts a hand involuntarily across her belly. Only to each other. This is how it is. Our dream of significance, of purpose or change, is just a dream after all. Just another trick of perspective. And she goes on walking in this new certainty of emptiness, the sky flying over, with rain somewhere in the back of its mind. She has to huddle in her coat, one hand still half across her belly, as if protecting it. She feels all the time now a warmth in her, the butterfly stirrings of her baby, an inwardness, her body concentrating on new life.

This is how the world goes, she says to her unborn baby. She looks at the sky, at the hawk, at the fields lying smashed with wind and rain underneath, so whipped-looking. This is how you'll find it. She thinks of Brilliana gone without trace, of herself, of Felipe looking through his camera at animals in the heat of Gabon, of her da.

Going, going, gone.

Nothing but this fragile chain of human echo, back and forth, calling and answering across the centuries, with no significance other than its own sound. Mia herself, and her child, her own mother, Syl and her boys, Brilliana and Ned, and her father and Sir Robert and Bill and so many others, over and over, as far back as time will allow, just so many voices echoing each other without knowing. As if life couldn't help but make itself up as it went along, patterning itself like music, out of little runs of repetition, little variations.

Mia raises her face to the rain. It seems precious to her to the point of tears, this intensely felt but ultimately pointless connection. And for no reason, as she looks up, there is a rift in the clouds and, on a wire, the slim silhouette of a rain-soaked kestrel, backlit with sudden sun, flares like a jewel. When he opens his wings to fly they are made of stained glass.

Mia stands with rain, or is it tears, in her eyes. Watching him climb, to hang cruciform at the top of the sky as the clouds close again, she cradles her belly, and utters what can only be called a prayer. I'm passing it on, she says, of this life that she sees now with the hawk's blinding severity. Even if there's nothing to show for it, it's sacred. Live, if you can find it, with conviction. Believe, if you possibly can. I hope you can believe.

Because sometimes, she says to herself, looking back at Brampton as she moves on, with the land dark and the wind blowing her hair forwards, sometimes it seems that havering this way and that, weighing things up with our noisy little minds, we have lost the stomach for the dedicated life, for the life lived even in passionate error. Just the flair, the clean swing of it, as it passes.

Look at me, Brilliana could have said, her eyes burning. I was so true.

BRILLIANA HARLEY'S FAMILY TREE

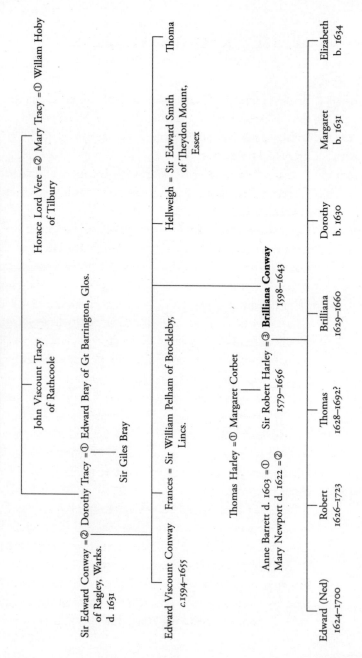

Horace Lord Vere =② Mary Tracy =① Willam Hoby
of Tilbury

John Viscount Tracy
of Rathcoole

Sir Edward Conway =② Dorothy Tracy =① Edward Bray of Gt Barrington, Glos.
of Ragley, Warks.
d. 1631

Sir Giles Bray

Thoma

Hellweigh = Sir Edward Smith
of Theydon Mount,
Essex

Frances = Sir William Pelham of Brockleby,
Lincs.

Edward Viscount Conway
c.1594–1655

Thomas Harley =① Margaret Corbet

Sir Robert Harley =③ Brilliana Conway
1579–1656   1598–1643

Anne Barrett d. 1603 =①
Mary Newport d. 1622 =②

Edward (Ned)
1624–1700

Robert
1626–1723

Thomas
1628–1692?

Brilliana
1629–1660

Dorothy
b. 1630

Margaret
b. 1631

Elizabeth
b. 1634

BILL RADIC'S TIMELINE

*c.*1598   Brilliana born in Dutch town of Brill where her father Sir Edward Conway is governor

1623   Brilliana marries Sir Robert Harley at Greenwich

1624   Edward Harley born

1625   Accession of Charles I. War with Spain over Frederick, Charles's Protestant brother-in-law's position as Elector Palatine

1626   Coronation of Charles I. Birth of Robert Harley. Sir Robert is returned to Parliament as senior knight for Herefordshire, takes up office as Master of the Mint, through the intercession of his father-in-law, Secretary Conway. Acts as Conway's aide, attempting to shield his patron, Buckingham, the Court favourite, from impeachment by Parliament. King dissolves Parliament rather than allow a conviction. War with France over French failure to pay royal dowry and anxiety over plight of French Protestants.

1627   Collection of forced loans by the King, to fund foreign policy. Several hundred refusers prosecuted or harassed. Five knights imprisoned. Attorney General caught trying to falsify the judges' findings. Failure of expedition to help the French Protestants under siege at La Rochelle.

1628   Petition of Right presented to King by Parliament and followed by Remonstrance, which sets out Parliament's fear of 'subversion of religion' by Catholics and Arminians, and 'innovation and change of government' as exemplified by the imposition of forced loans, prerogative imprisonment, the trial of civilians by martial law, and the billeting of soldiers on civilians. Assassination of Duke of Buckingham by a demobbed Puritan soldier. Birth of Thomas Harley.

1629	Peace treaty with France. Parliamentary anxiety about Crown's collection of customs revenues without consent. Complaints about tolerance of anti-Calvinist preaching and increase in use of 'Popish' ceremony in church services. Sir Robert Harley speaks in Parliament against Arminianism and in favour of a public declaration by the Commons of their religion, as set out by Elizabeth I in 1526 and James I at the Synod of Dort. King dissolves Parliament in anger. Seven MPs imprisoned and denied bail. Beginning of eleven years' personal rule. First large-scale emigration of Puritans to New England, escaping persecution. Birth of Brilliana Harley.
1630	Peace treaty with Spain. Birth of Dorothy Harley.
1631	Revival by the King of royal prerogative powers, long out of use, as a means of funding the personal rule, e.g. the distraint of knighthood, a tax of £40 per annum on all gentlemen of incomes who had failed to apply for a knighthood at the King's coronation in 1626. Death of Brilliana's father, Secretary Conway. Death of Sir Robert's father, Sir Thomas Harley. Birth of Margaret Harley.
1633	William Laud consecrated Archbishop of Canterbury. Institutes a commitment to ceremonial in church services, is pushed to outlaw many Puritan practices, and begins the move to rail off the altar table as the focus for worship instead of the pulpit. King crowned in Scotland. Thomas Lord Wentworth (later Earl of Strafford) sent as Lord Deputy to subjugate Ireland. William Prynne, a West Country lawyer and Puritan polemicist, denounces stage plays in a publication and is sentenced by the Court of the Star Chamber. He is imprisoned in the Tower and his ears are cut off. Sir Robert is among those who visit him in prison.
1634	Ship money introduced in all coastal counties as a way of funding the navy. Elizabeth Harley born.

1635	Ship money extended to all counties. Sir Robert removed from office as Master of the Mint.
1637	Attempt to impose new prayer book on the Scots. Star Chamber sentences William Prynne, Henry Burton and John Bastwick to life imprisonment for their writings. They are fined and have their ears cut off. Prynne has the stumps of his ears cut off.
1638	Case is brought against John Hampden for avoidance of ship money. Judges find narrowly in favour of the King. Scotland signs National Covenant pledging to resist innovations in religion. Ned Harley goes to Oxford.
1639	King declares war on Scotland (first 'Bishops' War') in an attempt to force them to conform. He is defeated. Truce signed at Berwick.
1640	King calls Short Parliament in April, to finance a second invasion of Scotland. Parliament uses it to air grievances about the eleven years' personal rule. Sir Robert speaks on behalf of Burton, Prynne and Bastwick, suggesting that they be released from the Tower to present their case to Parliament. He also speaks against the Scotch war. In May the King dissolves Parliament again in anger. Further religious reforms passed by convocation in May. Riots in Lambeth against Archbishop Laud. Two rioters executed. June, the King's planned invasion of Scotland is pre-empted by Scots. Scottish victory at Newburn. Brilliana's brother Lord Conway is in charge of forces and is routed. Subsequent Scottish occupation of Newcastle. September, the Council of Peers meets at York, recommends that the King call Parliament. Negotiations between English and Scottish peers over settlement between two countries. November, the Long Parliament is called. Lord Strafford is imprisoned. Archbishop Laud is imprisoned. Petition for

root and branch reformation of the Church is first presented to Commons, requiring utter abolition of all Church hierarchy.

1641   Act passed requiring Parliamentary elections every third year. Trial of Lord Strafford, who is sentenced to death under the Act of Attainder. Sir Robert and Ned Harley both present at the passing of the Act. Lord Strafford executed. House of Commons fails in its attempt to remove bishops from House of Lords. Act abolishing Star Chamber is passed. King signs Treaty of Edinburgh which results in Scots' withdrawal from Newcastle. Parliament calls for removal of all idolatrous and superstitious monuments from parishes. Sir Robert Harley personally supervises smashing of all windows in the chapel at the Palace of Whitehall, the breaking up with axes of the carved wood at Westminster Abbey, the removal of stained glass at Greenwich chapel, St Margaret's church and the chapel at Hampton Court.

September, Parliamentary recess. October, Irish rebellion breaks out. Thousands of Protestants are massacred. Refugees arrive in Wales and Herefordshire. Soldiers pressed to suppress rebellion.

November, House of Commons passes Grand Remonstrance cataloguing all the grievances of King Charles's reign and recommending remedies. Calls for measures to halt spread of popery and prevention of arbitrary rule by the King.

December, the Grand Remonstrance is printed by Parliament without King's or House of Lord's approval.

1642   King attempts to arrest five leading members of House of Commons and one member of House of Lords for treason. He fails. He leaves London.

Parliament takes control of all local defence forces. April, the King is refused entry to Hull where the magazine of his army is stored. July, the first man killed in a skirmish in Manchester. Earl of Essex appointed Captain-General of Parliamentary forces. August, King raises his standard at Nottingham. September, Parliament orders closure of theatres. First engagement of the war at Powick Bridge, near Worcester.

October, battle of Edgehill in Warwickshire. 1,500 killed.

November, Royalist army is faced by London militia and Essex's army at Turnham Green. King withdraws and sets up headquarters at Oxford.

1643   January, the King orders Fitzwilliam Coningsby to prepare for assault on Brampton Bryan. Plan aborted when forces are diverted to attack Puritan garrison at Gloucester. Eleven men sent to deliver a summons to Lady Brilliana demanding the giving-up of Brampton. Attack postponed to July. Ned Harley's horse shot under him during a charge at battle of Lansdowne. Prince Rupert storms Bristol. A day later, 26 July, Brampton surrounded by 700 men. Start of a seven-week siege. 9 September siege lifted. Royalist troops required at Gloucester.

31 October Lady Brilliana Harley dies.

1644   Siege and massacre at Hopton Castle. Second siege and fall of Brampton Bryan.

ACKNOWLEDGEMENTS

I would like to acknowledge the kind help and support of the following people:

David Beatty, Nicholas Beatty, Rosie Boycott, Caroline Dawnay, Jacqueline Eales, Claudia Fitzherbert, Edward and Victoria Harley, Sue Hubbard, Mary Keen, John Micklethwait, Violet Moller, Geraldine Norman, Alice Oswald, William and Alison Parente, William Seighart, Rupert Smith, Kim Wilkie.

Lines from *The Secret Life of Poems* by Tom Paulin © Tom Paulin, 2008. Reprinted by permission of Faber and Faber Ltd.

www.vintage-books.co.uk